SEMI-DETACHED

SEMI-DETACHED

Paul Heathorn

LITTLE, BROWN AND COMPANY

*Thanks to Antony Topping at Greene & Heaton, and Andrew Gordon at
Little, Brown, for their help with this book.*

A *Little, Brown* Book

First published in Great Britain
in 2001 by Little, Brown & Company (UK)

A CIP catalogue record for this book
is available from the British Library

ISBN: 0 316 85681 9

Typeset in Berkeley Book and Gill Sans by M Rules
Printed and bound in Great Britain
by Creative Print and Design Wales

Little, Brown & Company (UK)
Brettenham House
Lancaster Place
London WC2E 7EN

WILLIAM

When buying a house location is everything.
<u>4 WOOD ROAD</u>
So this is the main selling point for me, if it is ok I will take it.

**** OLDER STYLE THREE BEDROOM SEMI-
DETACHED HOUSE ****
** 25FT LOUNGE/DINER **
** 14FT KITCHEN **
** SOME DOUBLE GLAZING **
** OFF ROAD PARKING **
** REAR GARDEN APPROXIMATELY 50FT **

<u>DIRECTIONS</u>: **From the office in Oakley** *Spike the estate agent, who looks like Woody Allen without the glasses, and I* **proceed** *in Spike's blue car* **along Beech Road to the Old Elm Arms roundabout.** *(It starts to rain, just light fingertip touches but Spike puts his wipers on to imply he is a forward-thinking man.)* **Take the second exit into Maxtree Lane, then take the first turning on the right into Copse Hill. Continue into Mill Lane taking the second turning on the left into Wood Road where the property is located on the left-hand side, indicated by the 'For Sale' sign.** *The bedroom light is on next door.*

The accommodation in detail:

<u>**GROUND FLOOR**</u>
We go in through the
Part double-glazed front door to:

<u>PORCH ENTRANCE</u> **windows front aspect, part glazed door to:**
<u>HALL</u> **built-in under stairs cupboard, thermostat**

3

controller (un-tested), telephone point (un-tested), double radiator, Artexed ceiling. Red carpet (to remain). *The sole of my left foot starts to itch.*

<u>LOUNGE/DINING ROOM</u> 25′ 6″ (7.77m) × 10′ 9″ (3.28m) maximum, double-glazed traditional bay window to front aspect, part glazed door to rear garden aspect *where the wooden fence is too high to see over,* two wall-mounted gas fires (to remain), t.v. point (un-tested), double radiator, Artexed ceiling. Beige carpet (to remain). *I try and scuff my foot against the beige carpet and scratch the itch through the worn thin sole of my shoe.*

<u>KITCHEN</u> 14′ 10″ (4.52m) × 6′ 5″ (1.96m) window to side aspect, double-glazed door to rear garden aspect, fitted kitchen: range of wall and base units, sink and drainer unit, space and plumbing for washing machine, space for fridge freezer, built-in oven and hob (un-tested), part tiled walls, single radiator, textured ceiling.

<u>FIRST FLOOR</u>

I let the estate agent lead the way, so I can sit on the stairs, remove my shoe and scratch my hot foot.

<u>LANDING</u> window to side aspect, loft access point, Artexed ceiling.

<u>BEDROOM ONE</u> 13′ 5″ (4.09m) × 9′ 1″ (2.77m) double-glazed bay window to front aspect, sink with cupboard under, built-in wardrobes, telephone point (un-tested), t.v. point (un-tested), double radiator. Dark blue carpet (to remain). Cast iron double bed (to remain). *Maybe the room was built around the bed, it's big enough.*

<u>BEDROOM TWO</u> 11′ 4″ (3.45m) × 10′ 2″ (3.10m) maximum, window to rear garden aspect, built-in storage cupboards, double radiator. Mid-blue carpet (to remain).

4

BEDROOM THREE 7' 10" (2.39m) × 7' 0" (2.13m)
window to rear garden aspect *where I can see over the fence that Iman is reaching up to take in their washing from the whirlygig line. She hurries back to the house stooping as if the rain were hail, not realising she has dropped what I know to be Will's orange shirt.* Double radiator, textured ceiling. Sky blue carpet (to remain).

BATHROOM window to front aspect, bathroom suite comprising of wood side-panelled bath with shower attachment over (to remain), pedestal wash hand basin, low flush WC, part tiled walls, built-in airing cupboard, double radiator, textured ceiling.

OUTSIDE *I shake Spike's hand and say I'll take it.* The front area is tarmac with a shrub border enclosed by a brick wall. OFF ROAD PARKING FOR ONE VEHICLE. *Next door have a garage.* SIDE PEDESTRIAN ACCESS TO THE REAR GARDEN which is mainly laid to lawn, enclosed by a brick wall and timber fencing with a patio area and a vegetable patch. Timber shed (to remain). *This occupies the space where my garage would have been.* The rear garden measures approximately 50ft in length.

AGENTS NOTE: Please note that any Gas/Electrical or Plumbing appliances and systems have not been tested by ourselves.
I think these socks must've shrunk in the wash.

I'll say this for terminal cancer, it does give you the luxury of planning. I knew when Dad would die, I knew how much his life was insured for and I knew I would inherit the sweet shop and could afford a house. I made an offer on the place when the secondary tumour in his spine was identified and contracts were exchanged when it reached his brain. Even then he held out longer than predicted – but moves always have little hitches and I wasn't ready to go then either.

Had it been Will taking in the washing when I looked round the house I would have knocked on the window and shouted YOO HOO! I would have blown my cover before I knew I even wanted cover. But as I had never met Iman I decided I didn't want to be introduced as her new neighbour; I wanted to be introduced as Will's oldest friend. In the rain on the way back to the estate agent's office I worried about Will's shirt because the lawn would be turning into mud.

Will came to Dad's funeral but Iman could not make it, which suited me. I had enough to think about. Come the afternoon, 3.15pm, I couldn't think of any of it, though, so I thought of fuck-all. But sitting between the ancient Crabbe sisters I couldn't call it feeling fuck-all, so I told them I felt sombre. They sat there like OAP bouncers so fragile no one dare hit them, deflecting all the attention that came my way, telling relatives how sombre I felt and explaining Dad's last days to anyone who asked. When we left they each took hold of an arm, but I felt I was supporting them.

After all, I have the sweet shop. The Crabbe sisters still have their jobs.

I didn't expect Will to be at the funeral, because I couldn't think who would have told him about it. But it was obvious as soon as he spoke to the Crabbe sisters (because no one usually says 'Hiya!' to women in their sixties) that he must still use Dad's shop. Will doesn't smoke, he is not mad about chocolate, but he does buy the *Mail* each day. So I thought he must drive over two miles each way to get his daily paper from Dad. And I wanted to thank him for it, but I didn't. All that occurred to me in the crematorium was how much Will looked like Captain Kirk.

Will was the right age for Captain Kirk, he had his authority. The main difference between Will and Captain Kirk is that Will is balding slightly. Except William Shatner is infamous for his Kirk wig, so maybe what I was really thinking was how much like William Shatner Will looked. But I couldn't say that, because I hadn't seen him for a long time and there were a lot of people around. Once I thought it I was amazed I had not seen it before. Will mistook my amazement for emotion and hugged me.

It wasn't a coincidence that I bought the house next to Will's, but it did look like one. Instead it went like this: Will sent me pictures at university of him and his wife outside their new house. I thought: Will has a nice wife and Will has a nice house. Then I noticed in the corner of the photo the FOR SALE board. I tried to use the same estate agents, because if they are good enough for Will they are good enough for me. Will has that atmosphere about him – he is one of those blokes who is always all right. He could always sort out who owed how much in restaurants no matter how pissed he was, how large the group or if someone had not had any of the wine, drank beer and was vegetarian but did eat two desserts – that was me. So I thought he was bound to have chosen a great estate agent. I rang them up, mentioned the house I'd seen and said I'd like one just like it. The funny thing was that the house next door to Will's was the one FOR SALE. I was lucky, contracts had nearly been exchanged but the chain broke down when one couple got divorced and another was made redundant: I felt so lucky. The level of detail also gave me confidence in Spike the estate agent.

So I rang Will, used the same solicitor and surveyor as him and got the same mortgage from the same place. Except he doesn't know all this, he thinks I was just showing polite interest. Apart from the funeral I had not seen Will for the longest time. He had never actually managed to visit me at university and after missing their wedding and sending a toaster as a present (albeit the nicest toaster they received) I had not dared visit them.

I decided to give Tracey Crabbe the morning off. It never seemed proper calling such a venerable old lady Tracey, but she wouldn't answer to anything informal, especially 'Trace', and in a way I suppose she was blazing a trail into old age for all the Traceys, Mandys, Wendys and Sharons of younger generations. Her sister, Edna, worked the afternoons. This was how they liked it because it stopped their dog getting lonely during the day. Dad had said that Edna liked to stay up late and have a lie-in, and that Tracey liked to have early nights and afternoon naps.

Edna needed the afternoon off to go to the dentist, and once I was actually alone in the shop again I was glad. Everything was so familiar – I'd grown up among the penny chews. And it gave me something to do.

Will came in for the *Mail*; as he bent to pick one off the pile I got one out from under the counter which I was saving for him. He saw it was me just as our papers collided like we were shaking hands with folded copies of Tuesday's *Mail*.

'Liam! How de-do-de!'

'Do-de-ing just fine, Will. Considering, you know.' Now this conversation was ok for me. I didn't really want to talk about the funeral and I didn't want to talk about buying the house. Had I told Will I was thinking about buying the house when I was thinking about buying the house, it would have implied I was trying to get his permission, and that wasn't fair. I didn't need his permission: he didn't own the house. I'd paid off a massive amount of the mortgage with my inheritance, and the old owners were ecstatic. (After all, they'd been let down before, they'd already moved out, they had to sell; I wasn't about to let anybody down that late in the day.) Once Will got used to having me around again he might even like me living next door. We used to spend whole summers in and out of each other's houses. I would just move in, perfectly legally, keep quiet for a while to show him and Iman what a good neighbour I was, and then, when the time was right, when Will wanted me near him again like I wanted to be near him, I could tell him my new address. We'd probably have a beer on it.

A mumsy woman came into the shop and she talked about the funeral.

'Oh, hello, you must be Liam. Jerry, your dad,' she said like I didn't know his first name, 'talked about you, at university. I recognise you from the crematorium.' And I nodded a non-committal nod and she shut up.

'Can I help you?'

'Oh, twenty Lambert & Butler, red, please. That's my usual, Jerry sold me them thousands of times.'

So I gave her the fags and change together and said, 'The usual. Thanks,' after her.

Will was examining the cover of a porn mag. 'This one's dusty.' He ran his finger across the red star over the cover model's tit. 'Don't think Jerry liked touching them. Look, it's out of date too.' The shop door opened again and two schoolboys came in which made Will pull back from the top shelf in a neat role-reversal. 'Shit, I've got to get going, Liam. Come round some time – I'll ring you later, give you directions.' He gave me the money for the paper.

'I know the address, I know the way.' And just saying this without explaining made me feel guilty, but there was no reason for it,

9

I'd done nothing wrong. We were best mates and best mates is for keeps.

All the pornography was out of date. It took me over an hour to check this because whenever I thought someone was going to come in I would get off the stepladder. The oldest porno was just over three years. All the other, non-pornographic magazines were up to date. I couldn't imagine the Crabbe sisters shuffling the pornos into their neat line so maybe the dust was because Dad felt awkward handling the magazines when they were around, which was all the working day. Clearly no one was happy buying their porn from the venerable old ladies, they're like your gran.

I recognised the three-year-old copy of *Fiesta*, I remembered reading it in university halls my first year there. I thought maybe Dad was keeping it: the cover was dusty, yes, but the corners were well thumbed. Maybe he was uncomfortable keeping it in the flat, but happy keeping it in the shop: it was, after all, the best hiding place because it was public and just what you would expect to find on the top shelf of a sweet shop. The more recent the magazine the more hardcore it seemed to be. They were in date order, left to right, from the three-year-old *Fiesta* (WET 'N' WILD WOMEN) to last month but one's *Under 18* (GIRLS AS YOUNG AS THE LAW ALLOWS) tucked behind a copy of the more presentable *Viz*. Finally I got it: the magazines were well thumbed and dusty because terminal cancer stops you wanking. I wanted to have a wank and give off some of the lively stuff, just so I could stop thinking about all that death and filth. But now I knew Dad had been there before me I couldn't. It was bad enough to think we had both read the *Fiesta*.

When Edna Crabbe arrived, mumbling from the dental anaesthetic, I made her a cup of tea, partly because she assumed she would be making the tea and I wanted to establish that I would not be that type of employer. I took my cup upstairs. She'd just have to mumble at the customers.

The flat was still as Dad had left it. I had tried to tidy some things away, but there was no away place to put them. My old bedroom was full of stuff I should have thrown out before going to university. But I had retained my redundant possessions – school exercise books and seven-inch singles – just in case they might one day be needed as exhibits in the museum of my life. I had been using a thin path from the bed to the door through all the stuff. There were probably untrodden corners in this room, lush blue carpet preserved under boxes only inches away from carpet so worn-out it looked like Shreddies.

I touched the red plastic handle on the white wardrobe doors and, as soon as I pulled, the mass of clothes pushed the doors to swing fully open. It was like a rush-hour tube train. At the foot of the wardrobe, under a pile of old shoes and two pairs of football boots, both of which just had the front of the right boot worn out, was a Top Man carrier bag. This was familiar; this bag was something I had forgotten to do. Inside was a red shirt, still folded, with the receipt on top. Again I remembered Will's orange shirt in the mud, but now I remembered that his orange shirt was just his red shirt, faded and in disguise. Having bought a red shirt, the receipt said, on 19 December 1995, at 4.58pm when I was served by CRAIG, I had gone to Will's house (when he lived with his parents) on the way back here only to see him in an identical red shirt. So I had vowed (and my memory was specific about the word vowed) to return the shirt because now I couldn't wear it.

I pulled off my baggy black jumper and put the red shirt on. I could wear it now that Will's was orange.

The shop closed at 8pm. I let Tracey go home at quarter to eight and I worked the last fifteen minutes – but nobody came in. Lonely, lonely, lonely.

I decided on a really early night but couldn't face sleeping in my old room again. I thought I could quickly move all of Dad's personal belongings out of his, larger room, and just throw them into my old room, all piled up, and shut the door. This way I would be in what might feel like a new room to me. But Dad's room even had some of Mum's stuff in it, so I thought I would just sleep on it all and sort it out in the morning. Maybe I could hire a skip.

I lay down on the double bed and heard it crackle. It crackled again as I rolled over and I tried to work out if I needed to pee enough to get up again. I lay still and tried to relax but the thought of sleeping with an incontinence sheet on the bed was too much. What was I thinking not to even change the bedclothes anyway? But where did Dad keep the bedclothes? As a compromise I would strip the bed and, for one night only, sleep on the mattress with a cover-less duvet. Tomorrow I would buy new.

I pulled off the bedclothes, didn't find a plastic sheet, and snuggling under the duvet heard the crackling again. Paper not plastic. Under the mattress was a lot of pornography.

I got up, rang Will, and invited myself over. It wasn't long after eight – my early night could wait till later.

I made sure the taxi driver, who made me think of Robin Williams – which I put down to his very hairy hands on the steering wheel – dropped me off right outside Will's house. This way they could see me arrive and hopefully avoid the question of did I find the house all right. The FOR SALE sign on my house next door had been taken down. Will opened the front door before I rang the bell.

'Come in. Glad you came sooner rather than later. This is Iman,' and as Will turned to make the introduction Iman made a feline swerve past him and stood on the doorstep. We shook hands.

'Hello Iman, nice to finally meet you.' Our eyes were level, her on the step, me on the path.

'Ditto!' and she tilted forward and I was tempted to kiss her hello on the cheek but worried she might just be wobbling on the edge of the step and chickened out.

In the front room, which was just a lounge not a knocked-through lounge/diner like next door, I sat in the only armchair. This way I avoided the sofa and the possibility of Iman sitting

12

next to me, also if Will was seated next to me conversation would be harder. They sat on the sofa.

I didn't want to say 'nice place' because what would that mean in relation to me having bought next door? I could say 'these are nice houses' but that might get them off on a similar line of conversation ultimately leading to me revealing or concealing my interest in next door. Time was running out before this pause in conversation became a silence so I decided to speak to Iman. Speaking to Iman would establish that I had come to see her as well as Will, and that I was interested in her and regretted our long acquaintance without actually meeting – but I couldn't say that – and as I turned to her I was left speechless by the fact that she looked just like Whitney Houston.

Silence, not even the ticking of a clock.

'Would you like a cup of tea?' said Will and as I nodded he left the room. I wanted to call after him 'two sugars please!' to sort of check my voice was in good working order but Will knew how I took my tea. Just as I considered standing and walking into the kitchen saying 'I'll just see what's happening with that tea,' Iman spoke. 'I've heard a lot about you,' she said.

Iman seemed like a clever woman and I thought in the silence she must have rejected saying this, maybe more than once, and now she was just taking the easy way out. It was still difficult for me because this wasn't a question and so how could I answer her? Such a familiar opening gambit made it difficult to judge how to make an impression, so there was some more silence without even the ticking of a clock, except this time I thought I could hear Iman's watch.

'Iman?' She looked hopefully at me. 'What's the time?'

'I don't know, er,' she pushed up her sweater sleeve to reveal only a silver bracelet, 'about nine-ish?'

The cat walked in. I speak enough cat to get by, and like some people speak Holiday French I speak Holiday Cat: blinking slowly means 'All right?' and if the cat blinks back then you are both all right. So I blinked all right/hello at the cat and it blinked back.

13

'Nice cat.' I sort of said it both to Iman and to the cat.

'Yes, he's called Aslan. I've wanted a cat called Aslan since I was a child.'

'He reminds me of Felix the Cat, the black one in the cartoons.' Aslan turned and walked away from me.

'I called him Aslan after the lion in *The Lion, the Witch and the Wardrobe*. It was my favourite book as a child; did you like it?' But I was too preoccupied to answer. As Will brought through the tea tray I got up and brushed past him.

'Woah Liam! That was a close one.'

'Can I use your loo?' I asked, following the cat upstairs.

I needed to see Aslan again, I needed to know if he really looked like Felix the Cat because if he did it meant a very strange thing was happening. He was on the carpet by a closed bedroom door crouched into that folded cushion shape cats make when they rest, paws tucked in. I startled him by shuffling my feet; his eyes opened very wide, like Felix the Cat's.

The strange thing was that people had started to look like actors and now a cat looked like a cartoon. Why had I never noticed that Will looked like Captain Kirk? Was it a look he had grown into since losing his hair? Or perhaps it was the other way round; I had known Will from before I can remember seeing *Star Trek* and had never in fact thought that Kirk looks like Will. As for Iman looking like Whitney Houston, I now realised that I noticed this only when we were sitting down: in the wedding pictures, in the garden with the washing, and on the doorstep when I arrived, she had always been standing and then she had only looked like a short version of Whitney Houston, which is far less striking. Spike the estate agent really did look like Woody Allen without the glasses; he said people had commented on it before. The taxi driver tonight made me think of Robin Williams because of his hairy hands. I can't remember his face. And the Crabbe sisters do look like each other, but not like anyone else.

Will called up the stairs, 'You ok, Liam?' So I reached into the bathroom to flush the cistern and walked downstairs as if I was fine.

I sat down and said 'Shall I be mother?', confident that Iman would not have said it already for fear of sexual stereotyping, and thinking Will would assume he was going to pour the tea. When no one answered I tipped a dash of milk in each cup. Iman spoke as I did it, 'No milk for me please, Liam.'

'Oh, sorry. Er.' And I panicked, picking up her cup and drinking down the milk and now I had started I just went ahead and poured the tea quickly into each cup. I winced as if Will was about to give me a dead arm. Iman laughed, saying, 'You know what, with that milk moustache you remind me of James Cagney. It gives you his crooked smile.'

'James Cagney!' Will cawed.

'Who's James Cagney?' The name was familiar, but I couldn't place it. 'Was he at our school?'

'No! Black and white film star. Nineteen-forties gangster movies, BBC 2 in the afternoons, Channel 4 in the early hours of the morning. You students watch telly then, you must have seen Jimmy Cagney.'

I echoed him, 'Jimmy Cagney!' I suddenly remembered that Dad had liked Jimmy Cagney, in fact he did a drunken impression of him, but not knowing Jimmy Cagney I could never verify it or even remember it. I wiped the milk from my lip.

'*White Heat* and *Angels With Dirty Faces*,' said Iman.

I drank my tea quickly, then had a second cup. As if this made me appear hungry Will asked, 'Have you eaten, Liam? It's just we haven't, I was going to fix something, why not stay and join us?' Well, I definitely wanted to stay a bit longer so I accepted.

I said, 'Let me help you' as we went into the kitchen. I looked around, it looked about 14′ 10″, same as mine.

'Seems a bit strange seeing you again, Liam, I mean I'm a home-owning husband now. Not like tea after school anymore.'

'Don't you think?'

15

'Didn't Jerry do a Jimmy Cagney impression? Friday nights, I remember, your house for a few videos then he'd come in pointing at the telly people saying "Who's he? Jimmy Cagney!" before doing it.'

'Will, do you reckon Dad thought I looked like James Cagney?'

'He had a baby face look to him, Jimmy Cagney, and you were his baby.'

Will had assembled the food: bread, cheese and salad. I took Iman's through to her but she was not in the lounge. I found her in the dining room.

Iman taught art at a primary school. She was making space at the dining-room table, piling up a stack of coloured paper, putting three types of glitter and two types of glue into a furry yellow pencil case. Will and Iman took their seats, I pulled out a chair and, sitting down, felt a tube of paper crumple. I held it up and was going to apologise but as I opened it I just looked instead. It was an old-looking map centred on a city called Spare Oom in a land called War Drobe. The edges had been burned.

'I coloured that with a damp tea bag,' said Iman. I nodded; there was an X in the middle and an arrow at the top pointing to Narnia. The bottom edge had arrows pointing to Cair Paravel and the Lone Islands. 'Don't worry about the crumples, they add to the effect.'

So I said, 'Thank you.'

'That's just something to put on the classroom wall. We're doing a version of *The Lion, the Witch and the Wardrobe* for the Christmas show. It's amazing what eight-year-olds will believe.' Iman took the map from me and looked reverentially at it.

Will picked up the slack in the conversation. 'How are you finding it living in the flat again, Liam?'

'Not so good.'

'Well come round when you want, don't be a stranger.'

Iman said, 'Oh William! You can't say that!' and we both turned to her. 'I mean, say it but not in those words. Really, Will, makes you sound about fifty-five. It's the type of phrase my mother uses.'

16

She finished rolling up the map and clasped her hands together to impersonate Will: 'Don't be a stranger.' I thought of Whitney Houston doing Captain Kirk to her husband (the pop star Bobby Brown) over a light supper.

'Iman and I are going away, next week is half-term and I'm taking some holiday. I thought if the flat was getting you down you might like to house-sit here for us. You'd be doing us a favour; there have been a few burglaries in Wood Road.'

'And one on Mill Lane,' added Iman. 'And there was an attempted robbery at the petrol station by the Old Elm Arms roundabout.'

Spike hadn't mentioned any of this. 'Ok, that would be great!' and I feel the excitement and a sudden firm urge to pee at the same time. Tea can do this to me and beer used to have the same effect. I need a slash and my indecision intoxicates me: I could go, excuse myself then go – in deference to the fact we are eating – but both could seem a bit weird as they assume I only just went.

I need a whizz. I yearn to piss. Including the two cups of tea I have just had in addition to earlier coffee, today has been at least a five-cup day. And two cans of Coke.

'Coffee?' asks Will and Iman nods. He assumes I have nodded too when I am in fact rocking ever so slightly. I imagine Will saying, 'Lovely hot piss? Anyone?'

Iman excuses herself and I assume she is going to make the coffee but then I hear the rub of her stockinged feet on the stairs. I only have one toilet next door but I have a need to pee that fills my head with images of prize goldfish in plastic water bags. I seriously consider going next door to my beige, low-flush WC.

'Is she going to have a bath?' I say to Will but with the speech pattern of a drunken Skin saying, 'Did you spill my pint?' And in the shocked look on Will's face I can't see whether he knows the answer or just can't believe the question. I need to squirt. I could go in the street, I could go in the garden. I could offer to wash up and go in the sink, except I'm not tall enough.

17

Will leaves the room and I hear him filling the kettle. I could go out the window. I balance how pleased I am to be back in contact with Will, including the need to make an impression on Iman and my current need for a familiar nice friend, with the strength of the dam in my pants. I decide to stay, but it is close.

Toilet flush: I walk as if I have a pair of too-big tights on under my trousers which are sliding down with every step I take towards the foot of the stairs. Will is not in the kitchen. If he's queuing for the loo I will have to own up before the goldfish spills out of the water bag. But Will is now in the kitchen. Will is drying his hands. The flush I heard is followed by the sound of the cistern filling up outside the kitchen door. Will has two toilets! I feel betrayed and think of something to say for a few seconds while Iman flushes the upstairs toilet and vacates the bathroom. I make my point by ignoring Will's toilet and going the extra mile to Iman's upstairs, where I am certain the smell will be more interesting. We pass on the stairs. She seems to recognise my gait – either she has a weak bladder or has worn too-big tights.

In the time it takes to drink a cup of coffee, call for a taxi, wait for a taxi and suggest we go to the pub Friday night, so they can give me the house keys and I can buy them a drink, I need to go again. I decide I would rather be humiliated in front of a stranger than in front of my friends and neighbours and get the cabby to stop at the public toilets in nearby Oakley. I swear he thinks I'm cottaging because he doesn't talk to me for the remainder of the journey. And I'm glad I didn't tell him about his facial similarity, which stems from the angular tip of his nose, to Tom Cruise.

I decided to let the Crabbe sisters get on with running the shop. They know where we keep the supplies of Kola Kubes and they know how to change the toner in the photocopier. 4p A COPY – MISTAKES MUST BE PAID FOR! I hand-wrote this sign for Dad several years ago and I always thought of it as a good bit of free advice to customers. The price should have been increased by now but I suspect Dad didn't do it because he would have had to do a new sign.

Tracey Crabbe called up the stairs to announce Will's arrival as I was just waking up under the impression it was Friday. Will opened my bedroom door and snagged yesterday's clothes against the floor. He squeezed through the gap. He had the *Mail* folded under his arm. He got close enough for me to read that it was Thursday. My feet were freezing.

'Something fucking crap has happened.' And I sat upright in an attempt to read the headline, but realised fucking crap things happen to you – when they happen to other people they are disasters and tragedies. I was confused, having dreamt about Michael J. Fox, and now I was wondering what the J stood for because it seemed really important. 'We had a racial attack on the house.'

'What happened?'

'This came through the door,' he said, giving me a piece of folded-up feint blue-lined paper. 'I reckon it was kids and I reckon I know which one in particular.'

'Could have been an adult writing like a child.' I squinted at the writing because of how and what was written: *nigercowslagshiteaterwishingyoupiebaldspackkidswithtails*. 'Shit, I'm speechless Will.'

'Well, I reckon it was done by a Christing kid because of the size of the paper. It's been torn from an exercise book, only schoolchildren use those. And it should be nigger, not niger, kids can't spell.'

I considered talking about the etymology of the word nigger and its origins in the river Niger but wasn't sure I was right about this, so I said, 'How's Iman? Or is that a crap question?' Will stopped looking angry and exhaled a small laugh.

'Course not, Liam, all things considered she's not too bad. Well, she's been angry, had a cry, worried about the house – I mean it came through the bloody letterbox; they're not shy, they've been on our doorstep, and we've even talked about moving.'

I thought about this, how could this count as not too bad, this

19

really was fucking crap. But then I heard the frayed edge to Will's voice.

'The sad thing is she says she's had worse said to her, but as a child – which makes it a bit worse still.' Will was new to racism. 'I tried to be quite strong about it for her and I think she was trying for me too, but fuck, Liam, it needs sorting out.'

'What does that mean, moving?' Then I would be able to tell him about the house but then I could not live next door to him.

'No, we won't move.' He said it calmly like I was panicking to even suggest it. 'I love the new house, our neighbours are cool, the area is cool.'

'But I thought the house next door was unoccupied?' As soon as I said it I regretted it. Now I had lied to him. Now no matter what he said I would have to lie again. But I decided not to lie to him now, I wouldn't mention the house again. I would lie to him in the future, or maybe I just wouldn't tell him where I lived, I mean I don't want to lie to my best friend.

'One side's an empty house, the other side though, Mrs Price, she's nice and friendly. That's all the more reason why it was this kid, because he doesn't live in the area – only his little mate does – the actual fucker lives on the prefab estate.'

'Will, ok, you know it was a child but you don't know which one. You didn't see him.'

'Granted, but I saw him looking at me last night when we were going out to the police, and they knew who I meant too. We discussed him.'

'Well. Let the police sort it. They are bound to speak to him, aren't they?' I said this realising, as I spoke, I had no legal precedent for knowing what the police did about this type of thing.

'His name is Wesley and he isn't scared of the police. I want to know if you will help me scare him?'

I lay back on my pillow and rubbed each foot with the other. I learned at school that Will had a nasty side which supported the side of him that always seemed to be all right. I suppose one relied on the

20

other. He was a Lad, domesticated but all-knowing. He used to give me dead arms at school for laughing and 'digs', which was basically a dead arm but meted out for a different offence, like farting. It was strange to think in these schoolyard terms again, but a child had hurt some adults and something needed to be done, so I said, 'Ok, I'll help you do something. But we mustn't just give him digs.'

Will laughed at the very thought of the word.

That afternoon in his bedroom, Will showed me a side of him I would never have thought could exist: Will was into Country & Western line-dancing. He opened up the right-hand side fitted wardrobe, and there was a rainbow of different cowboy outfits inside. Cowboy hats were stacked one inside the other on the top shelf and at the bottom were three pairs of cowboy boots, one black, one brown and one orange.

'I'd only been going line-dancing for a few weeks when this old woman, Pearl, told me her husband had died.' Will paused, obviously worried about bringing up the subject of death with me. I just kept looking at the clothes, trying to take it all in. 'Anyway she told me her old man was about my size – in fact he was exactly six foot tall when he died, according to the undertaker. So I told her she's right, I'm six foot. She asked my hat size and I said I didn't know. Who the fucking Christ knows their hat size?' I turned to look at Will, trying to picture him line-dancing, then once I had managed that I tried to picture him line-dancing dressed as a cowboy, but I just couldn't do it. He thought I was looking confused trying to think who might know their hat size, and explained, 'I mean an old guy would have known his hat size years ago when people wore them, de-mob suits and that. Your hat size doesn't change, does it?'

In an attempt to sound vaguely like I knew what Will was talking about I said, 'I knew my hat size at graduation, for the mortar-board.' But I shut up when I realised I had instantly forgotten my hat size because I never dreamed I would need it again.

Will finished his explanation as briefly as he could, realising he was losing me.

'Anyway this old widow offered me all her old man's outfits. And I bought the lot for a hundred.'

I gestured towards the wardrobe. 'Why?'

'That's bloody cheap, the stetsons alone can cost sixty quid.'

'No, I mean why are you showing me these?'

'I thought we could wear them.'

'I'm more into rap than country and western, Will. No offence, but just take Iman.'

'No, I mean we should wear them when we go to shit up Wesley. It'll be so weird, we'll terrify him. How else can we harass a child without anyone questioning it or noticing us? We'll be just too strange.' Then, crestfallen, Will sat on the end of the bed. 'Iman won't come line-dancing anymore.'

'Will, can't we just clip him round the ear?'

'Shit Liam, we're not going to touch him! If you want to hit him you're on your own.'

'Can't we just go and tell his parents what we suspect? Let them ground him or something.'

'His family are known round here, loads of them have been through Iman's school, they don't give a shit. One hit a teacher! If we go round there we are likely to get a clunk on the face for our trouble. My way we scare him and no one will believe his story and knowing that he most probably won't tell anyone.'

Will was the orange cowboy, I was the black cowboy. We both got dressed there and then in the double bedroom. It's easy when you were at school together. Being the black cowboy was Will's concession to me, a groovy lure to get me involved: he banked on me thinking being the black cowboy was cool – and I suppose I did. Black hat, black neckerchief, black shirt with black rhinestones which was too big but ok tucked into my black jeans which I was wearing anyway. And I wore black cowboy boots with silver tips. We are the same shoe size, almost. The truth was I was more comfortable with the idea of intimidating a child than going line-dancing.

Will's orange outfit included an orange waistcoat with rhine-stones over his old faded orange shirt (he was wearing this anyway), orange jeans, orange cowboy boots and an orange holster on his orange leather belt. If he'd had orange underwear to put on I would have thought he was well weird, but he did not. Will got an orange water pistol out from under the bed, then he went to the toilet; maybe he was nervous too. He was a long time.

We drove to the prefab estate looking for Wesley. The car roof was too low for us to wear our stetsons; Will had already put his hat on the passenger seat so I sat in the back.

'The engine needs tuning,' said Will, tapping his dashboard, 'and I keep meaning to vacuum the interior, it wouldn't take long.'

School was not yet finished but it seemed a fair bet he would be hanging about somewhere near the school rather than being inside it.

We drove to the arcade of shops under the flats. We could not see him but daren't go into the arcade dressed as cowboys. We drove to the edge of the precinct – there were some kids there – so we drove to the other end to be closer and to see that none of them were Wesley. We drove to the recreation ground next to the school.

I saw a woman walking a dog across the football pitch on the far side and two tramps by a tree on our near side. In fact it was the only tree on the whole rec. Then Will saw Wesley walking across the grass. I knew the terrain, a mixture of stud marks and cigarette ends all along the edge of the pitch. Wesley detoured to deliber-ately walk along the touch line. Wesley was shaped a bit like a cricket bat, like the actor Kevin Bacon but as a kid, thin tall head on a long thick neck and a straight chunk of a body. Will parked by the tree and tied his neckerchief across the bridge of his nose and around the back of his neck. I copied him.

'Will, there's a couple of dossers behind the tree.'

'So?'

'Well, they'll see us!'

Will made a gesture that any watcher of war movies would know means 'follow me' to soldiers in the jungle. I tried to open my door but it didn't work, so I climbed over the front seat and followed Will. We crept behind the tree and I really thought for a tiny moment Will wanted to kill the dossers. As we were creeping up Will turned and whispered, 'We'll listen in on them, I reckon they'll be so pissed they won't believe their eyes.'

Then we were close enough to smell them and their pissy OAP smell, saying, 'I mean how the fuck would you like it – a fucking prostitute fucking stabbing you! I mean that whore, stabbing me! Course I went to the fucking police but if I'd had my hammer I'd have done her.'

'Yeah, the fucking coppers!' said the other dirty bearded voice.

'Yeah, the coppers,' said the first, impressively.

'And?'

'They told me to fuck off.' And they both laughed, then Will laughed a schoolboy snigger too so we ran back to the car. This time I put my hat on the passenger seat as well, Will's was on top.

Will started to do a three-point turn in the road. Then, before I could mention the woman and her dog, he stopped turning as we faced the rec and accelerated up on to the grass. Wesley ran. Will got out and ran; my door wouldn't open. I had an excuse and I thought about staying but I climbed over the seats and out of Will's door instead.

Putting on a stetson and running is hard. Will must have thought to tuck the string under his chin. I did not, and the black hat got blown off my head. I went back for it, then turned to see Will had Wesley cornered behind the changing rooms.

'Christing little fucker, you better start behaving or I'll kill you!' Then Will pulled the water pistol from his orange holster and held it by Wesley's thin face. Will ordered me to 'Knee him in the bollocks!' So I did, but not really hard. When Wesley screamed Will shoved the gun into his mouth and pumped the trigger. We left him, gagging and trying to puke.

We jogged back to the car, my door opened easy and the dog barked at us as we drove on across the rec. We did not speak until we were back in Will's garage. Sitting there with the engine running I imagined someone about to commit suicide. All we needed was to shut the garage door and that would be it. I should think we sat there just less than a minute.

'What took you so long?'

'I couldn't open the door. I thought you weren't going to touch him? Just scare him.'

'Shit yeah, it's got a child lock in the back. So did I, but then I got into character, you know. The orange mist descended!'

'Was the gun right down his throat then, to make him choke?'

'No, er, it was the piss I put in it.'

Will had some overalls in the garage. He put them on and did them up over his orange cowboy outfit. Then he went into the house and let me in through the back door.

'I saw Mrs Price next door, that was a piece of luck. She was bringing in her shopping so I said "Good afternoon" in the sunniest voice I could. Did you shut the garage door?' I nodded in reply and my stetson slipped down on to my eyebrows. 'Cup of tea, Liam?' he said as he filled the kettle.

As it boiled we both went back to the double bedroom and got changed. He didn't draw the curtains but the condensation on the windows hid us anyway. Will is very nice and he is very nasty.

Still shaking, I made the tea. The manoeuvres – kettle to teapot, teapot to cups, milk in – seemed as difficult as re-potting cactus. I knew if I crossed Will I would get more than digs now. Will was ruthless, what would he do if he knew about next door? Maybe he'd shrug his shoulders or maybe he'd go ballistic. But if Will was prepared to do that to a boy, what punishment would he mete out to a man? I couldn't think of one bad enough – but then I couldn't have thought of using a piss-filled water pistol in a child's mouth. I overmilked the cups and this time had to drink a bit from each, but I did it before Will came in the room. I felt some of the milk on my chin, but he hadn't caught me and I must be certain he never did. Will came in, still wearing the faded orange shirt. I did not hand him his tea or he would have seen me shaking.

'You know what, Liam, I think I smelt him shit himself.'

The Old Elm Arms on Friday night was hot and tense. The pub has no balance. There are three main groups of clientele: drinking men from the prefab estate, youths, and couples. Added to this are a few student-looking types. They made me feel a bit more at home; I am used to student pubs where it is not considered a weakness to drink half-pints, in fact it is considered economic.

I arrived first. There was one long table free but I didn't take it because I wouldn't have had the confidence to keep the vacant seats if anyone asked. Standing at the bar I didn't push myself forward to be served so was not served. This suited me really, as I was waiting for Will and Iman. If I knew what she drank I could have got the drinks in.

When they arrived Will insisted on buying the first round, he is that type of bloke, and now if I am to buy them a drink I must buy them two drinks because the first one would simply be me buying my round. Will handed me two half-pints and their house keys, saying, 'Before I forget, take these, Liam; actually we wondered if you'd hang on to them after we come back, in case we lock ourselves out ever, we'll keep a spare key for you too if you want.'

We took the long table, which was still free. Iman sat at the head of it, Will and I sat next to her. I was on the bench seat by the wall, Will had his back to the room and still looked relaxed. I offered Iman one of the half-pints, but Will cut in, laughing, 'No, they're both yours, I thought if you wanted a half I'd better get you two of the dinky little things!'

'Oh, cheers,' I said, then, to Iman, 'Will told me what happened with the note. How are you?'

She put down her wine glass. 'Which bit did he tell you?'

'Well, I read the note.' I looked to Will for approval, but he was distracted by a man asking him if the spare seats were taken. Will held out his palm, a gesture that everyone knows means 'no, you take those seats' and two other couples sat down at the long table. He didn't miss a beat of the conversation.

'Iman thinks she knows who sent the note.' Then, to stop me getting us into any trouble, he added, 'It was no one I had thought of.' I felt sick and put down my half. I realised I must act natural and picked up the other half instead. I looked at the ceiling; it needed painting.

'Yes, I re-read the note last night and the key word suddenly stood out. *Piebald*,' said Iman.

'Why piebald?'

'Because Indians rode piebald horses, or at least they are often drawn in books and shown on telly as riding piebald horses, so when we did Native American Indians as a topic piebald was one of the words of the week. So I have narrowed it down to one of the children in my class. I have thirty-one suspects, but I don't really suspect the girls which leaves me with eighteen suspects. Of those eighteen nine don't live on this side of Oakley and I doubt children would travel far to be insulting and also I doubt they would know where I live. Within the remaining nine, three are among the cleverest in the year so they are less likely to be motivated to insult me as I've never had to tell them off.'

'And they're less likely to be racist if they're bright,' interrupted Will, and I could have hit him, in theory at least.

'I suppose so,' continued Iman. 'Of the final six one is very behind with his writing and one always writes very scruffily, usually making the paper grubby, which leaves me four suspects. I looked through all the desks and in all the exercise books of the whole class. Will, did I tell you I recognised the page as coming from an exercise book? And anyway seven kids had torn pages out of the back but, of those seven, only two were part of my final four suspects!'

'So of these two children which one do you think did it?' I asked.

'I don't know.'

'Which do you suspect though?'

'If I don't know it's not fair to suspect, is it?'

'Yeah, but if you had to take a guess.'

Iman shrugged and sipped at her drink.

'No harm done, that's the main thing,' Will lied, and I cut him off, agreeing, 'No harm done!'

They both said, 'No' – Iman because she is forgiving, and Will because he is forgiving himself.

I drank quite a bit at the Old Elm Arms because I knew I would not sleep otherwise for thinking about Wesley, and also I decided I wanted to buy them several drinks. I wondered if Wesley had been able to brush the pissy taste from his teeth. Now it was Saturday I regretted drinking at all. I have never got used to heavy drinking and gagged a little as I yawned and coughed, like a small boy with a gun shoved in his gob. My room was stuffy, so after staggering along to the toilet for a rich alcoholic piss I went into Dad's room and lay on the double bed in the recovery position. The pillow was cool. I listened to the rhythms of the shop door opening and closing. I tried not to take in the mumbled voices, I just wanted a head full of silence. I wanted to pass out.

Since Dad's death I had found it hard to think of him. Yes, he was in my thoughts almost constantly at first, but I wasn't thinking of him. I could think of him as an old man, and as a very ill man (lumpy and thin: such a strange combination). But I couldn't think of him as himself. I had managed it when Will mentioned the drunken Friday-night Jimmy Cagney impressions. That seemed like a typical Dad moment. Except when Will raised it I had to wrestle with the notion that Dad knew I looked a bit like James Cagney but never let on. I decided it didn't matter, it wouldn't change how I looked, and thinking about it was preventing me from passing out.

I had a moment of clarity and I saw the thing that was forcing me to live in the present. It was the thought of being alone, this was the one thought that stopped me thinking of Dad as himself (or even of Mum). To really remember him was to admit he was gone and that would leave me, officially, alone. Now even Will and Iman had gone away on holiday.

I came to with an answer: get a lodger. This way I could delay telling Will and Iman about buying the house, which would then appear occupied and I would not be alone. When the shop had shut I went downstairs. I opened a jar of vanilla essence air freshener and just left it on the shelf. I wrote on a postcard:

ROOM TO LET IN PRIVATE RESIDENTIAL AREA,
WOULD SUIT STUDENT, NO D.S.S.

There was a problem with the phone number. If I put the flat number the Crabbe sisters would see it and might mention it to Will when he got back. So I put Will's number because it seemed the best way of him not finding out – I had a week to find a tenant before he was back. This put the pressure on so I wrote a second sign, exactly the same, and decided to put it up at the local language school to double my chances. My ideal tenant would have trouble speaking English to avoid interacting with the neighbours.

While I was in the shop with a black marker pen I decided to increase the cost of photocopying. I stuck a blank postcard over the 4p part of the sign and wrote 6p. I wanted to leave the rest of the sign alone.

Some of the signs in the shop window had faded, especially the one which said *Advertise here for 25p a week*. So I increased this to £1 and just to imply some improvement in this more expensive service I removed all the cards then cleaned the plastic postcard-holder in warm water. As it soaked I looked through the cards. It gave me a slight buzz to think of Dad inserting them. Each card had a date on the back showing when they should have been removed. I threw out the four really faded ones and the five which were over two years out of date. This only left me two, one for a DUNCAN'S LANDSCAPE GARDENING and my own advert. So two more were retrieved from the bin so the display would not look too poor. The survivors were KITTENS AVAILABLE, FREE TO GOOD HOMES, although they would certainly be cats by now, and MIKE WRIGHT THE BUILDER, NO JOB TOO SMALL because he had made the effort to use coloured pens to make his phone number more memorable, all the fours in red and the twos in green plus a single, blue three.

I decided to walk to Will's house. I preferred the idea of the crisp night air to a taxi, and anyway I had a nagging doubt I would get the Tom Cruise taxi driver which would embarrass me.

I had the whole building to myself. I had the keys to both sides of a semi. My house was cold as outside and all the ceilings needed dusting. But I told myself I preferred the knock-through lounge/diner in my house to the separate rooms of Will's. Then I allowed myself to imagine how this difference in number 4 Wood Road would be nice in contrast to number 2 Wood Road if I really did own the whole property. I could have a long dining room – bit like a castle's great hall. They had given their house a name, The Firs; it was cut precisely into a weathered ellipse of wood.

I let myself into number 2, The Firs, and walked round just to get the feel of the place. I turned on the central heating and listened to it. Iman had left the map of Narnia rolled out on the dining-room table. I studied it, and she was right, it was amazing what children would believe. It was also amazing that Wesley would not be believed.

If anyone had seen the orange and black cowboys and thought it was more than a game they may have told the police Will's car registration. This would lead them here and I decided I needed a strategy ready in case the police called. I decided I would tell them I was Will. Getting to know him again Will seemed unpredictable,

30

by pretending to be him I would sort things out with the police. I could predict what I'd do. So, when they came to the door of The Firs, number 2 Wood Road, I would say, 'Oh fucking Christ! Has there been an accident?' This way I would establish what the police represent to me. Anyone (particularly on the telly) who says, 'Who wants to know?' when the police ask for them, is guilty.

I thought we ought to hide the black and orange cowboy outfits. I went into Will's bedroom and opened his wardrobe. I couldn't see them, so I looked through all his stuff. There was a comedy leopardskin thong in his pant drawer.

Iman's side of the wardrobe was very crowded yet precise. She had a fabric shoe-holder, with two pairs shoved in each compartment, which hung from the top to the base of the wardrobe. Obscured behind this was a real fur coat hanging flat against the back of the wardrobe. This was strange because no one wears real fur these days. Tilting the fabric shoe-holder forwards I lifted out the fur coat. The black rhinestone cowboy shirt was inside the orange rhinestone waistcoat on the hanger inside the coat. This was a masterly stroke by Will. Even if someone saw us and even if they got our number (and if the police got past my clever line at the door) and the house was searched then this just looked like a fur coat. If the shirts were found inside the coat one may easily assume they belonged to a woman and one would also assume they belonged in the back of her wardrobe in an unwearable coat.

I had the idea Saturday night and it would not go away on Sunday: I really would like the run of the whole house.

Sunday morning I decided to go into number 4 and get the feel of the place. The house was as cold as the bottom of the sea. I stood in the hallway and coughed, deliberately, just to introduce myself once more. I decided to let the lodger have the back bedroom (number two, 11′ 4″ by 10′ 2″, with the rear garden aspect). I would have bedroom one at the front of the house with the fitted wardrobes. I stood in the wardrobe, but left the sliding door open

31

because, and I whispered this bit to myself, 'It is very foolish to shut oneself into any wardrobe.'

'Who said that?' I wondered out loud and waited for a few seconds for the answer to come to the front of my brain: 'The children in *The Lion, the Witch and the Wardrobe* say that.'

My Saturday-night idea must have come from the map and now my Sunday idea was to do something so simple and so strange that the adults would not believe it.

I rang Mike Wright the builder.

'Hello, sorry to call on a Sunday morning but can I speak to Mike Wright the builder.'

'This isn't the Wrights,' I heard, and as the woman said it I thought maybe I had remembered the wrong number of red fours or green twos, but then a man came on the line, 'I'm Mike Wright, well I was, sorry about the confusion but that was my building name – like Ian Wright the footballer. I figured he got so much press because he was Mr Wright, I mean had he been Ian Palmer – that's me, well it's Mike Palmer actually – then—'

And I interrupted him because I knew what he was going to say. 'Well if you're not a builder then I'm even more sorry for disturbing you on a Sunday morning.' But Mike kept talking, 'I could do it today cash in hand and that, I've nothing on, is it a small job you're wanting because no job is too—' and we both said: 'small.'

Mike Wright panicked me and I agreed to take the time he offered and as soon as I hung up I regretted it. Mike would be here 'around lunchtime'. This could easily mean anytime between twelve and two, but this was Sunday which could extend it a bit later still – the Old Elm Arms serve Sunday lunch until four.

Mike arrived within fifteen minutes of the phone call, before I could get a story straight in my head. He had a bag of tools in his left hand and he stooped slightly as he walked up the path as if unused to their weight. He paused and read the house name, The Firs, number 2, just as I'd told him over the phone. I opened the door and obviously looked surprised.

32

'No, it's not me!' said Mike Wright the builder.

'What?'

'Oh, sorry, it's just you looked so surprised. I'm forever being mistaken for Jeremy Beadle. That's what I meant by it's not me.'

'Sorry, no. I was surprised by how quick you got here. I thought you'd be here later.'

'Oh.' He sounded disappointed.

'You don't even have the beard. You look nothing like Jeremy Beadle.'

'No, but that's why I shaved it off. It ruined me, you can't be a builder and look like Jeremy Beadle. Where's the trust!'

I decided to trust him. Mike paused on the threshold and said, 'Right then, what can I do for you?' and he held out his right hand for shaking. In shaking his hand I expected a firmer grip and it took me a moment to realise his hand felt soft. I suppose I had been instinctively expecting a builder to have rough hands but I was still feeling surprised at just how little he looked like Jeremy Beadle. And then I was surprised that he'd resisted the temptation to say 'What can I do you for?' Had he said this I would have taken a dislike to him and put him off; instead I led him upstairs. If I had registered his smooth lotioned grip quickly enough I would also have had reason to put him off and called in a practising builder, but instead I led him into Will and Iman's number-one bedroom.

'What can I do you for then, sir?' said Mike, and I turned and just managed to smile in time as we made eye contact.

'I want a hole made between the two houses,' I said, and Mike nodded sagely. I can only assume he had already decided to nod sagely no matter what the request, to suggest he'd seen and done it all before, to inspire confidence. He answered, 'All right' like this was not the first time someone had asked him to join up two houses, and put his tool bag down on the bed.

So before Mike started improvising and saying what he really thought, I began a story that would be my story. 'You see, Mike, I own both properties, or I own the whole thing – two semis, the

33

one building – and I want a portal between.' I could see I was losing him. Mike started looking around the room and then looking around the ceiling. Maybe it was the word 'portal', it made it sound too fantastical. 'Yeah, so I need a little door between the two. You see my mother is going to live in this part of the house and I am going to be next door. She is elderly with heart trouble and wants me to have some emergency access in here in case of need.'

'Nice Artexing. A real pro job.' Mike stopped looking at the ceiling and just to prove he had been listening said, 'Well, we can't go through the chimney breast because, well, what would Santa do!' and he winked at me but I broke eye contact just as I saw what he was going to do so maybe the wink missed. 'No, seriously the chimneys are obviously well double thick, you'll have a cavity wall between the properties anyway but the best thing is,' dramatic builder's pause, the tip of the index finger raised briefly to his lips – it was all coming back to Mike – then, 'to take one of the wardrobes out, I mean an old woman can't have enough clothes for two wardrobes. Or, a cheaper option would be to go through the wardrobe. It's emergency access, you say? Well that way it won't show and you'll have it when you need it.'

'Would you like a cup of tea, Mike?'

'That would be excellent.'

'Sugar?' Then, as if remembering one of the finer details of his builder persona, Mike gave the correct answer.

'Three please. Lovely job.'

Mike took his cup of tea next door, and I saw a hint of relief register in his face when I gave him the house keys. He must have realised he needed some sort of corroboration before breaking a hole into another property. I hoped the tea would keep him warm in my cold house. My job was to knock on the wall at the position I wanted the tiny door. I took a final look at Iman's clothes and tried to take a mental photograph of them, so I could replace them all exactly. To aid my memory I took off the duvet and laid them out on the double bed in the order they came out of the wardrobe.

Then I put the duvet back over them. The hanging fabric shoe-holder and fur coat were put across the pillows.

Mike was knocking at the wardrobe, it was a gentle sound like a chick tapping from the inside of its egg. I stood in the wardrobe and returned the knocking, bottom right. Mike got louder, I got louder – I could feel the vibrations. Then Mike started knocking higher up the wall but I did not, I just kept my position. I would have to tell him I only wanted a tiny child-sized door.

Mike came back into the bedroom and handed back the house keys and his empty tea mug.

'I can probably do it today, if I can get what I need at the DIY store.' Then after a moment Mike realised he had dropped a stitch of his work outfit and said, 'I'll go to the DIY place, thing is, the builder's merchant, where I've a trade account, isn't open Sundays.'

'What about the quote?'

'Oh, er, "You've got to bet on the horses to win at the races" – Tommy Docherty!' Mike seemed so pleased to have recalled one of his builder jokes that I had to laugh but I was still laughing as he quickly said, 'Call it two hundred?' Now I could see the tactic, if they're laughing maybe try a high price and I wasn't sure if I could haggle or not. My secret fear was that Mike smelt something dodgy and knew he could ask a top price. But wouldn't it be more natural to haggle?

'I only want an emergency door for my mum's peace of mind in case every second counts, hopefully it will never be used. Let's make it a small door and we can enlarge it if she dies and I have the place to myself. Wouldn't a small door cost less? How about £150? You know what, Mike, rather than an actual door could you not make it a bit concealed, use the white board just like what's in there – so my mum won't feel self-conscious about it? That way if she ever did have to go into a home I could just brick it up and sell up?'

Mike got into the wardrobe and pushed against the back, 'Yeah, all right, we could even use this board, unscrew it, cut out a door bit – that'd work.'

I didn't want any hinges to show but I could not afford to tell Mike this, it would be getting too weird. So I thought of a solution.

'Tell you what, Mike, I have a pretty clear idea of what I need, how about you go to the DIY store and get what you need but just to make the tiny doorway. I'll do the rest and pay you £160.'

'Done,' said Mike reaching out to shake my hand from inside the wardrobe, but as I had a mug of tea in my right hand I just gave him that. He was still laughing as he left for the DIY store.

In the time he was away I hurried to find where Iman kept the bedding, then I got what seemed like some of the older sheets and put one on the wardrobe floor, one on the carpet and one on the bed. I wanted to do more, to tape them in place against the skirting board, but I wasn't sure if it would leave a mark. I looked for the tape to try anyway, but could only find a roll of red Christmas tape that had *Merry Christmas and a Happy New Year* on it, this was in a Christmas box in the cupboard above Iman's wardrobe. Iman might miss it. My search was cut short as the phone rang.

I wanted to answer by saying Will's phone number but paused as I looked for the number on the phone. I tried to remember it, and said, 'Five five four something. Hello?'

'Hellos. I'd like to be awarded the room,' said a voice that conjured up a mental image of Jean-Claude Van Damme.

'Awarded?'

'Yes, the room in the language school.'

'Ah, ok, when could you come to see it?'

'Where is it?'

'Four Wood Road, it's not a student house – I only need one lodger.'

'I can come now to view.' I marvelled at how he seemed to have accidentally hit precisely the right word in 'view'.

'Ok,' I said, to sound positive, because I knew it was an international word, friendly like Coca-Cola.

'Ok!' he replied then hung up.

I continued my search for the sticky tape, then settled for

nestling the edges of the sheets against the wall. As I worked I realised I had started a sort of race between Mike Wright and the voice of Jean-Claude Van Damme. Both were coming to see me, but in different houses. Where should I be?

My solution was to sit on the wall by the pavement. I sat just on the side of number 2, The Firs, because I thought Mike would come first as he had a van. When I saw the van approaching I would pretend I had been doing a bit of gardening – a natural occupation for a Sunday afternoon, even in late November. So I pulled out a daffodil bulb by its tied back leaves and rubbed the dirt into my fingertips.

A red car pulled up and a man with straight black hair and a wild curly beard got out. 'Number four?' he said and I tried to follow the voice back through the beard to see the face of Jean-Claude Van Damme.

'Yes,' I said, as I gestured next door with the daffodil bulb. As I did it I caught a momentary point of stillness in the racing after-noon. The bulb was beautiful, round and delicately warm.

I led him to the door. 'You've come to see the room?'

'To view it, yes. My name is Tymoteusz Wazyk from Poland.' And he held out a hairy hand for shaking. I took it tentatively hoping he would not mind the mud on my fingertips and trying to remember what name he had just said. He was obviously used to this sort of instant forgetfulness and continued, 'But people here just call me Tym.' Both his hand and his handshake were rough.

'I am Liam.'

'Oh, that's an unusual name,' said Tym.

I led the way up the drive and into the porch, unlocked the door and let Tym follow me through the hall and up the stairs towards the 11′ 4″ by 10′ 2″ bedroom number two. This was my way of showing some trust, to walk in front of him knowing he could jump me or stab me. Being from Poland I thought he wouldn't mind how cold it was in the house.

'This way,' I said when I knew he was following me closely. 'I'll

37

show you the room first.' Tym walked around the room, actually around the edges as if measuring it out in paces.

'Nice,' he said. 'I have some furniture.'

'Well obviously I'll get the basics in, chair, some drawers and a bed.' Then just to seem approachable and adult I asked, 'Would you like a single or a double?' Tymoteusz stopped walking as he reached the window.

'I don't mind. I am pleased easily.' Whether or not he meant to sound enigmatic he certainly did, very foreign and ambivalent. In fact he threw me and I found myself returning to estate-agent speak to fill the silence.

'Mid-blue carpet,' and I pointed at it because, even though I had not wanted to tell him the obvious, now I had started I wanted to appear confident. 'The carpet will remain.' And I don't know if it was the coincidence of my estate-agent speak and English as Tym might speak it, but he gave me such a lovely smile I decided he could have the room.

There was a knock at the door. After going down eight of the fourteen stairs I could see Mike calling through the letterbox. 'Hello! It's me – the builder, are you there?' I stopped on the ninth step down, saying, 'Tym, do you want to look round the rest of the house?' Tym came to the top of the stairs but I didn't decrease my volume as this was for Mike's benefit too. 'I'll be back in a minute.'

Tym nodded.

Mike was standing at the back of his van. He tilted his head towards the open van door, and I helped him carry in some small metal girders. Tiny girders, the sort that would be used for real Wendy houses.

'All right?' said Mike, but I didn't answer him until we were in The Firs' front bedroom, this way I did not risk pausing outside in case Mrs Price was watching.

'Fine,' I said in answer to Mike – which seemed to surprise him. 'A small door then, just there.' I pointed with a flat hand to the bottom inside right of the left-hand wardrobe like I was patting a child on the head.

'Ok, ok. Can you leave both front doors on the latch? So I can work it out from each side. Rather like making a pin-prick on both sides of an egg and then blowing out the yolk.' Then Mike paused, 'Or maybe not. I've never done a job like this, but I have done the egg-blowing thing with my youngest.'

I left Mike to his work. One thought filled my mind: I needed to get Tym out of my house before Mike entered it. Being so preoccupied was just perfect. It stopped me remembering that the story I had given Mike was a fib. I shut the front door on the sound of the electric drill. But as I climbed the stairs in number 4 I heard the drill note rising.

Tym was in the bathroom looking behind the sink. 'I like the house, and I would like much to move in.'

'Good.'

'How much is the rent; how much is the deposit?' I had not thought about this at all, I had no idea what my living costs would be and no idea what rents were in the area. I didn't want it to be too expensive for a student like Tym or too cheap to appear unrealistic.

'Forty pounds a week,' I said and Tym smiled so I pushed it slightly, 'plus a share of the bills.' He still smiled.

'And the deposit?'

'A month's rent, call it four weeks, one hundred and sixty pounds.'

He kept smiling and unfurled the deposit in cash, saying, 'May I receive a receipt?' Which I wrote on the back of a Christmas card that had come for the previous occupants. (Maybe it was from a previous Christmas?) Anyway, it was the only white paper I could find. I took the precaution of tearing off the picture of a robin first then wrote: 'RECEIVED WITH THANKS £160 DEPOSIT (BEING FOUR WEEKS RENT OF £40) FOR SINGLE ROOM AND HOUSE SHARE LODGINGS AT 4 WOOD ROAD'. Tym seemed pleased with the receipt, and he flipped his fingernail against its edge as he read it to himself. I realised I didn't know if we had just agreed a deposit and advance rent or just a deposit and thought I'd just see what Tym decided to do. Tym said 'Farewell' and was gone.

I went into the number-one bedroom in number 4, my bedroom, to listen for the drill. As I heard it burrowing into the brick I imagined how wet the mortar had once been. Someone could see this door as being wrong but I wasn't thinking about that, I was just letting the idea take shape. This was a strange calmness, like knowing a nightmare is a dream. I had not moved into number 4 yet, I had the flat, maybe I wanted to stay in the flat. I was pretty sure I could disguise the portal although until it was done I was not sure how. If no one ever saw the door they couldn't see it as being wrong. Will didn't even know I owned the house, but the fact remains I owned it and it was my wall I was removing too – well, nearly all my wall.

The sheer excitement, not the sound of the drill, gave me an erection. I lay down on it and felt the strength of the floorboards.

Hearing Mike call up my stairs, number 4's stairs, made me realise the drill had stopped. I raced out of the room and we passed on the stairs.

'Like the channel tunnel isn't it, when they shook hands through that hole on the news. Remember?' And I nodded to let him know I did.

Now he was working in number 4 I went next door into number 2, The Firs, to boil the kettle, not because I wanted more tea, just for something to do. But it didn't work and I began to feel guilty. Nothing sexual, I wasn't going to perv in on Iman. Then I felt dirty for even having the thought. Maybe I should have a cup of tea. Mike would probably want one. I only heard the kettle boiling once the drill stopped next door. Instead of asking Mike I would just make him a cup of very strong sweet tea.

'Finished!' shouted Mike from the top of Will's stairs right there in number 2. It gave me a start. I had carried the tea to the front door and had just opened it one-handed as he called and I spilt a dribble of tea on the carpet. I turned and scuffed it in. I looked at him in wonder as I climbed the stairs. Not because of who he was, but because of where he'd been. Mike was the first man to go through these two houses, to attach what had always been detached. The top stair creaked. I gave him his tea. 'Ah, that's the stuff, better than champagne to celebrate,' said Mike.

'That was quick. What about shaking hands through the gap and that, like the channel tunnel?' I stopped myself, I had more to say but realised I was rambling. What I really meant was that it only took minutes to puncture this building.

'Sorry, did you want to do that handshaking thing?' said Mike, so sweetly it made me think I bet he gets on really well with his youngest.

'No, it's just when you said it – well, it made it sound like a bigger job.' I followed him into Will and Iman's bedroom. The doorway was huge. Panic hit me like Jean-Claude Van Damme all over and at once.

'It's huge!' I mouthed, surprisingly audible.

'Yes! And at no extra cost!'

'No, we said a small door – I used the word tiny, you know as in Tiny Tim.'

'But the brick just went all dusty under the drill. I pulled the rubble through in the other side where it's empty. I put it all on a dust sheet. Just bundle it up,' said Mike helpfully. 'I wouldn't say it was huge, anyway, more approaching normal size. Youth-sized rather than child-sized.' Mike's tone became quite firm and fatherly. 'I had enough metal to give you firm edges, just wait a day for the cement to set. I'll cut the door into the white board after this cuppa.'

It reminded me of how I felt when Dad died – I just wanted to get into the future. I wanted Mike out, maybe another builder in and just get into the future when I would be able to think of an answer.

'Leave the white board.'

'It's ok,' said Mike, putting down his empty mug.

'No. Sincerely, leave it. I mean you've already done more work than we'd said for the money.' Before another flurry of panic punches could connect I remembered the deposit money. At least that fitted and I could pay Mike off right now. As soon as he saw the money I didn't need to persuade him.

'Let me know if you want anything else doing, cheers for the tea!' he called out walking backwards to his van. I waved. Then the panic that I had agreed to pay him cash in hand without any cash hit me. I sat down and worried that I was worrying about the thing that didn't go wrong rather than the doorway that did. I took deep breaths and tried to get into the present.

I had not missed Aslan until he appeared. Cats are often fearful of strangers and I was a stranger. The building noise must have scared him off too, but then I heard the flap of the cat flap and his mewing. His mew did not suit him, it was too squeaky, too mousey. Or maybe this was just how he mewed if he hadn't eaten for days. I put plenty of food down.

He was reluctant to eat while I was in the kitchen so I left him to it, but sneaked back. He looked up before carrying on, his back end curled up like the front of a boxing glove.

I had a week to sort things out. I thought about repairing the portal. Monday I went to the library, rejoined, and got out a book on bricklaying. I managed to get the heating working, and I was sitting in number 4 reading the library book when Tym arrived. Well, partially arrived. He had 'multiple' car loads of stuff and could only bring one today. I was still reading the book when Tym left. I gave him the spare key. There would be no need to give it to Will as I would not be telling him this was my house. As he'd suggested it I would give him a spare key, in case of lock-outs, for the flat. Monday night I read the book in bed between two duvets.

A storm started, no build-up of rain; it just got turned on. It made me feel at home because I was snug in a duvet sandwich and the wind and rain could not dislodge me. I wondered if Aslan was in or out next door.

Now, after spending forty minutes with a policeman, I know that the early hours of a stormy night are the worst/best time for burglaries. (Also to be aware of a repeat job a few months later when the insurance will have come and replacements go missing.) But Tuesday morning I just went next door to number 2, The Firs, and thought I don't remember leaving the cupboard under the stairs open. In fact I don't even remember opening it. Even then I only thought, could Aslan have opened it? Some cats can open doors with handles, but presumably only doors that open inwards. Then I wondered if the latch on the cupboard door was broken and reckoned if I could brick-lay I could mend a door latch.

The house was a quiet mess, not the type of mess burglars make when they rob during the day or when they know the house to be empty, but a methodical mess. Things were turned inside out, drawers were emptied out on to thick towels taken from the bathroom and downstairs loo. I went into Will's bedroom and put the white board over the portal before calling the police. It made me feel criminal. Two policemen arrived. They saw it was, 'A sadly all too common and routine occurrence, sir.' Then they were radioed (for something non-routine) and the shorter one, who looked a bit like a non-hirsute Bob Hoskins, left. I thought police always had to stay in pairs?

The telly was gone along with the video and stereo. In the dining room the chairs were gone but the table had been left. The map of Narnia had been unrolled and left on the floor, its edges curled up as if it had tried to roll back up. Some books were splayed out next to it. The policeman thought this meant they were looking for money tucked into the pages. It does happen.

Upstairs nothing was gone. I had to explain to the policeman that the number-one bedroom, Will's bedroom, already looked like that – he thought it was the work of the robbers with all the things laid out, but all they had done was pull back the sheet.

The policeman and I drank tea together. I had quite forgotten about Wesley until that point. This bare kitchen breakfast bar (microwave and chocolate biscuits nicked) made a passable interview room and I imagined the policeman wanting answers from me. But he didn't and I didn't have to justify myself, I didn't even have to say it was my house – he just assumed it was. Then I decided to tell him I was house-sitting and he assumed that meant I was in the second or third bedroom last night.

'In a way, sir, you were fortunate the criminals did not come into your room. Sleep with the door closed, do you?' I nodded as I sipped my tea.

'I'd had a few lagers last night, I was dead to the world.'

'Well then, that door was your salvation, burglars aren't into confrontation and you'd be surprised what a deterrent a shut door can be.'

I started to cry as the policeman spoke, I felt like giving myself up to him. He had such a warm voice and did not look like any actor I had ever seen. He looked like I could trust him. 'I've had it so rough – you know, really rough.'

'Have you been burgled before?'

As a matter of fact I had, it was strange, everything was tidied away before I got back from school. I wanted to tell him all about it. 'Well, yes, as a lad, about nine, living with my dad, and my mum in our shop. We were burgled. Except I got a message at school to go to my friend's house.' I pointed at the kitchen wall, meaning this friend, Will's, but it was too subtle for him to understand. I went on, 'So, I went there. We played Buckaroo, Operation and we watched *The Sweeney*. Will's dad went to help my dad, and by the time he came to pick me up the shop and the flat were all back to normal. My dad died last month.'

'I'm sorry to hear that, sir.' He was looking at his shoes.

'I was scared though, after being burgled at nine years old, lying in bed that night I felt there was a ghost in the house. Like kids do, because they can't be sure that ghosts don't exist and I knew someone had been through the house. They'd left a funny smell, like paint, or maybe ghosts smell like fresh paint – all white and that?'

'I'm sorry to hear that. *The Sweeney* was good though, wasn't it?'

'What?'

'That got me interested in coppering, *The Sweeney*.'

'Oh. Before I came back I was away, you know, living like a proper adult, no more studenting, going for proper jobs, now I've inherited my dad's shop and I thought it was good to be back, because of this friend, his house; now I've lost bits of his house. He leaves me in charge for a poxy week and I lose stuff.'

'There have been a spate of burglaries in this area, don't be too hard on yourself, sir.'

I was winding myself up, getting very emotional. 'And she had racism,' I blubbed and blurted. 'She was only down at the station last week after that note came.'

'Young woman?' said the policeman, as if that narrowed it down, which it didn't really. 'I think I know who you mean.' But that was good enough for me, it was a connection of sorts and I felt we were bonding because of our mutual friend and shared experiences of burglary.

Back in number 4 there was the smell of grapefruit. I smelt it in the hallway and followed it into the kitchen. The half-eaten fruit was on the work surface and the eaten half was in the pedal bin – lid left up. Tym's cupboard was full, the tins were stacked very accurately on the lower shelf, labels facing out, grouped like with like in a pile four long and three high, except there were only eleven tins, leaving a gap on the top right. Above them were the packets, rice, pasta, jelly and a block of six kitchen knives.

In the lounge Tym had placed his brown corduroy bean-bag in the corner by the double radiator. I could see two potted plants at the far end of the lounge/diner by the window and I imagined them looking longingly out at the plants in the garden while the plants in the garden looked jealously in on them. The leaves were tiny and shaped like hands waving.

In the bathroom Tym had put a brass presentation shaving set – still boxed – on the window sill. A can of lemon air freshener now sat on the toilet cistern. His toothbrush had a yellow dinosaur handle and his toothpaste was strawberry flavoured. There was a twelve-pack of economy toilet roll behind the bathroom door. He had obviously done the house-sharing thing before and I felt like I was being courted.

As I walked into his bedroom I only just remembered to knock on the door before I saw he was not there. There were three pregnant black bin liners, two tied and one with the ankles of some jeans hanging over the top. A computer on top of a suitcase flat on its side (just the right height for working at cross-legged) and a twin tape, no CD, stereo. He had put up two posters, one for a production of *A Midsummer Night's Dream* by the RSC and the other (a framed film poster) for *A Midsummer Night's Sex Comedy* by Woody Allen. Tym thought this was a joke and I wondered if to him it was a pun or just a funny coincidence. His wardrobe door was slightly ajar. But in the time it took him to turn his front door key, still not used to the particularities of the lock, I was out on the landing and leaning over the banisters.

'Hiya Tym!', then walking down two of the fourteen stairs, 'Need a hand?'

'Yes, these to go higher yes,' and he pointed up at me and placed two carrier bags on to the bottom step and walked into the kitchen carrying a single tin of beans.

He came out of the kitchen eating the remainder of his grapefruit without a spoon, looking very Jean-Claude Van Damme as the circle of the fruit obscured his beard which glistened when he had finished.

'Excuse me,' he said as he went to the bathroom and I heard him

46

wash his face. He walked down the stairs rubbing the beard dry with his paw and I think I was supposed to be pleased he had thought not to wash his face in the kitchen sink. He took the two carrier bags from the bottom step, smiled, then went upstairs.

I decided to make Tym a cup of tea. I could have asked but if I didn't it would make me seem considerate and would hopefully make Tym feel more at home. It would imply I did not mind him using my cups and saucers – and hopefully he would infer from the fact that I have cups and saucers in this mug age something of the man I am. I am nothing if not thorough. As the kettle boiled I thought that really these inherited cups and saucers said more about the type of man my Dad was but that Tym could safely assume I was similar. A wave of sadness broke over my shoulders and welled up behind my eyes. I could just see Dad resting his tea-spoon in the curve of pale blue flower saucer having just made two rhythmic taps against the cup lip. I could only breathe through one nostril, maybe I was getting a cold.

I did not want to cry, although I could see the advantages. I could just let things go a bit, think about Dad helping me learn to ride a bike and play football, all that stuff, but I didn't want Tym to see me and he was coming downstairs. As a diversion I counted his steps, twelve, maybe he has stopped, but then he was by the kitchen door. I poured the tea without turning to face him.

'Tea?' I offered the cup like a handshake.

'Oh, very kind, but no, thank you.' But I carried on, 'How many sugars?'

'NO!' and he gave the word the same definite shove to leave his throat that I would have to give the stubborn Polish word for no. 'I don't take tea.' I bit back on the tears. 'Then I will make you some coffee,' I said with a confident flourish I didn't feel.

'No. I do not take coffee, neither.' And for the second time that day I started to cry.

This seemed to make Tym feel at home, which made me worry about his home. He gave me a very European hug and it did the trick. Then Tym carried both cups of tea into the lounge and gestured that I should sit on the brown bean-bag. He sipped his tea thoughtfully, confirming it was just a prop for him to engage me. Then, just for something to say, I said, 'I like your potted plants. Nice pots.'

'Ah, you like pot too – good – I was a little unsure as they are illegal but we can take pot together if you wish.' Now I had been to university but I had never seen a pot plant. But that was obviously untrue. The fact was I had seen them but not known what they were. The leaves just looked like hands to me.

I felt very moral all of a sudden, I think it was holding Dad's cup and saucer that did it. So, I tapped the lip of the cup twice, as if calling order, and put the teaspoon into the flowery curve of the saucer and said, 'I don't think they are appropriate.'

'When?' said Tym and I wondered if that was the word he had wanted but tried to answer him.

'At any time, I am against them; it. They are yours but,' and I wanted to mention the police because they were on my mind, I mean should they come round about Wesley and I have to give them the line about 'Oh fucking Christ has there been an accident' I will definitely sound suspect knowing there are two dope plants in the front room. 'But I have a friend who is a policeman and if he comes round to visit he will nick you.' I said it as if I was proud of my imaginary friend's conscience.

'He will nick?'

'Yes.' I liked being in charge; of the Crabbe sisters, of Will's house and now of Tym. He took one of them upstairs and as he came back for the other said, 'This is a female plant, I will sell this for a lot of money at college. No worries.'

I bought some fishing line and the stuff to rebuild the wall: bricks, half-bricks and mortar, a trowel, a paintbrush and two tiny girders just the right size for building a doll's house. I was fucking angry when I bought all the stuff and I fucking forgot to buy a spirit level.

(I'd spent £32.60 including VAT because bricks are such a price and I'd said I wasn't trade – if I'd said it was for work and asked for a VAT receipt I reckon he'd have given it to me cheaper and less the 17½ per cent but my mind is not set right for fraud.) I even saw them by the door and thought there are the spirit levels. I remembered the paintbrush as featured on page 16 for wetting the bricks with water should you need to re-point any bit – it makes the cement dry more slowly, making a better bond. The spirit level was on page fucking 2, *tools of the trade*. I was so annoyed because I am nothing, nothing, if not thorough.

I didn't start work until midnight when I was sure Tym would not miss me. I could not wait another day to start, midnight made it officially Wednesday, time was passing and I couldn't risk not being ready in case Will and Iman made an early return. The weather said it was raining in Bournemouth so they just might.

Surgeons feel like this when they are committing murder. Like tree surgeons on bonfire night or policemen who beat their wives. The wall took shape quickly – I even improvised a spirit level (page 116, *appendices*: a key on a string plumb line for the vertical level and a measuring jug with some water for the horizontal level) – but I knew I was not going back. I had no plans to rebuild my part of the double-thick cavity wall and in Will's wall I knew I would leave a workable gap. The line between number 4 and number 2, The Firs, would remain crossed. The heating went off hours ago but the work kept me warm.

At about 2am I stopped working to leave a small aperture about twenty inches square in the bottom left of my wardrobe, making it the bottom right of Iman's. I wanted to try sliding through it but the mortar was still damp and I might undo all the good work. The tiny doll-sized girders had been bricked in at about 1.45am, one vertical, one horizontal – both dead straight. Even though I'd been assured about their torque strengths when I bought them I was not entirely certain what that meant. (And it wasn't in the glossary.) It looked like they could give way and I waited to see if either did.

I had been made aware, by chapter three and part of chapter ten, that the weak point of this wall could be the join I made between Mike Wright's doorway and my filler. This section looked well knitted and I risked a tap with my knuckle to check. It all looked like one of those medieval church doors, or the doors to a prison, where a massive door has a smaller door cut into it.

After I had made a small square brick plug of a door I had three bricks and two half-bricks left. The plan was that usually this brick door would be in place to avoid any tell-tale drafts creeping out past the white board. I've only got an electric drill so I went and got Will's hand-drill because it's silent. (I walked around and used the front door key.) With this I was able to make some pinpoint holes in the corners of the white laminated board that made the back of Iman's wardrobe. The holes went into the wood, stopped short of going right through, and out at each corner edge. By this time the mortar was the consistency of butter. I nudged the drill bit through the mortar, making holes for the fishing line from the corners of the backboard. This way I could pull the line taught on the corners, and always make sure the white board was flush to the wall after I had finished with the portal. It was a neat job, the fishing line was strong and the holes secure, like invisible stitches. Nothing showed on Iman's side.

Will had a tenpin bowling ball in the bottom of his wardrobe behind his cowboy boots. I took this back with me to number 4 and put the bowling ball, still in its box, against the back of the brick plug door. Next I nailed a strip of wood into the floorboard right behind it. I didn't care if the banging woke Tym because it was all over in about fifteen seconds. Now, even if the white laminated board was removed and the brick door spotted it would not move if shoved. (I decided, for extra thoroughness, that I wouldn't always put the bowling ball in place, and I wouldn't always tie the fishing line – its main purpose was to pull the board tight, not to secure it. Yes, these things were necessary when I was in my room, but say I wanted to get through from Will's side? If I

50

was round there legitimately I might want to disappear. I must never cut off my own escape route! Christ I'm thorough, if nothing else, I am thoroughly thorough.) Mike Wright had made a little threshold between the houses to cover the cavity, I cleared away the dust and left it looking like a polished front doorstep.

Taking the bowling ball made me realise I could take anything from Will's house and blame it on the burglars. Fantastic, really fantastical. But on Wednesday morning before I took anything I re-hung the clothes in the wardrobe and practised opening and re-sealing the portal. If I left the fishing line untied in number 4 I could prise the white board off from inside Iman's wardrobe, but it was hard on the fingertips.

What I stole from number 2, The Firs: an unopened jar of smooth peanut butter, a large part-eaten bar of milk chocolate, £7.56 in change and, from Iman's bra and pant drawer, her diary.

The diary was a mid-blue exercise book, obviously taken from the stationery cupboard at her school. The fact she had stolen it first made me feel a bit better about nicking it. Not that I felt that bad at all – it was fucking dynamite-fireworks-beer. I ate the rest of the milk chocolate as I started to read. A tobacco-like fragment fell from my lips and lodged itself into the spinal fold of the paper. My instinct was to weedle it out, but I relaxed and left it to smudge when it melted.

January 1
D.D. (Which I puzzled about, but guessed means Dear Diary, I skipped forward to check and sometimes it becomes Dee-Dee as if they are friends) *welcome to another year in the life of me. Well, so much changed in the last year that I can't predict where I will be when I write the sequel, except that we are in our lovely house and in our lovely marriage and I hope to stay put for a while.*
As is tradition, here are my New Year Resolutions:

1. To quit smoking (the traditional opening resolution) But she must have done it because I never knew she did it.
2. To get a cat (and keep Will)
3. To get more music
4. To be happier and happier
5. To stage a play at school – because the last one was two years ago
6. (The traditional closing resolution) To keep this diary for the eleventh year

P.S. As always there is no P.S.

Highlight: 83% 3am this morning (it is now 10.30pm and I am having an early night – the curtains need cleaning!) Will, dressed in a burgundy cardigan and pale blue pleated trousers and a blond highlighted wig singing Edge of Heaven by Wham at Jemma's 1980s theme New Year Party.

Every day had a highlight and a score. I fast-forwarded through the diary for them.

February 8 Highlight: 68% Thinking about summer holidays in the bath – Dublin or Italy. I wonder if I should take my fur coat to a charity shop, I never wear it.

March 23 Highlight: 56% Dancing on the bed to the Jackson 5 – originally scored 71% but I dislodged some plaster in the front room ceiling.

March 29 Highlight: 43% Sneaking a cigarette in the pub garden from a bloke called Steve. Decided definitely not to take my fur coat to a charity shop, it was my great grandmother's, that's an heirloom.

April 4 Highlight: 84% Intimacy, twice.

April 5 Highlight: 39% EastEnders, no actually just before the start of EastEnders.

July 15 Highlight: 60% Just before waking up thinking it was Monday and realising it was Sunday.

August 30 Highlight: 60% Tried Mars Ice Cream, would have *scored more as it was delicious and yummo but I felt sad I'd not risked it earlier in the summer.*

October 1 *Highlight: 85% First-class hug in the frozen aisle at Supermarket, tried again in the wines and spirits but it wasn't as nice.*

I re-checked the figures and marvelled at how an October hug in the supermarket scored one per cent more than intimacy twice in a day in April.

The diary stopped on 2 October and I realised there had to be a second volume for the remainder of the year, which Iman was obviously still writing in Bournemouth this week. I wanted to know what was written about me and at the same time I didn't want to know. I've often thought how easy it would be to record people when I am not in the room and then hear what is said about me. If I wanted to know this sort of thing I could, but it would be easy to think the stuff up or just eavesdrop. But a diary would tell me not what was said about me but what she actually thought.

I knew things about Iman Will did not know. Not just the occasional faked orgasm in the late spring but the detail, the arch of her back, the first grey hair in her pubic mound and the crooked smile of her head-teacher, Mr *Please just call me Terry* Armitage.

I finished the bar of chocolate, and went back into number 2, The Firs, and replaced the £7.56 in change, the fiver back on the mantelpiece and the change on the kitchen table because I am not a thief. I went back into their bedroom and examined the closed portal once more. Airtight.

The rest of the morning was spent doing my best to un-burgle the place. Drawers were re-filled. The books were closed and put back on the shelves. Iman and Will seemed to order their bookshelves according to colour. I picked up the first few from the floor and the covers were all black, two with gold lettering, one with silver – chunky holiday reads. Next to these were the blue books – from the navy cover of a Bible (a christening present from Uncle Mark to Will) to three mint-green Penguin Modern Classics (obviously Iman's). Although there were books scattered around the room I was able to re-establish a rainbow of order on the shelves. I finished putting back a yellow cook book and then two white books about art. I rerolled the map of Narnia and left it on the dining-room table. I thought about buying some flowers for each room.

The carpet under the table needed a clean. There was glitter and clippings of coloured paper, some breadcrumbs and flakes of mud and chocolate. It would be easy to vacuum with the chairs stolen and out of the way. So I pushed the dining-room table towards the window and searched the house, including the cupboard under the stairs twice, before concluding the vacuum cleaner had been stolen too.

In the front room I righted the armchair (I could see where Iman had dislodged the plaster on 23 March) and put the cushions back on the sofa. I put the spider plant back in its pot and stood in the corner where the TV and video had lived and the suite seemed to stare at me like a dog left tied up outside the shop watching the door. I've seen such things from behind the counter. I had to leave the room.

If I had brought the diary round from number 4 I would have read it on the toilet. It seemed a particularly disrespectful thing to do and I was glad I didn't have it. I did not want to disrespect Iman, the diary would simply be one of the many things that had been stolen. I was trustworthy, they had trusted me, I would not use the diary against her. I allowed myself to keep it. Iman had taken it from her school, it was an exercise book after all, paid for, no doubt, by public tax, so how could someone object to a stolen item being stolen? I would assume, for the thoroughness of my argument, that my tax had paid for this blue feint-lined exercise book so I could keep it. It wasn't stealing, not like the burglars. There had to be a second volume anyway; if I

54

took this one we were just sharing it. Primary school teachers like sharing.

But I did need the loo and rather than go back to mine in number 4 (and the temptation of the diary) I just went upstairs to Will's. I was house-sitting after all. Sitting on Will's toilet made me think about space and time. The portal between our two houses was such a neat job he need never find it. He need never know I even lived next door to him. We could share this building and all this space and I could be so close to him that I could feel the heat from his back without needing to touch him. I remember when Will used to stay with us he'd always get up early to use the bathroom first. He hated it if Dad or me used the toilet first. When I teased him about it he undercut my taunts with a chink of absolute honesty. It wasn't the smell he minded but the warm toilet seat. He had two older brothers, and always got the warm toilet seat. This never bothered me, not even in my student houses.

I looked around for something to read. Toilet cleaner would have done but there was none and they had taken the toothpaste with them. There was a bottle of anti-dandruff shampoo on the edge of the bath which I could read from the loo. RINSE AND REPEAT, FOR EXTERNAL USE ONLY – a familiar story but distracting enough for my purposes. BEST BEFORE *SEE DATE ON BASE OF BOTTLE* but I couldn't reach it. AVOID CONTACT WITH THE EYES, which seemed quite funny words to be reading, well not funny, but it did make me laugh. I reached for the toilet roll, there was none, which made me laugh even more. Not at my predicament but at the thought of the burglars bothering to take it and the fact I had a twelve-pack only next door.

WILLIAM

A338

A31

M27 (Junctions 1 to 3)

M271

A35

A3024

I get a tingle when we get on to our local roads, I feel at home because I can recognise the note of the tarmac under our tyres. So, as Iman drove into Oakley I waved an invisible hello to the Old Elm Arms as we went round the roundabout and down Maxtree Lane. I nodded as we went on to Copse Hill, then along Mill Lane (where the tarmac is patchy and rumbles and in need of replacement) to the smooth surface of Wood Road. I really should get the engine re-tuned, the sound's quite wrong.

'Wow, look, the lights are on next door,' I said.

'And the lights are off in ours. Where's Liam then?' Iman sounded worried, or it could've just been tiredness.

We sped towards the sweet shop, we only had five minutes before it shut. We parked in Liam's space. Through the glass door I could see Edna Crabbe picking her nose, but in the way old ladies do it, through a paper tissue. I pushed the door which was locked but rattled mightily. She stopped picking her nose which implied she could see us, but pretended she could not. I decided not to go to the side of the property where there is a bell for the flat because if Liam was not in ringing it could worry Edna. Instead I just stuck my face to the glass and called out, 'It's me!' because this is a useful thing to say when you want someone to make an exception. Edna recognised me. She recognised me from Liam's childhood, from the funeral and, of course, from line-dancing – in fact I felt her look of recognition was specifically from line-dancing, line-dancers share a specific smile. We're nice people.

Edna said, 'Liam's upstairs,' as she pointed us towards the side door of the flat. I wished she'd let us in: I was freezing my nuts off. She was at the side door before we were, silhouetted against the light she looked large and powerful. 'Liam's upstairs,' she repeated. 'If you'll excuse me. It's been a long day.' And she left us at the bottom of the stairs and walked out into the night.

I didn't feel comfortable just going upstairs to the flat and Iman was twitching her nose at the smell that was sinking down the stairs. It smelled like burnt sugar, familiar but hard to place. I led the way up shouting out, 'Liam! We're coming up, stop wanking!' and I could picture Iman's head shake at that without turning round. Sometimes I just couldn't help myself with Liam. For months now I'd been trying not to swear in front of Iman. Not that she's easily offended, it's just that I'm getting ready to ask her about kids again and I want her to know I wouldn't swear in front of them. I reckon less swearing = more chance of conception. (Also, I've been putting the toilet seat down after I've used it. She likes that too. It's considerate, why should it be left up? It's just sexist. I tried peeing with the seat down, but I usually had to clean it afterwards. She likes it when I put the toilet seat down – it shows I'm considerate enough to father her children.)

As we neared the top of the stairs Liam turned on the light in the living room and said, 'In here,' apologetically stating the obvious. I hadn't heard the telly and wondered if Liam had just turned it off, otherwise he must've just been sitting in the dark. 'Hello Iman, all right Will, tea anyone? I was just going to make some.'

'We thought you'd be in our house.' And Liam ignored me but said 'Excuse me' to Iman as he slipped past into the square kitchen. Square and yellow, it was obviously decorated with sunshine in mind but under strip lighting it looked tense to me. Liam filled the kettle and spoke extra loud to compensate, 'Do you want the good or the bad news?'

'The good news?' says Iman, tentative.

'The good news?' Liam asks himself, like he's thinking up the answer. 'The good news is I have given you a dozen quilted toilet rolls, from stock, and they are already in the house. And the bad news is,' he turns and takes three mugs from the yellow cupboard, 'shit, I thought people were meant to ask for the bad news first, sorry I think I am making this crapper than crap.'

'Just say it,' I said. Liam spilt a bit of sugar off the teaspoon.

'Your house was burgled and they took a lot, toilet rolls, video, stereo, loads of stuff.'

Iman turned and leaned on the work surface, bending slightly and breathing like someone who had just run a race. 'Where were you?' she said quickly, and it sounded for a moment like she was asking Liam for an alibi. There was no need for that.

'The policeman said I was lucky I slept with the door closed, it's a deterrent. The burglars must have—' and I tuned out from the rest of what he said, burglars plural, shit, I suppose my mind had got on to a lone cat burglar image, but that's shit as it was nearly always kids. Maybe Liam had been lucky.

'Thanks,' I said.

'Look, Christ Will, I'm sorry.'

'No, I meant thanks, really. It sounds like you were in danger, we all knew burglaries had been happening and you were still good enough to stay at our place.'

'Oh, thanks,' said Iman and I felt relieved we were in agreement until

61

I saw she was thanking him as he handed over the mug of tea.

The yellow kitchen walls buzzed.

Iman was driving us back before the tea had time to get cold in my stomach. I started talking in the hope it would slow her down.

'Try not to worry. We can get over it.' No answer, so I was more direct. 'Iman, come on, drive more normally. Try and concentrate.'

'Well, I've never been burgled and I have always worried about it. It's always lived in the back of my mind.' She talked fast to keep up with the car. 'And now it's happened I was hoping I could say I feel calm, you know like when a real fear becomes a fact and you can feel calm because what you feared was it happening and then it has happened and the fear decreases.'

'Yes,' I lied, and she could tell and carried on explaining the point to me.

'You know Will, like when people who've come back from near-death experiences say they felt calm, or people who are rescued from drowning just after they had accepted their lot and come to terms with death.'

'Yes.'

'Well, I don't feel like that. I feel frightened.'

'Yes. I always think those people are lying. I think, in the final seconds what kills everyone is fear. Not illness, disease, or even a bus, but the final momentary glimpse of realising that this is death and that is enough to make you breathless, choke or just stop the heart.' You'd never guess a bloke like me would think like that.

Iman said, 'Hmm. Does this engine sound funny to you?' before driving the car up the driveway and into the garage, where we sat in silence for several seconds.

'When we go in the house we'll be all right, you know that don't you?' and Iman managed a smile. 'It's still our house.' Iman got out of the car. She smiled and waited as I locked the garage door. I continued, 'I refuse to let this be too bad. If I were a betting man, I would back you to cope with this.' I stole a kiss as she turned to walk away down the drive.

62

As I opened the door I realised the light had been turned off next door. In the time we had taken to go to Liam's our new neighbour had either gone out or gone to bed. I fumbled for the light switch and felt surprised that it was where I'd left it. I didn't believe the nice stuff I'd said to Iman, I needed to calm down and get some perspective. I took two deep breaths and turned it on.

'So far so good,' I said to Iman. I put the heat on high, that would help.

'No, hang on, look at that stain on the carpet.' And she nudged the darker patch with her toe.

'Yeah, ok, but it's not excrement or graffiti,' and I looked at the lounge door, 'at least not yet.'

'It looks like tea to me,' said Iman and she knelt down and put her nose to the floor and sniffed.

'That'll come out. Maybe Liam spilt it?'

'I hope Liam would have cleared it up! And I can't imagine him spilling any of his precious tea. No, my point is the cocky gits had tea in my house!'

'Iman, get up, we have only just got over the threshold. If, after going round the whole house, our main worry is a blinking tea stain that would be great.'

'Great!' and she looked up at me like a puma about to pounce. 'You stupid cunt.'

'You can't say that!' I was genuinely shocked, primary school teachers should never use that word. 'It was a stupid thing to say but don't say that.' Iman laughed as she stood up. It was a lovely laugh, strong enough to split wood open like a fire.

In turn, left then right, I stuck my toes under the opposite heel and peeled off my shoes. It was supposed to make me feel at home. I have never owned a pair of slippers and although it can be well heavy on socks I like it this way. But I didn't feel at home, instead of the warmth of the carpet it felt gritty. My calf muscle twitched.

'After we've looked around I'll get the vacuum cleaner out and you can have peanut butter on toast,' I said.

'Peanut butter?' Iman asked quizzically.

'Well, whatever comfort food you want. That's what I'm getting at, we're hungry and tired. I think I'll just finish off that chocolate in the fridge.'

Iman darted into the kitchen. 'The fridge?' she said. 'Yes, that's still here. But couldn't we share the chocolate?'

I walked into the lounge without Iman, shut my eyes and turned on the light. In those moments before I opened them I pictured the room as I had left it, the room, in fact, as I had decorated it. I didn't want to lose everything at once so I tilted my head back to look at the ceiling. I opened my eyes. The ceiling was exactly the same shade of white I had rollered on to it, and the shade was just as we had chosen. Just like the one in the display house in the new estate we put an offer on. A bit of plaster had come down though, the bastards.

Eyes down, and for a moment it was like that kids' game where you have to look at stuff for a minute then look away and spot what has been removed. The chairs and the spider plant were in place. There was even a five-pound note on the mantelpiece which, had it been missing, I would never have remembered placing there. Obviously the television and video were gone, but they were both rented.

'Iman! Come in here, it's not too bad.' But she didn't come so I went and found her in the dining room.

'Look what they've done to the books!' she whispered and traced her finger down the crack in the spine of several in turn. 'Why? I mean they're ordered like a rainbow – what's it mean? This is too spooky, burglars who do interior decoration.'

'And do you think they have bent the spines back knowing how much it annoys you?' Iman looked close to tears, so I hugged her, 'I'm only joking darling, I'm sorry. I was trying to be nice.'

'But it does annoy me,' she said, and I felt like crying but she held me too tight to breathe. Finally she said, 'Let's sit down.' And when we reached for the missing dining-room chairs we both managed to laugh, Iman leading.

We sat in the lounge.

'Do you think they drank their tea in here?' she said.

'No. I am going to think they drank in whatever room I am not in. We need to get a tight grip of this, Iman. We don't want to be thinking of it in a year's time. Come to that we don't want to be thinking of it over Christmas. People get over it. We can get over it.' I felt a bit cheesy saying it, a bit too much like a motivational seminar for middle managers, but Iman smiled. I carried on, 'I'll get the vacuum cleaner out.'

When the vacuum cleaner wasn't in the cupboard under the stairs I thought maybe I had put it in the dining room. Then when it wasn't in the dining room I thought maybe I had left it in the bedroom. Then when I got into the bedroom I fell back on the mattress and thought what a prick I was. But I stopped worrying about the lost vacuum cleaner when Iman called up the stairs.

'Have you seen Aslan? Is he up there?' Now, I had just looked around most of the house and not seen him. But to be certain I went into the guest room and the box room to check (where for some reason the radiator was still cold) then to be definite I even looked in the bathroom.

'He's not up here,' I called back and was going to suggest Iman call him from the door, but she already was, so I had nothing to say and now the house felt heavy and empty.

'Aslan! As-lan!' she called to the night.

Iman walked into the kitchen and as I hugged her I could smell the night air.

'Chocolate?' I offered. Iman looked across at the kitchen work surface and smiled at the toaster, then she nodded her head at it saying, 'No, put some toast in for that peanut butter.' But we both had to settle for jam on our toast. I could have cried but chose not to.

In bed I couldn't stop thinking of the burglary. I thought of rolling over and holding Iman, preferably leading to full intercourse. But no sooner had the idea formed in my shorts than I thought about the burglary. The bedroom didn't feel private enough for sex tonight. A few minutes later and it was the sound of Iman gently sleeping that was keeping me awake.

I had been suppressing night-thoughts about Wesley with sleepy thoughts about line-dancing. The technique had worked admirably in Bournemouth partly because the two subjects were related and didn't feel completely like I was cheating. But now I accepted a few thoughts about Wesley because it was cosier than thinking about the burglary. Even though I wouldn't know how to start believing, or disbelieving, in karma I felt a bit that I had brought this burglary on us. Attacking Wesley just wasn't like me. I hadn't done anything remotely like that since I was at school.

Thinking about what I had done, with the type of late-night logic that can make you think your cold symptoms are in fact cancer, I thought I hurt Iman with Wesley. Her vocation is to teach children and I broke one. Another part of the answer, and this started occurring to me in Bournemouth but not in so many words, was maybe I *wanted* to hurt Iman. Without her I could never have felt the racism, and, after Wesley, I could never tell her my actual reaction to it. Now I was wide awake and tired. Liam would be water-tight about it and would never tell. It didn't bother me him knowing; in fact it made it better.

During the night I must have had rough dreams because I woke up with my head under the duvet. Iman came into the room, her voice so sunny I could have been forgiven for thinking I had hibernated right through to spring. I remembered I'd managed to forget about Wesley and sleep.

'Aslan's back!' she sang. 'He's having his breakfast. And I have had a fantastic idea!' I kept still under the duvet, my eyes shut in case she threw the covers back for dramatic effect. 'Let's have a party! Let's have a party tonight!' she said, folding back the duvet to see my reaction. 'It'll be good, honest, and it will reclaim the house for us. We can invite our new neighbour, I saw him this morning as I let Aslan in. He's young like us. You can invite Liam and your brother. I'll invite them from work. In fact Jemma was coming over tonight anyway.'

I thought about it, yes, parties are great ideas, I mean they sound great, but often the actual things are grey blancmanges. I slowly exhaled, 'Ok,' and thought about ringing my brother. Clive lives in Edinburgh, so I knew Iman didn't mean to invite him. She meant Jimmy – he's local.

Iman carried on thinking out loud, 'Or, maybe I should tell them it's going to be more of a dinner party but with a buffet? Or a buffet of crisps, nuts and stuff: party food.'

I sat up in bed. Iman was looking out of the window. She rubbed a window in the condensation.

I yawned, 'Or,' I finished the yawn, 'Or, you could tell them it's a buffet party and can they bring a quiche. People just love giving quiches away.'

'Look, he's coming out of the house. He could be younger or older than us actually, under all that beard.' Gripping the duvet round my neck like a cape I walked to the window before wrapping it around Iman. I saw our new neighbour walking away down the street, head down, body tilted slightly forwards as if walking against a massive wind.

Iman rotated inside the duvet. I remembered Wesley, and felt for a moment like I didn't deserve her so warm and close. Then I remembered the facts of the matter: I did it for her. She said, 'Do you want to go line-dancing this afternoon? There's a class, isn't there, and you did miss it this week.' Now usually I boycott the Saturday afternoon class because it clashes with football. Not that I go to watch the football, or even play football, but I like to know these opportunities are there. And I like to think I wouldn't like the people who can go on a Saturday afternoon for the same reasons. But today felt very different.

Although I would gladly have helped Iman prepare for the party, I took the hint and decided to go line-dancing. I would need an outfit. Last night we had not opened the wardrobes and I was rather expecting everything to just fall out when I did, like in cartoons. Actually in a cartoon all the stuff would fall out, then, just as I sat up inside the mountain of stuff, my bowling ball would fall on to my head. But it didn't happen, and I couldn't even find my bowling ball. Why would a burglar steal a bowling ball? (The holes are drilled specific to my fingers.) Somehow I felt offended that they hadn't wanted to steal my line-dancing gear, it is worth a lot of money.

The orange and black outfits were not in the wardrobe but I remembered hiding them at the back of Iman's. They were evidence now. After Iman left for the shops I opened her wardrobe to check the clothes were still in place. The wardrobe looked in perfect order, surprising what burglars want and don't want. Impersonal stuff seemed to have most value, and they'd even left the fiver on the mantelpiece, idiots. It didn't look like they had looked in her wardrobe at all. The clothes were closely hung and I reached through them for the touch of the fur coat to check on our criminal outfits. They were still there. It was a safe hiding place as she never wore the fur. It was inherited, twice.

I waited for Iman to go out before I read her diary, but I had a good reason, I wasn't sure if she had forgiven me for that business in the hotel restaurant. There were only bras and pants in Iman's underwear drawer. So I checked her luggage and found the diary in the bottom of her hold-all, tucked under the flap of plastic-covered card that makes the base rigid. I had already washed my hands (after the chip-grease-on-the-cover incident) and memorised the exact position of the diary, before lifting it. I turned directly to *November 22 Highlight: 70% Will grovelling after threatening waiter in restaurant. Dumb wally, good groveller!* I don't think I threatened him. I mean I didn't even swear! Still, this was a relatively high score, not the highlight of the week but it was nice to know I managed to salvage the evening. The 70 per cent probably reflected the cold walk we had along the beach before the restaurant and I think that was the day we had sex before breakfast. All of which pissed me off now, because, surely, if I scored 70 per cent after calling the waiter 'a waddling health risk', I might have got the year-high score if I had just kept quiet. Or if I had said it quietly, or if I had just left the fucking food and told Iman I was too in love to eat. The 1 October 85 per cent score was beginning to obsess me. I wish I had never hugged her in the frozen fucking food aisle, I can't rest until something else becomes the diary highlight of the year. I must go mad and even top the world record 96 per cent I scored on our wedding day.

Looking through, the whole week had been in the 70s. Seventy per cent was the lowest, twice. I stood and went to put the diary back in the underwear drawer before remembering I had to let Iman do it. For added guile, I unpacked the rest of her clothes and put them away, or put them to be washed, as required. Then I put the diary back in the bottom of the bag.

Why wasn't volume one of this year's diary in the underwear drawer? Presumably she had put it in the loft with the others. But the burglary gave me an itch, an itch on my neck and under my clothes like I'd just had my hair cut. I had the inclination to get into the loft, but it meant putting on the overalls and it was a risk. If Iman found me up there she could suspect my quarry and, well, it would be ugly. But the itch became an ache – the thought of the burglars reading the diary, even once, made me feel violated. So I decided the quicker I was up the ladder the quicker I could be out, so I got my overalls from the garage and got on with it.

The diary was not in the loft.

I chose a low-key outfit for line-dancing, it was the afternoon and I wasn't sure who I would encounter at the class. A denim shirt and white jeans would suffice, and I thought it best to put my cowboy boots on after I had done the driving. Men aren't used to driving in heels and I quite like driving in my socks, but you do need the heater directed at your toes. And it was gritty, I really must vacuum the floor. I left my spurs at home.

It was a good decision about the boots because I drove like a blanc-mange. I was too angry to drive. My ankles were tired. I was too aggressive and stalled at the lights. When stalled I was terrified I was going to see Wesley walk out in front of the car, Wesley and his father would be terrible. I locked the car doors. Finally speeding into the car park I braked so heavily my stetson slid off the passenger seat. Pulling on my boots and putting on the hat in the confines of the car just made me more hot and angry and I got out ready to fight.

There were kids in the church hall. The scent of weak orange squash (20 pence a cup) was in the air. I love the fact that line-dancing is all-encompassing but some of the kids looked young enough to be in Iman's class. In fact I decided, to be sure, I'd only use my first name just in case any of them made the connection. Sandra was taking the class, she had her back to the lines (so everyone can see her feet and so everyone's left and right is the same) and she was calling out the steps over the bluegrass country music.

'Now do the vine!' and the lines did the three steps to the side and the toe touch of the vine, and Sandra smiled at me, knowing they had moved as one millipede by the rippling sound of their feet. I resisted the urge to tip her hello with my stetson. As a rule of thumb, what looks cool in films is crap in a musty, low-ceilinged church hall.

Pearl recognised me from the far end of the hall. And as she picked her way through the two lines of dancers (like they were all playing a gentle game of British Bulldog) I thought perhaps the warmth of her smile was aimed at my stetson. It was one of the ones I bought from her which had belonged to her old man and right now I felt a bit ghoulish in it. At least I wasn't wearing one of his complete outfits.

'How,' she said and she paused and in that instant I thought two worrying things – 1: was this an unfinished utterance of the word 'howdy', which is considered the height of bad manners at a line-dance? Or, 2: perhaps this was the only syllable of greeting she was going to use and was hoping for an embarrassing cowboy-and-indian-type exchange. But she coughed, hand over her mouth, then hanky over her hand as she coughed again, louder than the music. 'How are you, William? How's Bournemouth?'

'Bournemouth and I are just fine, thank you Pearl.' What a nice lady.

'I don't usually come to the Saturday class,' said Pearl.

'I was just going to say that!' I said. 'But I missed the evening class this week.'

'Because of Bournemouth,' nodded Pearl. 'Orange squash?'

We sat at the edge of the hall, each drinking our orange. The class was divided into two lines by age. The front line were children, and the back line, presumably because they could see over the children, were adults. I was the only male in the place over fifteen and under sixty-five. It was like being on the bus.

I finished my orange squash, watching the shortest old man in the back line. He was so short I reckoned he was really a dwarf, not just because he was a little old man with a beard, but because of his shape. He was a lovely little mover though. Even though he couldn't see Sandra's feet from the back row, he stood his ground with the grownups. He was one of the best, but I had to pity him because nobody made line-dance clothes that would fit him. If he had the gear I reckon he'd win competitions, he danced so well.

'Sandra takes the Saturday class on her own,' said Pearl between sips. 'Where's hubby Claus then?'

'Apparently he has a season ticket for the football, but my John went every fortnight for twenty years, before he died, and he never saw him up there.'

I didn't know what to say, so I just stood and said, 'Shall we dance, Pearl?' Then the music stopped. But Pearl stood as well, the music stopping was a good sign, it meant the next dance would soon be beginning.

'This is the Cowboy Hip-Hop,' said Sandra, facing both the lines but only making eye contact with the children in the front row. She covered the basics for them. 'This is a one-wall dance – that means we will always end up facing the starting wall. The Cowboy Hip-Hop is part of a new young craze in the States.' Sandra spoke like a primary school teacher, it's a specific tone Iman uses sometimes – and I have to hug her. 'Now, in this dance we'll be using steps, touches, and first off the vine – which you all know from the last dance. So, can you remember the difference between your steps and your touches?' A hand went up in the front line. 'Yes?'

'On a step change the weight from one foot to the other, and on a touch, don't,' said a girl who I decided would be one of my enemies if these were my school peers. But, of course, I've grown out of such behaviour.

'Excellent,' said Sandra, turning her back on us. 'So first without the hip-hop music. Vine to the right, big step to the left, and touch to the right.' The lines moved, but like seaweed. As I went through the motions I thought of Liam. He said he was into rap which is something to do with hip-hop I think.

'Vine right, big step left, and touch to the right. And again.' Sandra

71

spoke to the whole class, like an aerobics instructor. 'Come on, you can do it.' We did it. 'All right,' she said, but not like an American, it was just an ok type of all right. Sandra looked back over her shoulder, taxi-driver style. 'Now, follow me: jump-jack,' and we all jumped our legs apart then back, 'but to do the hip-hop we jump-jack with a half-turn.' And she was facing us. We jump-jacked about face. 'Now chugg to the front.' Which I did, only to be facing the children's line who didn't understand chugging – turning round, one foot as pivot. Such innocence.

When we could all: **VINE,**
BIG STEP LEFT,
RIGHT TOUCH,
JUMP-JACK WITH A HALF-TURN,
CHUGG FRONT,
RUN ON THE SPOT,
HIP ROLL,
HITCH,
AND ELECTRIC KICK ...

And repeat ... Sandra turned on the hip-hop music. It was different. It was obviously country style hip-hop. It clanked along, and rather than hopping it seemed to stagger. I didn't get it, but when we danced, I got it.

Just as I was going to leave, Pearl walked over with Edna Crabbe following; Pearl gave me a cup of weak orange squash, which I accepted out of politeness. I was so hot I would rather have just had water. Edna said to me, 'I love this dancing, I think it loosens up my arthritis.' And Pearl must have been able to see the question floored me and answered on my behalf.

'I know what you mean, Eddy.' *Eddy!* I was speechless. Pearl turned her attention to my hat. 'You know, William, that's one of John's hats, isn't it?' The question disorientated me, I drank hard on the orange squash to avoid answering, then I nodded with the cup to my lips, so a little bit dribbled down my chin. I wiped it away feeling the rough Saturday

72

stubble on the back of my hand. Cowboy stubble. 'In fact it's nice to see you wearing his things, William. I like it.'

'It was all far too nice to throw away, Pearl. I enjoy it.' And Pearl smiled a goalscorer's smile at me.

'Iman and I are having a few people round for a bit of food and a bit of a party tonight; would you like to come?' I said to Pearl.

'That sounds nice.'

'Yes it does, I've found before that the word "party" can actually be nicer than many of them,' I said, but wasn't sure Pearl heard me.

'Yes,' she said and left, without me knowing if she agreed with my theory on parties, or, yes, she would be accepting my invitation

I said to Edna, 'How's Tracey?'

'Jealous. She's jealous of me coming to the dance class on a week night because it means we swap our shifts, and she misses her afternoon nap, but today, she's still jealous, even though Liam's working the shop. I told her I'd walk the dog.'

I looked at her like I cared (really: like I cared), but she ignored me, saying, 'I didn't see you this week. I'd kept you a copy of the *Daily Mail*.'

'I've been in Bournemouth.'

'Ah, Bournemouth!' but before she could carry on I cut her up, 'Actually, don't worry about the *Daily Mail* any more, I'm stopping, for economy.'

I was glad Edna had told me Liam was working in the shop, it would give me a chance to cancel the *Daily Mail* and invite him to the party. Actually, I decided it would be better to invite him to the party first, then cancel the paper.

I went to the shop and left my stetson in the car. Walking without a hat on I suddenly felt very bald. I was thinning, yes, but the downside of the stetson is the feeling of baldness without it. Liam was behind the counter, leaning. He seemed to manage to lean sideways and forwards, into the counter, and downwards, on to the counter with his forearms flat against it.

'How-de-do-de?' And he slowly stood up straight before answering, 'De-do-ing ok. Yes, not bad Will. And you?' I raised my thumbs to him, to signify the post-line-dancing buzz, and slight stiffness I was feeling; he laughed.

'Do you want to come to a party?'

'A party?'

'No, make that *the* party. I can guarantee you a rockin' good time and a cheese roll.'

'Where and when?'

'My place at nine, and that includes a coolly late arrive estimate.'

'Tea?'

'Why not.'

'Do you want to mind the shop or make the tea?'

'Well, it's your shop and your tea – do you want a break from the shop or a break from tea-making?' Liam laughed, and I heard him run up the stairs two at a time.

I had worked in the shop one summer with Liam, when we had both finished school. His mum had just left his dad, and his dad was suffering, then, suffering with drink; then finally, as autumn moved in, he was suffering from alcohol withdrawal. But I had a brilliant time.

The shop had been a great adventure, we took turns to take wank breaks with anything, and everything, from the top shelf. We even tried to negotiate a special sale-or-return deal with the jazz-mag sales rep. At the same time, we used our power, refusing to sell porn to people from school because they were under eighteen. But then, we would relent if they paid a pound over the cover price. We were firmer about cigarettes though, only giving in for double the pack price, although we would sell anyone a single cigarette. We even gave them away sometimes, in an effort to get girls we fancied hooked on both fags and coming into our shop. The sun poured in through the glass door all summer and we had ice creams for lunch.

Now we drank tea and ate Kola Kubes. Liam wanted to come to the party. He gave me some Neapolitan ice cream, and tinned fruit, from stock for the buffet. Things seemed unchanged between us. When I told him I'd given up the *Daily Mail*, he said 'good idea'.

*

74

Jemma was at the house, Iman was out, so when I let myself in it felt a bit like I had walked into someone else's life. Well, it would have if I could really imagine Jemma being married, cohabiting, or even having a boyfriend in the first place. My toes were sore from line-dancing in cowboy boots, and going from the cold into the warm house my toes started to sing.

'Howdy Iman's partner!' she called out from the kitchen. Then in answer to my unspoken question, she said, 'She's gone to buy some paper plates because we knew you wouldn't want to do the washing-up.' Before talking to Jemma I went into the lounge and poured myself a massive brandy. I could afford to take my time, this was my house. I gulped at the brandy and it raced right down my body to warm my toes.

'Hello Jemma. How's it going?' I walked through and saw a jelly with fruit suspended in it. 'Nice jelly!' It seemed the right thing for a primary school teacher to be making. Sometimes, talking to Jemma felt like reading between the lines of Iman's diary. I was very familiar with both sensations, and more comfortable with the diary. 'Yes, that is one of the best-looking jellies I've ever seen.' I decided to stay with the jelly theme, because it sounded almost rude.

'Was it ok, at the OK Corral line-dance?' she said, along similar lines, but I embraced her taunts like the proud cowboy I was.

'Yep,' I drawled, swigging down the brandy and wiping my lips, before putting Liam's donation of Neapolitan ice cream into the freezer and the tinned fruit on the counter by the jelly. 'Couldn't you get any whole-meal jelly? I was sure I saw some in the health food shop.'

'That's as maybe, I can't eat it anyway – it's not vegetarian. Gelatine,' she said in a tone I was sure her pupils were familiar with. 'Would you like some tea, Willy? I was just going to make some.'

'No thanks, you go ahead. I was just going to sort out some music for tonight.' I took a beer instead.

Jemma made two cups of tea anyway, and Iman was back just as hers finished brewing. Uncanny. Then Iman found me in the bedroom, standing in my pants, having just put my line-dancing gear away.

'Good news Will, Jemma's lent us four of her dining-room chairs! She's got a set of six, and thinks she only needs two.'

'Huh, she only needs one chair. She lives alone! Don't we just need to borrow two?' Iman looked at the ceiling and sighed, like I knew nothing about chairs, she didn't spell it out, but I was pleased when she changed the subject.

'So what music are we having tonight?' She sipped her tea. I imagined the steam, dampening her top lip, and the rim, resting on the bridge of her nose; like glasses or an early morning kiss.

'Well, I thought either Johnny Cash and/or Elvis. Oh buggeration! No stereo, no music! They've stolen the stereo – how can we have a party?'

'Jemma's brought her portable round, and there are plenty of CDs left unstolen,' Iman said coolly, and I thought about saying *Hooray for Jemma! Hooray for her chairs! Hooray for her stereo!* but decided not to in case she could hear. 'You are thinking of playing Elvis, as in Elvis Costello?' Iman asked, sounding genuinely surprised.

'As fucking if!' It just slipped out, the f-word. I regretted it as soon as I thought to say it, but could only think of saying *Hooray for Jemma!* again – which was never going to happen. I think I would rather Iman heard me swear than praise Jemma. It's not that I don't like Jemma, it's just that, as Iman's best friend, I sometimes feel I'm in competition with her. Once I had sworn, I decided to stand my ground. Luckily, Iman was more interested in my pants.

She pointed as she walked up, over, and across the bed. 'What are they?'

'These are my line-dancing support pants!' All this attention on my pants gave me an erection. Iman looked fantastic walking over the bed to me, but I felt she turned away momentarily before Jemma called (like an actor in an Australian soap). 'IMAN! Iman, your new neighbour's at the door.' Then the doorbell rang.

I heard Iman at the door and I heard our new neighbour, and just as I was tucking my shirt and semi-erection into my jeans, feeling somehow sad that thieves don't covet Elvis or Johnny Cash, I heard Iman saying goodbye.

He said, 'Farewell,' and she shut the door.

I went downstairs and asked, 'Well? What's he like? Our age? What did he want?'

'He seems nice. He looks about our age, but his beard looks older than both of us.'

'His name's Tim,' said Jemma, but I ignored her and Iman carried on, 'And Tim wanted to know if we could direct him to a supermarket.'

'Oh. Did you tell him about tonight?'

'Certainly did. He said, 'I know Saturday night,' whatever that means, and not to worry about the noise.'

'Weren't you going to invite him?'

'Yes. He's going to bring us some sour barley soup from the supermarket.'

'Soup?' And, if Jemma hadn't been there, I'd have said, *What's that?*

I rang Jimmy. He was out, probably at the football, but I left a message on his answerphone. 'Hi Jimmy, it's Will, we've been burgled, so we're having a party tonight. Come round, anytime after eight if you want to. Bring a bottle, or a TV and video.' I hung up and wished I'd said goodbye at the end of the message. I rang back, 'Me again. It would be great to see you if you can make the party. Goodbye.'

At 7.50pm, even though no one had arrived, the party officially started as I opened the wine and played 'Come In Stranger' by Johnny Cash (1958). I pushed the repeat button and just let the song revolve over and over again. It only lasted about one and a half minutes each play, but Iman was losing patience after about three minutes and twenty-four seconds.

She said, 'Come in stranger, it's good to have you home.
I hurried through cos I knew it was you,
When I saw the dog waggin' his tail.'

It's a kind of old car of a song, rumbling along over a rolling piano. I felt it was very appropriate for tonight's guests. I was treating them as I would wish to be treated. Johnny Cash could be used for line-dancing, but he is part of popular music. I wanted people to feel they had timed

77

their arrival perfectly. And by playing the song over and over, the first person to arrive would feel it was lucky; almost like in a film.

> She said, 'Come in stranger. I know you're weary from all the miles.
> Just sit right there in your easy chair,
> And tell me all about the places you been.

I turned it down slightly to be sure of hearing the doorbell.

> How long it'll be before you leave again,
> I hope it's a long long while.'

Iman said, 'For God's sake Will, must we have this on? I thought you were joking about Johnny and Elvis. Why not just line us all up and, and, shoot your guns?' I pretended I couldn't hear her by singing along. I was at least pleased she had moaned during the guitar break, then I was back on track.

> She said, 'Come in stranger. Oh how I miss you when you're gone.
> I walk the floor and I watch the door,
> And then I lie awake and wonder where you can be,
> I'd give anything to have you here with me . . .

Iman said something. I shut my eyes, to concentrate on the vocals and savour the tropical fruit flavours of the Chardonnay.

> I get so lonesome all alone.'
> She said, 'Come in stranger. And won't you listen to my plea.
> Stay long enough, so that the one I love,
> Is not a stranger to me.'

The song ended. Liam was stood in front of me, looking at his shoes. I started to speak, but the song started up again from the beginning. I switched it off.

'How-de-do-de, Will?'

'Yes, how-de-do-you-too, Liam. Yes, hello, thanks a lot for coming. You're a bit early though.'

'You said it started at eight.'

'Ah, yes I did, but I gave you nine as your entry time, so you could seem a bit cool and groovy. You know, make a bit of an entrance.'

'I was going to bring my stereo, as yours went, but – well, it was too heavy to carry, and anyway I'd forgotten you had that one.'

Iman called from the kitchen, 'You should have brought some music!' Then she came in and introduced Liam to Jemma, and Jemma to Liam. Everyone seemed more comfy than me. For one night only, never to be repeated, and something I would deny, under oath: I decided to give up on Johnny Cash and Elvis Aaron Presley.

'Wine, Liam?'

'I'd prefer a beer, Will.' And we went into the kitchen. 'So who else is coming to the party?' And when we were alone in the kitchen, and Iman and Jemma had put on some alternative music, I answered the question I believed he was asking.

'I don't think there will be anyone worth pulling.'

'But what about the Pamela Anderson lookalike? Well, if Pamela Anderson was taller, and thinner all over, with short hair.' Liam pointed his beer towards the front room.

'What are you talking about?'

'Jemma!' Pause. We both laughed our dirty schoolboy laughs, except, our voices are much deeper now.

'No, I er, don't really know who's coming. I've only invited you, and maybe a couple of others.'

'From work?'

'No no, none of them. I've invited Jimmy.' And I paused, expecting Liam to ask after him. When he didn't, I carried on. 'Our new neighbour's coming as well; well, he's been invited. Iman's spoken to him, in fact. I'm not sure who else she has invited. We'll call it informal; unless loads of people turn up.'

Liam opened and shut his mouth a few times, like a fish, before saying, 'Are those things for the buffet then?' He pointed at two trays of cheese and pineapple cubes on cocktail sticks, sandwiches cut into quarter triangles, and fruit suspended in jelly. Even though it was obvious they were I still paused, looking at the food before saying, 'Yes, of course.'

We each carried a tray into the lounge. 'The neighbour is bringing over some barley soup!' and I expected Liam to comment, to say *What's that when it's at someone else's home?* But he seemed to almost ignore me. Then he opened the lounge door and the music was too loud for talking.

Iman and Jemma were dancing. I compared the wobble on their tits. They didn't stop dancing as they started laughing, at, and with, each other. I saw Liam check his trouser fly was done up. It was a complicated manoeuvre, he put his left hand under the centre of the tray and balanced it, like a waiter. Then, as he tugged on the tiny metal tongue of his zip fastener, the jelly wobbled. Perhaps he did it as an instinctive reaction to the girls' unexplained laughter; perhaps because he was nervous, or perhaps he wanted to ignore my advice about Jemma.

I put both the trays on the table.

There was a banging against the window. Insistent, more like burglars trying to smash it than rain or hail. I went to the door and was pleased when Liam followed me. I turned to speak to him, not really because I had anything to say, just to check he was with me, in case. But Liam had gone, presumably to the toilet.

I turned the door lock slowly, before swinging the door back in one quick, smooth motion. There was no one there. I leaned out, looked into the garden and said, 'Hello?'

The man stopped looking through a chink in the curtains, stood upright and answered, 'Good evening. I'm Terry Armitage, Iman invited me.'

'Oh hi. I'm Iman's husband, Will. You're the headmaster, aren't you? Come in.' And he did, and he wiped his feet which annoyed me because I wanted to be able to say, *Could you just wipe your feet?* He even shook my hand.

Bosses must feel compelled to dance when their employees are danc-ing. It must be one of those boundary-breaking things, which actually confirms a boundary, that managers get taught on courses. Terry strutted his funky stuff. I hadn't smelled any alcohol on his breath and he only had an orange juice in his hand, but he moved and grooved with his staff like an uncle with the bridesmaids at a wedding disco. When Liam got in the room I would have to point it out to him, I would have to suggest he imagine our old headmaster dancing to techno. It would make us smile. I read the compact disc box, this was happy hardcore house music.

Liam didn't return and I felt quite alone. I could have danced over to Iman, Jemma and Terry, but why should I. This is my house, and if I don't want to dance, I won't. I got two more beers for us from the fridge. Even though there were plenty of seats at the edge of my lounge, I stood, not even leaning against the wall, gripping the beer cans till my hands were the shape of boxing gloves. I drank my beer, sipping it at first like wine, then tipping it up and shaking it all down. Tired of waiting, I made the other beer mine and drank that too. But, so Liam wouldn't feel the loss, I went and poured us some huge whisky chasers, which required me collecting two more beers to make it clear that they were chasers. In passing, I wondered, is that radiator on?

I thought I heard the doorbell, and even though I was far from cer-tain, I went to check because it gave me something to do. Pearl was stood next to a man, who by the fierceness of his beard, and big saucepan of soup, I assumed had to be Tim, from next door.

'Hiya! Hiya, we are together, but not together,' said Tim.

'Good evening, Will,' said Pearl. And I was so dumbfounded I handed them both a can of beer (also to make carrying the huge whiskies easier) and invited them in. Pearl looked at the can, and asked for a glass.

'I know you can drink out of the tin, but,' and I handed her a pint glass because it was the first that came to hand, and I didn't want her to wait and feel she had to justify wanting a glass. She said, 'Oh, now I can't get the ring pull off.'

'They don't come off any more.' I reached out to help, and she took it as an offer to pour the beer for her, which I slowly did. I wished I had taken the trouble to find her a smaller glass. She'd be more comfortable with a half-pint glass, but it would probably have been dusty from the back of the cupboard and needed washing up anyway.

I took Tim and Pearl's coats upstairs, one on each forearm, so I could still carry the huge whiskies. Pearl's coat was the heaviest. Although Iman and I had not discussed it, I assumed we would put guests' coats in our bedroom. On the bed is traditional, and it wards off any rogue shaggers. When I saw someone burrowing under some coats (Terry and Jemma's?) on the bed I felt a mixture of: at least I was right, we are putting coats on the bed, and, stop that, you rogue shagger. I put down the huge whiskies (on top of the paperback Iman had thrown out of bed), and then the coats (by the door), and put on the light, pretending I hadn't noticed the furtive movements.

I decided to say 'Oh do excuse me!' as I flicked the switch. First I recognised Liam's shoe, then his trousers sticking out from under Jemma's coat. I pieced together the bulges of his body before deciding I hadn't interrupted him, and could ask, 'What are you doing?' The answer didn't sound like Liam.

'Ha ha, just sleeping,' in a kind of Welsh, kind of made-up, regional-type accent. He was obviously mucking about, but I didn't understand what the joke was. Maybe it was a bit like hiding in the cupboard at school – which I do remember him doing, and it seemed hilarious. Anyway, I didn't know what he was doing, and I don't know why, but I jumped on him.

Liam screamed with his normal voice. My knees pinned the coat down around his body, and the more he struggled and shouted the more muffled his cries became. When I could barely hear him, I got off and pulled back the coat. He gulped in air.

'Oh, it is you,' I said ambiguously, to check if we were still playing. He kept gulping and looked so hot and flustered it could have been either tears or sweat on his face. 'What are you doing in here?' Again no answer, but less gulping. 'I thought you'd only gone to the loo. You left me down there on my own with our new next-door neigh*bear* – a right grizzly-looking furry-faced fellah. Some mate you are.'

82

Liam regained his composure. 'What's he like then, this neighbour?'

'I told you, like a bear; neighBEAR I said.'

'I didn't feel well. I came in here for a lie down.'

'And I suppose you were trying to sniff your way to feeling better on my bed, or under Jemma's coat – I don't know which is worse!'

'Don't be crude.'

'Oh, ok.' Maybe he really wasn't feeling well.

Tim was in the kitchen heating barley soup. He stood with his feet slightly wider apart than his considerable shoulders. It saved him from having to lean as far forward to slurp a taste of the soup. Then he sprinkled in a few flecks of (my) salt and watched it bubble. He looked rather at home there. I presumed it was because he was so new next door. Perhaps our kitchen was similar, and similarly new to him.

When Iman opened the lounge door I noticed that the music wasn't on.

'Darling, what are you doing standing out here?' And I couldn't answer her question, because I just stood there, listening to the word darling. It sounded so sweet I hugged her. When I finished the hug, Tim had turned slightly away, and pushed the kitchen door half shut.

I asked her, 'Where's the music gone?' She led me back into the lounge like we just might find some. Terry Armitage was peering into the top of the stereo, Jemma was stood at his shoulder. There was a man I didn't know standing next to her. Presumably this made him a primary school teacher too, but then he touched Terry Armitage on the shoulder, and pointed something out to him in the music-less darkness of the stereo. Surely no one would touch the boss? Pearl was on the sofa looking at a cushion. I went and sat next to her; I decided I would introduce Iman and be the perfect host.

'Would you like some food, Pearl?' I beckoned towards the buffet.

'I'm fine, thank you, Will.' Then, after putting the cushion down, she reconsidered. 'Well, it would need to be something that can't get stuck under my plate.'

'Fruit suspended in jelly?'

'Perfect.'

The doorbell rang and I left Pearl with that thought. Now Iman was looking at the stereo too.

People can look very strange in the wrong context. When I opened the door, and saw the Crabbe sisters there, I felt about nine years old. I wanted so much to say, *Party? What party? No Edna you must have misheard me speaking to Pearl at the class today. No Tracey, I don't know what party Liam was talking about either. I don't even know where he is.* But even reluctant gatecrashers are guests, of sorts.

'Good evening, William,' said Edna, and handed over a bottle instead of a handshake. I was obliged to let them in because they had made the effort. They walked ahead, and the music started up once more. I looked down at the bottle of sweet sherry they had placed in my hand, and decided to stay in the hallway for a while and let things sort themselves out, perhaps.

'Soup! Who is souping?' Tim bellowed. I expected him to come out of the kitchen with it, and he obviously expected everyone to rush in clutching bowls and spoons. But the happy hardcore house music was back on and too loud, and the old ladies wouldn't rush; so Tim came out of the kitchen with two bowls of soup and came right at me.

'Soup! *Krupnik* — the real thing.'

'Isn't Coke *the real thing*?' Which I was rather pleased with, thinking it to be a friendly, international little joke. But maybe the ads have different phrases in different countries.

'No, this is the real soup. You have never had *krupnik* like it.' I took the hot bowl (last used for my Corn Flakes). Tim looked expectantly at me. I smiled then went to walk past him to get a spoon, but tiring of waiting for his own *krupnik*, Tim cupped the bowl to his mouth. He grinned at me with a broad barley-soup moustache. Keen to show willing, I put the bowl to my mouth, but had to use both hands to tilt it. I took a tiny sip.

'This is the family recipe, not like the new shop-bought piss,' said Tim. Being stuck for a reply I did what people on TV soaps do, I just kind of repeated what he'd said. I have learned a lot from TV.

84

'Your mother's *krupnik*?' It sounded like an insult. But to Tim it was magic.

'Ah! Mother's *krupnik*, yes, grandmother's *krupnik*, great grandmother's *krupnik*. And my mummy's mum's mother's *krupnik*. Except, I bought the barley instead of growing it.' I looked at the carpet, we could really do with a new one, definitely. Tim swigged down more of the soup, then went to the kitchen to refill his bowl.

'Liam! LIAM!' I shouted up the stairs, wondering where he'd got to. I felt like I needed an ally.

Edna Crabbe came into the hallway.

'Is Liam here then, William?'

'Somewhere.'

'I was just looking at your compact discs. They're lovely, really lovely.'

'Yeah? Which ones did you like?'

'Oh, well they all have such a beautiful shiny rainbow pattern on the back, it's lovely.'

'LIAM! LIAM!' I called up the stairs.

'I am partial to Johnny Cash,' she said, thinking out loud. I stopped shouting.

'Johnny Cash?'

'Yes, and Elvis Presley; you've got some lovely Elvis.'

'Elvis Presley?' I realised I was doing the telly dialogue thing instinctively.

'In fact, I saw Elvis Presley.'

'You saw Elvis Presley?' There I go again.

'Yes.'

'On television, the '68 comeback special?'

'No. I saw Elvis Presley in Hawaii.'

'*Aloha from Hawaii*?'

'Yes.'

'On television?'

'No.'

'Are you sure?' Edna Crabbe looked hurt. Genuinely hurt, like I had accused her of insanity, like I was the doctor telling her she was senile and she was just sane enough to take the fact on board.

'No. I was on holiday in Hawaii in the summer of 1973 with a gent who was courting me, and, he said, had I heard of Elvis Presley. Admittedly I hadn't really, although the name did ring a bell, but I wasn't into popular music then; classical, yes. Anyway, he had heard of Elvis, and we went to watch the performance.' I was open-mouthed, how could someone who had never heard of Elvis be lucky enough to see Elvis? 'The concert was like nothing on earth. He looked like a spaceman crossed with a Shogun warrior. It was beautiful.' For a second I couldn't think, then, I wished I was her, but only for another second. 'That was the same holiday I first heard country and western music, but of course there wasn't any line-dancing in those days.' When I could speak again, I wished I hadn't.

'You lucky bastard.'

'Bastard?' said Edna, trying on the word.

I turned away from Edna, annoyed with myself for swearing and annoyed with her for seeing Elvis.

Terry and Jemma opened the lounge door and came into the hall. The happy hardcore house music was still on, but much quieter, and I could see that no one was dancing. I saw Pearl was at the buffet, having seconds of fruit suspended in jelly. Edna saw her old friend and went to join her. Terry was leading Jemma towards the kitchen.

'Paris is absolutely perfect for Christmas,' Terry was saying.

'Perfect?' said Jemma, except I blocked off her view of Terry as I stood my ground in the hall.

'Yes, Paris is perfect. Did you know Barry Manilow *never* releases records in France?'

'Barry Manilow never releases records there?' repeated Jemma, and I turned and joined in their conversation, childishly confident. Ideally Liam would've been with me to join in too.

I asked Terry, 'Is that what makes Paris so perfect then? You're guaranteed not to hear Barry Manilow.'

'No,' he said with a cough of disbelief. 'N-*cough*-O! He doesn't release records in France so he can have Paris for himself; to wander the beautiful streets in solitude.' The tone of his voice got right up my nose, then it got into the aggressive bit of my brain. I spoke quickly in reply, 'Or, maybe Barry Manilow doesn't release records in France because he's a heap-o-poop not fit to re-string Johnny Cash's guitar.'

There was a stand-off, me and Terry in the hall with Jemma in between. She looked at me in disbelief, then she looked at Terry, her headmaster, her boss. I had picked on the wrong cowboy.

'Will here likes line-dancing music,' she said to Terry. The cow, she said it like it was something to be ashamed of.

'Really?' he said, dead slow. 'What's that? Country and western?'

'Could be,' I said, even slower, not wanting to give anything away. I needed time to think. Here I was arguing with Iman's headmaster, he was her boss too. What was I thinking? At least I'd not sworn.

Terry smiled, and said in a sing-song voice, 'That sounds super, I've always thought I'd be rather good at that.'

'It's great fun, really, I love it.' I smiled too and Jemma turned her back on us both and went into the kitchen.

Terry went and turned off the happy hardcore house music and announced that we were all going to do a bit of line-dancing. Iman managed to look pleased too – because it was her boss telling her to line-dance.

'LIAM! LIAM!' I called up the stairs, I didn't want him to miss out. Sometimes I feel quite evangelical about line-dancing. He didn't reply.

I burst into my bedroom and turned on the light. 'Liam?' Aslan the cat was curled up on the coats, he blinked at the light. I checked under the bed. I checked the bathroom. I looked into the front bedroom, then I stuck my head round the door of the small box bedroom.

I checked the downstairs loo. It smelt of barley-soup piss. Liam had vanished like a burglar, and the thought scared me. I had been in the hallway all the time, where did he go?

Liam had to be in the lounge, but he wasn't.

Terry spoke loudly, like this was morning assembly. 'Ok everyone, now this gent here.' Then he whispered to me, 'Sorry; Will?'

'Yep, I'm Will.'

'Ah!' Then he addressed the assembled party guests again, 'Will here is going to teach us all a bit of line-dancing! Over to you, Will.'

'Oh, right, well, first things first; everybody line up.' The guests formed into two lines. Terry was at the back.

'Hang on,' he said. 'We're in two short lines here, they're columns and rows really. Shouldn't we be in a line, line-dancing?'

I thought quickly, maybe Terry was trying to make me look a fool – maybe he was getting me back for the remark about Barry Manilow. But I outwitted him, me, no A-levels, outwitting a headmaster!

'Ok everyone, let's use the hall!' And they did, Terry even led them and organised everyone into one long line: Jemma, Iman, Edna, Pearl, Tim, Terry and his mate, from the kitchen to the front door. He told me to stand on the stairs for the purpose of demonstration – and again I thought he was trying to ruin me, making me line dance on the stairs. But I was too good for that. I was so good I could easily show them the difference between touches and steps. (On a step change the weight from one foot to the other, on a touch, don't.) Then I showed them how to:

Chug in a circle	*use one foot as a pivot, taking rocking steps*
Kick	*flick the foot out, from the knee down*
Electric kick	*hard to explain – watch this …*
Jump-jack	*jump your legs apart, then back*
Hip roll	*self-explanatory*
and hitch	*with your thumbs, hitchhiking!*

It was beautiful, Liam was really missing something.

Then we put it all together to Elvis. That was Edna's choice, 'The Devil In Disguise', by Elvis. For me line-dancing on the stairs evened things out, like we were all beginners, like we were all learning something together. Even though Iman didn't want Elvis and she didn't want line-dancing, she did want to please her guests. It was perfect, no one was in time with anyone else, but it was an icebreaker, it made everyone feel at home, including me.

The only person who didn't like it was Jemma. She was the first to stop, stopping before she'd even started. Then Tim stopped, but the rest of the line carried on, doing the moves we'd learned over and over, changing the order, getting better, getting more and more co-ordinated. That's the key, the submission of the individual to the group.

In the end it was just Pearl and Terry left and I had to stop it, they weren't a line, they were just a pair. And Jemma had put the happy hard-core house music back on again.

I looked again for Liam, I wanted to get drunk with him, he had to be here somewhere. But I couldn't find him, which spooked me out a bit. The only explanation was that he slipped past me when I was talking to Tim or to Terry before the line-dancing.

I got drunk and didn't worry about it.

I got drunker and went for a pee. I must've forgotten to lock the door, because Jemma opened it just as I was about to start.

'Oh God, Will! That's gross!'

I had my back to her and didn't know what she was so worried about – it's my house, my bathroom door, my lock. I turned round to tell her, but I was drunk and forgetful, I couldn't remember the words.

'Christ! Put it away, Will!' Jemma covered her eyes. I swayed and fumbled with my fly. 'First you make us all line-dance, now you make me look at that, that ...' She searched for the word to best describe my penis. I helped her, 'Wife's best friend?' I ventured.

'Hardly!' said Jemma, even more annoyed that I should suggest anything other than her was my wife's best friend. 'I should've known only small-dicked men go line-dancing.' And she went to the downstairs loo.

I tried to pee again, but couldn't relax. She could have a go at me, but I didn't see why she should have a go at line-dancing! I drunkenly planned my revenge. It was so funny I nearly peed myself.

I went and got the water pistol, staggered back and straddled over the toilet pan and peed over my hands (yikes that's hot), ha ha, I'm so funny and Jemma is so smug. Then I put in the stopper and washed my hands.

I turned on the bedroom light shutting the door behind me. Aslan blinked, then ignored me. He was lying on Jemma's coat, perfect. He ignored the first few squirts of the pistol. I thought he might object to the hissing sound of the gun but instead his nose twitched at the smell. His smug furry face started to look very confused: tiger pee? No, surely not, not in suburbia? Aslan moved out of the way and went to cower by the door. I emptied the gun on to Jemma's coat. When I'd finished, if I could have got my chunky finger into the child sized loop round the trigger, I would have spun the pistol around. It was that funny and I was that cool.

I was going to open the door for Aslan, but to make things complete, I decided Aslan needed to be shut in the room. It made things more plausible. So I shooed him away from the door with my foot and slipped out myself, then shut the furry little straight-man into my joke.

I went into the spare room and tried to pass out.

Sunday morning sunlight is no different from any other morning sunlight, but the hangover made it apocalyptic. My brain was too big for my head, my head was too hard for the pillow. I was colder than the bed. I worked out a plan with my eyes shut: get up, throw up, put on my puffa jacket and pass out.

Step one: Getting up, was easy, my head woosied around like your stomach does when the car goes over a humped-back bridge.

Step two: Throwing up, didn't happen at first, I could only belch so I gripped the toilet rim and breathed in, hoping the smell would make me cock-crow it all up; but Iman keeps the toilet so clean.

Step three: My puffa jacket was not hanging at the foot of the banister or by the front door. But looking did make me nauseous, so I threw up in the downstairs loo (which was cleaned less regularly and had the faint smell of barley-soup piss in it, which, for once, was a help). I drank a pint of water and took three aspirin.

Step four: Passing out can be a hard thing to plan. If I went back upstairs I would be cold again. And, I remembered about Wesley, I remembered what I had done. It was the worst time to think of it, when

90

I needed to be unconscious. What kind of piss artist was I? First Wesley, now my Aslan joke. At least that was meant to be funny, not nasty, but right now I regretted the lot; it just wasn't like me to do things like that. Most unusual, at least Iman need never know.

I turned on the heating and went into the lounge. I found my niche on the sofa, but under the seat cushions. They should keep me warm, the base was a bit gritty as I slid in, but I didn't mind that, and I had to fold up my legs. I found a fifty-pence piece. I rolled over so my head was between the tilted seat cushion, the arm and the back of the sofa. Hibernation.

I heard Iman and Jemma come into the room and go out again. I pretended they could not see me in my furniture camouflage. I slept but I was aware of things. Time passed and I drank it down knowing it was the only thing that could make the hangover go. What a beautiful afternoon was coming.

I woke up cured. I remembered about Wesley and my Aslan joke on Jemma. Yes, I'd done a bad thing, but now, I'd done a good joke. It was only the use of pee that was weird. It makes sense to threaten a kid who (you thought) did you racism. Aslan peeing on the coats is plausible – it makes sense.

The house had been tidied up and it looked like the burglary had been lifted. I walked into the dining room, it was ours. The map of Narnia was open on the table, Iman had propped it open with a book on each corner. She came in the room behind me.

I spoke, tentatively at first, but found my mouth to be in perfect working order. 'The map looks good, almost as if the crinkles the burglars added make it look older, cooler somehow.'

'Will, have you seen Aslan?'

'No; is Jemma still here?'

'I'm very worried about him.' Then she looked at me and I saw how worried she was. 'No, she left about an hour ago. But I've not seen Aslan at all this morning.'

'You were right about the party. When I woke up then, I really felt this was our house. In fact, I think I even feel it's our home more than I have ever felt before.' She was looking under the dining-room table, where the chairs sit underneath. Jemma's chairs had higher backs than ours.

'Sometimes he sits on there, doesn't he?'

'Yes,' I said, but only because I felt I had to say something to get her attention. Technically it wasn't even true, these were Jemma's chairs after all, I expect Aslan had sniffed them suspiciously. 'Didn't you hear me, I said how at home I feel, after the party, you were right it was a great idea, the party, and all the tidying-up after it really helped it feel like home again.'

She was hardly listening and walked off looking for Aslan, leaving me talking to an empty room. As is the way when people are looking for things, Iman came back into the dining room to look for Aslan again. She looked behind the curtains, saying, by way of an explanation, 'He sometimes lies here, when it's sunny. Actually, maybe he's in the garden? Jemma insisted on helping clear up before she went.' Iman spoke in a slightly different tone, less tense, like she was stopping actively looking for Aslan, in the hope he would just slink in. Cats don't like being sought out.

'Good old Jemma.'

'Yes. She was well annoyed with him actually – he'd peed on her coat. I was actually glad he wasn't about this morning, or she might have wrung his neck.'

'Maybe he got shut in the bedroom last night, I mean to pee on her coat.'

'Maybe. But he wasn't there when I went to bed.'

'Wasn't he?'

'No. Probably a good job too. I must've been a bit drunk myself, not to notice the pee smell I mean, and I could've rolled over and squashed him.' Iman left the room again. I watched her walk round the garden – arms folded against the cold – bending into the bushes looking for him. I watched her lips call his name. I reassembled last night inside my head; I was certain I had shut him in there for the purposes of my great joke, which had actually gone rather well if Jemma was annoyed. I didn't like the thought of Iman sleeping with the smell touching her. Aslan must have made a break for it when people collected their coats. It was only to be expected. He would be back when he was hungry, and Iman had obviously reached the same conclusion when she put down a saucer of food outside the back door. My only regret was that the joke was also a secret. Maybe I could tell Liam.

When Iman shouted out my first thought was of an intruder. I suppose it meant I wasn't as over the burglary as much as I imagined.

'OH, FUCKING FUCK; FOR GOD'S SAKE!' And I was up the stairs in time for the end of the sentence, ready for a fight. Then I saw there was no fight to be had.

'What is it?'

'This.' She pulled out her underwear drawer and tipped the contents on to the bed. What it was, was what it wasn't: the missing diary. I knew it was missing, but I remembered to play dumb (especially after the chip-grease incident).

'What? Did they steal some of your underwear?'

'No.' Iman started refilling the drawer.

'What then?' I lied.

'Well, I've been keeping a diary – as usual – and this was my hiding place.' Iman sat on the bed with the drawer on her lap. 'They've nicked it. Why would anyone nick it?' For a second the question frightened me so much I was terrified of the possible answers. I felt cheap that I hadn't thought of these angles before. I thought through the possibilities. 1: Perhaps they are not burglars, but a single stalker? Or 2: Perhaps the burglar was someone we know (Jemma?); someone implicated in the diary? (Except I've read it and no one is implicated in it – but maybe the thief didn't know it and had a great interest in our lives.) Instead, I decided to play innocent.

'Are you sure that's where it was?'

'YES! Of course.' I tried to look hurt but didn't really feel it, I'd had time to get used to the diary being gone.

'All right,' I said, 'don't get angry with me.' I picked the underwear

93

drawer up from her lap and put it back in the chest. I made sure the runners on the drawer got stuck, twice, as if I wasn't used to its smooth action.

'Eleven years of diaries, and I'd only missed about eight days in all that time. Now I've lost a year. What's the point?' I nearly said it, I nearly said about her having only lost volume one, January–October, of this year. Those school exercise books get filled so quickly, she still had the second volume of the diary in her hold-all where I'd left it.

'What will you do? I mean, it would be a shame to let them win. Why not start a new diary? Today?' Iman seemed to avoid looking at me. 'It could be like Year Zero; or, you know, Chinese new year, or the financial new year – it doesn't have to start in January.'

Iman smiled, 'That's sweet of you, Willy.'

I burped.

WILLIAM

It was my CV and not my CV.

LIAM FOX
Curriculum Vitae

A Graduate with varied work experience and
considerable transferable skills

EMPLOYMENT

Account Manager Cokely Design & Image Co. (Dec '98
to present day)
I have overseen many projects, including the re-launch of two
high street brands and several pharmaceuticals, most recently
working on the launch of a non-prescription sleeping tablet.
*I pretended I was Will for this bit, he agreed to give me a
reference and I borrowed the facts from him.*

Office Assistant Fox & Sons Estate Agents. (July '98–Dec
'98)
My duties involved filing, data entry and supporting the
Estate Agents in their everyday tasks.
*I thought it best to have had more than one job and chose this
just because it would be plausible to give only a mobile phone
number. The coincidence of names was lovely too.*

Youth Trainee Southampton Football Club ('92–'94)
I performed maintenance tasks around the ground and, on
occasion, trained with the full squad. I was twice a reserve
in actual reserve team games.
*If asked, I failed due to a dodgy knee, this would guarantee me
respect and possibly even sympathy. What more could I ask for.*

97

WORDPROCESSING AND TECHNOLOGY SKILLS

Yes.

Enough said.

EDUCATION AND QUALIFICATIONS

'95–'98 **English Literature BA Hons degree, First Class**
King's College, Cambridge. *I gleaned enough facts about this from a programme on television.*

'94   **A-Levels**   **English Literature A**
                      History A
                      Politics A
                      Sports Science B

'92   **11 GCSEs**
Winchester Boys School, Winchester. *Why not?*

PURSUITS

After being a football apprentice I decided to play hockey at university, where I was team captain and society secretary. I have a passion for jazz music and the films of the Marx Brothers. *Actually this is not me, this is Woody Allen.*

I took a gap year in Poland between my A-levels and taking up my place at Cambridge. *Surprisingly this was the riskiest bit, I was banking on picking up a few anecdotes from the lodger, Tymoteusz Wazyk. It made me feel nervous.*

PERSONAL INFORMATION

D.O.B. 21-10-76

Address 23 Lime Street, Oakley

Marital Status Divorced *I regained my confidence with this lie, it was one of those things which is implausibly plausible. And it would be in keeping with the facts of the matter for me to be evasive about the details.*

REFERENCES

William West
Cokely Design & Image Co.
Will's work number

Fox & Sons
Oakley
A mobile phone number, Dad's old one – it's disconnected.

I missed Dad more in death than I ever had in life. I missed him for two days solid. Then for the next two days I just missed him part of the day, the morning then the afternoon. The sweet shop was a mixed blessing, some days I felt it held me together but most days I felt it holding me back. As a child in a sweet shop I was happy, happy as a child in a sweet shop! Now, it made me sad. I felt it especially in the sound of the door closing itself when the customers left. Dad was everywhere and he was nowhere. I was him and I was alone. So I decided to get a job, a proper graduate job like a grown-up would have. A job with a pension included.

In spite of my better judgement, I photocopied my CV and sent it everywhere I could think of and to fifty companies I found in the phone book. (Including SAEs it cost me £30 in postage but at least the photocopying was free.) I knew it was best to apply for advertised jobs and I knew it was best to only send original CVs, preferably on heavy quality paper, but I didn't give a shit. Achtung job, schnell schnell, blitzkrieg applications. It only took a few days to put my plan into action. Applying for jobs focuses the mind and, despite being a homeowner, I felt quite free to leave the area. Well, free in principle anyway, because I had only just come home here and the thought of leaving again made staying all the more exciting. I missed Dad less at the mere thought of it all.

The party at Will's was so frightening I decided not to answer the phone for a few days, and it gave me the time to do the job applications. My two worlds had nearly collided. I nearly met Tym in the wrong house. I'd tried to avoid him by hiding under the coats in Will's bedroom. After Will found me, I hid in the box bedroom, this time under the bed for extra safety. I needed it too, Will looked into the box bedroom at one point. I could see one of his feet, well, cowboy boots.

I took some confidence from the fact my methods were thorough enough to escape through the portal from the other side. I'd not tied the fishing line – you don't want to get caught in your own trap.

My confidence took a real knock too when I felt a draft coming through the portal. This is what happened. Once I had escaped from the party I waited up for Tym, sitting in the lounge acting all natural, trying to look at home in case he came back from the party early. After a few hours I got tired and went to bed. My wardrobe doors moved ever so, ever so, slightly. It was next to nothing, but I'm too thorough not to check it out. I opened the door and felt a gentle draught. I deliberately hadn't put the brick plug in place, for speed – in case Tym trapped me in my own room and I had to return to the party for sanctuary. But the other error was unforgivable, I'd tied the fishing line to secure the white laminate board but it had snagged on one of Iman's shoes. It was quick, easy and silent to reach through and free up the shoe and secure the laminate board, but it was a serious mistake. Even in the excitement and success of using the portal the wrong way round I should have been more thorough.

Now it was all over I couldn't explain myself to Will but he would want an explanation. So, when I was certain both he and Iman were out and the answerphone was switched on – I used the front door key this time – I rang and left a message.

'Hello, how-de-do-de and that. Just calling to thank you both for hosting such a rip-roaring party. Sorry I overdid things a bit and had to go home early. [Pause.] Well, that was it really, no need to ring back, I'll call again later. Cheers then.' I was pleased with the message and particularly liked the fact it was kind of true, because I had gone home; they just didn't know it was next door.

That morning I decided to decorate my bedroom. It was a great idea, an elegant idea. Once I had the project under way it would furnish me with loads of excuses for Tym. I could say things like, 'Oh, I couldn't sleep in there because of the paint fumes.' And, 'Hang on – DON'T OPEN THE DOOR! – there's a pot of paint on that ladder.' While all the time making it feel like it was my house and I was busy in it, regardless of where I was actually staying. Also it would help me make the break away from the flat, it was like living in a museum, this way I could just write it off by getting the house exactly how I wanted it. Decorating was the natural thing to do, and anyway, I know enough about applying for jobs to know that everything takes fucking ages. For once I had the time to watch the paint dry. I considered dyeing my hair blond again, but decided against it.

I stood in my room considering the dark blue carpet. It was quite dominating and I wondered if it should go. I wondered about the cost of carpet and then I wondered about the cost of paint, or wallpaper. I wondered how I could get the double bed out of the room to get a new carpet fitted. The previous owners had left the bed in the house. It was to remain. It was a Victorian island, it was older than the house, maybe the house was built around it and they'd had to leave it here? It was obviously way bigger than the door, but just in case it made a difference, I tried to lift it. Back straight, knees bent, very thorough, because I wasn't a total novice at physical work. The bed tilted at the corners and I ruffled up the bedding and felt embarrassed by the stainless steel bolts. Maybe the bed wasn't Victorian, but I could see it all, I could see the last owners divorcing and selling and leaving their bed behind them. When a marriage breaks up no one wants the marital bed.

The wallpaper was a floral pattern, pinky flowers and green

102

curvy stems. The background had obviously been white at some point in time but the previous owners had definitely smoked in bed. I looked around for a likely point to start, some flap of paper. When I lifted an edge, by the bay window, I could see other layers of paper underneath – but only in profile, like the end of a bit of wood. I tried to split them with the scraper blade but they only moved together. I tore them off. Two things happened, first the motion of the tear arced across the wall and revealed another layer, and second, a lot of plaster dust snowed on to the dark blue carpet. I tentatively chipped away at the seam of paper and more dust fell, I imagined this happening all the way round. I imagined great chunks of plaster falling off, but then I remembered Mike Wright the builder and the fact that no job was too small for him. He gave me the confidence to carry on.

Chipping off the wallpaper was surprisingly noisy and I made a mental note to only do it during work days when I knew Will and Iman were out. They could hear it, especially on the connecting walls, and if they heard it they might ask Tym how it was going and he might mention me.

At first I was content chipping away at the plaster and peeling the paper off in one great wad. But, working my way along the arc of the first great tear, I began to study the old wallpapers. Beneath the current floral pink with curvy stems was a layer with geometric interlocking shapes in various blue shades. Perhaps the carpet had been bought to match this? No matter, what I could deduce, in archaeological terms, was that this paper was the 1970s in a big way. Some of the blue dividing lines were even delicately touched with orange.

It was time for a tea break but I also had a secondary motive for putting the kettle on. I used the steam on a torn-off hunk of the paper, working the 1970s and the layer below apart over the course of two boilings. It was a bit soggy, a bit translucent, but the theme was definitely a linear arrangement of a white/cream background with thin black lines and broader orangey/yellow/sunshine

103

lines. Rather nice in fact. I took my tea back up with me. Before drinking any of the tea I got back into removing more wallpaper, it was that satisfying, like a good nose-picking.

Wherever the paper was seriously stuck I left it and just followed a seam of loose paper around the big wall. Revealing the wall below was a lovely satisfaction. I even found a bubbled spot where the pink curvy floral paper and the 1970s paper were not even fixed together. I leafed the pages apart and saw a more vibrant blue in the 1970s paper and realised that the geometric shapes were in fact stylised flowers. I couldn't decide if it was lovely or ugly. So I went to sip my tea and think about it, but the tea was dusted with an icing of plaster. I went to re-boil the kettle.

The doorbell rang. My initial instinct was to just ignore it. The kettle started to rumble, the doorbell rang again. The fact that I was ready to offer whoever was at the door a cup of tea pleased me. It made me feel organised. So I took two mugs from the cupboard (Dad's cups and saucers were too macabre) and went to open the door. I could see enough through the frosted glass to know it wasn't Will or Iman at the door; in fact the frosted glass was squarely filled by the silhouette. A debt collector's silhouette, definitely.

'Hellos! You're in, fab,' said Tym. 'My key is inside!' he said as he walked in.

'You forgot your key?' I said.

'Forgot?' He kept walking into the kitchen. 'No, I knew it was here.' And he picked up his bunch of keys from the kitchen counter. Why so many keys? I thought, but felt it would be rude to ask.

'Tea?' said Tym. When I didn't answer he assumed I meant yes and put a tea bag into each mug. He had the enthusiasm of the converted about tea. Living with me he had learned to love it. I had given him tea; it gave me a warm glow.

'You're home early,' I said.

'No, this is a usual time. I mean I often go to the library, but today I came straight back because I was nervous about not having my key.'

I watched the tea brew, then remembered the stuff about Poland on my CV and decided to start the ball rolling.

'Tym. What's Poland like?' He looked at me in a new way, like a parent when their child says fuck for the first time.

'Who wants to know?' he said, which was rather strange.

'Well, me, obviously. I'm interested.'

'No, I mean why? What about Poland?'

'Anything.' Well anything would be a start, we could build up to the more personal stuff. Tym was quiet. I finished assembling the tea, when I handed him his mug it broke his reverie and he answered.

'Well, in Poland, in the public lavatories, well, here the gentlemen's often has the sign of a man on it—' he paused and looked out of the window, 'or sometimes I know the gentlemen's has the word *gents* on it.' He looked me in the eye. 'Well, in Polish public lavatories, the gentlemen's is marked with a triangle.'

'And the ladies?'

He exhaled across his tea, 'Yes, the ladies is marked with a circle.'

'Thank you,' I said. Tym looked out of the window and said, 'Do you think this house is haunted?' then sipped his tea.

I tried to think of something else to ask about Polish toilets. Um, 'Is there a toilet attendant?'

Tym answered impatiently, 'Often yes, he has to take the money for the toilet tissues and soap and towels. But please talk of ghosts in this house.' I didn't like the idea, let alone the certainty in his voice. I was terrified of ghosts as a boy, particularly after we were burgled when I thought ghosts smelled like paint. Tym continued, 'Last night, when I was in bed, I heard a terrible scratching noise. It didn't wake me, I was walking along the upstairs corridor when I heard it. I tried to ignore it, you see it was coming from your room and I thought it was your business.'

'Scratching? My business?'

'Well then, I mean I had just flushed the toilet – because I thought you might hear it and stop scratching, or whatever – but I heard some howling. Howling like a tiny flimsy thing. Then more scratching. I stood outside your room but didn't dare go in.'

'No, I mean I would really rather you never ever went into my room.' Which seemed to both alarm and console him, as if I was the source of the noises. 'No, what I mean is obviously we need to respect each other's private areas.'

'Yeah.'

'What did you do?'

'I went into my room, shut the door and pushed my bed against it. I thought about even saying some prayers.'

Now I had a choice, I could tell Tym I had not been in the house for the past two nights, and therefore didn't know anything about any noises. Or, I could accept responsibility for the ghostly noises. But Tym is a resourceful man, and said, 'If you don't think it was ghosts and don't think it was from your room, maybe it was from inside the chimney – you know, sometimes pigeons fall down the chimney and sound spooky as they die. I mean a death like that could take weeks.'

'Did it sound like a pigeon?'

'No, not at all, I just thought this way I could think it was a ghost in the chimney and you could think it was something else, like a pigeon or something.'

'Thank you,' I said, but I wasn't really sure why. I was sweating, but it was only because I'd forgotten to put on any of my Happy Shopper deodorant. I knew there weren't any ghosts. (There wasn't even the smell of fresh paint.)

Tym put down his tea on the kitchen counter next to the wallpaper scraper. 'What is this?' he said.

'I've been decorating. Another good reason not to go into my room. There's a paint pot on a ladder behind the door.' I realised this might have made sense as a thought earlier on, but just sounded weird when I said it out loud as a lie. But Tym looked excited.

'That's it! You were doing some of this scraping last night! That was the noise I thought was a ghost.' And he made a little up-and-down scraping movement with the tool. I smiled at the neatness of his explanation and at the fact he seemed to be forgetting the ghostly howling, but Tym obviously didn't want to believe in ghosts either. So I just said, 'Yes.'

I own three kettles: one from number 4 Wood Road, one from the flat and one from the sweet-shop storeroom – which still works even though Dad told the Crabbe sisters it was broken just to reduce their tea breaks. I got all three boiling away by the big wall in my room, steaming up the atmosphere. Chipping away with the scraper was too much hard work.

Some of the top layers came away easy; the consistent problem was the bottom layer, black and yellow/orange lines on a cream background. I tried again and the scraper took a bite from the plaster. I relaxed, and teased the metal edge into the lip of paper and wall. It worked quite well, so I went and tipped away half the boiling water, put in some fresh cold, and started all three up again. This time the blade caught on some fabric in the wall. I tried again, and there was a ruffle of brown goo with more firm fabric. I clicked off the kettles and got a sponge from the bathroom. I used the water from one of the kettles to saturate the spot. The water was pulled through the fabric under the paper, redefining the slightest rumples in the surface. I scraped again, there was more brown mush revealing more fabric. I picked off the brown mush and, just as I was going to flick it on to the floor, decided to examine it.

It was a mountain. It really was, I recognised those concentric height lines from geography. By flattening out the paper I saw a few letters, then I put it all flat against the wall and re-stuck it so I could read the words: RED HILLS. Under the word RED it said

Beinn Dearg, and just below the word HILLS was Beinn na Caillich.

Faintly on the reverse of the fabric there was the imprint of a fourth layer of wallpaper. It was something new with red vertical stripes of several widths. It was all a secret, a remnant of the decent job the first home-owner had made of decorating his room. I tried to imagine the scene all those years ago when this was a new house with stiffly plastered walls. But the likelihood was that this was a professional job by actual painters and decorators, tradesmen from the 1940s with flat caps, coveralls and smoking Woodbines who prepared these walls for their jazzy red stripes of varying widths. Suburban archaeology. The first home-owner probably pasted the map on top and I would never know why. Maybe to cover a stain on the stripy wallpaper?

I held up a boiling kettle and used the damp hot sponge to edge out a bit more of the landscape. I found STRATHAIRD, before moving up to discover that this was a map of S K Y E. It was a beautiful word. I stood back and looked at the part-exposed map the way a painter studies his canvas. It was beautiful, from the RED HILLS in the bottom next to STRATHAIRD which in turn was below LORD MACDONALD'S FOREST. (Who's he?) From this segment I'd gone straight up to reveal an edge of somewhere that began RA but the rest was lost in the removal, yet the ease with which it was lost just made me more pleased about the bits I had found.

I stopped scraping and heard some scratching. Instinctively I called out, 'Tym?' because I hoped it was him playing about, or, it was the instinct to get reinforcements. There was no answer and in that gap I listened hard for the scratching. Nothing. Then Tym made me jump, he tapped on the door and it opened a tiny amount.

'Hellos? Did you call? I had my radio on,' he said, and I was over there by the door, ready to protect whatever it was I'd found from him. He couldn't see past me.

'Er, no, I didn't call you,' I lied, but casual. 'Sometimes I think I can hear the phone ringing in the back of music, so I'll turn it down and there'll be nothing there.'

Tym nodded and went back into his room but didn't shut his door. I shut mine and listened again. Nothing, except the trace of Tym's radio. Then I heard it more faintly, followed by a sigh. I thought about running, but it was still daylight outside and that made it more scary. There was nowhere to run to because this was my house and I had to confront whatever was in it. I couldn't run away home when I was already at home. More scratching and another sigh, I took some very deep breaths which sounded like an answer to the sighing. I tried to locate it, was it in the chimney? Not a bad starting point, and I put my left ear against the chimney wall (and wondered if there was another map sandwiched inside the wallpaper). With my left ear covered I heard the noise with my right ear. It wasn't in the chimney. It was in the wardrobe. I felt it in the back of my thighs, something was in the wardrobe. I picked up a kettle in each hand because anything is better to fight with than nothing. Anything, especially for someone like me, a paperclip is good for stabbing, a shoe is good for hitting and kettles of hot water would be good for throwing. It was an effort but I breathed very deeply.

Kettles of boiling water would be even better, so I plugged them both back in and turned them on. My knee joint clicked, but it didn't hurt. As they boiled I held on to the third kettle, just in case someone/thing came out of the wardrobe. My imagination took over – Will could be in the wardrobe, he could have found the portal and he could be watching me through a pinprick in the door. Will could be shitting me up with scratching and sighing. If he had found the portal he might think I'd robbed him, which was really unfair, I'd only taken the chocolate and the peanut butter, oh, and his bowling ball. I thought about Wesley and Will's revenge on him, which was revenge for not very much and I felt

109

my legs were going to give way at the thought of what he might do with a reason.

Then I thought again, did he know this was my house? How much had he seen? If it was just me starting to decorate then I could say it was as a favour to Tym. I picked up the bubbling kettles anyway, just in case I didn't get a chance to say anything.

I slid open the wardrobe door, using my knuckles as I gripped the kettles. They are the type of doors that can only be opened one at a time, because as soon as one is slid open it covers the other closed side. There was nothing there but darkness. The kettles were very heavy. I slid shut this door and opened the other side. Nothing again but darkness. I shut it and put the kettles down by my feet. If it was Will in the wardrobe he must have been moving from one side to the other as the doors were opened in turn. (The type of hiding that happens in pantomimes.) Sticking my head in to check would leave me open to attack, so I just swung the doors open and shut in turn as quick as I could.

As I whisked across the second door for the second time it bounced instead of shutting. *MIRAOWL!* I jumped back, kicking a kettle with my right foot, it burst, some spilt forward, some sank into my sock and fucking burnt. I grabbed off the shoe and sock – still burning hot to the touch – and scrambled for the other kettle. I looked at the darkness and the darkness looked back at me.

It was Aslan making tiny crying dolly noises. He was on his side, his chest was moving quickly but his head and face were still. There was no damage on his face, I went to stroke him under the chin and recoiled at the touch of blood. The blood was really hot, then I saw he was wet all over and all the water was still hot. He really smelt bad, quite rotten. He was steaming.

I thought Tym might come in and find me. Aslan had made such a noise. I listened for his radio, and heard its imprint coming through the door, but surely Aslan had been louder than that? Maybe he wouldn't investigate, but it made me feel like I had at the party, that if we met now everything would just unravel. He would see the cat, he would tell Will, Will would kill me, or I would have to kill Tym. Christ, it just didn't make any sense, I only wanted to be close to my best friend, I didn't want all this.

As I'd done on the night of the party I found myself again hiding under a bed. Before, when Tym had me hemmed in upstairs at Will's, I hid under the bed in the box bedroom and accidentally shut Aslan in my wardrobe. Now, I deliberately shut Aslan in my wardrobe and hid under my own bed. As I lay down on the floor, about to slide under, I saw at eye level two of Aslan's claws embedded into the deep blue carpet. I had heard of this – I had heard of cats' claws getting stuck in the road when they are hit by a car and in the final moment grip the tarmac for purchase. I slid over on my belly and examined the claws; by the way they sloped, left to right, they had been torn out sideways as Aslan had reached out and gripped in face of the oncoming door.

Maybe I could use this, maybe I could pretend to Will and Iman (oh Christ it's Iman's cat) that I had found Aslan like this and taken him to the vet's, I could say, 'He must have been hit by a car! And that's what the vet thinks too – just look at his missing claws.' I wouldn't mention the hot water burns, that could be a mystery. Yes, or if his injuries are more minor, then I could say, 'The vet thinks he must have been hit by a bicycle! Just look at his missing claws.' And I could point at where the pedal had caught him just under the chin. Only I need know he'd been hit by a speeding wardrobe and a crashing kettle.

I opened the wardrobe door. The darkness was quiet and furry with the smell of ill cat. I reached in for Aslan, but he was so heavy, too heavy for one hand, that I knew he must be dead. I felt bad enough already about not securing the portal, catching the laminate board on Iman's shoe. It was a grave and serious error, particularly for someone as thorough as me. But how could I have not noticed Aslan when I freed the shoe and secured the laminate board? It was dark, his fur's so dark, maybe that's how? Maybe he was asleep? No matter how unlikely, unlucky and unlike me it was, it had happened.

The heat of the water had dissipated, but he was still wet and the room was so humid. Even though his face wasn't damaged his head was very floppy – I think the door broke his neck. When I put him down on the deep blue carpet his head flopped back and got tucked under his body. It looked so uncomfortable I had to ease it back round. He did smell. This gave me some comfort, it must have meant he was a bit ill anyway, a bit smelly. I mean, a cat's reflexes should be fast enough to avoid a door. He must have been a bit under the weather not to make more noise in the wardrobe, not to mew or howl at being shut in. (Or maybe cats don't think like that, maybe they just accept it and wait it out, it's not as if he knew where he was.) Still, death was a heavy price to pay for straying through the portal.

'Hellos?' said Tym, through the door. In one movement I bundled Aslan into my arms and rolled over under the bed. Tym tapped the door with his fingernails.

'Hellos? Liam?' I heard the door inch open. 'Would you like the cup of tea I am making?' he said, it didn't sound like he had come in. 'Hellos?' A bit louder, like he stuck his head round the door but I couldn't be certain. But what would he see anyway? My wardrobe door open? What else, he didn't know I was in here and if I kept quiet he wouldn't know. He didn't come in. Could he recognise the smell of a dead cat? I listened for the sound of the bedroom door shutting. It didn't happen but I did hear Tym go downstairs. He couldn't make any tea though because the kettle was in here. That was all that was amiss to him, he could know no more.

I rolled out and pulled the cat after me. I found a white carrier bag and put Aslan in it, but gently; I ruffled the bag up, like some people do when putting on a sock, and eased it around him. Tym came back up the stairs and I could smell dope, Tym must be having a sneaky puff thinking I was out. I was annoyed at the deception but then elated because for once it was a good thing, the

112

talk of tea was a smokescreen, not even the kettle would be missed – and more importantly, he believed I was out.

But I was stuck. I could hear Tym's radio and it sounded like the door was open. My door was ajar and I had a dead cat in a carrier bag. I daren't risk going out the front door, the only thing for it was to go through the portal.

I got in and shut the wardrobe door behind me. (Remembering, as I always seemed to, that 'It is very foolish to shut oneself into any wardrobe' and delighting in ignoring it.) I slackened off the fishing line at each corner of my wardrobe. Then I moved the bowling ball (still in its box) and lifted out the brick plug at the bottom left. Nudging out the white board, as usual, I was able to tip it forward to rest against Iman's clothes rail. I slow-dived through the bottom left corner of my wardrobe into the bottom right corner of Iman's. I reached back through for the white carrier bag. Nice and easy.

As is my rule, because I am nothing if not thorough, I opened the wardrobe door a fraction of a fraction first, then eased it back to see the whole bedroom. Now with this light I carefully refitted the white board and straightened the clothes on the rail before shutting the door. I even checked the spot where I had put the carrier bag for any leakage.

The only problems I could foresee were the possibilities of being seen leaving the house by either neighbours, Tym or Mrs Price. Tym seemed not to be any problem because his room was at the back of the house and he was enjoying a crafty spliff. Mrs Price was an unknown quantity, but if I worried about her I would never do any of it. (I did think it was a good sign that she hadn't been at the party, I mean it was fair to assume they were not that close.) I saw the answerphone light winking reassuringly with my message on it. After the tropical climate of my bedroom Will's house was cold. My sweat stank and I hoped they would not be able to smell me later.

I was worried about leakage, particularly on the beige hall

carpet, but it was all over so fast and then I'd shut the front door behind me. Nice and easy does it.

To minimise the Mrs Price risk I went up Wood Road past my own house. Aslan was very dense and made the bag swing vigorously with my walking. I got on to Mill Lane then headed for the recreation ground, it seemed just the spot to dump a dead cat.

Passing by the arcade of shops at the bottom of the flats, I felt safe enough to worry. I sat down on a bench and put the carrier bag between my feet, keeping it upright just in case. Even in the open air I could smell it. I weighed up the pros and cons of either burying Aslan or leaving him in the roadside gutter (at the Old Elm roundabout?) to imply he'd been hit by a car. The advantage of the Old Elm roundabout was that Will would see him and it was so busy as to be entirely plausible. Burying Aslan was a good cop-out though, it would solve the problem for me and get rid of this unhealthy smell. But I would need to wait until dark to do it. I tried to think of it from Will's point of view: either way the cat was dead. I thought of it from Iman's point of view, finding the cat run over would be painful. Not finding the cat, which had already been missing since the party, would be more lingering. Perhaps less painful, but in its own way it did rather suggest Aslan had met the same fate. The Old Elm roundabout was a good idea but I didn't like the thought of Will driving and seeing it, what if he stopped concentrating on the road? Also what if he was concentrating on the road so much he didn't see it? And any cat that lies at the edge of the road either gets all bloated or run over again – or bloated then run over again. No, it was just too messy. The best thing to do was to put the cat on their doorstep with a note of explanation. It was too cold to hang about thinking anymore.

I went into the newsagent's in the arcade of shops at the foot of the flats. I had to carry Aslan with me much as I would have liked to stash him outside the shop and take a chance. A smelly carrier bag could attract some kids, or maybe even the keen nose of a local dog, or even other cats – and what would they think of me! I

114

gripped the top of the bag shut, got in, bought a biro (20 pence) and asked for the receipt when I realised I didn't have anything to write on.

Under normal circumstances I would have been interested in this rival newsagent's, where the assistant looked like a dark-haired version of the comedy actor Steve Martin. I would have compared their layouts and checked the sell-by dates on their chocolate because that's an excellent barometer of how well a shop is doing. For the most accurate assessment of a rival shop check the dates on a Mars bar as a sort of control reading. These usually shift themselves and should therefore have quite a distant sell-by date, anything over a year away. If the date is less than a month away then the shop is in trouble. Next, compare the Mars bar date with a middling brand of chocolate, say a Crunchie. If this date is also distant then the shop is in a strong position. (N.B. Remember, if the shop is doing really badly, and has had to chuck out-of-date stock away, it could have deceptively distant dates on the new stock. But often these shops try to sell the out-of-date stuff cheap to kids. A bad sign for them, let it go, if it goes wrong just accept it and move on.)

I consoled myself with the fact that biros in my shop are two pence cheaper, and the fact I'd been lucky enough to get quite a long receipt; he'd mispriced the item and had to cancel it and I had the header of a previous transaction on it. I returned to the bench. Christ I was tense, I thought of the map of the Isle of Skye and how relaxing it must be there at this very second, walking up the Red Hills or picnicking in Lord Macdonald's Forest. Cold though, colder than here.

I scribbled with the pen until the ink flowed nicely and got on with it, using an extra finger to hold the nib and with my hand at a different angle to disguise my writing. I imagined the words in a Scottish accent.

Something terribly terrible has happened. I asked about and

heard this was your cat. Christ knows I am so sorry about it, I
hope it is of some consolation to you that the little cat must have
died instantly, because I stopped right away and was going to
take him to the vet. Sorry I can't face you in person but I am in
a terrible hurry. Again, I am so, so, sorry.

Both sides of the receipt were full and I was rather pleased with it.

Back at number 4 Wood Road I shut myself into my bedroom. Even though Tym was out he had left the heating on. I waited for it to get dark and wished it smelled of flowers in my room. There is a certain balance in waiting in a dark room for the evening to come on. Light tilts: one moment the room is the dark bit and the next the street is the dark bit. The street lights wobbled into action, I got used to the smell of the dead cat, which seemed like a terrible thing to be used to, so I opened the window a fraction. Iman called him in for his tea.

'As-lan!' Then, quicker, 'Aslan!' It seemed like he would twitch the bag at the sound of his name. Then she came to the front door again, rattling a fork inside the can of food. 'Aslan! Aslan!'

At 7.15pm I saw Will leaving the house dressed as a red and blue cowboy. He put his cowboy hat on for the walk to the car, put it on the passenger seat and drove off. I waited half an hour to be certain Iman had shut the curtains, then went down and put the bag of dead cat on the doorstep (next to a bowl of cat food) and jogged back to the sweet shop, it kept me warm and burnt off some nervous energy.

I was a shit for killing Aslan. I left the lights off in the flat. It wasn't murder though, nothing like it, accidental death was all. (Still death though.) Yes, still death but nothing like murder – I mean cats is cats – they can't be murdered, or, come to think of it, even manslaughtered. (Iman will be crying now.) Not necessarily, Will will probably find it when he comes back from line-dancing. He'll find it and he'll break the news to Iman, it couldn't be better, I mean he is her husband after all. And I wrote the note, it was a very nice note, quite a personal touch. (Will is vengeance.) No wonder no one would want to knock on a stranger's door and say, 'Sorry, here's your dead cat.' It could be dangerous – Will would be dangerous, I mean look at Wesley. And I felt much better for thinking it all through logically, nothing must jeopardise my closeness to Will.

One of the good things about losing a parent to cancer is that it gives perspective to people mourning the death of lesser family members. So, I decided for this reason, and as a friend, I was just the person Will needed to talk to, if he only but knew it, so I rang him. As the phone rang I thought how great it was to live alone and always find things where you left them. The phone was on the dinner plate – I didn't even need to turn on the light to know that. I didn't even need my eyes open to talk to Will on the phone, phones are great when you are too nervous to make convincing eye contact. The phone rang and rang and rang.

I imagined the scene in number 2, The Firs, as the phone rang through the empty rooms, if only Will were there to hear it. I imagined the faint sound of the ringing phone in number 4, if only Tym were there to hear it. I was in all three places at once.

'Yes?' said Will. Now I was on the spot rather because I had let the phone ring for an unnaturally long time. 'Hello?' said Will. I took a deep breath and dived in.

'How-de-do-de-ing!'

'I'm right in the middle of something, let me ring you back.' And he hung up before I could agree. But it couldn't be sex! No way, I mean he's done that to me before, I mean I've been certain that was the reason, but not now. No way, their cat's dead.

I made a cup of tea in the dark, using a saucepan to heat the water because the kettles were at number 4. It was easy, I used the light inside the fridge when adding the milk – the only part of the exercise where precision was required. I waited for Will to ring back, but the tea was getting cold so I drank it.

Now it was done and I was out of danger, I allowed myself to

117

think of Aslan and how sorry I was, not just sorry for Iman and Will, but sorry for the furry little man himself. I felt better after getting some of the feeling sorry out of the way. I put the telly on silently because it makes a lovely flickery lamp.

I rang Will again, this time he only let it ring twice and didn't bother with how-de-do-de or hello.

'Liam?'

'Mmm.'

'Yeah sorry about that.
Iman was very upset; about
Aslan.'

'Oh no, what about him?'

'He's died, hit and run. Terribly sad.'

'Oh no. Well give her my condolences won't you.'

'What did you want?'

'Hmm?'

'When you rang me, what did you want.'

'Oh no.'

'What?'

'Oh, no, I er, was just thinking about Aslan. Poor cat. How was line-dancing?'

'Yeah? It was nice. Learned the American Pie.'

'No, I was ringing, when I rang you, to check you got my message, on the answerphone, when I rang earlier today, I left a message. American Pie as in Bye Bye Miss American Pie?'

'Yes,' and Will played their messages: *'Hiya Iman it's me, I've typed up the script and thought we could start rehearsals on Thursday – send the permission slips home with the little angels tomorrow. Let me know tonight, or in the morning. Enough already! Byee!'* Then I heard him call out, covering the receiver, quietly shouting, 'Iman! Did you hear that? Message from Jemma.' I could just be heard in the background: *'Hello, how-de-do-de and that. Just calling to thank you both for hosting such a rip-roaring party. Sorry I overdid things a bit and had to go home early. [Pause.] Well, that was it really, no need to ring back, I'll call again later. Cheers then.'*

'Will?'

'Yeah, sorry about that, just checking Iman got the message. School stuff.'

'Did you hear my message?'

'Yes, "no need to ring back, you'll call again."'

'I rang to thank you for the party, and to apologise about having to go home early. I was ringing now just to be thorough.'

'Yeah, you stitched me up leaving me there with Edna Crabbe and a quiche.'

'Did she enjoy the party?'

'I'm not sure.'

'Wasn't she at line-dancing?'

'Yes. She said she'd enjoyed getting out. But she didn't like the American Pie.'

'So, how did you find Aslan? I mean, well, I suppose he was

119

'at the side of the road for you to think hit and run.'

'I don't *think* it was hit and run, we know it. They left us a message, he was too scared to face us.'

'Or she?'

'Ok smarty pants, he or she, was too scared to face us.'

And I think I heard Iman crying in the background.

'Christ she does sound upset.'

'Yeah. It's very sad.'

'It is! It's such a sad thing to happen.'

'Yeah.'

'She'd wanted a cat called Aslan ever since she was a child.'

'Yeah. And now he's dead.'

'Will! Did she hear that?'

'No, no, she's shut herself in the lounge. Just like at the party, eh?'

'Yeah. Did I miss much then?'

'You missed line-dancing to Elvis.'

'Wow.'

'Really? Really wow?'

'Yeah, wow.'

'I had everyone doing it – but it wasn't even my idea. Iman's headmaster, Terry, suggested it.'

'Exactly. Never mind, eh. Maybe next time?'

'So, I missed out.'

'What have you done with Aslan then?'

'Nothing.'

'Aren't you going to bury him? It's hygienic.'

'True. Between me and you Iman is hugging him at the moment. She's got him on a towel on her lap and she's stroking him.'

'Ah. That's sweet though, really it is.'

'Leaks a bit, mind you.'

'Reeks?'

'A bit'n'all; but I said *leaks*. L-L-leaks.'

'It's just from under his chin, not really blood, it's a clearish fluid.'

'Ok, enough, don't get grim about it.'

'Will! Enough! She's had a hard time of it recently. You both have.'

'We all have. But we don't hear you moaning about it do we?'

'No.'

'Well, maybe we should, hear you moan I mean.'

'Come on, I was at the funeral.'

'Why should I?'

'Ok then, answer me this,
Mr Fine, are you sitting in
the dark?'

'I'm fine, Will.'

'What's that got to do with
anything?'

'Answer it then. Because when
we came round that time you
were in the dark. I've been
thinking about it and I reckon
you've been sitting in the
dark a lot.'

'Too much sitting in the dark?'

'Yes.'

'Why's it matter?'

'It's like you bottling out of
the party!'

'Sitting in the dark is like me
leaving the party? You just
played my message – I overdid
the drink.'

'No you didn't. You can't face
people and you keep the flat
lights off most of the time. I've
been past, I've seen it.'

'I've got the lights on. You're
wrong.'

'Ok, what can you see?'

'The usual: a plate I've left
from yesterday's dinner, the
telly, my mug of tea – the
yellow mug with the blue
rim – which is three-quarters
empty. Oh, and it's got a ring

122

round the inside where I didn't
wash it up properly.'

'No. I'm sorry mate, I don't
believe you, because I came by
the shop today and Tracey let
me upstairs, I left two letters
for you and you've not mentioned
them, I left them on top of the
telly, you would have
mentioned it . . .

PAUSE

Got them?'

'Yes. But this is addressed to
you.'

'Blimey Liam, that one is to me
asking me for a reference and I
presume the other one,
addressed to you, is asking
you to interview.'

'That was quick: I only started
applying the other week.'

'Read it! Of course it was quick,
it stresses the need for speed in
the letter. At least it did in my
letter – wouldn't want you to
think I'd been reading your
letters.'

'That's excellent news, isn't it?
Excellent news.'

'Yes. Look, you write your
reference, there's some of our
Cokely Design headed paper in
the envelope, then bring it
round here and I'll sign it.'

123

'Thanks Will, that's excellent.'

'Look, I better go. Dead cats
and that.'

'Yes, I know. Bye.'

'Bye. Thanks for ringing.
Keep your chin up.'

I decided sitting in the dark was actually an excellent thing for Will
to think I did. Yes, I did do it, sometimes, but also it would allow
him to think I was in the flat when I was out, particularly good
when I was at number 4. I turned on the light and started to read
the letters. They were from a company called Brown Advertising.
Then I got that feeling that feels like the end of the school summer
holidays. A feeling which concentrates the mind and the bladder.
The feeling of having too much to do and too little time. Like
diving off the high board with only the shallow end to aim for. The
interview was tomorrow.

I wore my suit. Inside the inside pocket a ticket is sewn into the
top seam:

PATTERN USED BY CUTTER 20/149
E/H 68453
MONTAGUE BURTON LTD.
FOR REPEAT ORDERS PLEASE
QUOTE NOS. ABOVE. DO NOT
REMOVE THIS TAG WHICH SHOULD
BE SEWN INSIDE THE BREAST POCKET.
(POCKET TYPE 65)
2.2.66

I loved it, the suit is very 1960s with a high-buttoned jacket, thin
collar and thin pleated trousers. It fitted me and my new CV. It
seemed just the type of suit someone who'd been an account

124

manager with Cokely Design & Image Co. would wear. And, most importantly, it looked brand-new. I would put money on the fact that today was only the third time the suit had ever been worn. It was my graduation suit and now my interview suit. First time round it must've been someone's funeral suit; for the funeral of someone who didn't live to see England win the World Cup. It was beautifully made to measure, with a furry edge inside the top of the trousers to grip the shirt (blue with an orange tie) and it fitted like a glove.

My interview was at 5pm which did give me some time, but I needed this to familiarise myself with my CV. I was fatalistic, this would at least be practise. Brown Advertising was based in a three-storey converted town house, occupying the basement and ground-level floors, all the rooms smelled like a glossy magazine. I felt half-prepared as I had read half a book on interview techniques.

I realised I was totally unprepared when a man whose name I instantly forgot after introduction (but who looked like a young Ronald Reagan, he was about forty years old but this is still young for Ronald Reagan) asked me why I wanted the job and I didn't know exactly what the job was. I looked at my feet and noticed I was wearing odd socks, one navy and one black. I crossed my ankles to hide it and made eye contact. I pretended I was being interviewed on the news and repeated the question.

'Why do I want the job?' I mused aloud. 'I suppose that from my CV you know the factual reasons why I should want the job.'

'Yes,' said Ronald Reagan. 'Actually, about your CV. What was the non-prescription sleeping tablet you were working on?' I felt a little island of calm within my chest, one difficult question had been replaced by the opportunity to lie. I had given this imaginary brand considerable thought late at night while trying to get to sleep.

'I was in charge of a new range of sleep aids, called *Peels*. I was even responsible for the name.'

125

'*Peels*? I haven't heard of it.'

'Well, we're launching it in the New Year. The research indicated there is a knock-on effect from people stocking up on hangover remedies, as well as cold and flu treatments, to an increased acceptance of a new lifestyle tablet. And all that stress and debts over the holiday period will have given people sleepless nights.'

'And the space is cheaper after Christmas.' Ronald Reagan nodded with an approving smile.

'I developed the name *Peels* to cover the range of two tablets, one organic, one not; and a liquid, organic, form of the preparation. *Peels*, you see, it's sleep backwards.'

'Doesn't that rather imply staying awake? And you have the package blanks with you Mr—' and he paused, turning over my CV, 'Mr Fox?' The island of calm in my chest sank to my bowels and I felt my bowels relax.

'No.' And there was a heavy pause. 'They are the intellectual property of Cokely Design, and, well, I would be equally confidential about the work I did for you.' I felt like sighing but didn't risk it.

'Quite. You have fitted a lot of different experiences into your young life. Tell me, which was best: Poland, Cambridge or being a trainee with Southampton Football Club?' Which was a bit of a dirty question and without thinking I said, 'Poland.' Not because it was (or would have been) best, but because he'd said it first and I just wanted to answer as quickly as possible.

'Poland?' and when he said it as a question I couldn't help but answer him again.

'Poland,' I confirmed.

'Really, I went to Cambridge and thought it an enchanting place.' Oh Christ, I tried to head the conversation off before it got too personal.

'Really, which college did you go to?' I said, hoping to God it wasn't King's. I had prepared an imaginary anecdote about going around Cambridge dressed as something amusing but I hadn't decided what (a parrot? A policeman?) and ending up in the river for Rag Week. But it was most predictable and had in fact been something I'd seen on television. What if he'd seen it too? I'd look like a fraud, worse still, I'd look like an unimaginative fraud. Why hadn't I put Keele University, it was the truth, why did it all have to be lies?

'Oh, we went to them all, on a sort of day trip, Mrs Brown and I were celebrating our anniversary.' I had it, he was called Mr Brown and this was Brown's Advertising Agency. What could be simpler, impress him and get the job. 'Sorry. I, er.' And he lost the thread of the interview and fell back on to one of the regular questions which I'd been expecting. 'Was there anything you wanted to ask me?'

'Yes.' And I took out a piece of paper and a pen and tilted them towards me so he wouldn't be able to see that the paper was in fact a shopping list. I looked studiously at the shopping list, I turned it over being sure to keep my hand over the words. I tried a compliment. 'You've been pretty thorough and I don't think I need ask most of these.' Mr Brown smiled his simple Ronald Reagan smile and I banked on him forgetting that we'd barely spoken. It seemed a fair bet because he had probably been interviewing all day and things would be getting hazy underneath all that slick hair.

Then I asked a question to lead us back to the beginning of the interview and the definition of the job.

'So, Mr Brown,' he smiled at the use of his name, 'what would my initial targets be?'

'Well, we've never had a dedicated Inserts Manager before.' I nodded, I'd decided to do it irrespective of what he said, nod and listen, that was the plan from here on in. 'So, in some respects you would be able to write your own job description. Responding to the briefs and anticipating the needs of the clients. Building up relationships with insertable space vendors.' I stopped nodding. 'Magazines!' laughed Mr Brown, and I got it, inserts had to be those bits of paper that fall out of magazines. 'How do you feel about that?'

'Excited!' And I really did. 'I think inserts are the future of advertising. They occupy the purest advertising space because they're real. They exist in real space. People actually have to interact with them, even if they don't want to. They represent a heady mix of passive and aggressive marketing and I love the way they just lie between the pages.'

'Really?'

'Oh yes. They're persuasive like the wallpaper that the last people left under your wallpaper. They're hidden but present, like stuff in the loft, like the warm blanket people put under their bed-sheet in winter. They are out there, really, really out there!'

'Ok,' said Mr Brown. 'What would your ideas be for expanding the market?'

'I would put inserts into pornography.'

'Don't they already use them?' Which I took as a green light.

'No. I would suggest advertising in pornographic magazines, nothing too hardcore, to companies which had previously ignored the market. Some of those magazines are bestsellers – irrespective of subject matter. Did you know *Fiesta* sells a quarter of a million copies a month?' Mr Brown didn't seem to know that. 'I reckon a real bonus would be when people take a sneaky peek inside the pornos in the shop. Imagine it, someone, anyone, man, widower, young man, boy, head of an independent advertising agency, anyone, opens the magazine to stock up the old spank banks. Then as they take it from the top shelf the inserts fall out. Well, they are going to pick them up, no doubt about it, they are going to pick them up and put that advert into their pocket! And later they won't want to admit to anyone that they got the add from a porno, they're going to pretend – even to themselves – that they wanted the advert!'

'And the advertisers could track the origin of any responses from the usual numeric codes,' considered Mr Brown.

'Exactly,' I lied.

There was a lovely pause in the conversation, it felt very peaceful. Either Mr Brown was digesting my comments, or we were both listening to his watch tick. He had his hands linked together with his index fingers pushed up as the church steeple. He pointed them both at me and said, 'Would you like a cup of tea, Mr Fox?'

'Yes please,' I said, confident that for once I really knew an answer. Mr Brown must be very keen on tea because he then asked me, 'Ceylon all right for you?' Which was another difficult question.

'That's great,' I lied.

'Do footballers really drink tea at half-time?' he asked as the loose-leaf tea brewed in the stainless steel pot.

'I don't know,' I said, then remembering my CV, said the words again but with a different inflection. 'I don't, no. Or perhaps that should really be, I didn't when I was a player, no.' I thought I'd got away with it as Mr Brown poured the tea without a pause.

'Football is the most marvellous thing,' he said. 'We have a team in the local five-a-side league here. Maybe you would like to play for us? We have tea at half-time.'

'Oranges are more conventional,' I offered.

'And yet, you still say Poland was a better experience than being a trainee at Southampton!' He said it like the oranges could have tipped the balance.

I sipped my tea and thought of an answer. 'Poland was a revelation – not at all like you'd imagine it. Being a trainee was great, but leaving broke my heart.' Mr Brown nodded like he also knew the pain of loss. Then he offered me a chocolate biscuit and I thought the job was nearly won. I broke the biscuit in two and left half in the saucer. I finished the tea, but didn't get a chance to eat the second half of the biscuit before Mr Brown offered his hand for shaking.

I went back to the flat to type my reference on the headed

Cokely Design paper Will had provided. I decided to keep my suit on to make writing the reference more businesslike.

Confidential Reference

MR LIAM FOX

Mr Fox joined Cokely Design in December 1998, initially as an Office Assistant, but within a month his talent and ability allowed him to act up as an Account Manager. Once in this post he, quite literally, made the position his own.

Mr Fox has an excellent rapport with his staff and is considered by his superiors to be a bedrock of the working team. His inscrutable nature and keen sense of business make him a credit to this organisation.

In the time he has been with us he has not had any days off due to sickness; and is in fact slightly under his entitlement on holiday taken. To my knowledge he has never been late for work.

I would be sad to lose the services of Mr Fox, but feel duty bound to advise any prospective employer that he is a first-rate employee, and, as we shall probably find to our cost, quite irreplaceable.

Please do not hesitate to contact me if you require any further information.

I went round to Will's so he could sign it, I was buzzing. The job seemed just the ticket, it would occupy me and test me. It was the type of opportunity I deserved, not just because Dad was dead, but because of all my qualifications and all my potential. And the inserts! The space between magazine pages was just right for me. I could happily have a career there.

I'd put Aslan out of my mind until Iman opened the door of number 2, The Firs, and the smell (not her face – not at first)

130

reminded me. It smelled of leathery rotten eggs. Iman turned away and said something, but I didn't catch what it was. I followed her in and hung my coat over the top of a red hooded jacket. I recognised this as one I had hidden under at the party, I guessed it was Jemma's coat, and with that, the atmosphere in the house seemed to change. The hallway became more public, I became more public. I had expected to just pop in, get Will to sign, and leave. I did feel much better about Iman since reading her diary, like we knew each other more. But now I knew Jemma was here and wasn't even sure if Will was.

'Will?' I called out, there was a pause before he answered from the back room.

'In here, Liam.' I followed his voice from the hallway into the back room.

My eyes adjusted to the candlelight and I acknowledged first Will (with a nod) then Jemma (with a nod and a smile) and then Iman (with a nod a smile and an 'Ok?') – Iman ignored me. All three of them were sitting around the dining table like they were about to eat, but there wasn't any food, only a ring of scented candles. Now, even for someone who likes sitting in the dark I was starting to feel uncomfortable. No one spoke to me, I moved a step closer to the table and looked over the ring of candles. I could feel the heat under my chin. It was hard to see what was on the table, it was very dark, and as the heat started to prickle I moved my head from side to side to avoid it. In the middle, like the wick inside the flames, was Aslan, laid out in state. This was Aslan's smelly wake.

Jemma stood up, took my hand by the wrist and led me out of the dining room.

'Come on, you can help me make some tea.' And even though, for once, I didn't want a cup, I didn't dare refuse her. She confided in the kitchen, 'I think they need to be alone.' The kitchen was nice and cool after the heat from all those candles.

'Well, I only came round because I need Will to sign something

131

for me.' As I said it I regretted it. Rather than actually explaining myself, I only begged other questions.

'What?' she asked. Now I could either tell her the truth and let her in on our secret, or lie. But what else could I possibly need Will to sign? So I took the plunge, 'A job reference. For me.' Jemma looked teacherly, so I fudged it into a half-lie, 'Will offered to be a reference but was very busy this week and delegated the writing of the reference to me – because I know more about the specifics of the job – then he's going to ok it and sign it.'

She saw through me. 'So, if you've written your own reference why do you need Will to sign it? Why not just sign it Will West yourself?'

'That would be cheating,' I said and she laughed, but not at me. As she laughed she leaned forward and I could smell her. It was a familiar smell from hiding under her coat, a safe and exciting paradox of a smell. Jemma smelled of powdered lemons.

'What's the job?' she said. I loved the attention.

'Advertising.'

'That sounds—' and she looked around the kitchen for the right words, 'that sounds, well paid? Smartly dressed?'

'I don't know yet.' And I began to worry that Mr Brown and I had not talked salary, did that make me seem like a novice? Or perhaps it meant he wasn't keen. But, I reminded myself, remember the chocolate biscuit.

'Well, that suit you're wearing now, now that's very smart. Very advertising executive. And the orange tie, very now.'

'Now?'

'Yes. Now.' She was so confident it gave me an erection.

'Now is good I suppose in advertising.' And I put my hands in my pockets.

'They're very 1960s trousers,' she commented. I adjusted my hands in my pockets as her attention shifted downwards. 'And the 1960s are very, very much now, aren't they.'

'They are, they are,' and I crossed my feet to free up a bit more fabric in the crotch, I hoped she wouldn't notice my odd socks.

'I've an idea. If you don't want to sign your reference Will West, why don't I sign it Will West?' I looked around the kitchen for a reason and instead noticed that they had replaced the peanut butter. The jar was open on the counter opposite me with a knife sticking out like someone had stabbed it. 'You see you've no answer to that, have you?' said Jemma. I hadn't.

Jemma went to get a pen. She came back into the kitchen carrying her open carpet bag in her left hand and delving down into it with her right.

'Ok.' She withdrew a pen and dropped the bag on the kitchen floor. The bag hardly made a sound, it just sort of crumpled there. 'Where's this reference then?' I reached into my inside jacket pocket and withdrew the reference, rather like James Bond would take out his gun. I stood with the envelope pointing up and considered again whether I should let Jemma sign it.

'Thanks,' she said, taking it, and I thought of the anxious looks customers give me in the sweet shop when I roll up their wrapping paper. They want it done smoothly, that takes patience, when they look at me curling over that paper they are probably thinking of the present they will use it on, or the person they will give it to. But Jemma undid the envelope like opening a bag of crisps and she snapped open the paper with one hand. 'Right, where do I sign?' Before I answered she saw the spot for herself and, leaning on the kitchen counter, wrote *Will West*.

Before I read the signature, I held the paper up against the light to check for any peanut-butter stains. Then I read it, hoping to see that the name looked like a signature, not just a name, but instead, I saw red.

'You've used red!' I couldn't think what more to say, or even what to call her.

'I am a teacher!' she said and I felt glad I'd killed her best friend's

133

cat. I told Jemma I was going home and went next door. It was nice to tell her a truth that she couldn't possibly understand. I didn't need to say goodbye to Will and Iman because I'd not even said hello.

Tym was ready for me, the smell of pot was gone and he was sitting at the back of the knock-through lounge/diner. He wasn't really doing anything, which was slightly disconcerting. The radio wasn't on, he didn't have a book or a magazine to hand, he wasn't eating and he didn't even have a cup of tea on the go. There was a formal atmosphere around him, he was sitting quite upright on his bean-bag – perhaps he was trying not to look stoned.

'All right, Tym?'

'Hellos.'

'What are you up to?' I said, which sounded a bit like the type of thing Dad used to say to me.

'I am listening.' And he interlocked his fingers. 'The lady next door is very sad and has been crying.'

'Oh dear.' Sometimes when I need the toilet I feel very agitated and worry about all of life. I had that feeling.

'Yes. She is very sad and I was worried she was alone until I heard a second voice.'

'You can hear their voices!' Then I took a firm grip on my temper and asked the question, light as air, 'Can you hear what they are saying?'

'No!' he sounded offended. 'I would not listen if I could hear all the words.'

'So, you can hear some of the words? You can hear their speaking voices?'

'I have heard a lot of crying, that's not words.'

'Never mind.' And I felt the relief, like a long hot piss when the agitation about life goes down the toilet too. I felt like the king of the houses, and I felt like I was the new dedicated Inserts Manager for Brown Advertising. I decided that in the business we are probably known just as Brown's.

Tym shifted uneasily on the bean-bag, managing to make it look uncomfortable. Small talk was required, I decided to combine it with my new work persona and gather some more information about the Poles.

'Tym, being from Poland, I mean, well, when you were learning English, didn't you find it funny that Polish looks like polish – you know when you're cleaning?' I gripped my shirt cuff and rubbed the air in a polishing motion.

He said, 'No,' before I had finished my demonstration.

'Oh, but what about the term Pole, I mean what about that one meaning the long things too?'

'Actually, this misunderstanding amuses all people who know Slavic languages. Pole means field. The original Polanders were mighty farmers in the lowlands.'

'Really?' I said, incredulous that that could amuse anyone, although I did feel annoyed. I had always thought of poles when thinking of Poles. 'Fieldland.' I tried it out.

'Perhaps,' said Tym.

'Might as well just be called Land,' I mused.

'No,' Tym said firmly.

'Or Landland,' I went on, ignoring him.

'No!' and then he was standing.

Iman started crying again. It pushed through the wall like a damp patch.

'She sounds like a ghost,' said Tym.

'I thought we agreed there weren't any ghosts and that what you'd heard was just a pigeon in the chimney, or me decorating, or something.'

'Sort of.'

I felt an enormous weight descend on to the conversation: if Tym and I couldn't agree then that would mean that ghosts could exist. (And what about my dead Dad then? And what about

Aslan?) It was a chance I couldn't afford to take, so I left the room and kept walking.

'Where are you going?'

I was halfway down the driveway before I answered, 'I am going to post a letter.' It was reckless, anyone could have seen me, Will, Jemma, Mrs Price, anyone.

WILLIAM

An ornate Turkish Delight box
A red bulb and battery to go in the box to glow like Turkish Delight
A tiara for the Queen Witch
Glasses and a beard for the professor/narrator
An old suit for the professor/narrator
A big star
2 bolts of fake fur – brown and yellow
A cheap wardrobe

Jemma leaned forward from the back seat of the car, curling her fingers over both sides of my driver's seat. 'I think we got everything on the list,' she said. 'Everything except for a cheap wardrobe.'

'And except for that mask,' I said. 'What I mean is, that mask wasn't on the list.'

'What, this mask?' And Iman took the plastic lion mask from her lap, put it on and roared. We all laughed. The mask was a good fit on Iman because she only has a child-sized face. I'd tried it on in the joke shop, I'd been the one who found it, but it didn't fit me.

She kept the mask on, saying, 'Put the car away, Willy,' and got out to open Jemma's door. Jemma put on the plastic tiara and it winked and flashed in my rear-view mirror. She said, 'Actually you'll need to wait and let us get everything out of the boot first.' So I did wait, then they went into the house and I put the car away. I made a mental note to get the engine tuned, it was sounding worse and echoed in the garage.

139

I considered getting the car valeted too, if I did both it would be good enough to sell.

They had left me the box for Turkish Delight and the suit, beard and glasses (without any lenses) on the doorstep. I put the glassless glasses on and carried the rest in. I went into the lounge and checked my reflection in the television. Glasses suit me, they make me look intelligent. Actually, I am cleverer, and nicer, than I look. I tried on the beard, it didn't suit me, and it made me look simple, but I knew it would amuse Iman and Jemma and left it on. I was reaching to put the television on when I heard Iman scream.

I had two thoughts, side by side: I thought, is it Aslan? (But I knew he was very, very dead.) And I thought, we've been burgled, again. But I was looking at the television, so we hadn't been burgled.

I ran upstairs and met Jemma, still wearing the tiara, and Iman, the masked lion, on the landing. Iman pointed at our bedroom door like a scaredy cat. Neither of them seemed at all amused by my beard and glasses, so something was most definitely up.

I had a third thought which caught up with the first two, then overtook the other two ideas as I toe-ended the door open. I thought there was going to be some racist graffiti daubed on the walls. There was a strand of silver Christmas tinsel on the floor and the door snagged over it.

The walls were clean. The dressing-table chair was tied to the dressing table with tinsel, and tied to the chair was a youth done up like a Christmas tree. His hands were taped to struts in the back of the chair with that tape that says *Merry Christmas and a Happy New Year*. His elbows were tied close to his sides and round the chair-back with some shiny green string that Iman uses on the presents. It was wound round and round him, so thick it took me a moment to place it. I went round the end of the bed and saw his ankles were also fixed to the dressing-table chair, and then tied to the dressing table, this time with gold tinsel. He kept glancing at me in the table-top mirror, like a driver looking to pull out.

There was more of the *Merry Christmas and a Happy New Year* tape round his open lips and round his head. It was wound tight several times because his collar-length hair made it hard to stick to his head. Between it, behind his teeth, I could see the red of a Christmas bauble. This bauble was something of a family heirloom. I knew it from childhood Christmases. It was so old it was made of glass.

In the mirror I saw (princess) Jemma and Iman (the lion) look round the door, and I saw the eyes of the youth, done up like a Christmas tree, bulging as he saw them. Then he shut his eyes and kept them shut. He coughed, and sort of swallowed, and sort of couldn't.

I whispered, through the fake beard, 'What's going on? What is going on?' as I watched all of our reflections in the mirror. I couldn't see if they were looking at me or at him, so I turned and said, 'What – in the name of ginger Christ on a BMX bike – is going on?' They didn't even shrug, we all just waited, until Iman said, 'I was thinking about the box of Christmas decorations only the other day, I couldn't remember where it was.' Then, in an attempt to solve at least the seeds of this very strange situation, I thought, and answered.

'It was in the cupboard over your wardrobe, I think. Yeah, I remember putting it away there last year.'

The youth opened his eyes, and, just as he was about to shut them again, I asked him, 'What's going on?' without any swearing this time. It was an ideal opportunity to show Iman that I wouldn't swear in front of our own, hypothetical, children, no matter how extreme the situation. An answer rumbled in his throat. I went closer as if it was a distant sound, but he went quiet.

I picked a pair of scissors from the dressing-table top, pointy little things for cutting your toenails. He shut his eyes again, but this time they were really screwed shut, his breathing hardened, a bit of snot dipped in and out of his nose.

'I'm not going to hurt you,' I said, then I reassured Iman and Jemma in the mirror. 'I'm not going to hurt him.' Maybe he didn't hear, but he did open his eyes and started to convulse, he was tied so tightly that in effect it was little more than a wriggle. Cutting the tape was tricky, especially with him pinging his head around, so I called Iman and Jemma to

141

hold him steady. Iman pushed down on his shoulders and Jemma took his head. Even so, some of his hair got cut too. He had deep brown mustang eyes.

'We're not going to hurt you,' cooed Jemma.

'Sit still and we'll let you talk,' Iman echoed. And he was still.

'Now, open wide and I'll take that out,' I said and reached for the red glass bauble, but stopped and thought, what if he bites me? So I said, 'Don't bite me.' This was stupid because I now feared I had given him the idea to bite me, so I said, 'Hold him' again, and they did. 'Come on, open wide.' He grunted and puffed nasally. 'Come on. Come on,' I encouraged because I so wanted to hear him explain what the fucking hell was happening. 'Open your mouth.' Presumably, this wild youth was a burglar, but I needed to hear it from him. Then I thought, why would he be honest enough to tell me he was a burglar, if he was a burglar? But what else could he be? I withdrew my hand and told Iman and Jemma to leave go of him.

'Ok, now then son,' the word son was for Iman's benefit, not his, 'listen to me. Nod me some answers. Are you on your own in the house?' He nodded but it didn't stop Iman and Jemma spinning round to check – but he would have to have had a vampire as a mate because I'd been checking the mirror.

'Were you trying to rob us?' Again he nodded, then I wondered if he was just going to agree with everything I put to him. My face was getting really hot under the beard. I pushed the glassless glasses firmly to the bridge of my nose, leaned in and asked, 'Did you rob us before?' No answer. 'Ok; are you a racist cat-killer?' And he even managed to look more amazed than us.

'He can't answer that!' said Jemma.

'Why not? I mean why is he here?'

Jemma couldn't answer me, but did say, 'He can't answer anything complicated just by nodding.'

I answered her, 'Why not?' Again I held out my hand and asked him for the bauble; he bared his teeth like a horse and tried to open his mouth but he couldn't hinge it back any further. I risked him biting me and slid my thumbnail and forefinger into his mouth and gave it a tug. It slipped, rotating a little, but stayed fast. He breathed heavy and snotted on the back of my hand, then gave a little whinny.

'That sounded like an apology,' I said and he nodded furiously. 'You see Jemma, an apology, something complicated by just nodding.' Iman tutted, sighed and said, 'Don't bicker, look just get that thing out of his mouth and get him out of here. I'm going to make some tea, and I'll even make him some and Jemma will help me bring it up here.' She led her best friend away. 'He can tell us what's been happening over a lovely cup of tea and a biscuit. And I'll put the heating on, it's freezing.' Although I bet her face was getting hot too under the lion mask.

We really needed to understand this surreal burglary. I slid my fingers around the bauble and pulled. He gave a noise familiar to dentists and I stopped. I picked off more of the *Merry Christmas and a Happy New Year* tape and tried to think of a different line of attack. I remembered hearing that if someone puts a snooker ball into their mouth they cannot remove it. The only solution is to knock out a few teeth. I thought about knocking out a few teeth. But how can I knock out his teeth when there is no space to knock them into? Removing the teeth would require proper medical assistance, or else it's assault. So, I figured if pulling wouldn't work, pushing might and rested my fingertips on to the line of his jaw. He was just too young to have stubble, although it felt like he did shave.

I walked my fingers forwards. 'Open it, come on, make like one of those snakes with those jaws.' I felt a mini-movement, then it broke. He was very tense and very still, he stifled a cough like a stifled sneeze. He leaned forward and some broken glass fell out. There was a little blood. Now I had a choice: either I could pick out the rest of the broken bauble, or I could free up one of his hands so he could do it. But I decided not to free him until I knew what was going on.

I have cowboy gloves, leather wrangler's gloves, and they were just perfect for picking pieces of broken Christmas bauble from the blood-ied mouth of the youth. They got a bit bloody, but maybe that's the way cowboys' gloves should really be.

I got two towels, one for the glass which I put on his lap and one to stop any blood getting on the carpet. I thought I'd got it all out and asked him, he looked as if to answer, but was silent, so I ran my finger between his cheek and gums. I felt a bit of glass cut him and he cried out. I could pick it out easily though with finger and thumb, the leather on these gloves is so flexible.

I went into the bathroom to wash my gloves, time was of the essence because blood is such a tricky stain to remove. It rinsed off easily because the surface of the leather is impregnated with a special chemical and they are just so flexible it was easy to rub the fingers together. Then, on the perfect surface I felt a dimple, I examined it and saw a scratch, then I feared what I had found was in fact a cut. I filled it with water to check and it bulged and leaked like a defective condom. This burglar hadn't stolen anything but he had ruined my wrangler's gloves, and I was owed. I took off the beard so he was surprised to see me.

'Have you got any money?' I asked him. I kept the glassless glasses on to look intelligent.

'Er.' It didn't even sound like his voice had broken.

'How old are you?' Then I remembered and asked again, 'Well, have you got any money?'

'Fourteen.' His speech was tentative with pain.

'Ok, fourteen. So, have you got any money or not?'

'Yeah,' he confessed.

'Good, I'm afraid you owe me some money.'

'Why?'

'You cut my leather wrangler's gloves, they cost me eighteen pounds. I was helping you, with that bauble, so it's only fair you pay for the gloves.'

'I haven't got eighteen quid.' But I ignored him, just in case he was lying and because I remembered that, 'In fact, they cost me eighteen pounds and ninety-nine pence. So you actually owe me nineteen; it would be fair to give me twenty quid.'

'I haven't got it,' he said again with a growing confidence.

'How much have you got?'

144

'Dunno; some change.' He swallowed hard, probably on blood.

'Right, well just give me all of that. I'll have to settle for what you can afford.' With kids you have to use logic like this, agreeing to pay half for stuff if they save half, things like that. I was showing this youth some proper values.

'Help yourself.' He nodded down at his pockets.

I wrung out the wrangler's gloves before putting them back on, damp. I slid my hand into his front jeans pocket and saw him check his rear-view mirror and acknowledge Iman and her two cups of tea before whispering in my ear.

'Are you trying to feel my cock?' I should have Wesleyed him when I had the chance! He smiled at Iman, who'd taken off the lion mask, and spoke like nothing had happened, 'I hope that's got sugar.'

She smiled back, 'It has actually, I wondered, then thought you'd take sugar.' She put the teas on the table and said to me, 'What are you doing, Willy?' I found three pound coins, pulled my hand out, and said triumphantly, 'Look!'

Jemma brought in two more cups of tea. She offered me mine but saw I was holding out the money. 'Are you robbing him, Will?'

'No.' I laughed as if it was absurd and took the tea with my other hand.

'Have you found out what he was doing here?' said Iman and I was relieved to be able to say I had.

'Yes; he was trying to rob us.'

'Who tied him up?' said Jemma and she sipped her tea and I noticed anew how she always seems to be able to drink her tea hotter than anyone else. She holds her lips back from the mug so they don't get burnt.

I confessed, 'I don't know.'

'Who tied you up?' she asked him directly.

He answered tentatively, 'Adam Ant?', maybe seeing if Jemma would accept it, maybe taking the piss, maybe he wasn't sure who Adam Ant was, or, maybe he hoped we had never heard of him. Jemma smiled, she's used to children.

'He's taking the piss!' I implored first to Iman, then to Jemma direct. 'He's taking the piss out of you.'

Jemma looked at him again, widened her eyes and nodded. He cleared his throat, 'Well, I saw the back window open downstairs and it tempted me in. I looked about downstairs and then came up here and when I got to this dressing table I saw the other burglar in the mirror. It gave me such a fucking fright.'

'Well, that just about takes the biscuit! A burglar gave you a fright – you are a burglar!'

'William!' said Iman.

'What?'

'Calm down.' She walked towards the bedroom door.

'Where are you going?' I said.

'It's silly but you reminded me, biscuits!'

'In the name of ginger Jesus Christ on Evel Knievel's motorbike, woman!' I was going to some lengths not to swear properly.

'All right Will,' said Jemma, but she was looking at him, prompting him to continue.

'Well, yeah, it did frighten me, I am only fourteen. And anyway he was bigger and older and he was here first, so I said I'd go but he said no. And when I said, no I'll go, he grabbed me and done all this.'

Jemma looked at him then at me and said, 'Why not give him his money back?'

Iman was back. Munching through her biscuit she said, 'Yeah, why not cut him free and give him the three pounds back, Will? It might be bus fare or something.'

'He owes me eighteen pounds ninety-nine for the leather wrangler gloves.'

Jemma gave an arrogant laugh and said, 'Huh, if he had eighteen pounds ninety-nine on him I doubt he would be in here trying to rob you!'

I couldn't think of an answer to that, all she made me want to do was punch her in the face. I thought about it, but it was only ever an idea, I wouldn't want to be the type of person who hit anyone. Iman and

146

Jemma could justify being annoyed with me much more than they could justify having found a youth done up like a Christmas tree in our bedroom. Then I realised I could justify being annoyed with them too.

'Don't be so naïve, Jemma.' Naïve, oh I saw the word hook her as her head bobbed like a fishing float. 'It's naïve to think he is short of eighteen pounds ninety-nine and that he's come here for it. He's probably robbed hundreds of houses,' then I cast a glance at Iman, 'and it probably was him who robbed us last time – remember the police warned us we could be targeted again?' I think she wanted to nod, but didn't want to get between me and Jemma.

'Will,' said Jemma, 'I am not naïve; I am understanding.'

'Ok, then, how can you understand this?' I pointed at the youth.

'Well, like he said, the other burglar, the interruption, the attack,' and she looked at him, not using the mirror this time, but actually into his eyes, 'which must've been very traumatic.'

'But it's naïve to think that.' The word was making me feel quite drunken. 'If he interrupted a burglar why haven't we been burgled? Not so much as a television's been taken.'

'Who's being naïve now!' she cawed. 'Are you suggesting he did this himself?'

The urge to hit her ran down my wrists. 'No, I am not suggesting that, that would be silly. It makes more sense to think he knew the other burglar and that the other burglar hated him and tied him up as some sort of set-up.' I found my stride. 'The other burglar realised that if he robbed us, then this boy here would be able to grass him up – so he left.' I leaned forwards towards the youth, resting my hands on my knees. I got close to his face, but not close enough for him to see there was no glass in my glasses, and whispered, 'And don't tell me it didn't go through your head, when you saw us, that maybe he'd set you up with some paedophiles. I bet you were terrified thinking – he has sacrificed me to evil.'

'William, what are you saying?' I knew Iman couldn't hear, and it made no sense as she'd missed what he'd said about me trying to feel him up. He'd started it. I stood up and finished, 'It's a thought though, isn't

147

it? You can't deny that, I mean you're safer with us than with him, but I like to think we gave you a frightening thought. It's what you gave us.'

'That's enough, William.'

And Jemma backed her up, 'Yes, give me the scissors, this really is getting us nowhere.' They opened him up like a present and gave him away.

I waited in the lounge and heard them cooing to him and heard him answer confidently. They even gave him back his three pounds and wished he would stop burgling. After he had been gone a minute, I went into the bedroom and saw they had tidied all of the Christmas stuff away. It seemed like he had never been there. Then I thought hard and it seemed like he had been there, but much longer ago. They had missed a bit of tinsel by the door; I went outside and put it in the dustbin.

*

December 1 *Highlight: 86% Will made a lovely little speech when we buried Aslan, it could have been a prayer.*

Yes! I had cracked it, 86 per cent is the new diary high score for the year and it pisses on a first-class hug in the frozen aisle at the supermarket on 1 October at 85 per cent. This was life and death, this was real. This was a triumph over adversity, this was me managing to help her grieve.

I didn't have long, Iman was only in the bathroom getting ready for bed. I put the diary back at the bottom of Iman's underwear drawer, then I ruffled all the bras and pants back over the top and shut it. I got in bed, then straight out again and opened the drawer an inch, remembering this was how Iman had left it.

We had buried Aslan days ago but Iman had taken a while to write it up in her diary. We put him under the woody shrub (that grew tiny yellow flowers) where he loved to sleep during the summer. We all wrapped up warm, Jemma had held the torch, Iman held Aslan, and I tried to get into the soil with a trowel. It was no go. So I had to get a long chisel and a claw hammer to beak up the soil. Soon it was easy to lift out all the loose bits with the trowel. Iman laid Aslan down. But the hole wasn't deep enough and his flank bulged out. She picked him out and dusted him down like a potato. She was the only one who didn't mind the smell. I turned the claw hammer around and used it to pull out even more of the deeper, softer, earth. Iman laid him to rest.

All the work had made me feel nice and warm but Jemma and Iman were shivering. So I knew my speech had to be quick and I knew I couldn't wait around to see if either of them said anything.

'Thank you for being such an excellent cat to us, Aslan. We will miss you everyday, and all the people who ever saw you, in the street and in their gardens, will have to make do with lesser cats.' It was what I wanted to say, but I didn't know then that it was what Iman wanted to hear.

'All right?' I said when she came back from the bathroom.

'Goodnight,' she answered.

'It's weird to think of him in here, isn't it?'

'Oh, did you have to mention it?'

'I thought you might want to talk about it.'

'No. And why have you stopped putting the toilet seat down?'

I was in trouble. I didn't know why she was bringing the toilet seat into this. Putting the toilet seat down was a goodwill gesture, showing consideration and maturity, I didn't have to do it.

'I haven't, have I?'

'Well, it was up earlier. Why should it be left up?'

'I don't leave it up, that's virtually sexist. Perhaps the burglar left it up?'

'Do you have to keep mentioning him? Anyway, he told us what happened, he didn't mention using the loo, there wasn't the time before he got tied up.'

'Maybe it was the other burglar, the one who caught him?'

'Ok, can we stop mentioning the burglars!'

This wasn't fair, I was being blamed for the sexist toilet use of the burglar and I couldn't even mention him in my defence. I didn't want this to develop into an argument, but couldn't see a way out.

'Surely we can mention it, I mean he was in here. Were you going to just go to sleep and not think of him, over there, all done up like a Christmas tree?'

149

'I was going to try. I was going to think about Aslan.'

And there it was, my way out of the argument, 'I've been thinking of Aslan too, you know.' I played my ace. 'His death has affected me too, I meant every word I said when we buried him, and more besides that I couldn't get into words.' She snuggled into my side. Bingo. No more talk of toilet seats and burglars. Iman happily followed me away from the argument.

'Mrs Price has asked if we can look after Tinkerbell, her hamster.'

'Oh,' I said.

'She's going away to her mother's.'

'Can't we just go round and feed him, like last time?'

'No.'

Last time I took the opportunity to have a snoop around Mrs Price's and I would quite like the chance to look again. She'd gone away and left the washing-up.

'Why do we have to have him here?'

'Apparently Tinkerbell gets lonely. She'll be away all week at least, and she doesn't want to have to leave the heat on for the sake of one hamster.'

'Ok.'

I listened very carefully to the house. I listened as the radiators ticked and cooled and I listened to Iman's breathing. It was a good way of convincing myself I wasn't listening for burglars.

God, I wish I hadn't hurt Wesley. At least with the Christmas tree youth I'd tried to help him out. It was weird, but not as weird as what I'd been like with Wesley. That wasn't like me.

Iman whispered, 'Will, are you awake?' and spoke at her normal volume to make sure I was. 'Will, I feel scared, I feel like tonight I know I'm going to have a nightmare. Is that window shut downstairs?'

I got up to go and check.

On my way downstairs I remembered the fact that Iman had never wanted to know which room the old lady, who owned this house before us, had died in. Mrs Price had told me it was the dining room. I wondered if this uncertainty about her death, that was meant to console Iman, was working against her, at this exact moment. That, perhaps, she was lying in bed wondering if the old lady had in fact died in our bedroom. But chances are Iman was not thinking about the old lady at all. I was thinking about the old lady because I was about to open the dining-room door and was trying not to think about the burglary. I was sure I'd shut it, I didn't need to check. I waited a moment and went back to bed.

She asked, 'Was it shut?' and I wanted to lie to her and when I couldn't I marvelled at the man I am. That I could squirt urine into the mouth of a boy called Wesley and not feel the need to confess, but can barely tell a white lie to my wife.

'Ah, no.' I consoled myself with the thought that if Iman had asked me directly have you ever hunted down the person you thought had sent us that racism last month and attacked them orally with a pissy water pistol – I wouldn't lie, I'd explain myself. But I was confused.

She hissed, 'What? I could've sworn I'd shut it!'

'No, sorry, I meant no I forgot to check if it was shut.' I was up and gone before she could hit me. I turned on the lights as I went: bedroom, landing and hall. The window was shut. I opened it, so I could shut it, just to be sure. But as I opened it (and all the warm air, containing the last traces of body heat from the different burglars rushed outside) I smelled the night. It smelled great. I was very aware of what I was wearing, standing in front of the open dining-room window, curtains back, light on. In bed I wear old shirts. I prefer them to T-shirts because of their long sleeves. During the day I like to wear boxer shorts, but at night, I choose briefs. I prefer them and so does Iman. Tonight I was wearing my old orange shirt, in fact it is really an old red shirt that has become an older, faded, orange shirt. I like this shirt and since wearing it as part of my orange cowboy outfit and attacking Wesley I had hidden it in Iman's wardrobe because it's evidence. But then I realised, why not just make it into a night-shirt, get the use of it. It is a really good fit, comfortable.

I was just about to shut the window when I heard a noise, like a really big, really loud hedgehog eating in the garden. I took a kitchen

151

knife, put on my lace-up work shoes without lacing them up and went outside. I was fearless.

I couldn't see any big hedgehogs, but I could still hear the sound. The noise was coming from next-door's garden. Not Mrs Price's, but the other side, which is divided from us by a tall wooden fence.

I had a dozen thoughts at once. 1: It's burglars! 2: Run next door with the knife. 3: Run away. 4: Call out. ('Fuck off out of it'?) 5: Call the police. 6: Maybe it is Tim next door; gardening perhaps? 7: Gardening? But it is midnight in December. 8: Yes, but according to Jemma, Tim is Polish, and maybe there is some sort of Polish seasonal time difference in gardening. 9: Bang the wooden fence really loud and call out to my brother Jimmy, to suggest there are two of us, to scare the burglars away. 10: What is going on today? 11: It's a really, really big hedgehog. 12: A really big hedgehog eating really loudly.

I chose thoughts 4 and 9, and ran to the fence, kicking and screaming, 'Fuck off out of it! JIMMY! OVER HERE!' and I pounded the wooden fence with the flat of my hand and the butt of the kitchen knife. I stopped kicking it because I didn't want to scuff up my work shoes.

The noise stopped and listened to me. I said, 'Jimmy, give us a bunk-up,' and made a jump at the fence, wriggling against it. I saw an average-sized someone, but fell back just as Jimmy would have been pushing me up over the fence if he was here. I doubt even my brother would have wanted to push me up and over by the seat of my pants. I listened, and heard a door slam.

I went back into my house. I put my puffa jacket on to warm up and went next door to investigate. It was the neighbourly thing to do. No lights were on. I knocked on the door, long and hard, until finally the lights came on. Tim opened the door wide.

'Hellos? Yes? Hellos?' he said, not looking at me, but rubbing his eyes like he had a sore head. His confidence reassured me, he was big enough to open his door wide in the middle of the night and not even need to see who was there.

'Hello. I'm your neighbour, we met at the party. Remember?'

'I remember.'

'I was in the garden – my garden – because I heard noise in your garden. And then I heard them, I mean him – the garden burglar – go into your house.'

'A gardening burglar?'

'Yes! In your house.'

'What is this gardening burglar?'

'A burglar who was going to steal stuff from your garden!' I enthused.

'No no. That would be a burgling gardener,' said Tim, with an accuracy and understanding that obviously pleased him.

'I heard him go in your back door. I've come to warn you.'

It seemed like he understood when he said, 'Ok and thank you.' But then he shut the door. I knocked again, he opened up again.

'The man may still be in the house.'

'Yes, thank you, we can sort it out,' he said and just as I went to step in he shut the door again. So I knocked again, harder and harder thinking maybe his English was worse when he'd been woken up as I expect he dreams in Polish. So I used only the words he had used, to ask, 'We can sort it out?', pointing at each of us with different hands, but that meant I pointed at him with a kitchen knife.

'Yes we can, thank you,' he said as he shut the door. I shouted through the letterbox after him, 'I'm not drunk, you know. Even if it isn't a gardening burglar or burgling gardener, you have an intruder.'

After line-dancing I went to the pub. The Old Elm Arms, on a Tuesday night, seemed a safe enough place to wear my line-dancing gear. I couldn't leave my stetson in the car, it might get stolen; they are worth about sixty quid. I was the first to arrive. I walked over to the bar, using a very definite walk so that no one would be able to accuse me of moseying, and ordered a lemonade. I was driving and could only have one pint, which I didn't want to drink alone.

I put my hat down on the high stool next to mine. There was a tiny risk that someone could sit on it, but I felt less self-conscious than having it on the bar (where there was always the risk of spillages and splashes).

The lemonade was on draft from one of those mixer-drink guns. The barman smiled at me and quick-drew the mixer gun from its plastic holster. He whooshed lemonade into the glass before sliding it down the bar to me.

'Ninety pence, please.'

'Can I ask, why did you do that?'

'What?'

'Slide the drink down the bar. Look, you've spilt some. Is it because of my line-dancing gear?'

'Yep,' he drawled, and slid the mixer gun back in its holster. I narrowed my eyes at him, but stopped when I realised he might think I was trying to look like Clint Eastwood in *The Good, the Bad and the Ugly*. Instead, I decided on action, and went over to him, leaned in, and picked up a bar towel while maintaining wide-open eye contact. I cleaned up the spillage, and checked none had dripped on to my stetson. I slid the glass back down and said, 'Fill her up!' A little more spilt over his hand as he stopped the glass and he made it back up to a full half-pint of lemonade. He gave me the drink.

'Ninety pence?' he said. I agreed and gave him a pound.

I drank my lemonade in silence and looked around the bar. It was as busy as you'd expect for a Tuesday night, but it was far superior to staying on at line-dancing for orange squash with Edna Crabbe telling me again how she wagged off work today. I told her no one says wagged off work any more, and recommended she say skived. Liam arrived and I beckoned him over, saying, 'How-de-do-de?' confidently.

'De-doing just fine,' he answered. 'What are you drinking?' and I didn't take him literally as I finished the lemonade and answered, 'A pint.'

Liam ordered two pints. 'Is Jimmy coming?' he asked and when I nodded he ordered another pint for my brother.

As we walked to the nearest table Liam said, 'Don't you think the barman looks like Michael J. Fox? Only of course the barman's much taller.'

'Hmm, yes, he does look a bit of a wanker.' I did enjoy being able to swear with Liam. 'Very 1980s, both of them.'

154

'What do you think the J stands for?'

'Don't know, maybe you should start using it: Liam J. Fox.'

'I think it stands for Jesus,' Liam laughed.

'Anyway, how the devil are you? Not got the flu?'

'I'm fine.' There was a third seat at the table which I used for my stetson. I left it pulled out so I could see it.

'Edna *was* at line-dancing.'

'Of course.'

'But she asked me not to tell you she was there. And she told me you're in danger of wearing out the photocopier.'

'But she goes on a Tuesday. And all the photocopier needed was more toner.'

'Yes. But it's a bit rich to go line-dancing when she didn't go to work this morning, isn't it?'

'Didn't she?'

'How come I know this and you don't?' I said, and Liam just shrugged. I was becoming increasingly worried about Liam's depression. His father's death seemed to have cut him adrift – he had obviously stayed in bed until this afternoon not to have missed Edna this morning. So I said, 'So do you fancy Jemma or what then?'

'What? I mean, why do you ask?'

'I ask because I am a bloke, we are mates, and I reckon she has nice tits.'

'Tits?' I didn't know if he was questioning my use of the word or thinking about the appeal of Jemma. 'Isn't that your dad over there?' and as Liam pointed Dad came over, quiff bobbing with each loping stride.

'Evening lads,' said Dad as he went to sit down, but he heard my sharp intake of breath and saw the stetson, just in time. He put it on the table.

'This is lucky,' I said, 'you're just in time to see Jimmy.'

'I know,' said Dad, 'he invited me. I don't spend all my free time in the pub on the off-chance.'

'Anyway, back to Jemma's tits,' Liam continued and I felt like I was being torn apart by wild horses.

155

'You know my dad, don't you Liam?' I said pointedly.

'Of course, I've always known him,' and they exchanged a nod. What I meant was, look Liam, this is my dad, so now I am a son, and we can't talk about Jemma's tits. Dad obviously took it to be some sort of test he needed to meet, to show that either he was unshockable, or that he had an opinion on Jemma's tits.

'Iman's friend?' said Dad.

Now, instead of explaining to Liam that I felt he was being a bit strange since his father's death and maybe was talking like this because he knew I could never embarrass him in front of his father again, instead I just said, 'Would you say that in front of your dad?' There was a pause, I looked at Dad and Liam, they were already looking at me. 'Sorry mate,' I said. 'That came out wrong.'

Dad said, 'Yes, I was very sorry to hear about the death of your father, Liam. I would've liked to have come to the funeral, but work only let you off for immediate family.'

'Thank you.'

'Jimmy should be here soon,' I interrupted.

Dad asked, 'How's Iman?' But Liam interrupted my answer, 'You know what Mr West, you know who you remind me of? I mean I have known you for ever, but it has only just occurred to me that you look like an older version of Eddie Cochran.'

I tried to join in because I knew this would please Dad. 'It's the hair,' I said.

'Yes, it's the hair. But I've always had Eddie Cochran hair.'

'Yes,' said Liam, 'but I only saw a picture of Eddie Cochran the other day; young of course.'

'Well, Eddie was only ever young,' Dad said, and took a sip of the pint Liam had bought for Jimmy.

'Only ever young,' Liam repeated. 'But you look like him old.'

'Cheers,' said Dad, and raised Jimmy's pint in acknowledgement before drinking from it as if it was his very own.

Liam said, 'You're welcome.'

I thought for a second and remembered Dad's question. 'Since you

156

asked how Iman is, she's been having a bit of a crappy time. Her cat, Aslan, died, and we were burgled, again.'

'Burgled!' said Liam.

'Burglaries are crap son, I'm sorry,' said Dad. I nodded at his accuracy.

'Yeah, really crap,' said Liam. 'I remember when the shop was burgled and I was only nine.'

Dad answered him. 'Oh, I remember that one too. I helped your dad with the decorating. He brought you round to ours, and I went back with him, and we worked like niggers getting that place straight again.'

'Dad! Must you use that phrase?'

'Oh, of course, sorry son. But this all happened back in the days you could say that. Your dad's shop was a mess. They'd really gone for it, a load of stock was taken, things were chucked about, LPs were scratched,' he paused to tilt more of Jimmy's beer down, 'yes, and they wrote stuff on the bathroom wall like it was a pub toilet. Terrible graffiti, stuff about your mother.'

'Dad! Do you mind?' I told him off like we were rehearsing for his old age. 'Maybe Liam doesn't want to talk about his dad right now?'

'No. I like it,' Liam reassured him.

'Well, your dad was adamant that you shouldn't see any of it. He wanted it put right for you, and we had to get rid of that graffiti before your mother saw it.'

'What did they write about her?' Dad paused, so Liam prompted, 'I really want to know.'

'Well, they wrote about your mother and a big-dicked dog.'

'A big-dicked dog?' said Liam, trying out the words we were obviously all allowed to use now.

'Exactly, we painted it all out. Painted over the lot.'

Liam grinned and asked, 'You painted over a big-dicked dog?' probably just because he had never got to ask it of someone before.

'Yes, and more besides, I painted out *granny monkey sex*.' Liam interrupted him, the smut was over-stimulating his brain, 'Is that sex between old maternal monkeys, or a type of human OAP sex?'

Dad answered him seriously, 'Or maybe they meant a position.'

157

'Dad! For fuck's sake!' and he had the balls to look shocked.

'All right son, there's no need to swear.'

'Yeah, Will, it could be a position – like doggy style's a position,' Liam told me, like I didn't know.

'Funny isn't it, how I can remember it so clear. I reckon I can remember everything they wrote. I just had to keep reading it as I rubbed the paintwork down. Then I read it all again as I painted the new paint on – then it was gone for ever: *big-dicked dogs* over your bathroom mirror, *cow-pat burgers* on the back of the door, *furry udder witch* over the sink above the tiles.'

'Granny monkey sex,' added Liam, like they were naming the 1976 FA Cup-winning team.

'Granny monkey sex was on the ceiling!' said Dad.

Liam finished his pint. 'So, of course, the house smelled of paint. Thank you, thank you so much for telling me that. It's much clearer now.' He sounded really reassured, or maybe it was an especially satisfying pint.

Dad finished Jimmy's pint and said, 'Pint?' pointing at Liam.

'Pint,' he replied.

'Pint?' said Dad, pointing at me.

'No, just a lemonade, please, thank you.'

'But a pint of it? Or, have a shandy?'

'Ok, thanks. Half a shandy.'

'Pint?'

'Ok, pint of shandy. Oh, and get a pint for Jimmy, he should be here soon.'

Before Dad was out of earshot Liam told me, 'Your Dad is brilliant.' Then when he was out of earshot, 'I never liked him when I was a lad.'

'Well, I don't think he liked children much.'

I considered helping Dad with the drinks because he had four pints to carry. But I didn't want to go near the barman again. Dad would just have to make two journeys, or get a tray for them.

Liam asked, 'When's Jimmy due?'

'Now.'

Dad came back carrying four pints, he had asked for the drinks to be put in those chubby pint glasses with handles and the little windows all over them, so he could hold two handles in each hand. Crafty and clever.

He put down the drinks precisely, like chessmen. The table was full, one ten-gallon hat and four pints. Then Dad moved a chair over from the next table in readiness for Jimmy.

'So, what went missing when you were burgled this time?' It was a conversation I didn't want to have with Dad. I couldn't tell him, or anyone for that matter, about the youth because it just didn't sound possible. And I didn't want to tell him nothing had gone missing, because he would then want to know what kind of a burglary was it if nothing had gone missing?

But I needed to say something. I had a think and considered asking Liam if he had got the job. But what if he had not, then what would I say? Anyway, all the job stuff seemed a bit strange. I didn't object to helping him out with a reference on moral grounds. Not a bit. But maybe I was going to help him get a job that just really wasn't him. It seemed best to wait and see what he said about the job, I mean if he'd got it he probably would have said so. I calculated that I had three options: 1: I could ask either of them a question about football. 2: I could wait and hope Jimmy turned up. Or, 3: I could say, to either of them, that I liked their shoes.

This is a trick Iman taught me, it triggers a conversational reflex. Iman taught me the trick after I (genuinely) told her, on our first date (in this very pub), that I liked her shoes. She started to tell me how they had been reduced, because the left one was slightly faded, but stopped and got very defensive. She said, 'Are you bored?' Now this panicked me because I wasn't bored, I was the absolute opposite of bored (erect?) and I worried that maybe I just had a bored-looking face. I was up front with her, I said, 'No, I'm not bored. They're really nice shoes.' Then Iman let me in on her secret. She told me that if all else fails she was taught by her mother to ask about shoes. Whatever you say about someone's shoes, say it a bit like a question, and they cannot help but answer you.

Iman tried it on her mother's friends when they told her she'd

159

grown. The question flattered them and allowed them to complain about bunions and the cost of shoes.

As a teenager, Iman used the question when she changed schools, twice. All she had to do was pick the girl with the most interesting-looking shoes, and say, 'I like your shoes, are they new?'; it is a sound basis for a friendship.

It has a different effect on men. I had never had to use it before, but Iman had. She used the question on the first headmaster who employed her, he assumed she wanted to date him. It flattered him, but he couldn't accept compliments because he believed in monogamy. He said, 'Thank you, but my wife bought them for me.'

When Iman told me all this on the first date, I wanted to ask her if she had ever used the question to ask out any men. I didn't, I waited, and I reminded myself that I am still waiting to ask her. It would have worked on me.

I looked down, realising a brilliant thing about Iman's question; when it is hard to think of something to say, it is natural to look at your own shoes. So I did, I eyed up the leather. I noticed the fact that the sole at the front of each boot was worn from all the steps, touches, vines and big slides we had been doing at line-dancing recently. It looked good to me. I leaned forwards and gripped my ankles so I could look under the table. Dad broke the silence.

'What's wrong, son? Tired of talking about the burglary? Have you dropped something?'

'No,' I answered but wished I hadn't said anything — by answering him I only begged more questions. I stuck to my task. I noted that Liam was wearing Nike trainers. So I decided to say it to Dad.

'I like your shoes, Dad.' I stayed down under the table, watching his black brogues.

'Yeah?'

'Yeah. Very smart.'

'Yeah, they are smart, aren't they? Very comfy though. I've had them ages.' I maintained my position, as if I was on a plane about to make a crash-landing. Liam crossed his ankles.

'Liam?'

'Yeah?'

'Your trainers stink!'

'Yeah! But that's not me, that's the air that Nike use in the soles.' Then I heard Dad let me down and say, 'What do they use then – farts!' They both laughed. I stayed down.

They both twitched their feet at the same moment and Dad called out, 'Jimmy! Over here.' The trainers and brogues shifted in anticipation.

I decided to stay down for a moment or two longer because the only alternative (sitting up) might draw more attention to what I was doing. My flushed face would be the first thing Jimmy saw, and it just wasn't me. This way, I would be able to see Jimmy's shoes, which meant I would be able to say, *Like the shoes Jim. Are they new?* and it would get the evening off to a flying start.

I heard Jimmy say 'Cheers' to his pint as he sat down, wearing slippers.

I sat up and we all said hello, I was stuck for anything else to say. Jimmy said, 'You all right, Will? Just you're looking a bit flushed.' Dad answered for me, 'He's been looking at our shoes.'

'And smelling my trainers,' said Liam.

'Each to their own,' said Jimmy. They all laughed at me, politely. I stuck to the plan.

'I like your slippers, Jimmy,' then to make it sound natural that he might be wearing them to the Old Elm Arms, on a Tuesday night, added, 'are they new?'

'Yeah! They're dead dead comfy. Got them as a Christmas present in fact. I got your message the other week, about your party. I was going to come but—'

Liam interrupted his explanation, 'But it's not Christmas yet, they haven't even got the decorations up in here.'

I said, 'What do you mean by that, Liam?' and he couldn't work out if I was being defensive on Jimmy's behalf or not. So I made myself clear: 'Jimmy comes in here, into the public bar of this public house, wearing his Christmas-present slippers and the strange thing about it – according to you – is that he got the present early?'

161

'Well,' but I didn't give Liam a chance to finish, I continued, 'No, that's not strange. I get presents early some years. Dad even used to give us presents early some years.' I looked at Dad for confirmation of my memory.

'Yes, if it was something really big, like a bike, or that snooker table we had in the back room – but there was nowhere to store that.'

'Yes, thank you, Dad. So, Jimmy, why are you wearing slippers?'

'Well, I was just saying, about your party invite the other week, and the thing is—'

I got a bit impatient, I was tired of things happening I couldn't understand. (I couldn't understand why I'd done that to Wesley.)

'Yes, yes, but why are you wearing slippers?'

'Yeah but, when I got your message, it was weird.'

I cut him off again, 'Answerphone messages are always weird. It's weird if they're not weird, and that's weird. Why are you wearing slippers?' And Jimmy looked at me with an older brother look that never needed explaining.

'Why are you wearing that shirt, with the tassels?'

'They're not tassels; it's a fringe. Tassels would be longer.'

Jimmy was unmoved, he narrowed his eyes and said, 'So what; why?' Liam and Dad shifted their chairs back ever so slightly, like in a Western when someone draws a gun under the table.

'Why? Well, I suppose the movement of the fringe emphasises the movement of the line-dance.'

Jimmy looked down and I thought he was accepting my answer, but he saw my hat on the table, 'Well, why wear this?' and he touched the brim of the stetson with the bottom of his pint glass. It left some moisture there.

I had no answer. There was a Mexican stand-off.

'Why wear the slippers? I've answered one of your questions.'

'Well, why wear the cowboy hat? You think you're Wild Will West?' he answered as we both regressed.

Dad tried to mediate, changing the subject, telling Jimmy, 'Will's been having a bit of a bad time of it.'

I explained, 'Yeah, we've been burgled; again.'

'Like before the party?' he added to show he had been paying attention to my life.

'Yeah, just like before the party. Except,' I couldn't talk about the Christmas tree youth, so I changed tack, 'except nothing was stolen; we interrupted them.' Jimmy was silent, he didn't look at me but he knew his silence would hold my attention. Silence in a pub, even the Old Elm Arms on a Tuesday night, is as golden as the beer. I was captivated by my older brother and wanted to confess all. I wanted to tell him about the Christmas tree youth, about how we frightened him and I wanted, for a second, to tell him about Wesley.

'Yeah, funny things have been happening.' But the second passed.

We waited for Jimmy to speak.

'What you need is a burglar alarm.' Simple. Brilliant.

'You're right!' I said.

'I know; I know a bloke who can get you a really good one, really cheap.' Dad's eyes lit up as he saw an opportunity to do a bit of fathering.

'Hang on, that sounds dodgy – it's not nicked is it?'

'They are bankrupt stock, that's why they're so cheap.'

'Oh, I see.' And Dad seemed content with this greyness. Jimmy carried on and reminded me of what I learned on jury service: that legally, the definition of an expert is the person who knows most about the subject in the court. Jimmy explained, 'The beauty of any burglar alarm is that it doesn't have to be brilliant, it just has to be better than your next-door neighbour's.'

'My next-door neighbours haven't even got one!'

'There you go then, get one and you will never be burgled again.'

Liam joined in the conversation, 'What if your next-door neighbours get one?' Jimmy paused at this cross-examination.

'Then their neighbours had better watch out.' He paused and measured his words, 'Ah, hang on, you'd need to be careful with your cat though, these systems have very sensitive infra-red detectors. A cat gives off enough infra-red to set it off.'

'The cat's dead!' said Liam, a little too pleased, but I appreciated the sentiment and added, 'Yeah, no problem with that.' So Liam wouldn't feel bad.

'It's like the old joke,' said Dad, we tried to ignore him, if it was one of his old jokes then it probably wasn't worth encouraging him, but he didn't need encouragement, 'the joke about two explorers, in the jungle, who see a lion about to chase them.'

'Mrs Price wouldn't buy a burglar alarm, she's scared of electronics, I've had to set her video before now.'

'And, the first explorer drops his pack and puts on his running shoes.'

'There's a student living the other side, he's not going to want to invest in an alarm either; it's a brilliant idea.'

'And the second explorer says to him, "What are you doing? You can't outrun a lion!" And the first explorer says, "No, but I can outrun you!"'

Jimmy laughed politely, smiled at me, and said, 'You're right.'

Liam stood, picking up the four empty glasses: two in each hand by their handles. 'I could help you install it, if you want, Will. I saw Dad fit ours in the stock room. Piece of piss.' He went and got another round. I wanted to drink and decided to walk home, then after we'd all bought two rounds (or was it three?) I decided to stagger home.

Iman came back from the bathroom, she'd been quick tonight and I was glad I hadn't tried to read the diary. It would have been tight. She handed me a large glass of water.

'I had the greatest evening tonight.' I was triumphant/drunk.

'That's nice.'

'Oh, did you have a nice evening?' I was sensitive/drunk.

'Ok. I tried to ring Jemma, got the answerphone, so I left it.'

I was impressed/drunk, 'Jemma!'

'Yes, Jemma, well I did leave one message first thing this evening, but that was only pick up if you're there, after that I just left it each time.'

'Oh. Maybe she's out with a man.' I was insightful/drunk.

'Was line-dancing good?'

164

I was forgetful/drunk, 'Line-dancing? I saw Jimmy in the pub and he had a brilliant idea. A brainwave in fact!'

'Yeah?'

'Yeah! We should buy a burglar alarm off a bloke he knows!'

'Ok.'

I was amazed/drunk. 'Ok?' Amazed by the speed with which she made the decision, I had all the arguments ready, all the virtues of a burglar alarm at my fingertips, I had a joke about explorers and a lion.

'That sounds like just what we need.'

'Liam reckons he can help me install it.'

'Even better. How's Jimmy's toe?'

The water was drunk. I didn't have an answer and I looked at Iman like she was a very bright light. 'Which one?'

'Which one do you think?'

I worked it out – drunk – and decided I had a one-in-twenty chance of getting the right answer. But realised I was drunkenly including fingers, and the odds halved to one in ten. I decided it was not going to be his little toe, and who knows the names of the other toes? So I guessed, 'His big right toe?'

'Yes.'

'Fine.' I was confused. Iman was happy with my answer, thought about it, then was unhappy.

'Wasn't the left big toenail the in-growing one? I'm sure it was.'

And I was so drunk that the unexplained bits of life came into sharp focus. 'Ah! Slippers!'

WILLIAM

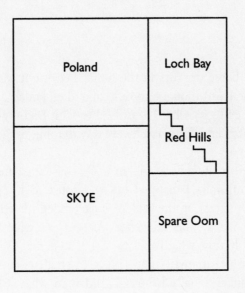

169

I preferred being upstairs in the house because it was more like being in the flat. I thought about that and reckoned I liked being upstairs because it's what I was used to with Dad. Being upstairs felt like flying, and flying is a lovely way to think of the dead. Dad has flown.

I didn't decorate downstairs, in case I was seen. After I finished decorating upstairs I mapped out my house and kept the map under the mattress, in the middle. I pretended I lived upstairs in the land of War Drobe. Like everyone, I know what War is, and like no one I know what Drobe is, it's just a name. I wondered, in silence, if it meant anything in Polish. My halfway upstairs house was not conventionally beautiful, but then what would be the point of that because no one I knew was going to see it.

The Red Hills made lovely stairs. The idea was nice, I bought a deep russet runner carpet and stripped down the walls. When the old carpet was up I painted the right name on to each of the fourteen steps. To make it clear, even when the russet carpet was down, that the stairs were the Piccadilly tube line, I painted the skirting board the appropriate shade of navy blue. On the bottom step, step 1: *Earls Court*. Step 2: *Baron's Court*. Step 3: *Hammersmith*. Step 4: *Turnham Green*. Step 5: *Acton Town*. Step 6: *South Ealing*. Step 7: *Northfields*. Step 8: *Boston Manor*. Step 9: *Osterley*. Step 10: *Hounslow East*. Step 11: *Hounslow Central*. Step 12: *Hounslow West*. Step 13: *Hatton Cross*. And the top step,

step 14, was *HEATHROW.* I let the paint dry before fitting the carpet. It was beginning to make sense. The landing was for landing.

I put a sign on the box bedroom door saying SPARE OOM, and I don't think Tym noticed a thing wrong with it. So I did the same on the bathroom door, a small plaque I got made in the precinct at the foot of the tower block, it said LOCH BAY. Tym didn't even read it, but I knew I had to be more subtle with his door, after all he paid rent. I couldn't just put POLAND on his door, that would be rude, so I compromised. I stripped this door down to the wood and made sure it was highly polished. Then for good measure, and to be absolutely clear, I gave it a polish again and again and again.

My room had to make sense. On the ceiling I wrote S K Y E in big big big letters, and, when I lay on the bed and read it, I felt like it wasn't there and like I wasn't here.

To complement this I made my own wallpaper which I wanted to put up in the whole house but I knew that was just a fantasy. Edna Crabbe was getting suspicious about the photocopier when it kept jamming and running out of toner and anyway what would Tym have thought? When I say I made my own wallpaper, I don't mean for a moment that I pulped the wood and pressed it. I am thorough, but not that thorough. I mean that I bought blank lining paper from the DIY store and cut it into A4-sized sheets, which I then loaded into the photocopier.

In the evenings, when the shop was shut, I enlarged every section of every segment from a new map of the Isle of Skye and copied it on to the wallpaper. (The first night I turned out the lights in the shop to do it. The sweep of the copier light attracted some kids to the door, so I turned on all the lights. This meant they were in the dark and I couldn't see them, but that was ok now. If they saw me, from their distance, it looked just fine to be photo-copying.) After two weeks I had copied the entire island and pasted it on to my walls. The giant jigsaw was complete. So now, when I lie back, and look at the word Skye hiding the sky from me and I think of the map walls and the stairs that brought me here, I feel like I'm in the middle of an onion. It's nice.

Sometimes, mice get brave. At university I had a friend and the mice in her bedsit got brave. They came out during the day, and at night, once, they ran over her duvet cover and she wet the bed. She wanted to get a cat but she made the mistake of asking her landlord, who called it a studio flat and not a bedsit, and he said no pets. Now I was beginning to feel how those mice must have felt, except I wasn't getting brave, I was getting stupid. But then how stupid could I be? The limit was my imagination, and I decided that getting stupid was no bad thing. Instead it was like the difference between being sane, and saying something mad knowing what a mad thing it was to say, and being mad, and thinking you are making sense. Brave and stupid as a mouse.

I was pleased when the burglar had come in. It gave me an opportunity to make it up to Will and Iman; after all, I should have been house-sitting properly when they were robbed the first time. In fact, when the burglar came in, I was in the loft of number 2, The Firs, because I knew it was a stupid place to go. For a start, I have to bring a sheet from my house, number 4, just to put on the ground below the loft hatch to protect the carpet from dust. And, I have to feed a ladder through the portal because the alternative is getting one of Will's from the garage and that means going outside. Then I have to take the precaution of pulling the ladder up after me and closing the hatch. And once, after all that shit, I forgot the torch.

The rewards of the loft are considerable, there's Iman's old diaries, Will's school books, financial records, old vinyl records and an Action Man tank with two Action Men. The rest of the stuff up there just looks like the stock in a shit charity shop, and it's dead cold.

So, I was in the loft reading Iman and Jemma meet Leigh (16 May 1990) and trying to work out if Leigh was a man or woman, when I heard the burglar. Except I thought it was Will. I didn't dare turn the page, what would he think when he saw the sheet? And I needed a piss, and I needed a piss more with nerves.

I could either sit it out and ride my luck (for about twenty minutes tops, unless I found something to piss in), or I could escape. Escaping meant through the roof tiles or down the hatch and running. If I went out the tiles I'd still have to get off the roof, so I would have to go out the hatch, dropping down without the ladder was quickest, and then leg it. I knew it was a stupid thing to do as I lifted the hatch quiet as a mouse.

It really was too stupid though, Will is an old friend, he'd recognise me. As the intruder came up the stairs I had an idea. I took a copy of the 1980 Adam and the Ants album *Kings of the Wild Frontier* and dropped out the record and inner sleeve. Then, I pushed and tore through two eye-holes into Adam's face, split the side of the sleeve about halfway along, and pulled the record sleeve over my head. It was a good fit. By pushing the side I opened it out well to give Adam a real 3D look.

I heard the bedroom door open (it catches on the carpet with a sshh) and decided to make a break for it. I hung down from the loft, doing that cartoon running action in the air because I needed to make my escape a.s.a.p. As I hung there an intruder reached the top of the stairs. It wasn't Will. I registered the fact it was not Will as my already running legs hit the floor. He ran, shouting, 'Shit!' So I let out a *Kings of the Wild Frontier* Native American scream (much as Adam Ant himself did). And he kept running and shouting, '*Shit!*' He was so loud I wondered if Mrs Price could hear. This meant another someone was still in the bedroom, and the fact they hadn't come out of the bedroom meant it was not Will.

I stuck my Adam Ant head round the door and caught sight of the intruder in the mirror. He was fucking scared. He turned around.

'Oh Christ!' he said.

I said, 'No,' like he was the stupid one.

173

'Oh Jesus Christ. Please, let me go?' I waited, he would have to do better than that, I mean I was just going to run out past Will and this dumb boy was *asking* me. He asked again, 'Please, please, let me go?'

'No, you are going to stay, I insist, I'm adamant. Get it? Adam Ant.'

He sat down on the dressing-table chair and put his face in his hands and held it.

Now I had a dilemma. If I left him he would try and escape, possibly out of the window. (Why not? I had considered going off the roof – but then I knew what Will could do.) If he did try to get out of the window it could be dangerous, he could hurt himself. Maybe, if I left him, he would take his chance and run out of the house while I was looking for stuff to tie him up with.

I shut the door and leaned against it. He looked up and I thought he was going to ask me to let him go again. I widened my eye-holes so he could see my disapproval and would not ask. He didn't ask. He held his face again.

When the idea came to me I snapped my fingers. Then I pulled out the Christmas box from the cupboard at the top of Iman's fitted wardrobe.

First things first, I thought, and taped my mask on – over the shoulder and under the arm several times each side – using some tape that said *Happy Birthday!* which had found its way into the Christmas box. I used up the whole half a roll because I didn't want to reveal my identity. (Like those mask-wearing wrestlers when they lost on Saturday afternoons.) He watched through his fingers. I got some tinsel and tied him up, then I got more and more stuff and tied him up, and then I tied him to the dressing table. I didn't say anything until I'd got him still. I told him to open his mouth, he didn't, so I hit him in the guts, dropped a bauble in his gob and taped his trap shut. Then I said goodbye and went for a pee in Will's toilet. Of course I can use his loo whenever I want, but this time it was a big relief. I just flipped up the seat and went immediately and copiously. I make it a policy to clear up any splashes, always flush, and always spray the air freshener – which is probably more than Will does.

I went out the back door and over the fence with my mask still on. This way, if Mrs Price or Tym saw, they would think we were being broken into by a burglar or by Adam Ant, which was fine by me.

I waited for Will or the police.

Now there would be no more burglars. Come Saturday I would help Will install the alarm. I was confident about it. I'd helped Dad fit ours at the shop, and, if anything, they would've got simpler to install. I was relieved he decided to get an alarm. It was a good idea. In fact I wish I'd thought of it. That way I would have more control and I could ensure it wouldn't mess up the portal. But I'd already started to change things, and changes can be frightening.

The very next time I went through the portal into number 2, Wood Road, The Firs (two days after the second burglary) I tidied up the loft. I had to use a chair to climb up there and retrieve my ladder. I put the records back in order. After this, I knew I needed to replace the *Kings of the Wild Frontier* album cover. My first thought was to order it, and it wasn't until I walked into the music shop that I realised this was madness. I didn't need a new copy that would look like it had fallen through a loophole in time from the future to sit alongside Will's Ultravox albums. I may as well just buy him it on CD. What I needed was a copy from 1980.

I looked in eighteen charity shops before I found it in the Samaritans. The charity shops were all run by Katharine Hepburn (really old like in *On Golden Pond*, but fatter). Except the Samaritans shop, which was run by someone who looked like a very, very, very old Marilyn Monroe. The record I bought wasn't quite right, it looked fine, it wasn't too frayed or too perfect, but it was a 1982 vintage. I bought it for sixty pence and tried six more charity shops before conceding that 1982 would have to do. I didn't like it, it was wrong, like an air bubble in the wallpaper (behind a bit of furniture). It was a change.

It took me two days to look through all these charity shops and the night between them I spent at the flat. A good thing was, that by visiting these twenty-four charity shops, I found some perfect wallpaper for the Red Hills stairway, which I had feared would be left stripped bare. The wallpaper was a mountain scene: a photographic pattern of tree trunks, flowers, water and mountains. The mountains locked together every third roll to form a mini range, and over the diagonal of the rising stairs, the effect was breathtaking. There weren't enough rolls to do the landing as well, but that was all good too. I painted the landing walls blue. Not sky blue the colour, but blue-grey like winter sky. It even looked black at night when the lights were out. So I stuck on one of those night-glow fluorescent packs of stars and planets. Everything in my house was starting to make sense.

I no longer wanted a job. Brown's didn't want me and I didn't want to look for anything else, so I would take a year off. Dad was against me taking a year off before university, but Dad was dead. Taking a year off gave shape to my shapelessness. I decided to do the garden. It was an elegant idea because gardens are annual things and December is as good a time to start as any.

Except the ground was like concrete and I could only work quietly at night for fear of being seen. It was cold. After the incident with Will nearly catching me outside I decided to make it policy to only work in the early hours of the morning. It was even colder. The dew made the ground marginally softer – before the dew became frost. Mostly I was pulling up (snapping off) weeds. But I had grand plans. If my room was the Isle of Skye then this was Lord Macdonald's Forest, surrounded by the sea. So at the end of the garden, in the old vegetable patch, I began sculpting waves from the earth, making a virtue of the hard soil, chiselling away ripples and building swells.

I knew I was doing the right things to everything when I finally had a dream that made sense. One night, when I wasn't working in the garden, I dreamed I was working in the garden of my house, number 4, Wood Road. It had become such a natural thing to do at night that the dream was lucid. The work was hard and cold, just as it really is. The moon was full and bright, like it often is.

I looked around and saw a tool I had not used before. It was a scythe, beautifully balanced but too large for me. I picked it up but could only reach one handle at a time because it really was so very big. Instead I gripped it along its arm ignoring the handles and gave a few practice swings. It whoooooooshed.

Then I tilted it until the blade caught the moonlight. I whoooooooshed it again, this time letting the momentum of the arc turn me and wondering if this scythe could fell a tree.

I said, 'Hello, is this yours?'

Death turned round and said, 'Yes.' (And I don't mean 'turned round and said' like most people mean it as a shit phrase when they say 'and he turned round and said' to imply . . . I don't know what. I mean Death actually turned round because before turning round he was standing on tip-toes and jumping to try and look into Tym's bedroom.)

'Are you looking for Tym?' I said helpfully.

'Who?' said Death. I remembered that Death probably worked on full names to avoid confusion.

'Tymoteusz Wazyk.' Death paused thoughtfully before answering, probably because he stores names alphabetically like everyone else.

'Er, no, not yet,' said Death.

'He believes the house is haunted, you'd give him quite a thrill.'

'Well, it's not his time yet.'

'Oh I know, but couldn't you just rap on his window with a bony finger or two. It'd be a laugh.' I found a cheeky tone of voice, found it like I found Death's scythe and the two were definitely connected. Anyone can afford to be cheeky when they're holding Death's scythe.

'A laugh?' said Death.

'All right, it would be an evil bloodcurdling cackle.'

'Ah,' said Death, nodding. He stopped nodding. 'Shouldn't Tymoteusz Wazyk be in Warsaw, near the multiplex cinema?'

'Why? Is that where he's from? Wow, I know he's Polish.'

'No, it's not where he is from.' Death gave an evil bloodcurdling cackle, leaned across and took back the scythe. If I had held on he would have pulled my hands off.

'So, does this mean I am about to die?'

'No,' said Death. 'You are already dead.'

That whole myth that only the mad die in dreams is a load of crap. I woke up, nearly pissing myself, but I knew it was a mad dream, that's the difference. It was a mad dream to have, and the madness ended with the dream because I woke up.

After the dream I got up and turned on all the lights in the house and made a cup of tea. I made a mental note to buy bananas.

I suppose I was a bit worried about the burglar alarm. I mean, it would be ironic for someone like me to get caught by a burglar alarm when I wasn't even breaking into the house. It could be that me being inside the house would set the alarm off. There was no point worrying about it yet, all I could do was make the most of my open access to the house, so I decided I would go in every day until Saturday – Wednesday, Thursday, Friday – and make the most of it.

I couldn't stop now and I didn't want to stop now. I'm nothing if not thorough, which made me pretty confident I wouldn't get trapped by an alarm. It wouldn't apply to me, I would help Will and he didn't want or need to be protected from his oldest friend. It was only prudent to make the most of the house though, just in case this was my last hurrah.

Night-time gardening was leaving me very tired. I couldn't sleep in all day because I needed to go into number 2, The Firs, during primary school teaching hours. School finishes at 3.30pm. It was the only way I could be certain I wouldn't get caught. I had to stick

178

to this rule because getting caught wasn't something I even wanted to think about. It wasn't going to happen. There was no point doing this if I was going to be tense in Will's house. So, the rule about attending during school hours had to remain.

Will's house was really cold. If I got in just after they left for work it would still be warm from the central heating being on. But I didn't like to do this, it was feasible that either of them could come home to pick up something they had forgotten when they left the house. Also there was no point having a year off work and getting up early. But this week I would have to make an exception, just in case I couldn't work around the alarm. I must be in the house as much as possible.

So, Wednesday, mid-morning, I toyed with the idea of turning their heating back on. It was highly unlikely that they would catch me and it was so cold that my hands were going a bit numb. The more numb my hands the more likely I was to make a mistake, to drop a cup of tea or tear a page of a diary. But I couldn't turn the heating on. I needed to be able to leave that house in an instant. The problem with the burglar had shown me that. If Will or Iman came home unexpectedly I could escape – but even if I turned the heating off it would still be warm. That would be very weird for them. It would probably cause an argument about who's responsibility it was to turn the central heating off. Or they might think that the timer mechanism on the heating was broken, maybe they'd even have to call out a heating engineer. I hate having to call people out myself, so I wasn't about to make them do it. I don't want any heating engineers coming round here.

There was no need to get carried away with all these *ifs* and *ands*. The simple reason why I couldn't put the heating on was because it would cost them money. If I come in here and keep costing them money that's a kind of theft, and I wasn't about to become a thief.

A more elegant answer was called for, and I found it hanging up at the bottom of the stairs: Will's coat. Will had two coats. The formal one he wore to work and this one. This padded puffy one. So I decided I could wear this when I was cold in his house. I was only borrowing it, it didn't cost him any money, and I would always put it back where I found it, at the bottom of the stairs.

The coat was perfect. It smelled of Will. Not that Will smelled, but in the way that you can start to notice the imprint of someone's odour when you know them well enough. Something about the brand of soap that they use, their deodorant combined just with the way that nature made them smell. I remember this from being a boy, I could smell a lot more people then and get away with it. I remember how Will smelled when I met him. Maybe it's one of those things that gets lost in adulthood. The smell of the shop and the smell of Dad are one and the same.

I wondered if Will could smell me? I mean it could make sense, I smell like everyone else – but I can't, I mean, not like everyone else. I smell like me, individual. Will must know that smell, what would it be? Me plus Happy Shopper deodorant from stock. I wondered if he could smell me in the house, in number 2, The Firs, I mean. But it was unlikely though, really unlikely. Whenever I even peed in his toilet I was sure to flush it. Smells are on a molecular level. I didn't leave a smell behind, surely. I considered stopping using deodorant, just to be sure. It was a decent idea. Worth trying, just to be thorough. Now I come to think of it, I hadn't worn any for a while.

Will's was a very warm coat. Really warm. It was the very essence of what I needed. I needed to be close to him and I needed to feel his warmth, the warmth of friendship. Wearing his coat, walking round his house, sitting watching his television and drinking his tea I felt really, really warm. I never wanted it to end.

I stood at the bottom of the stairs, warm in Will's coat and turned to go into the kitchen to put the kettle on. But there on the doormat, I saw the post had arrived. There was so much post I couldn't ignore it. I picked it all up and shuffled it into a pile like a deck of cards.

Of course I had looked through the post before, I don't mean for one second that I opened any of the letters, but I had flicked through the pile of mail on the mat to see what they'd got. It was sort of being helpful. You can easily spot junk mail without having to open it. Bank letters have the logo on the envelope. Private letters are marked *Private and Confidential*. I would never open anything like that, it's clearly confidential and private.

I took the post with me into the kitchen and flicked through it all as the kettle boiled. As my tea brewed I read each envelope in detail.

The first, addressed to Iman, I was almost certain was a credit card promotion. I don't have a credit card and I get these pretty often. You can tell before you open them because the interest rate is on the bottom corner (8.9%, not bad).

Next was a letter from the bank. The logo was in the top left. It was addressed to them both, so presumably they had a joint bank account. I was tempted to open it in the hope it was a statement, but if I really wanted to know I'm sure I could find a bank statement in the house somewhere anyway. Who cares how much money they've got? Not me.

I could see the next envelope before I even flicked it to the front. It was yellow and big. Some sort of corporate branding was going on, I tried to ignore it. Were they a phone company? Cable television? It was pretty hard to ignore! So big, so yellow. I put it to the back of the pile before I had to give it another thought.

I squeezed out the tea bag to hurry up my cup, and retreated to the front room. I turned the television on using the remote control and continued to read the post. Will's television is much better than mine. You can tell even without looking, the sound is a different class.

There were only two more envelopes, and a flyer for a pizza company. The flyer was neat, *BUY ONE, GET ONE FREE, on presentation of this flyer (includes pizza delivery)*. I put it in my pocket. It was free so couldn't possibly be seen as stealing. Then I realised

181

that one of these flyers had most probably been posted through next door, number 4, too. I already had one! I took it out of the pocket, it was crumpled, too crumpled to put back with the post. I mean that could be just the type of minute error, the dropped stitch, that begged the questions that unstitched my position. I had to remain thorough. I was better off taking the flyer than putting it back crumpled. I folded it twice and put it in the inside pocket. I like pizza, I love it, and could definitely eat two for the price of one.

The next envelope was handwritten. This is very rare, not just in this house, but rare everywhere nowadays. The writing was big, but neat and curly, addressed to Iman, and I was overcome with the desire to read it. I held it up to the light (the light coming from the window, as I never turned on the lights in number 2, The Firs, if I could help it). It blocked out the light and any hope of seeing through the envelope was lost. But I did learn something. The envelope flexed like it had a card in it. It didn't feel like a letter at all. I pressed down on the back of the card to try and make out the image. But it wasn't on this side. I could see something that could be the maker's mark, but beyond that I couldn't see if it said Happy Birthday or Happy Christmas. The picture was under the address, and the address was so big and curly I couldn't make anything out for sure.

I didn't know what to do, but I had time to think. I turned off the television to help me concentrate. The house was very, very quiet. I thought I could hear the sound of Tym's radio next door, in the middle distance, but couldn't be sure.

A car drove past the houses.

It isn't Will's birthday, I know that much for certain. It could be Iman's birthday, but it's unlikely. Unlikely for many reasons. She would get more than one card surely. I mean I'd send her a birthday card, if only I knew when her birthday was. I could check a diary for her birthday, but it wasn't necessary. I knew what this was, this was their first Christmas card of the year.

182

I put the Christmas card to one side, unopened on the coffee table, and turned my attention to the final letter. This one was different, this one was addressed simply to *The Occupier*. How exciting.

I knew I was going to open it as soon as I read that. The Occupier, yeah, that's me. But I didn't open it straight away, I drew the moment out, like it was a decision. Like I was weighing up both sides of it. In fact I was telling myself that opening this one was the exception because it was addressed to The Occupier, opening it didn't mean I could open all of them.

I picked up my cup of tea and the coaster came with it. As I sipped the coaster fell off. The tea was delicious. I'd started buying the same brand of tea bags, I liked them so much. We didn't even stock them at the shop and I had to go to the supermarket especially. I turned the envelope over in one hand and looked for the coaster to stand the cup of tea down. I couldn't see it straight away and decided to look properly in a minute. I stood the tea on a bit of paper instead, I daren't leave a mark on the coffee table. They're always called coffee tables, aren't they? Even by people who don't like coffee and only use them for tea.

Taking The Occupier letter in both hands I prepared to open it. I was excited about this. It was recognition of sorts. A secret and public recognition of my status. I flipped up the stuck lip of the envelope and delighted in tearing along. I made a mess of it, it was ok though because this letter was addressed to me.

In as businesslike a manner as I could muster (bearing in mind I was taking a year off from work and the pursuit of work) I opened up the letter and read:

Dear Home-owner,
We are the premier Estate Agent in your area.
We are actively seeking to sell houses just like yours.
*   If you would like a free estimate of the value of your property,*
without obligation, please call us, or call in.

183

That wasn't fair, it just wasn't fair. The envelope said The Occupier, then they ask to speak to the Home-owner at the top of the letter. How was I to know?

Quite flattering though. Flattering all round really. This was a different estate agent from the one me and Will had used. These houses must be really sought-after. Mine cost quite a bit more than Will had paid, they must be going up all the time. Moving here made so much sense. I picked up my tea and drained the last drops.

My heart nearly stopped.

What had I done? As I picked up the empty cup the handwritten Christmas card envelope came with it. This was a grave error. I could've kicked myself, I mean really kicked myself in the teeth but there was no way I could reach. What an error in my excitement at The Occupier letter. Maybe it was because of the night-time gardening leaving me so tired and all. I'd mistaken the back of the envelope for a bit of paper. Of course it is a bit of paper, it's just not mine to put tea cups on.

If you do anything enough mistakes become inevitable. It was only to be expected. My first instinct was to peel the Christmas card envelope away from the cup. But I didn't, I kept calm, realising that I needed to find the coaster first. I stood up and looked at the carpet. It wasn't difficult, I found it in the middle of the floor, the coaster was round and must've rolled away. That was lucky. It was hardly credible it had rolled so far. Even that made me worry about the ripples of my actions in this house.

I separated the cup from the envelope and put the cup on the coaster. I had a decision to make. I could open the card and hope that Iman would think Will had opened it, and that Will would think Iman had opened it. Or, I could leave it as it was and hope that Iman would think Will had put his tea down on it, and Will would think Iman had put her tea down on it. Or, I could steal the card.

I wasn't happy with the idea of stealing from Will and Iman. In

184

fact, I had been considering returning the things I had taken: the diary, the chocolate and peanut butter. I had read the diary, and many more besides in the loft, I didn't need it any more. And I had eaten the chocolate and peanut butter and very nice it was too. I could always buy a new bar and jar, put them in the back of the cupboard, anyone finding them would think *I don't remember buying that*, but in a pleased kind of a way. I still needed the bowling ball.

Stealing the card made sense. This way I could not be caught out. If I opened it and put it on the mantelpiece that was bound to make waves. I mean, do they even put their Christmas cards on the mantelpiece? I decided to open the card, it couldn't hurt – or at least it couldn't hurt any more.

Behind the picture of a Robin dressed as Santa was,

Dear Iman and Will,

SEASON'S GREETINGS

Looking forward to seeing you both,

Love,
Mum
XX

Two kisses, this was serious.

Will's mum would have put his name first, this had to be from Iman's mum. And, as she was coming to visit she would expect to see her card so I couldn't steal it, in a way I was relieved. I decided it was too risky to put it on the mantelpiece. It would cause comment, especially as it was the first Christmas card of the year. The only thing to do was to borrow it and slip it in among the other cards when they arrived.

I checked the back of the card for any tell-tale circles of tea that might have seeped through the envelope. That was something at least, I was in the clear. I even thought to take the envelope with me and put it in my bin.

I took The Occupier letter with me too, just to be thorough.

I woke up suddenly in the early hours of the morning. One of the problems with the night-time gardening was that I couldn't set the alarm to wake me. It would probably wake Tym if I did. But what had woken me today was not the thought of night-time gardening, it was remembering my mental note to buy bananas.

It was so dark I couldn't see my Isle of Skye wallpaper, but I knew it was there. It was nice to know. Luckily I didn't even need to get dressed because I had fallen asleep in my clothes. There wasn't even the need to take my shirt off and apply some Happy Shopper deodorant because of my decision to stop using it – in case Will could smell me. This was just as well because it was so cold that if I'd had to take my shirt off I think I would have just instinctively rolled over and gone back to sleep.

Instead I padded down the Heathrow landing, past the highly polished door and into the Loch Bay bathroom for a pee, then didn't flush to keep things quiet. I wished I had Will's padded puffy coat on because it was really cold. I went down the Red Hills stairs and put on my own coat. The mountain wallpaper took my breath away in the half-light.

For once I was able to stride confidently out of my own front door, certain no one would see me. It was a pleasure. The supermarket had started opening twenty-four hours a day. It was an experiment over the Christmas period with a view to keeping it open all the time in the future. I wasn't even the only one in the store, it was pretty popular which probably means it will stay open for ever.

I bought some milk, tea bags, sugar, chocolate, peanut butter and two hands of bananas. It was lovely walking around at night, really lovely. The exercise even made me warm by the time I started my gardening. There is little point having a garden if you can't sit back and admire it from time to time. I did this for a while, and ate a banana. I stopped admiring when the cold kicked in and started sculpting another muddy wave at the foot of the garden. The Isle of Skye, protected by Lord Macdonald's Forest, surrounded by the sea. It was so dark I worked by touch.

The light changed in the garden, and I looked up to see the bathroom light on in number 2, The Firs. This was nothing to worry about I told myself, but I didn't quite believe it. When Will had nearly caught me before I'd panicked and run into the house. It was reckless. So reckless I could have learned one of two contrasting things from it. I could have learned that if I hadn't got caught then (or in the loft) I was never going to get caught. Or, I could have learned to be more careful. I was more careful about when I gardened. But maybe I had learned both things. This time, just to be thoroughly thorough, I went back into the house, quickly and silently. I'd only managed one wave, but even a small amount of progress is progress, think of water creeping through rock.

It took me some time to get back to sleep, listening all the time for any signs of life next door. But why should I worry? I'd woken up to go to the toilet too, there was nothing strange in that. And, I'd come straight back in from the garden so they couldn't possibly have seen me. Tym opened his door and it sounded loud as a wave breaking over my head. I gasped and hugged myself. It didn't matter. It didn't matter, he'd been the one who kept Will at the door when he nearly saw me in the garden. Tym was not my enemy, Will was not my enemy, with friends like these I didn't need enemies to make me frightened in the middle of the night. Fucking hell it was dark.

I could hear voices next door. Will and Iman were talking,

definitely. I got out of bed, luckily still fully clothed so it wasn't too cold and put my ear to the wall. They were talking all right but I couldn't make out the words. Quiet as I could I slid open my wardrobe door, stepped in and shut it. Quiet as I could I removed the bowling ball (still in its box) and crouched down to put my ear to the portal. They were still talking but I could only make out the odd word . . . *'Ok?' 'Yeah?' 'No.'* What use was that? So, quietly as I could, and it was near silent, I removed the brick plug, edged it back and stuck my neck out between the houses – ear flush to the laminate board.

'Is that better?' said Will.

'Hmm,' Iman replied. But 'hmm' meaning *yes* or 'hmm?' meaning *I don't know*. 'Probably just period pain,' she explained.

'Well, if you want anything else, wake me, won't you?'

'Hmm,' said Iman, meaning yes I will wake you if I want anything else. What a nice man Will is.

'Period pain doesn't give you diarrhoea though, does it?' I was so involved in the conversation I nearly answered him, no. I suppressed the words and involuntarily shook my head, no, in answer anyway. It made me nuzzle the laminate board. I froze. They can't have heard, though, because no one mentioned it.

'Actually, Will, there is something.'

'What?'

'Could you rub my stomach?'

Then nothing, not a murmur more.

Reassured, I fell asleep in the wardrobe.

I slept like the proverbial baby. It was a fantastic night's sleep, until I opened my eyes and didn't know where I was. It was dark. I felt like I'd slept for ages, but it was still dark, and it was cramped. I tried to remember if I'd been imprisoned in a Turkish jail cell barely bigger than a man. So far as I could remember, I had not.

The contrast between the lovely sleep and my confused awakening made it all the worse. Turkish jail cells probably smell worse than this, I reassured myself. It happens like that sometimes, waking up just before the dreams all pop, anything seems possible.

I wondered if I'd been buried alive. I went through the check list. It was dark enough. It was cramped enough. I was alive. It seemed like a possibility, a remote one, but terrifying even at that distance. I tried to move and felt very, very stiff, so stiff that my first thought was of that embalming fluid that undertakers use. I wiggled my toes. Bit cold, but working. I prepared to sit up. I couldn't. I thought about panicking, but it wasn't the roof of the coffin that prevented me from sitting up, I just couldn't. Then I remembered I had to be quiet. For some reason, I knew I had to be quiet.

Maybe I wasn't awake? I tried pinching myself, reaching my left arm over to my right arm. I couldn't feel the pinch. I did it again, harder. Nothing. Shit me this was getting spooky. I tried to take a deep breath, but there didn't seem to be enough air for that.

It sounded like a *Tyrannosaurus rex* belching. Now I knew I was awake because it woke me up, properly, fully. The stuff about the Turkish prison cell, thinking I was buried alive, I wasn't right awake then. Now I was. It was that loud. Iman was throwing up.

My right arm was still asleep. I pushed myself up with my left and shook my right hand, like I was meeting a stranger. I remembered to be quiet. It's pretty nauseating hearing someone else throw up. But I couldn't get out of the wardrobe until the feeling returned to my hand. It was ok though, I didn't want to leave Iman all alone and ill.

At least shutting the wardrobe door had kept me warm. Iman threw up again, sounded like she was down to the bile. Under cover of the noise I took the chance to shake my right arm back into life and open the wardrobe door. Even my room smelled fresh and I took some deep, deep breaths. Iman stopped, I stopped.

The next time she chundered I would replace the brick plug. I had to wait. It was quite pleasant though, much as I wanted to replace the brick plug and get the bowling ball (still in its box) back in position so it couldn't be moved, I didn't want her to throw up again. I was happy to wait and lay back down with my head by the portal with just the membrane of the laminate board between me and Iman. I hoped she would be feeling better soon.

She sighed a little, or so I thought. Last night I had heard her much more clearly, but she seemed to sigh. Probably with relief that the nausea had passed. I was drifting back to sleep when I heard Will, his soft voice woke me up.

'Ok, love, I'm off then.' Another sigh from Iman. 'I'll come back at lunchtime and see how you're doing. I'll empty the bowl again then if you don't fancy it. All right? But call, promise yeah? Call if you feel worse and I'll get the doctor out.' My ear was back against the laminate board, I heard them kiss. It sounded like they kissed on the lips. After all she had brought up that was love, it was a sound of pure love.

I had painted myself into a corner. Iman was lying a few feet away in a state of pained hypersensitivity and I dare not make a sound. I needed some cover to get the brick plug back in, it's heavy and nearly always makes some noise. Until that point I needed to be silent because any sound going through the portal would sound different, it would be too loud. It would be a tell-tale sign. If Tym called out for me I was in trouble.

I lay there willing her to be sick.

Tym got up. I heard him close his polished door and go into the Loch Bay bathroom. I couldn't even close the wardrobe door to shield the laminate over the portal. They must have heard the distant muffled swish of these wardrobe doors under normal circumstances, if I did it now it would be too loud. The laminate board looked like the skin of a drum to me.

Tym flushed the toilet. The bathroom door slammed behind him. So loud it had to be the wind taking it, he always chooses to open the bathroom window rather than spray the lemon air freshener. Why? He bought it. Then, when the door had slammed the bastard even apologised, 'Sorry! The wind!'

Why was he doing this to me? If he thought I was asleep and the

190

slamming door had woken me why make it worse by talking? Tym thought I was downstairs, I heard him walk downstairs and call out, 'Good morning.'

He wouldn't shut up and Iman wouldn't throw up. It was a bad combination.

I could hear Tym in the kitchen, then I could hear him directly below me, in the lounge part of the lounge/diner. The television was on. I wanted to focus my hearing on Iman, to listen out for any changes to see if she was all right. But hearing's not like that. If she sighed now I wouldn't hear it.

As my toilet filled I thought I heard Iman's flush. I couldn't be certain. There was too much aural interference. But I think it flushed. I had a mad thought to stick my head through the portal and see if she was there. It was a mad urge and I bit back on it.

Once more I put my ear to the laminate board, but this time I heard Iman's wardrobe door open and she rattled the clothes on their hangers. Of course she wasn't doing this just to rattle them, she had to be choosing her clothes. Something baggy and comfortable would be best, I thought. The moment didn't last, of course it didn't, I mean, it doesn't take long to pick out something to wear, not when you're alone in your room, ill, and going nowhere.

Maybe getting dressed meant she was feeling better. But that momentary thought lasted even less time. She sighed and flopped on the bed, I heard it, nothing else could make that sound. Iman had not closed her wardrobe door.

We were virtually face to face.

Tym slammed the front door.

Will came home at lunchtime, it was an improvement though, he brought her a radio, and just before he turned it on and re-tuned it for her, I heard Iman say she felt better. She certainly hadn't been sick for several hours.

We listened to the radio all afternoon.

*

191

The next morning I watched from a chink in my curtains to be sure Iman went to work. She did. I felt like I was at the bottom of the sea with all the ocean weighing down above me. This could be my last day with both houses, my last day with the two semis of this whole house. Tomorrow, Saturday, the alarm would be fitted and that would be the make-or-break moment. Would I be able to work around it? I had to make the most of today, just in case I could not.

I decided to make everything all right. If this was the end, and I prayed that it wasn't, I might not get another chance to make things right with them. I got into my wardrobe and shut the door behind me. I removed the bowling ball (still in its box), removed the brick portal, untied the fishing line at each corner of the laminate board, pushed it forward to rest on her clothes rail before edging my way through the bottom left of my wardrobe and into the bottom right of Iman's.

I reached back for my bag of groceries then pushed the laminate board back against the wall. After checking the bedroom, with the wardrobe door open a fraction of a fraction, I was home and dry.

The only thing in the grocery bag for me was a banana, the rest was all stuff I had to return. Well, I didn't have to, I wanted to, there is a difference. Truth be told, I was guilty about it. I am not a thief and once I had replaced these things I would have proved it. I'd even bought the stuff and not taken it from stock.

The house wasn't too cold today but I took Will's coat from the bottom of the stairs and put it on anyway, it was too nice not to. First off I went to replace the chocolate, but remembered that the bar I had taken was part eaten. Surely this entitled me to eat part of this one? And what could be better with a bar of chocolate than a cup of tea? I put the kettle on. I tried to remember how much of the bar I'd taken had been eaten, but erring on the generous side I just broke some off and replaced the rest in the fridge. I had it open anyway for the milk.

Then I remembered the answer to the question, what could be

better with a bar of chocolate than a cup of tea? A banana. Luckily I had thought to bring one with me, I was practically living off them. The best method is to push pieces of the chocolate into the soft flesh of the banana. Peanuts work well too.

Which reminded me. I took out the jar of smooth peanut butter from the bag. It was identical to the one I had taken after the first burglary. I was feeling pretty pleased with myself, pretty virtuous. I opened the cupboard and put it behind their existing jar.

Never change horses in mid-stream, that's a phrase isn't it. Well, they'd only gone and done it, they'd only gone and changed. How was I supposed to know. They'd only gone and bought crunchy peanut butter instead of smooth! How could they? I mean if you like smooth you like smooth, you don't go and buy crunchy. My world started to reel around me. I got angry; I mean, wouldn't you? Imagine always buying your friends red wine, year on year, dinner party after dinner party, only to find out at their wake that really they preferred white. I could've got crunchy if only I'd known they liked crunchy.

Fuck 'em, I'd taken smooth and I'd replaced smooth. That was all there was to it. I had made right my debt, we were even. It didn't matter to me, it wasn't like the Adam and the Ants record being from the wrong year. This was not from the future, this was just a jar of smooth peanut butter, at the back of the cupboard. They were bound to be pleased to see it, thinking they had just forgotten about it, same with the chocolate. It wouldn't get discussed, and even if it did, they would never in a million years think, *Liam did that*. And even if they did, they would never in a billion years work out how this trick was done.

I drank my tea and ate my chocolate banana. Very nice.

The only thing left to replace was the diary. Now this was more difficult. It wasn't like food, like when you buy the same things over and over and you stop seeing them as individuals. I should know, in my business. The brand overcomes the item. Chocolate bars and jars of peanut butter are interchangeable. Diaries are not.

And the problem was further complicated by the fact that Iman would know the diary was missing. What I had to do was make her think that she had found it again.

Easy. I went back into their bedroom, where I'd found the diary in Iman's bra and pant drawer. I took a look in this, it was full to bursting point. There was no way I could put it back in there, what I had to do was put it somewhere near, but far from it. Removing the bra and pant drawer, and then both the other drawers, the middle one with T-shirts and tops and the bottom one with socks, tights and leggings, I revealed the space I needed. The floor beneath the drawers. Putting the diary there would just make Iman think it had fallen out the back of its drawer. It didn't even matter if she'd checked here before because it could've got stuck behind another drawer before falling all the way. It didn't really matter how plausible it was because she would have the proof of the matter in her hand. I put the diary on the floor under the drawers, folding it slightly into the back corner.

The lounge was a mess. There were metal take-away containers on the coffee table, one still had half a curry in it. My instinct was to clear them away, the curry was starting to whiff, but I stopped myself. Yes, there was a strong chance that each of them would just assume the other had cleared them away. It was unlikely to be my downfall if I did it. But I was increasing the chances of them talking about me with every action I left in their house. Returning what I'd taken was more important than clearing up, it would be nicer to sit here watching television without the smell of old curry, but I would just have to put up with it. It was a price I had to pay.

I turned the television on and decided to watch cartoons. The cartoons were followed by more children's programming, which was followed by schools stuff.

I couldn't help but look at the take-away cartons. It didn't look like they had bought enough for two. There were only three metal cartons. I guessed at the order, based on trace colours and odours: possibly pilau rice with a prawn curry; my guess, based on the half left, was prawn dansak. Evidently served alongside something delicious because the other carton was completely clean. There was also a paper bag with a metallic lining, nan bread no doubt. I peeked in and sniffed, garlic nan almost certainly. It was possible that one of them had eaten curry and rice and the other curry and nan. That would make sense if one of the curries was a balti, but it didn't look like it. I re-examined the clean carton, a balti would leave a trace, this was nearly spotless. I guessed it was a side order, there was a little touch of green in the corner, possibly spinach, leading me to think sag aloo, the spinach-and-potato side dish favourite. Maybe Iman had only wanted a little bit because she'd been ill? But if you'd spent the day puking and had suffered from diarrhoea it's unlikely you would order sag aloo, and you certainly wouldn't order prawn dansak, although that could explain why half was left. No, what I had here was the remnants of Will's comfort eating. He hadn't bothered to cook, but made a virtue of it by treating himself to a curry blow-out. He'd over-ordered, not eaten everything and not even had the good sense to put it in the fridge for another meal. How thoughtless. Such waste made me quite angry. Iman must've been ill in bed all evening for him to leave this rubbish.

I really had to stop myself clearing it away, it would be better in the fridge, but I knew I couldn't do it. (Anyway, it was too late for that, the prawn curry had been out all night already.) As lunchtime neared the smell of the food started to make me feel hungry.

Iman came home for lunch.

If the key hadn't stuck in the lock I would've been caught straight away. And in that second and a half it took her to turn the lock, as I dived for the remote and turned off the TV, I had a mad thought. I thought, how embarrassing to be caught and not to have at least cleared away the curry stuff.

I got lucky: Iman's first action was to walk upstairs. I heard her lock the bathroom door. I looked around the lounge for somewhere to hide. There really wasn't anywhere. The sofa was too close to the wall for me to get in there, the best I could come up with was behind the door. I was panicking, I mean the situation had already changed, she'd come in and gone upstairs, I could make a break for it. The odds of being seen leaving the house were far better than the odds of staying in the house. I went into the hall, quite slowly to be quiet, although I swear she could hear my heart beat.

The bathroom door unlocked. (Why was she bothering to lock the door when there was no one else in the house?) I couldn't make it to the front door in time, but fortune favoured me, there was a bolt-hole. Under the sound of the cistern filling I opened the cupboard under the stairs and got in. Time went slow, like when you fall off a motorbike. I slid the (new) vacuum cleaner to the left and got in between that and the gas meter. I hooked my finger round the door and pulled it to, the friction with the carpet prevented me pulling the door hard enough for the latch to catch, but it was close. Time went back to normal speed. I heard her walk downstairs over my head.

For once I wished I wasn't wearing Will's coat because it made the cupboard an even tighter fit. But who cares, tight fit or not, I was invisible. I thought through all the ripples I had made in the house today, the stuff I'd planned to do was all ok, but in addition I'd left a tea cup (thankfully empty, so the heat wouldn't betray me) and taken Will's coat. Probably no problem. The tea cup was just a part of the mess on the coffee table and Iman wouldn't miss Will's coat, all she would think was that he'd worn it to work.

So long as the gas man didn't come to read the meter I was safe.

My eyes adjusted to the darkness of the cupboard under the stairs. I started to think more calmly. I pondered. How did I know it was Iman who had come back for lunch? I assumed it was her because I hadn't heard the car. But I was watching television. The thought that it was Will sank down my spine. I didn't want him to see me like this. And it was worse still, he would know it wasn't his tea cup on the coffee table, he would know he hadn't worn his

196

puffy coat to work. I started to shake with fear, but I was protected, there wasn't enough room in here to shake violently, the coat padded all the space out like I was bubble-wrapped. I had to keep still though because it was the only way to guarantee silence.

I wasn't uncomfy, I was too psyched for that, the adrenaline was in full flow. The cupboard door was slightly ajar, but I don't think either Will or Iman would think it too strange. When I came back into the house after the first burglary the open door of this cupboard under the stairs was the first thing I had seen and I didn't think it meant burglary. I thought it meant the latch was broken. At least while it was open I had more air, it was hot in there.

I tried to judge from the weight of their footfalls whether it was Will or Iman. Whoever it was made several journeys between the kitchen and the lounge, probably clearing away all that take-away rubbish. The footfalls suggested it was Iman, a lighter step. What I really needed was for whoever it was to start talking to themselves. Or if the phone went they could answer. If I had a mobile phone I could ring up and see who it was. It mattered a lot, I was in the dark, Will was more dangerous than Iman. But at the same time it didn't matter at all because I wasn't about to reveal myself and didn't intend to get caught.

It was intense. It had to be Iman, didn't it? She worked closer to home, which made it much more likely she'd come back at lunchtime. That was some source of comfort. I wasn't in any physical danger if it was her. I prayed she didn't want the vacuum cleaner to clean up after the take-away. If she opened this door to get it I didn't know what I would do.

That was a thought, the thorough thing to do would be to have a plan, in case she wanted the vacuum cleaner. It was a possibility and much more likely than the gas man coming to read the meter. If she came for the vacuum cleaner I would have to run. What alternative was there? I couldn't explain myself, not in so many words. I made a pact: if she comes for the vacuum cleaner I move to the Isle of Skye.

197

Whoever it was had their lunch watching television. It was tempting to make a break for it. Really, really tempting. The door of the cupboard under the stairs would open silently because it wasn't totally shut. There could be a slight whisper against the carpet but not more than the volume of the television. The problem would be opening the front door silently. If the front door made a sound they'd see me, either from the lounge window or by investigating the noise in the hall. The only other alternative was to use the portal. But that wasn't without considerable risk. Not that it made much noise, and what noise it did make, moving the laminate board around, would be further from the lounge. But using the portal would take a lot longer. I would need to get up the stairs in silence and move through the bedroom, immediately over the lounge, in silence. If I was going to go upstairs I may as well just wait it out hiding under the bed in the box bedroom like I'd done at the party. That was the tried and trusted spot.

I calculated that the odds of being caught moving about the house, to whatever end, were greater than the odds of them coming for the vacuum cleaner, or the gas man calling. I decided to sit it out. Odds are funny things though, the improbability of being struck by lightning isn't very reassuring when you are sheltering under the tallest tree during a thunderstorm.

The television was turned off and in the silence I became very aware of my shallow breathing. Despite the crack in the door it was stuffy and hot in here. I wanted to press my lips up against the gap and suck in some air, but that meant moving and moving meant more sound. As they walked into the kitchen I held my breath.

It never ceases to amaze me the speed at which people leave. Often when they've gone I think their leaving was very sudden. No amount of, 'I'd better be making a move,' or, 'I'll see you later,' quite prepares me for it. But without the need for goodbyes they leave the house really quick. Just straight from the kitchen, down the hall, past the cupboard under the stairs – pausing only to nudge the cupboard door shut (and I was glad I didn't have my mouth by the gap) – and out the door and back to work.

I breathed again, starting with a sigh of relief.

Often the moment at which a disaster happens is not immediately evident. As they clicked the cupboard door back into place, my first instinct was relief, it meant they didn't question why it was open. It was too quick for me to be worried they were going to open it, I wasn't expecting it, it was just step, step, from the kitchen, click shut, step, step, step, front door opens and then slam. I was in the clear. Except I wasn't in the clear, I was in the cupboard.

The door wouldn't open. I tried not to panic and to bring to mind all I knew about the way this cupboard shut. How the latch worked, how the handle worked, how I could escape. It was a struggle to stop my mind racing away, wondering if I would die of asphyxiation or starvation first. That was madness though, surely I'd be better off getting caught than dying here. I looked at the door, which was very difficult in the dark, but I could make out some faint lines of light around its edges. I hoped these would let in some air.

To conserve energy I decided to keep still, but I was getting so hot I decided to take off Will's coat first, then keep still and conserve energy. Imagine taking off your socks without removing your shoes – it was like that, I was packed into the coat so tight and the coat was packing me into the cupboard so tight I could hardly move. Panic loomed, I took some deep breaths, extravagant breaths given the circumstances, and tried to remain calm. I tried to nudge the vacuum cleaner backwards, and it went a little way. I tried to get the coat off again and eventually succeeded, but it was tight. I had to puff and pull and struggle and when I'd finished I looked at the darkness and thought it was tunnel vision and I was about to pass out.

It wasn't. But my effort to keep cool had made me hotter and even shorter of air. I thought about the handle and the latch again.

The only time I had really noticed the handle on the cupboard under the stairs before was after the first burglary. I called the details to mind, what had I thought about it? How did it work? At that time the thought had occurred to me that Aslan could have opened the door. So it was obviously the type of handle that a cat could, in theory at least, manage. I had it, it was a horizontal, thin, silver thing. Now how exactly did that help me on this side?

If only I had accepted one of those credit cards I was always being mailed about! Curse me for not having a credit card! If I did I could have slid it into the edge of the door, flicked it against the mechanism to release the latch. I checked the pockets of Will's coat for a credit card. All I found were some mints, at least I wasn't going to starve for a while. I sucked on one of the sweets and felt a little calmer. If there really wasn't enough air getting in here surely I'd have passed out by now? I waited for a while longer, wondering if I would pass out. I decided the encroaching darkness I'd seen around my eyes was just the darkness in the cupboard under the stairs, it wasn't tunnel vision, I wasn't about to pass out.

When I came round I thought I was in the wardrobe, like yesterday morning. But it all came back to me. Nothing seemed to have changed, I was still sitting up because there was no room to fall. Wondering how long I had been unconscious I listened out for Will or Iman. It was all quiet. If only I wore a watch, preferably one with a light, I would know how long I had left before they got home. I listened, wondering if they had a clock that might strike the hour, or if there was a church or civic clock that might strike the hour. It was so silent and so dark. Time to panic, I decided, like it was going to be my last rational decision of the day.

Then I stopped myself by sucking on a mint again. It was the same mint! Surely I couldn't have been unconscious too long if I had the same mint in my mouth! Surely the mint would have dissolved?

I ran through my options once more: stay here and pass out

again, stay here and be discovered, or break the door open. It was no contest. Looking at the light around the edge of the door I found the spot at which the latch blocked the light. I leant back the fraction I could and used both hands to pick my leg up and place my foot against the latch. I couldn't manage an actual kick, so tried to do a Bruce Lee one-inch punch, but with my foot. At the second time of asking the door opened.

The first thing to do was find a clock. I fell forwards on to the floor and crawled into the lounge. The video clock said it was 2.22. It didn't look like a very likely time, all those twos, so I went into the kitchen and checked with the microwave, 2.23, that looked more plausible. I had some time.

The handle of the cupboard under the stairs looked ok. Examining the wood around the cupboard door frame, it all looked ok. The metal plate on the door frame, which the latch clicked into, had bent out of shape. I tried to find a hammer to knock it back into shape, but had to use a meat tenderiser instead. It worked well and only slightly roughened the surface. To see the difference you would have to really know where to look. I had to be pleased, I mean I was faced with discovery or death and all I'd left was a slightly bent and roughened piece of metal. I shut the door, it looked ok, but it didn't click shut. When Iman (or Will?) had walked out of the house and nudged it shut there was definite click. The click was gone. I examined the edge of the door. The piece of metal (the male part to the female recess in the door frame) was jammed inside the door. I jiggled the handle but couldn't release it.

It would have to do. I couldn't replace the door, I mean it wasn't like an Adam and the Ants record where replicas are available. This door was a very specific shape, I could never get a perfect match. The cupboard door still looked the same, at least both the changes weren't visible when the door was closed. I opened it up again, retrieved Will's coat and moved the vacuum cleaner back into its original position.

The coat was a problem. It wasn't too dusty, I brushed most of it off with my hand, but I didn't know where to put it. If it went back at the bottom of the stairs whoever had come home at lunchtime could think, 'What's that doing there?' But I couldn't just take it, could I? Not after I'd returned the things I had taken, to take something new would be madness, it would be theft. I could risk putting it somewhere else – with the other coats by the door, perhaps? This way Iman could think Will had put it there, and Will could think Iman had moved it. It would hardly be worth them commenting on.

I went to the toilet, flipped up the seat and let out a contemplative piss. That's it! The answer to the puzzle about who came home for their lunch. It was Iman! I laughed to myself, feeling really clever. The first thing they had done was come rushing up to use the loo. That was what saved me. And now, when I came to use the same toilet I had lifted the seat. Ergo, a woman had used it last: Iman.

This fact had great implications for the coat. Iman would not have noticed it was missing from the bottom of the stairs, at most she would think Will was wearing it. And she would not have thought the tea cup I left on the coffee table was out of place, she would assume Will had used it. I just put the coat back where I'd found it. That would do.

I checked on the living room. The take-away stuff had indeed been cleared away, how kind of her considering she hadn't even eaten it. The room could do with vacuuming, so I'd been lucky there. It was something Will should really do, they were his crumbs of garlic nan, after all.

The Quest Intruder Alarm was sitting on the sofa, in its box, but without any cellophane wrapping. I sat down next to it and my weight made it tip towards me, showing that the staples on the lid were already open. Iman must've had a look at it over lunch. I was getting lucky and I knew it. A lucky chance like this made up for

202

the bad luck of Iman coming home. The pay-off for the risk. This was all making a lot more sense. She'd come home to drop off the alarm they'd got from Will's brother Jimmy. She'd had a specific reason to come home for lunch, it didn't mean it would be happening again, today she didn't want to leave the alarm in the staff room all afternoon where it could get nicked. That's only sensible, she hadn't started behaving in an unpredictable way.

There was no reason not to have a look. This alarm could be the end of me and Will, the end of my living with him like this, so I should at least be able to meet the enemy. I considered smashing it up before it had the chance to come between us, but that was premature. Imagine a husband meeting his adulterous wife's lover in a divorce court, that was the type of atmosphere the alarm created in the house. I wanted to know about it and I didn't want it to exist.

The component parts were wrapped in plastic and I couldn't see the instruction manual. There were a lot of parts. I lifted up the box to see if the instructions were written on it anywhere. They weren't – it was made in Macao. Maybe this was a stolen burglar alarm like Will's dad feared. It certainly looked dodgy without an instruction booklet. Each unit was sealed and separate, there was no way to break it without the damage being obvious. I went to make some tea, I had just enough time. It was another lucky masterstroke because the instruction booklet was on the kitchen surface by the kettle. I memorised its position before picking it up and carefully analysing it, paying special attention not to break the booklet's spine. The kettle boiled up and clicked off, but I didn't make any tea.

I would've liked more time to read the booklet thoroughly. But I shouldn't be greedy, today I'd used up a lot of good fortune. I remembered to take the empty banana skin back with me, I wasn't about to slip up on that. Yes, I had made a lot of waves, but the house would be calm again by the time Iman and Will came home.

WILLIAM

THE QUEST INTRUDER ALARM

Contents:
External siren housing
Control panel
Movement detector
Door and window sensor (x3)
Remote control unit

Tools required:
Screwdrivers, slotted and cross head
Wirestrippers
Hammer
Drill
6.5 Masonry drill bit
And Liam

Liam was as good as his word, turning up bright and early Saturday morning carrying his dad's tool bag. He had inherited a cordless electric drill. There was a funny smell in the hallway, he was so early I'd not had time to wash so I excused myself.

'Make yourself at home, Liam. I'll be a few minutes.' I went upstairs for a shit, shower and shave. I thought Liam would be making tea but I was gone so long I thought mine would have gone cold and I'd have to microwave it. Instead I came downstairs to see him reading the installation booklet, having already drawn out a plan of the house. It whiffed a bit in the dining room too. Maybe Aslan's smell was back to haunt us. I had a look at his plans.

There were two squares for the front and back rooms, an oblong for the hallway, and a smaller square for the kitchen. On the back of the paper he had traced through the same images to represent the upstairs. Except there was an extra small square for the box bedroom. I studied his plans. He spoke, sounding concerned.

'It's only meant to be schematic; the book strongly advises *Step Two* of *Preparing the Installation* is to make a schematic plan. There is one movement detector and three door or window sensors in the pack, we need to plan where they go best. And, we need to fix the control panel.' I kept on studying and he kept on talking. There was something not quite right with his drawings and it was hard to concentrate for thinking about the smell. What was it?

Liam continued, 'The book recommends housing the control panel in the cupboard under the stairs.' He reached past me and drew a line on to the hallway oblong to indicate the cupboard door. Did his breath smell? For the first time in the dozen years I'd known him, did Liam have smelly breath? He continued talking, totally unselfconscious. 'Or, I thought, you could use the old larder space.' I leaned back, he drew another line, further down, and this time I saw what was not right with the drawings.

'Yeah, but you've got stuff the wrong way round. The layout is right, but it's all arse about tit. The hallway isn't on the right of the front room, it's on the left.' Liam was silent, he picked up the plan from the table and angled it, like a map, to the geography of the house. Then he blew his top.

'Oh for fuck's sake, what's it matter! I'm only trying to help. You can do it all yourself if you want!'

'Ok, ok, it doesn't matter.' I remained calm, I didn't want him to leave and take his tools with him. Iman came in.

'Problems?' she said. Liam seemed to respond well to the presence of a primary school teacher. He answered calmly, 'No, not really, I just drew the flipping plans arse about face.'

'Good. It's too early for shouting. I'm making some tea, anyone want some?' We nodded.

We sat on opposite sides of the table with the plan between us, this way, we had left and right on different sides of us and the plans didn't seem quite so wrong. Liam resumed, 'The book says more movement detectors and sensors are available separately. And, you can get magnetic contacts for either windows or doors. I reckon they'd be worth a try.'

I wondered if I should tell Liam about his bad breath. I mean that's what best friends are for, to tell you things like that. It was a delicate matter though, I couldn't just come out with it. So, I said, 'What do you want me to do?' just to be polite. Liam answered quickly, snatching at my words.

'I want you to get the ladder from the garage, put it against the front of the house and drill through wherever you want the siren to go.' He tapped the booklet. 'Somewhere prominent is best. *The siren housing is your first line of deterrent.* Why not on the corner of the house, by the front, but just on the side, then you can use the box room air-brick to feed the wires through?'

'I could do with some help getting the ladder out of the garage.' Maybe we could talk outside.

'I'll help,' said Iman, handing us the tea. We got the ladder. I went back and put my puffa jacket on.

INSTALLING THE SYSTEM (cont.)
How to fix the external siren:

Step 1. *Remove the screws to separate the front of the housing from the back plate.*

I hate following instructions, but there was no alternative.

Step 1. a) Go down the bleedin' ladder, get a screwdriver from Liam, and remove the screws. Go back up the motherloving ladder, wearing leather wrangler gloves for warmth and grip.

Step 2. Move the anti-tamper device until the contacts touch both the housing and the back plate.

Step 2. a) Go down the fucking ladder and get pliers from Liam to adjust the anti-tamper device. Go back up the motherfucking ladder.

Step 3. Run the necessary length of cable from the control panel to the proposed external siren position.

Step 3. a) Go down the bloody bastard ladder and get the cable from Liam. Bite lip, sigh, grip the end of the cable with your teeth and go back up the ladder.

b) Listen to Iman, at the bottom of the ladder, who calls up and asks, 'Why have you got the cable?'

c) Pretend you can't hear Iman.

d) Listen to Iman calling to Liam, asking, why has he got the cable?

e) Shout down, and drop the cable as you open your mouth. 'Step three! Can't you see it's step three!'

f) Throw down the instruction booklet for emphasis.

g) Feel disappointed when the instruction booklet falls like a feathery leaf.

h) Wobble as Iman leaves her post and goes inside.

i) Climb down the piss-wanking ladder, carefully.

j) Pick up the cable, dust off the end and put in mouth, before climbing back up the lovely ladder, quickly, when Iman returns to her post wearing her coat, hat and gloves.

k) Say slowly, 'I am doing step three!' when Iman calls after you, 'Liam says why have you got the cable?'

Step 4. Hold the siren housing in the intended place and mark the cable entry hole against the wall.

Step 4. a) Open your mouth, let out a silent scream, and, as the cable falls to the ground, climb down the ladder in silence while you think of new swear words. Raise a finger that says, *just don't say anything* to Iman.

210

    b) Pretend you dropped the cable deliberately because
       you needed to get some chalk from Liam's tool bag.

    c) Climb up ladder, fast, cable in mouth, chalk in back
       pocket, mark the position for the cable entry hole
       with the chalk.

Step 5. Drill the cable entry hole (we recommend you wear safety
goggles when operating an electric drill).

Step 5. a) Don't bother with safety goggles, it's just an
       insurance disclaimer.

    b) Feel the force of the drill push the ladder back
       slightly, then feel it fall forwards as you finish the job.
       Excellent, dusty.

Step 6. Using the screws provided mount the backplate to the wall
– ensuring the cable entry holes are aligned.

Step 6. a) Open the pack of screws, and those orange plastic
       sleeves they go in, carefully.

    b) Realise it would have been better to drill the holes,
       then open the pack, but it's ok, put them in your
       back pocket.

    c) Go down the ladder to change the drill bit.

    d) Say to Liam, 'Can I have a little bit?'

    e) Go and get the cable and give it back to Liam, after
       he points out that step three meant you to run the
       cable from the control panel – which he has installed
       almost arrogantly – through the house.

    f) Say, 'Well it should fucking say that then,' but don't
       listen for an answer, just repeat the question, holding
       the drill like a six-shooter, 'Can I have a little bit?'

    g) Go back up the ladder, listening to Iman say, 'I didn't
       think the cable would go up the outside of the
       house. It's too thin for exterior use.'

    h) When you get to the top of the ladder feel free to
       answer her. 'Then maybe you should be up this
       knobrotting ladder risking everything!'

i) Regret using bad language at Iman.
j) Drill the holes.
k) Bang in the little plastic screw sleeves with the butt of the drill.
l) Screw the backplate to the wall, ensuring the cable entry holes are aligned.
m) Drop two screws.
n) Climb down.
o) Find one screw. (Because Iman watched it fall and bounce.)
p) Climb up, secure the backplate, leaving the bottom right hole empty.
q) Smile.
r) Start to climb down, look up to see the internal cable waggle through the cable entry hole, and Liam calling, 'Yoo hoo! This needs wiring in. Yoo hoo!'

INSTALLING THE SYSTEM (cont.)
Wiring the siren unit to the control panel:
Step 1. *Strip back 6mm of all cable strands.* Liam had already done this and, under normal circumstances, I would've thanked him.
Step 2. *Double over and twist the cable strands together,* (all done) *then connect to the terminals on the siren and anti-tamper unit . . .*

I could hear Iman talking, and thought Liam must have run down the stairs. Then I heard Iman laughing, warmly, and thought Jemma must've come round. In fact it was Tim, just stopping by to say, 'Hellos.'

'Did you find the gardening burglar?' he called up, and I assumed Iman must've thought he'd got that bit of the English language wrong, so I just went, 'Thank you!'

'Do you need any help?' he offered. I looked at Iman for the answer, she thought about it and then went inside to ask Liam.

I couldn't keep eye contact with Tim, the last time we had spoken I had waved a knife about. I was relieved when Iman came back quickly and said, 'Thanks, but no thanks. We're nearly finished.'

Liam called me through the air-brick. I couldn't smell his bad breath.

'Read all the instructions first this time.' I did as I was told, but wished I had asked Tim for his help, he was obviously good at languages and this instruction book could've been translated from Polish.

INSTALLING THE SYSTEM (cont.)
Wiring the siren unit to the control panel:

Step 2. *Double over and twist the cable strands together (which Liam had already done and I had already read),* then *connect to the terminals on the siren and anti-tamper unit: connect the red wire to the point marked positive, the black wire to the point marked SW, the green wire with yellow band to the point marked negative, connect the white wire with black band to the return point. Then undo the retaining clip on the strobe light holder base, before connecting the dark blue wire with yellow band to the positive strobe point and the yellow wire with light blue band to the negative strobe point. Clip the strobe light holder to the base.* **Do not fit the front cover yet**.

I started with the last instruction, it was the only one I understood. Really, I was waiting.

'All right? Any problems?' called Liam.

'Yes and no.'

'Good,' he said.

'Sorry, I meant no, I'm not all right, and, yes, there are problems.'

'Just read through it step by step, word by word if you have to, and do each syllable.'

It was obvious. It worked, like learning a new line-dance or unravelling three balls of wool.

In the time it took me to wire the siren unit to the control panel,

Liam fitted sensors to the front and back doors. Iman told him to put the third sensor on the window the burglars had used. Now this window was secure I felt like we'd stemmed a leak. No one else would be getting in my house. I thought it was all over and said to Liam, 'Thanks ever so, Liam, I don't think we could've done it without you. Tea?'

'Not yet,' said Liam and he installed a movement detector at the top of the stairs before he would accept a cup.

As he made an adjustment to the side of the unit, Iman asked him, 'What happens if we walk through that? I mean can we have the alarm on at night?'

'Yeah, no problem, just create a *walk-through zone* on the *night set final exit*.' Liam finished adjusting the sensor and translated, 'All that means is that at night the movement detector won't work, the rest will. I've just adjusted the range of the unit from ninety down to forty-five degrees, so it only covers down the stairs to the front door.'

As I made the tea I thought about Liam and I thought about Wesley. It's a shame that Liam knows this thing about me that is really not like me at all. He's a great friend and after all his help with the alarm I felt like I owed him even more. I owed it to him to tell him about his bad breath. Liam was by the control panel, fingers poised like he was controlling a spaceship. He spoke with authority.

'You need to think up a four-digit number, of personal significance preferably, so it can't be forgotten, to programme into the system. You can't use one-two-three-four – that's the factory pre-set.'

I sipped my tea and looked at Iman. 'We'll use our wedding day,' I said. 'The fourth of the sixth, ninety-seven.'

'Yes!' said Iman with a spark.

'Four-six-nine-seven,' said Liam, 'four-six-nine-seven.' He programmed the unit. 'That's the code you need to turn it off then.' The control panel buzzed and stopped.

I tried out the user code, 4 6 9 7, it made a nice pattern, sliding across from the 4 to the 6, then down and back, from the 9 to the 7. Remembering it would even help me to remember our anniversary.

Iman went upstairs to have a shower. I had a moment with Liam.

'Thanks, Liam.'

'You're welcome,' he said. I leaned in just to confirm what I knew about his breath. There was definitely a smell, but now I couldn't be certain it was his breath. It smelled a bit like sweat.

I wondered if it was me. I felt under my armpit. Yes, I was hot and sweating slightly from the work. As I withdrew my hand I felt something in my inside coat pocket. It was a piece of paper about pizza. Two for the price of one. I don't remember that. Funny how you can do things without remembering them.

'Do you want to stay for lunch?' I held up the flyer to Liam. 'Pizza?' He looked worried, like he had something important planned and needed to get away. I encouraged him, 'Go on. Let me get us some pizza, you've been a such help with the alarm. Let me buy you lunch.'

'Ok. I'll have what you're having,' he said. Nice that. I rang up for two stuffed-crust veggie deluxe, that would be enough for the three of us.

The smell coming from Liam wasn't bad breath, it was body odour. Now we'd stopped he was sweating, I saw the sheen of sweat on his forehead and I could almost taste how much he stank. We went into the lounge and I opened a window before we sat down. Liam looked nervous. 'Are you too hot?' He motioned to the window. This was my chance, I owed it to him, if I smelled I would want him to let me know. And there was still the other dimension we'd never properly talked about – grief.

'No, Liam. Can I ask you something?'

'It's just if you're hot, take your coat off, don't open the window. I'm cold.'

I ignored him, it was my window. 'Listen, I want to talk to you. Can I ask you something?'

'Maybe.'

'Do you prefer shower gel or soap?' I was so vague. It was all I could think to say, but it was too vague.

'Shower gel,' said Liam.

There was a moment's silence. I wanted to ask him how he was coping, about the sitting in the dark, about how it smelled like he'd not washed for, well, I don't know how long. But I didn't know how to begin. He was my oldest friend and I didn't know how to begin.

'Liam, if I had a bogey hanging out of my nose I would want you to tell me.'

'Right. Me too. Have I got one dangling?'

'No.'

Another moment of silence. Followed by another and another. Iman unlocked the bathroom door and padded, over our heads, into our bedroom.

'The shower's free,' I said.

'Ok,' said Liam. 'I'm feeling a bit sweaty, mind if I have a shower?'

'Be my guest,' I said. And he was.

He went without another word. I went to tell Iman and to get him a towel. Iman is beautiful. So beautiful it's a fact. Somehow it still took me by surprise to see her naked in our bedroom.

'Hello,' she said.

'Wow,' I said. 'Hello.' I touched her skin, she was nearly dry. 'I've just phoned out for pizza. Two for the price of one.' It was the least romantic thing I could have said, but it made her laugh.

We heard the shower turn on and she looked a little startled.

'Liam,' I explained. She seemed to accept it without me saying anything else. I didn't have to tell her about how he'd smelled, she'd probably noticed. Hearing the drumming of the shower I remembered about getting Liam a towel. I'd missed my chance, he was in there now, I couldn't just pop my head round and drop in a towel. When we have people to stay properly Iman puts a towel on the bed in the guest room. It avoids situations just like this.

Iman was moisturising her skin with cocoa lotion. It smelled great and I just watched her with her foot up on the end of the bed. Then she switched foot and carried on. I love watching her. It proves how close we are, time and time again. Jemma never gets to see this.

'What type of pizza?' she said. It made me laugh, were we really so

216

close, I mean there I was watching her and there she was thinking about pizza.

'Veggie.'

'Veggie,' she repeated, nodding.

'Deluxe,' I added.

'Have we got time to make love?' she whispered.

'If I'm quick!' I promised.

The shower drummed on and on.

The doorbell rang, unanswered. It rang again, this time the shower stopped. Iman and I stopped, still locked together. It seemed so funny, the risk of discovery giving the lovemaking a whole teenage edge.

We listened as Liam ran down the stairs and opened the door. A brief mumbled conversation later and he called up to us.

'Pizza!'

'We're just coming!' I shouted back.

We heard Liam climb the stairs again. 'Have you got any money?' he called. At that moment we were all pocketless. I didn't know what to say. The doorbell rang again. He went back.

'Iman, it's Jemma!'

Iman put on her robe and walked downstairs. I followed almost immediately.

Liam and I passed on the stairs, he had a small hand towel around his waist. It was my fault, but he looked a lot happier for the shower.

'All right?' I said.

'Lovely,' he replied.

I walked down the stairs following in his damp footprints. Jemma gave me a smug smile, like she'd just interrupted Iman and Liam in the shower or something. Like she was pleased that Iman had finally decided to cheat on me. It was a bit of a farce I suppose. But I couldn't be bothered to tell her why Liam was showering here. And I certainly didn't want her to know that she'd interrupted me and Iman making love. Somehow I thought she'd see that as a triumph.

We had half a veggie deluxe pizza each. Jemma too – after all, she had paid for them. There wasn't anything for dessert, but Iman found a big bar of chocolate in the fridge which Liam and I shared. I thought about the chocolate, about how it smelled like Iman's cocoa lotion. I ate more than half, Liam didn't seem to mind at all and went home looking happy.

WILLIAM

8

9

I opened doors eight and nine on Will and Iman's Advent calendar because it was an audacious thing to do. It was more fun than laughing. There was a picture of a Christmas tree in eight, which was a little disappointing. Nine was a picture of a pair of socks, which threw me until I realised it was obviously meant to represent Christmas stockings waiting for Santa.

Iman's mother, Candida, was visiting and this meant I could open the doors with impunity, knowing that all three of them would assume that someone else had done it – and of course they would be right. Tonight, Will, Iman and Candida were in London. They were shopping during the day, seeing *Cats* during the evening, and staying in a hotel overnight. Which meant none of them had remembered to open the doors before they left. Door nine was a bit more of a risk, just in case they checked the calendar as soon as they returned, but they wouldn't. The first thing they would do was make tea. Anyway if Iman or Candida saw door nine open they would assume Will had opened it before they went away, all organised, for their return on the ninth.

I looked forward to reading about the shopping trip, *Cats* and Candida in Iman's diary. It would probably include what they were getting me for Christmas, and of course, there would be Iman's Christmas wish list to guide my present-buying. Nice. I know they have discussed inviting me over for Christmas Day and plan to ask me at the last minute. This year they are having Will's dad over too, hence Candida's pre-Christmas visit. They can't risk having both sets of in-laws, not since Christmas 1996.

I was sitting in the spare room at number 2, The Firs, sniffing Candida's perfume, when I heard the front door of number 4 slam. So Tym was in. I listened for him climbing the stairs and shutting his door (his room being parallel to Will's guest bedroom) before getting ready to return through the portal. If Tym had noticed them going away with overnight bags I couldn't risk being heard here. And if I couldn't risk being heard, I couldn't re-arm the burglar alarm because it beeps and whizzes on activation. So I left it off and slipped back through the portal, tying the wall laminate behind me, intending to activate the alarm later.

Since re-decorating I have started locking my bedroom door. Tym likes the mountains on the stairs and the sky on the landing but why risk him liking my map room? Also, with it locked, I know I won't be disturbed in the wardrobe. It means I can see to replace the bowling ball (still in its box) behind the brick portal plug with the wardrobe door open. It's a small refinement but these little improvements are the details of life.

If only Aslan were alive I could offer to feed him when they're away, and we could blame any false alarms on him.

There was a sweet smell on the landing. Not dope this time, but aftershave. I tried and failed to imagine Tym without his beard. He is as hairy as a bear: without his beard I think I would struggle to recognise him.

'Tym!'

'Yes, hellos?' he answered from his room.

'Have you shaved off your beard?'

No answer. I waited for a reply and thought about growing a beard, it would be something to do with my year off, a year off from shaving. (Not washing had been a wash-out; madness in fact, Will would have smelled me. I'd got sweaty working on the alarm for him – he'd owed me that shower. Now, I was back on the Happy Shopper deodorant almost every day.) I heard the pssst of

223

Tym's deodorant and smelled it mixing with the aftershave. I repeated the question, getting more specific.

'Well? Have you shaved off your beard, moustache and sideburns?'

Tym stuck his head around the polished wood door and even though the answer was plainer than the nose on his face, said, 'No, I have a beard, moustache and?'

'Sideburns,' I offered, patting the side of my cheeks (in the motion of applying aftershave).

'Ah, sideburns,' Tym said, as if my use of English was impressive.

'It's just I thought I could smell aftershave.'

'Yes.' He ducked back into his room, so I spoke a little louder, 'Well, and that made me think you'd shaved.'

Tym came on to the landing and showed me the bottle. 'Alpine Breeze aftershave. Is the right smell.' He motioned towards the wallpaper.

'Ah,' I said, as if I understood Polish.

'I am against this shaving,' he said, rubbing his beard, and I copied him and rubbed my considerable stubble. Our eyes met and Tym, seeming pleased with the connection, said, 'Shaving my hairy arse! Huh?'

I didn't know what to say, and waited, hoping he would repeat it, so I could deduce his tone. Surely he meant 'Shaving, *pause implying the next bit is a comment on shaving and the comment is* my hairy arse! Huh?' Surely, I mean, we share a bathroom. In the ongoing silence I tried to think laterally. Why would anyone even consider shaving their arse? By the time I had the answer to that Tym had gone back into his room. So I called through the polished wooden door.

'Tym, do you have a date for tonight?'

He came out of his room, smelling mightily of Alpine Breeze, and smiled. He walked down the Red Hills stairway and I enjoyed seeing him so much that I nearly forgot to ask the question again. I leaned over the stairwell and called down to him.

'Tym! Do you have a date for tonight?'

Tym paused in pulling on his coat. 'A date for tonight?' Then as he zipped it up, pulled on his Russian-style hat, and opened the door, he called back, 'Tonight is the seventh December!' and he was gone.

I went into the Loch Bay bathroom and opened the window a fraction to let the Alpine Breeze escape. I peered into the bath for any hair. All clear. But really it should be cleaned as a point of principle anyway. I ran the hot tap and rubbed my hands in the stream until the heat hurt.

'Oh fuck!' I said, washing the water around the bath. 'That's weird, I don't usually talk to myself,' I went on. 'Fuck, it's the seventh and I've opened the eighth and ninth doors!' I explained, and I was silent in acceptance of my explanation. I cleaned the bath, twice.

Another benefit of locking my bedroom door, and so not having to shut the wardrobe door, is that everyone knows it is very foolish to shut oneself into any wardrobe. I still thought of it though, and missed the foolishness a little. I pocketed the remote control for the alarm and Candida's Christmas card and moved the bowling ball, still in its box, from behind the brick plug. After undoing the fishing-line ties on the laminate board, and removing the brick plug, I pushed out the laminate board and squeezed through. I opened Iman's wardrobe door the regulation crack and checked the room.

I commended myself, silently, that my first instinct now was to rush to the alarm with the remote control unit, but I stopped by the movement detector knowing I hadn't set it. The picture of the Christmas tree and socks I had revealed behind the eighth and ninth doors were messages from the future. Like the Adam Ant album from 1982, not the original 1980, like the smooth peanut butter, not the crunchy, and the broken door latch, I had displaced things. And Iman's mum had arrived before I could put her card in place. I could still put that right. But why did she pay postage for a card when she was going to visit so soon? Some people just didn't make any sense to me.

The Advent calendar doors wouldn't shut properly. When I held them flat the crease down the left hinges was all too visible, and, letting go, the doors opened ajar. The ninth was worse than the eighth.

'Shit.' I bent the calendar back against itself and the doors did shut, tucked slightly under the right edges. But no matter how carefully I stood it back on the mantelpiece it would always straighten and the ninth would ping ajar. I considered stealing the Advent calendar. But that idea was madness – they have a brand-new burglar alarm and no burglar would steal a part-used Advent calendar. No burglar except me. Like the Adam Ant album from the wrong year I could just leave it. Except the record was hidden in the loft and did at least look right. (Even the smooth peanut butter was in the back of the cupboard.)

At least there were now lots of Christmas cards on the mantelpiece, they covered the Advent calendar a little. I used these cards as cover for the card from Iman's mum. I hid it well and hoped it wouldn't ambush me.

The phone rang. I jumped, knocking down some cards. Will said, 'Please leave a message after the tone . . .' Jemma spoke, as I picked up the cards and tried to put them back in position.

'Hiya, it's me. I was ringing to say I'm going to Mum's late tonight myself and can't take Tinkerbell cos of Bessie – she's got to see the vet anyway. But, shit, of course you're away or I wouldn't be looking after it for you for her at all! Anyway Iman I've got big news, big throbbing news.' She laughed, 'Say hi to your mum for me, or I'll even say it myself if I can pop round tomorrow, maybe 'bout five when you're back, depending on how Bessie gets on. Anyway, didn't mean to worry you about Tinkerbell, I can vouch for who's looking after it.' And she laughed again and giggled into

226

the start of 'Byeee.' Jemma then waited for a second before hanging up and in that second I covered my face in case she could see me. Jemma makes me feel like that, especially since she saw me in that little towel.

I activated the alarm with the remote and raced past the movement detector before it had stopped buzzing. To be perfect, to be airtight, all I needed to do was come to the house just as they got back, about five like Jemma, and then I could open the doors officially myself. I could say something like, 'Oh, look you didn't open yesterday's door; I'll do today's while I'm about it.' They might say 'It's not your turn!' but I would have done it.

It was a simple plan with little to go wrong, yet it worried me during the evening. So to relax I took the opportunity to do some gardening, and I could really relax because Tym was out, Will and Iman were away and, by the look of her dark house, Mrs Price was away too. If only it was summer and I could garden in the nude. It was so pitch black I could have gardened in the nude without being seen, but it was fucking cold. So I wrapped up warm and after sculpting some earthy waves at the back of the garden I warmed up and was sweating. Aslan was deep frozen in the ground, he wouldn't rot until the spring.

Gardening in the dark is like developing your own photos – you don't know quite what you are going to get. I have sculpted some earthy waves that felt magic, but in daylight were more ripples than waves. The best waves give the garden zen lines, and the best plants are in Lord Macdonald's Forest. I want the garden to look like it makes as much sense in the daylight as it does in the dark.

I had a hot bath and went to bed, tired, with my door locked.

It sounded like bed springs going ey-or like a donkey. I awoke to the thought of Tym's arse (shaven of course) bobbing about. I tried to ignore it for several minutes. Then I thought if I'm ignoring it for this long it cannot go on much longer, surely. Not without a break at least. There were pauses yes, then the rhythm would resume.

227

Tym must've brought his date home, which was a shame because if he was on his own in there, making this much noise, I could ask him to stop. Then why would he be making this much noise if he was alone? I was tired from an evening's gardening and that's what it does to you. The bed springs went ey-or again and again like a donkey derby.

Then it stopped and I listened and waited and it was still stopped. Then ey-or ey-or ey-or, and he was off again, like a donkey derby race winner, elegantly striding to victory. It was such a long race I had to marvel at the stamina, but surely this meant it was coming to an end. Again there was silence, and again I listened for it to start again, and again there was a moment's more silence before ey-or ey-or ey-or.

It lasted hours, like a full season of donkey derby races, like all the donkeys on the beaches raced and the winners of those races went forward to regional finals. Then these finals were like the best of three races and the overall winner went forward to the national finals and these were over like five races. Then this super donkey went on to race horses; great snuffling beasts who never talked to each other.

I attained a strange kind of sleep, always aware of the noise but never touching Tym's privacy. Had they been calling out I would have had to say something, but they were very quiet and if the bed made noise then that made me, as landlord, culpable. In the late, early hours it was over.

When I woke a little less early I was tempted to wake up Tym. Nothing nasty, loud exercise noises would make the point about how thin the walls were. So I did some star jumps and some squat thrusts and then had to have a lie down, panting out of breath. Perfect. I finished off with eleven press-ups, fourteen sit-ups, some running on the spot and lots more breathless panting.

As my tea brewed Tym wandered into the kitchen.

'Hellos.'

'Good morning, Tym,' I said, trying not to sound too knowing.

'Do you have any muesli?' he asked.

'No.'

'Aha!' and he pulled a small packet of muesli from the back of his own cupboard.

'Where did you get that?' I asked, and he looked at me and I hoped he wasn't going to say 'the cupboard' but he said, 'It came through the door, like post.' He read from the packet, *'Free sample not to be resold.'*

Without thinking I reacted, 'Doesn't that make it mine?'

'You like muesli? Why not buy some muesli?' he said and confused me as he offered the packet.

'No it's ok, I don't like muesli.' Then, to try and save face, 'But I like shampoo and washing powder, have we had any free samples of them through the door?'

'No,' said Tym, 'I don't like them.' He took the muesli upstairs without a bowl or a spoon or any milk – unless he is keeping them in his room.

I went to the shop to help with the papers. I don't have to go but I know how heavy Tracey Crabbe finds the *Sunday Times*. When Dad still had paper-boys he let them start late on a Sunday. The tallest paper-boy was called Craig and he ran his round: awesome. I wanted to be out of the house to give Tym a bit of space too, so his date could leave or have a shower or whatever. When I arrived at the shop the cold walk and the exercise had made me so tired I slipped in the side door and went to bed in Dad's old room. The thought of spending Sunday morning with Tracey Crabbe while Tym and his lover ate muesli was too much, so I slept super-soundly.

Sunday 8th December. I started waiting at the end of Wood Road from 4.30pm to time my run to perfection as soon as I saw Will's car turn on to Mill Lane. It was cold. I jogged on the spot. I waited. I got cold. I hoped they had not got home early while I was still at the flat or really early while I was still asleep. I jogged on the spot again.

At 4.55pm I saw Tym walking up Wood Road, alone, towards me. I stopped jogging on the spot and walked very slowly down Wood Road. I didn't want him to see me waiting and I didn't want to be seen talking to Tym.

'Hellos!' said Tym.

I tried to just nod my reply and keep walking past him. But Tym had stopped and stood in the middle of the pavement. He could block out the sun. His big coat and Russian hat made him look more beary than ever, impervious to the cold. He looked me in the eye and said, 'I tried a little of the muesli, I sampled it, and now I am going to buy some of that brand. It is the best.'

I asked Tym, partly to try to annoy him and keep the conversation brief, 'Did your friend like it?' I maintained a distance that I hoped would suggest to Will, should he drive past, that we were two strangers talking about muesli in the street, a little more than arm's length.

'You are my friend and you don't much like muesli,' he answered, not the least bit annoyed.

'No, not me. I meant the friend you had stay over – it's ok – but, well, did she like the muesli?'

'Nobody stayed over,' said Tym. I resisted the urge to argue and to ask if the donkey had enjoyed the muesli (he'd never have understood that, even if I explained it, explaining the noise and donkeys and how I didn't mind but . . . and everything). I looked him in the eye and said, 'But there was a lot of noise last night.'

'You think it was the ghost!' His eyes widened. I didn't want to get into it and I didn't argue because it was nearly 5pm and Will, Iman, Candida and even Jemma were due any minute. And anyway I don't want to believe in ghosts, especially not now Will's dad had explained about the paint smell. So I just said, 'No. I'll see you later then,' and walked round him, putting one foot into the road. We walked away from each other back to back like duellists, except I don't think Tym knows what a duel is.

Tym would be at least quarter of an hour going to the shops,

230

more if he went beyond the precinct. That was good, so long as Will wasn't late.

Will was right on time, Jemma was late. He slowed as he saw me and stopped just outside number 2, The Firs. He parked in the road.

'How-de-do-de?' said Will, getting out of the car. Iman got out of the passenger seat. We nodded. Candida looked straight ahead, possibly giving me a sideways stare, then Iman remembered she had to open the child-locked door to let her mum out of the back seat.

Will was at the front door, he burst in like the SAS and ran for the alarm.

'You've got plenty of time,' I called after him, but realising this was my opportunity to get to the Advent calendar I moved quickly too. The alarm stopped sounding excited. As expected Will went to put the kettle on and I was left holding the Advent calendar. I think my wisdom teeth are starting to come through.

'Tea?' he called.

'Of course.' I waited for him to witness me opening the doors.

Candida came into the room, she was wearing a *Cats* T-shirt which made her look like an American tourist. (She was so small I wondered if the T-shirt was an adult small or a medium for a child. If she can wear children's clothes that's great, there is no VAT on them.) We looked at each other because there was no one to introduce us. I blinked slowly, she didn't look like any actress I had ever seen, which after the way things had been going seemed strange. Everyone looked like a twist on some actor or other; but Candida was an exception. I was speechless. I tried to think of any old female black movie stars and drew a blank.

Iman brought in the tea-tray.

'Oh, Mum, this is Liam, that friend of Will's.'

Candida said, 'Hello, Liam' in a voice that was somehow American, somehow familiar. I wondered if we had ever spoken on the phone.

231

Will came in and took the Advent calendar from me, saying, 'We've got a day each to do Iman, unless you'd like to do one, Candida?'

'Yes please, I love Advent calendars. Last year I had an Advent candle and they're just not as good.' So everyone in the room wanted to open the doors. Will gave her the calendar and she opened one.

'Door ten: holly and ivy,' she said.

'Traditional,' I said.

'Door ten?' Will said. 'It's the ninth. Or is it the eighth?'

'No, I'll do the ninth,' Iman said, taking the calendar from her mum. She examined it. 'There is no ninth.'

'There is, it's today!' insisted Will, grabbing the calendar. 'Or is it tomorrow?' I could own up or shut up. 'You're right,' he said, 'hang on.' He counted, then shut the doors in turn. 'They're open.' He showed Iman, who got defensive.

'Well I didn't do them. You know I only do the odd numbers and I didn't even do that.'

I didn't own up and I didn't shut up because it came to me that Candida sounded like Al Pacino, she even had his short and mean demeanour.

'Candida, has anyone ever remarked on the fact that you sound like Al Pacino, the movie star? The similarity is striking, the short-pitched phrasing, it's almost American.'

'Who's Al Pacino?' she said and Will paused in his argument with Iman and answered her, 'The Godfather.'

Iman said, 'No, Marlon Brando is the Godfather. Al Pacino is his son.'

'It's a man!' said Candida, sounding a bit like when Al gets quietly angry in *Glengarry Glen Ross*. 'I thought Al was short for Alice or Alishia, I thought your friend was complimenting me.'

'Or it could be short for Alison?' I offered and they all looked at me and I blushed.

Will spoke, he was my best friend after all and didn't want to see me struggle, 'Anyway, what I want to know is who opened the eighth and ninth doors?' He looked at Iman and I got the impression he thought maybe Candida had done it. Perhaps he was even suggesting Iman ask her.

'Maybe it was Macavity!' hissed Candida.

'Who?' I said.

'Macavity, the Mystery Cat.' Candida sang, *'For when they reach the scene of crime . . .'* Then whispered, *'Macavity's not there.'*

'If only,' said Iman.

'He's a *Cats* cat, is he?' I said to none of them in particular, but Iman answered, *'He's the Napoleon of crime.'* Then to Will, 'One of the songs near the end.'

I interrupted, 'Was Napoleon a criminal?' and realised I was starting to piss them off one by one. So I pissed off Will as well.

'Actually, I opened the doors while you were making the tea.'

'You . . .' he paused and appeared to censor his anger, but I was still a 'bastard!' Now I was glad Iman and Candida were in the room keeping me safe. I needed to be near him, but I needed protecting from him. Will stomped out of the room and out the front door. Iman went after him.

Candida smiled at me, nice.

'Have you seen *Cats*?'

'No, I've never been. Did you like it?'

'Oh ever so, when we got there I thought these aren't great seats I don't know why Will went on about these. Then the stage turns like magic and they are good seats.' Candida talked faster and faster in her Al Pacino voice, think of Al as *Scarface* doing all that cocaine. 'And all around the stage and in the audience there's rubbish. Giant rubbish as big as it would be to cats and they come in the audience and they're always moving like cats.'

'Did they bury their . . .' and I was going to say shit, but my brain registered mid-sentence that this was Iman's elderly mother – not Al Pacino – so I couldn't say shit. 'Did they bury their own dung?'

Candida managed to both look right into me and ignore me simultaneously. 'And they dance like cats.' She paused and I didn't dare contradict her. 'The story is for an old cat, Grizabella, who no one wants to touch and she dies and goes to heaven.' Then she whispered, 'It made me think of Iman and poor Aslan. I might get her a cat for Christmas and call it Grizabella.'

I joined in the whisper, 'Then she could always call it just Bella – that's a name.' But Candida stopped the whispering.

'Anyway, she, Grizabella, sings "Memory" and ascends to heaven. The effects are really,' she thought of the right word, 'special.'

'Special.' I thought out loud, we were bonding now. I took my chance and picked up her card. 'I was looking at the cards, I like the one you sent.'

'Oh, thank you,' said Candida. We shared a smile.

Will and Iman went up and down stairs and in and out to the car, carrying armfuls of Christmas shopping. Candida followed me into the hallway. I glanced at the cupboard under the stairs, the door was looking normal. Nice and closed. Candida confronted Will, he stood still, his packages looked increasingly heavy.

'I thought you said yesterday, my card hadn't come?'

'It hadn't.' He moved to go round her, his armfuls of shopping slipping.

Candida held up her card. 'Here it is, and it must've come yesterday because there's no post on a Sunday.'

Will allowed the shopping to slip from his grasp to the floor. He took the card and revolved it in his hand. He looked confused, which was ok by me. Candida was doing my strange work for me.

Will handed her the card. 'And *Season's Greetings* to you too.'

I called out to rescue him, 'So you got what you wanted then?' Will walked into the kitchen like a gunslinger. Candida retreated to the lounge.

'No. We got what you want. Got you something great.'

'Yeah?'

234

'Yeah.'

I whispered again, 'What did you get Iman?'

Will whispered, 'Not much, I'm a bit stuck for her. She's difficult to buy for.'

There was a knock at the door, which had been left on the latch for bringing in the presents. Jemma pushed it open.

'Hiya!' she called out. Candida called back, 'Jemima! Come on in darling.' They met in the hall. 'What a lovely surprise, what are you doing here?' Jemma didn't answer, she just extended her index finger and pointed at the answerphone until the pointing became a prod on the PLAY button: '*Hiya, it's me. I was ringing to say I'm going to Mum's late tonight myself and can't take Tinkerbell cos of Bessie – she's got to see the vet anyway. But, shit,* (Jemma winced as Candida heard her say shit) *of course you're away or I wouldn't be looking after it for you for her at all! Anyway Iman I've got big news, big throbbing news. LAUGHS* (And winces once more.) *Say hi to your mum for me, or I'll even say it myself if I can pop round tomorrow, maybe 'bout five when you're back, depending on how Bessie gets on. Anyway, didn't mean to worry you about Tinkerbell, I can vouch for who's looking after it.' LAUGHS AND GIGGLES INTO 'Byeee.'*

Jemma waved at Candida. 'Hiya!' she said and they hugged. Iman couldn't wait to tell Jemma and they didn't even say hello, 'I got you the most marvellous Christmas present.' And Jemma said to Candida, 'Oh! That sounds nice.'

'Yes it is nice! Iman did really well.'

They all smiled as Jemma asked, 'So what did you get me?'

'First you tell me your big throbbing news.'

'Not now,' and she shot a glance at Candida. Will waded into their conversation, 'Look, you can't tell her what you've got her anyway. It's just not the proper thing. Where's Tinkerbell?'

'With a friend,' Jemma said and looked down.

'Ah-ha!' said Iman. 'Why don't you just tell me about this friend who's hamster-sitting for you then?'

235

'Hamster-sitting?' I said, and they all looked at me as if I wasn't making any sense. They all paused, not the waiting type of pause, but the pause as if there was a pause button and things were on hold. They paused again to get things moving. Jemma asked, 'Did you all enjoy *Cats*?'

Will nodded, Candida beamed and said, 'Oh, yes!'

'Very special effects,' I added.

Jemma ignored me and said, 'What did you think, Iman? Any ideas for the school play?'

'Well, I did keep thinking of Aslan. The real one, and the one in our play.' Her face cracked, 'Silly isn't it, they were nothing like real cats but I thought Aslan was such a Rum Tum Tugger.' She turned to Will, 'The song quite near the beginning.'

'The *curious cat*?' he asked.

'Yes.'

'But he's *a terrible bore*,' said Candida.

'I don't mind,' said Iman getting closer and closer to tears. Candida carried on talking, almost singing,

'*When you let him in, then he wants to be out; he's always on the wrong side of every door.*' Iman started crying and went into the lounge. Will followed her, and Candida followed him.

'I'd better apologise,' she said. 'It's just such a catchy tune the words are so easy to remember.'

Jemma and I were left in the hall. I said, 'Grief is a funny thing. I remember when Dad—' but Jemma had interrupted me.

'Yes. I've been wondering whether or not to get Iman a cat for Christmas. I mean I know you shouldn't give pets, but I think it would help her get over the loss of Aslan, don't you think?'

I couldn't believe she'd interrupted me talking about Dad to talk about a cat. I covered up my anger, 'Yes, I think that would be a most marvellous idea.'

'Maybe I should check it out with Will, I mean maybe he doesn't want another cat and it would be his responsibility too.'

'But I know Will loves cats, and you know he doesn't like to

236

know what they're getting.' And I quoted, '"It's just not the proper thing."'

'You're right,' she said. 'It's a marvellous idea. I could even give it a name for them.'

'Why not get a tomcat called Tom?' I offered.

'Like in the cartoon!' said Jemma. 'She always liked *Tom and Jerry* cartoons.'

'Excellent,' I said. 'You know, it had crossed my mind to buy them a cat, but I think it would be so much better coming from you.'

'Oh thank you,' she said. 'You are thoughtful to think of it as well, and thoughtful to think of me.' She caught me looking directly at her tits but didn't seem to mind, she'd seen me in just a small towel after all. 'What was it you were going to say about grief?'

'How it's a funny thing. That's all,' I lied. I even managed a light laugh. Jemma smiled because she didn't know what I was laughing at. Obviously, I would have to buy Iman a cat for Christmas myself. I had the right to buy her one because I killed Aslan – I owed her a cat. But this way, if Candida and Jemma gave cats my cat debt would be repaid time and time again. The more the merrier, that's a phrase, that's a truism; the more cats the merrier Christmas. I went and poured everyone a cup of tea; it was really strong.

There was muesli on the floor: just inside the front door, in the kitchen by the fridge, on Tym's brown bean-bag in the lounge/diner and a piece of muesli on each step all the way up the Red Hill stairs, from Earls Court all the way to Heathrow. There were fragments of muesli in the doorway of the Spare Oom bedroom, the Loch Bay bathroom and at the foot of Tym's highly polished wooden door.

None of this worried me, it was unusual, but not worrying. I wondered if it should worry me, but rather than stay and worry I was keen to go to number 2, The Firs, to check out all the Christmas presents and catch up on Iman's diary. The muesli looked so strange on the floor that there just had to be some explanation. Maybe Tym's lover had laid a trail?

I unlocked my door, opened it and it sshhed against the carpet. This worried me. Will's bedroom door sshhs against the carpet, not mine. Something was wrong. There was a mist of muesli dust spread out by the arc of the opening door. A raisin had rolled with it and pressed against the dark blue carpet. It wasn't much at all, but it was something. It was the difference between nought and some. I locked the door behind me.

I know it is lovers' sport to fuck everywhere but this room was mine. I couldn't care what they thought of my Skye ceiling or map wallpaper, but together they could look strange to a stranger. I checked my plan of the house was still in place under the mattress, in the centre. It was. I sat on the edge of the bed and faced the door, considering the implications. The bedroom door had been locked, but that didn't mean I always locked it. I tried to, but maybe I forgot one time. Unlikely, because I am nothing if not thorough, but it was at least possible.

The alternative was that Tym had a key. For starters that would mean he knew I locked it and I was disappointed in both him and me if he did. It was a safeguard, I would like to be able to trust him. To have a key Tym must've duplicated my key, which meant stealing it, at least for a time. It made no sense and I needed to peer across at the muesli again to believe it. It made no sense to think that Tym would steal my key, duplicate it and unlock my door, put down some muesli and then lock the door again. But the facts were on the floor, there was even the raisin!

I froze as an alternative emerged, because there was another way into the room. I couldn't keep the thought out because it was a possibility. Perhaps Will was on to me and if he was then he was more than on to me, he was all over me, he was inside me. I needed to be near him but this was too close. I was the next

Wesley, I'd seen it, I'd helped him hurt that boy, and now, for this, it was going to be me.

Could Will have just been playing me along with Candida's Christmas card? He accepted it so easily from her. How could he have known? The unlikeliness of the truth about the Christmas card was outweighed by the fact she'd put the card in his hand. And here I was, he might know, it was unlikely, but there was the muesli – a fact on the floor.

The pull to turn round and look at the wardrobe was equal to the urge to run to the bedroom door. I sat still. I was stuck and I had even locked myself in for safety. I was in a magic trick, from one point of view it looked like muesli had been spilt, which is fine and normal. Until it is all over the house, and until it is in a locked room.

I prayed it was Tym, even though he's much bigger than Will he is not as vengeful as Will. I am tied to Will for ever, I am locked into this.

There was an answer, but I wasn't brave enough to check it. All I needed to do was check the portal. Simple, because if Will had come through he could replace the board and perhaps even get the bowling ball to fall into place, but he would not be able to tie the fishing line. Just in case he was in the wardrobe I unlocked the bedroom door as an escape route. I cleared my throat and said (being sure not to call out or raise my voice at all, just in case he was in his house, in number 2, The Firs, even, maybe, in the bedroom), 'Will?' There was no answer. I went to the wardrobe door and said it again as a whisper. 'Will?'

I went in the wardrobe, and because the bedroom door was now unlocked, I shut the wardrobe door behind me. I felt for, and found, the tied fishing line. I was saved – unless Tym had a copy of my bedroom door key?

Perhaps all the bedroom doors had the same key? I mean it works for old Ford Cortinas, Tym could have used his own door key, which was bad, but not worse than Will. I had to try Tym's door, it was already shut and possibly locked. I inserted the key and tried to turn it right – nothing – then left – something. The lock locked and I sighed.

Tym knocked on his door like hail and feeling I had the tiger by the tail I considered not unlocking it. He called out, sounding like Jean-Claude Van Damme, 'What the fucks! Hellos! Unlock these!' I thought about it and about how big he was, as big as a bear. I imagined Jean-Claude Van Damme fatter and with a beard – it took some doing. I decided to unlock the door at arm's length just as Tym unlocked it himself.

I said, 'So you do have a key to my door then?' which was enough to confuse me let alone a Polish student. Tym paused in the doorway and I stood back at arm's length.

'Hellos?'

'Hello, Tym. Can I explain?'

'Well, I cannot,' he said aggressively, eyes narrowed.

'There is muesli in my room.'

'Yeah, so what?' he said, like it was nothing strange, like he got the words muesli and carpet or air mixed up.

'Muesli,' I emphasised and used my foot to nudge some of the muesli on the floor by his door. 'There's muesli in my room and I had the door locked. So I thought, have I lost my keys and has Tym found them and unlocked my door to return my keys, and finding me out, left some muesli?'

He earnestly answered, 'No.'

'So then I thought,' I paused and thought, 'then I thought, maybe Tym's key works in my lock and he came back and opened my door by mistake, say he was drunk?' Tym nodded in consideration. 'And he left some muesli in my room.'

'Drunk?' he said.

'Yes. So I was trying my key in your lock to see if this was possible.'

'Ok. Thank you,' said Tym and started to shut his door until I strode forward and put my foot in it.

'Why is there muesli all over the house?' Tym was now on the back foot and he got defensive.

'I didn't opened your door!'

'So why is there muesli? I don't much like muesli, I don't eat it – you know that.'

'Yes,' he said and looked down and I started to wonder just how hard Jean-Claude Van Damme is himself, I mean he plays hard men but I bet he doesn't want to get cut in real life. I bet Jean-Claude Van Damme is a frightened little girl. I thought, right now I could have Jean-Claude Van Damme, I had the anger for it.

'I am looking for the hamster of Mrs Price,' said Tym. 'I was minding it for her this weekend but he has escaped. He is a muesli fan, so I am trying to tempt him.'

'Ok.'

'I put muesli under your door. I put it on the floor and pushed it through with a ruler.' He went and got a 30cm ruler, then held it up.

'Ok, ok,' I reassured him, and me.

'Yes, ok, and I even put a raisin in through the keyhole because Mrs Price's hamster is a raisin fan. I pushed it through on the point of a pencil.' He went and got the pencil. It was very sharp.

'Ok. So where is the hamster?'

Tym confessed, 'I don't have him – but it is true. I need to give the hamster back and I don't have him any more. I am hoping he has homed himself already.'

I loved Tym's explanation, it made sense. 'Your method is all wrong, let me help,' I offered.

'Thank you,' he said. 'How do you find hamsters?'

'Well, at the moment you have put down so much muesli that he could take some and you would never know. So, let's just put all the muesli into one pile and watch it.'

'Yes please!' said Tym and he was off. He vacuumed up all the muesli, except the stuff in my room which I locked up. We met on

241

the landing, Tym holding the muesli box. I took control, 'Now, all that vacuuming will have scared the hamster. I think it best you put the muesli down near to where you last saw him.'

'But that was in my room.' Tym sounded worried.

'Ok, let's do that.'

'But I have checked my room.'

'Yes, but isn't his cage in there?'

Tym said, 'He has a house in there?' checking this was the same.

'Even better. Now let's look in the house and see if all his bedding material is there. Hamsters love to move their bedding, and then they move it back.'

Tym went into his room, shut the door, then came out carrying the hamster house with the muesli box balanced on the top. The hamster house looked great, like a sort of Bauhaus-inspired living complex. Magnificent.

'Magnificent!' I said, and Tym held it up slightly proud, the muesli box slid a little and I took it. 'Is that all the bedding?'

'I think so.' And Tym peered into the top module which was stuffed full. Tym tried to hold the hamster house with one hand and shut the polished bedroom door with the other. It was obvious he didn't want me to go into his room, so I wanted to go into his room. In the moment it took Tym to re-orientate the hamster house and reach for the door handle I took action.

'Let me help you,' I said and opened his door like that was what he wanted and walked in. I looked around for Tym's secrets. The room was much as I remembered it, the bed was in the same spot, the posters were the same, *A Midsummer Night's Dream* by the RSC, and a framed film poster for *A Midsummer Night's Sex Comedy* by Woody Allen. Tym had even left his computer on top of his flat suitcase. He must work at it cross-legged, it is just that height even for such a big man. He had a twin tape deck, with no compact disc player, although he did have three compact discs. There were some ornate brass scales on the windowsill, they were new to me and seemed a bit old-womanish.

I held up one of the compact discs, 'Are these CD-Roms for the computer?'

'No, that is The Beatles, they are a pop group,' he explained.

'Oh yes, we do have The Beatles in England, but you don't have a compact disc player.' I pointed at his tape machine. He nodded and said, 'So I play them on my computer. Would you like to hear The Beatles?'

'No.' I was indignant but said in a whisper, 'Noises scare hamsters.'

Tym put the hamster house down in the centre of his room. The main room, the hamster's living room, had a large yellow wheel on one side, so maybe it was more like the hamster's gym. There was a ladder from this room to a second higher chamber, with a water bottle fixed into it like a bent Fisher Price hypodermic syringe, and above this room was the room full of bedding. I crouched down and felt I could empathise with this hamster who wants to sleep upstairs. It makes more sense, sleeping upstairs is like being in the flat and being in the flat is a bit like flying and flying is a bit like being dead.

'They don't live long, you know,' I thought out loud.

'I know, we do have hamsters in Poland,' said Tym.

The front door of the hamster house was already open. I poured a little mountain of muesli outside it and put a raisin on top.

Tym said, 'Thank you, I can do the waiting if you want.' He seemed so keen for me to leave that I wanted to stay. I did want to go and read Iman's diary and check the Christmas presents next door, but that would have to wait anyway because Tym was in and I now knew my lock wasn't secure.

I whispered, 'I don't mind waiting. We must be quiet now,' just to try and end the conversation, and it worked. Tym lay on his bed, occasionally propping himself up on one arm to check the hamster house. I stayed sitting still and we waited. Gradually, as we waited, I moved from sitting upright, to leaning back, to lying back on my elbows, until after about half an hour, I was fully reclined. Then I lay back with my head on the carpet and thought about sleeping.

Tym kept his room nice and warm; hot as tea and toast.

Lights make a noise. But it wasn't until I rolled on to my side, and saw the dotted line of light at the bottom of Tym's fitted wardrobe, that I heard the sound of the light. It was a tiny buzzing miniature whirr. The light was constant. I didn't know what it was, but knew it had to be a secret. I decided not to ask Tym what was in there, because if I asked he would know to try and stop me finding out.

We waited. Tym lay back on his bed luxuriantly, he is so big and the bed is so narrow I wondered how he'd managed to get someone else in with him. She must have gone on top. I whispered, 'Not much room.'

'What? This room, or his room?' Tym motioned at the hamster house.

'Well both, but I meant your bed, I mean if you had someone else in there you'd need a bigger bed.'

'I would, yes,' Tym said, not sure what to make of me.

'Do you want a bigger bed?' Tym looked bewildered and more than a little frightened, so I tried to explain and put his mind at ease, 'I mean I am the landlord, I could get you a bigger bed.'

'This bed is fine, fine for one,' he said. I felt the need to explain myself more: to talk about my responsibility as landlord, how I didn't mind him having his date back but . . . and maybe what I meant was a bed that didn't squeak, rather than a double bed if he didn't want to lose space in the room.

'The hamster is in the bed bedroom!' he shouted with relief.

'The bed?'

'Yes, the bed bedroom.' Tym pointed to the top of the hamster house, but I thought he was pointing past this at me, at the bedroom, and I sprang up like I had a rat on me to see a slight ripple going on in the bedding. Then it stopped and we waited, so long that it seemed like we were wrong and the ripple was a mirage. Until the honey and caramel hamster climbed down his ladder sniffing the air.

244

'Of course!' I said and the hamster paused to listen and sniff, so I shut up and he walked down his stairs and ignored his water and then ignored the muesli outside his open door. The hamster got on his wheel and started to race. The wheel went ey-or ey-or ey-or.

'Like a donkey!' I said and Tym said, 'Yes,' and nodded like he understood how hamsters can sound like donkeys. 'Sometimes he's on that wheel all night.'

Traditionally Christmas presents should be kept in, or on, wardrobes. Iman knew this, which made using the portal doubly difficult. I heard the presents slide and the plastic carrier bags crackle as I pushed forward the laminate board, inch by careful inch, until it stuck. Fuck.

I pulled the board back, tied it in place, replaced the brick plug and put the bowling ball, still in its box, behind it. But really it was no use, I had disturbed their universe; again. The presents would be pushed all back in the wardrobe and Iman would think, *why are they pushed all forwards in my wardrobe?* Maybe she would accuse Will of looking in there and he wouldn't like that (but I bet he has looked in there).

I opened up the portal again, thinking surely nothing is that stuck, and this time I pushed it with my foot, then, when it stuck, nudged it with my foot. The gap was tempting, if I was four I could have got through. I nudged it again with my foot, then tapped and when it didn't move, kicked. Something broke like bone china and the board gave way like snow underfoot. Still I couldn't get through, I would have needed to be about nine to fit.

I put the portal back together before I panicked. Then I felt sick, until I remembered the spare key Will gave me in case of lock-outs, and now I was locked out. I kept the spare key at the flat. I had to, because if Will ever needed it he would come looking for me there and one of the Crabbe sisters would be able to give it to him. The key was nothing compared to the portal, using the key meant going in the front of the house and Mrs Price, Tym, or anyone could see me leaving my front door, going down my driveway and up their garden path. It would just look weird.

The portal meant I was actually in Will's life with him.

It took me sixteen minutes to walk the two miles to the shop because I jogged most of it to keep warm. By this time Edna Crabbe would be at work. I didn't go in the side door, but went into the shop to try to see things like a customer. Edna wasn't there.

A mumsy-looking woman, who I recognised from both the crematorium and the shop, came in. We stood side by side, then I ducked under the counter.

'Excuse me! Can I help you?' she said.

'Twenty Lambert & Butler, red, isn't it?' I replied.

'Oh, it's you again isn't it? Jerry's boy from university.'

Edna called in, 'Hello, Liam. Sorry, I was just getting the cigarettes I needed for facing up.'

'Fine, give this woman twenty Lambert & Butler, the red, please.' I left them to each other.

The shop was warm and the flat was cold. I kept my coat on, got the keys and left by the side door, quietly, so Edna might think I was upstairs, unless she knew how cold it was up there.

It is hard to know exactly what time primary school teachers get home. Although school finishes at 3.30pm Iman often seemed to be back at 5pm or later. I turned off Mill Lane and into Wood Road, I didn't hesitate or even look round as I marched up the path to number 2, The Firs. Mrs Price must be away if Tym has her hamster and I don't even know the name of anyone else in Wood Road so they don't know me. I stopped by the door and slackened off my shoelaces.

Inside the door I slipped out of my shoes and put one in each of my coat pockets. Of course, I would have preferred to be wearing Will's coat instead of my own. But that's what it's like, coming in from the outside instead of coming in from the inside. I answered the alarm before it sounded too frantic with the user code 4 6 9 7. Nice. Everyone was definitely out because the alarm was on. This felt a bit like housebreaking, not that I have ever broken into a house. I had forty-six minutes till the school bell, assuming they still had bells.

The bedroom looked different from this angle, the door sshhed open and I allowed myself a peek through the hinge before I went in. The presents in the wardrobe had buckled up inside the door, like a chunky wave, with space behind now the laminate board was back in place. I was pleased with how solid the back of the wardrobe looked, I tapped it over the portal and you really would never know.

Pushing the presents back into position made the broken pieces of china tinkle. They were at the front. The carrier bag said LINE DANCE PRO TIGER. Is anyone really a pro line-dancer? Inside a layer of bubblewrap was a broken man. I pieced him together, he was very fat, rotund in fact, and he had a cowboy hat. But it wasn't a cowboy hat, it was a lid, and the man was a teapot, short and stout, here's his broken-off handle, here's his broken-off spout. I put it back in the bubblewrap and back in the bag. I started to reorganise the presents into a wider, thinner order to give me a chance of opening the portal, but it was no use. Even if I could get through the portal I wouldn't be able to get the presents back into position behind it when I left.

It seemed more important than ever to look at the other presents too, because who knew when I could come back. There were two pairs of slippers, one female and more mature, for Candida, and one pair of moccasins, probably for Jimmy – very thoughtful now he was wearing his other, early Christmas present, pair out. He could wear these moccasins just in the house, like slippers. There was a bottle of Irish single malt whiskey, in a presentation box with a free glass, and I was relieved it was not this that had broken and spilt everywhere. I reckoned it was for Will's dad and that I might even get a taste of it on Christmas Day. Two Body Shop presentation packs of toiletries which could have been for anyone. Eighteen power balls in four different colours and thirteen giant pencils, six with the Union Jack on them. I didn't know who these were for until I counted them together, thirty-one, they must be presents for Iman's class. In this bag there was also a presentation box of the Narnia books, *Voyage of the Dawn Treader*, the lot, so maybe these were for the school as well. Maybe it was a prize, or maybe it was for Jemma. There was a bag of new Christmas decorations, baubles and tinsel, plus a three-pack roll of wrapping paper and some tape that said *On the first day of Christmas* which I unwound to read on *my true love sent to me*. I wanted to read more, to see if it went on to all the leaping lords and that but I knew it would be too hard to rewind if I did. Anyway, I would need some surprises on Christmas Day.

Will also knew keeping presents in the bottom of the wardrobe is the right and proper thing to do. He hadn't bought as much. Iman got lingerie. She has a 34B bust and takes size 12 pants, at least he'd got that right. He'd also bought two of those thick airport books with the author's name in gold, possibly for his brothers. It would be easy to send a book to Clive in Edinburgh, heavy though, especially the hardback one, and time is running out for posting. There was perfume for Candida and aftershave for his dad, at least I hoped it wasn't for me. There was a sweater that I wanted. Not only because it was cold in here but because it seemed the friendliest present. That's how warm Will makes me feel, even when he's not around.

Now it seemed more important than ever to read Iman's diary, because who knew when I could come back. I had time. She was running low on underwear, probably since the trip away to London. London's heavy on pants. The diary was only under one pair of pants (which, strangely, were size 14, maybe why they are her last pair?) and two bras (both 34B), which was a bit of luck making it a cinch to replace.

December 8 Highlight: 70% Found the line-dancing shop and bought Will's presents. Left him and Mum to go there –

nice to be alone. Cats was crap. No intimacy in the hotel, Mum was next door.

December 9 Highlight: 60% Coming home! The alarm was a great idea and I felt the benefit all the way home. Why are there so many adverts for ice-cream this winter? Mum still next door, but it's the last night. Waiting's exciting.

Iman's focus on the highlight of each day had seemed like a lovely positive primary school teacher thing, but it was beginning to annoy me. I wanted to know more: details, thoughts, dreams, desires. I left the room and the house as I had found them, set the alarm, and I took a chocolate digestive biscuit back next door. (They could easily spare one, they had a double pack and I had none, except at the shop.) I didn't put my shoes on, I just walked down the damp path and home in my socks, it was quicker and so looked more natural.

I made a cup of tea, took my wet socks off, put my shoes on, and ate the biscuit and wanted another immediately, but it would be a reckless thing to go back for and Iman would be nearly out of school. So I checked Tym's cupboard and had one of his biscuits. The presents in the wardrobe were a problem but at least they would be gone in a few weeks, but even so that was a long time for me not to go to Will's house. We're best friends, I need to be with him. I consoled myself with the fact that I was due to go into Tym's wardrobe and investigate that light. Maybe it would be nothing, but at least it was something to do in a wardrobe.

Tym put on his aftershave and went out. He had locked his door, but that's fine because now he knows I have a key that works. The dotted line of light under the wardrobe door looked great. I stood silhouetted against the light of the Heathrow landing in the land of War Drobe, and there, across the dark polished land, at the edge of Lord Macdonald's Forest, was somewhere waiting to be discovered.

I turned on the light and saw that the pile of muesli remained and the hamster house was gone. Still standing in the doorway I started to plot my course across the room, then I turned out the light and barefooted towards the light.

As I started to open the door I felt the heat, it was summer in there. I paused to let it touch my face. There was aluminium foil plastered against the side wall and I wondered if Tym had gone mad. Then I slid the door right across and saw Tym's pot plants, one in flower; it was a tropical forest wrapped in aluminium. I didn't know what to do or what annoyed me most: the disregard for my wishes or this abuse of my electricity. I slammed the door shut and went downstairs. I would ring the police! They would know what to do!

Then I got to the phone and thought about it. This is my house, the police would come round and find cultivated dope plants in my house and I didn't know what they would do. I considered retreating to the flat and calling them, but Tym knows who I am, it could still lead to me and worse Will could get to hear that I lived next door if it went to court. Maybe I would have to compromise. I locked the door on the problem and waited up for Tym, who didn't come home.

I woke up feeling strangely moral, and in this spirit decided I had to replace Will's teapot. It had felt good replacing all the things I'd taken, so I should replace what I'd broken. (I'd even done my best with the door on the cupboard under the stairs.) If I did it today then Iman would never notice anything was wrong and they would not have a surreal argument about how it had been broken which could result in one accusing the other of lying and undermine their marriage. That was the last thing I wanted. But I couldn't be bothered to go to London.

So I rang directory enquiries for the number and telephoned Line Dance Pro Tiger. I even remembered to give the sweet shop address for the express delivery. If Iman didn't find it was broken in the next few days, then she need never know.

*

250

I slept at the shop. The next day I was woken by Edna Crabbe calling up the stairs.

'Mr Fox! *Mr Fox!*' The first thought to creep into my sleep was who is Mr Fox? Then I thought Mr Fox is Dad and I opened my eyes and for a mini-moment seeing myself waking in his room I thought maybe Dad, Mr Fox, was there. But nobody answered to the name of Mr Fox. Edna called again, louder, as she was halfway up the stairs.

'Liam! There's a package here and they need your signature.'

Luckily it had been too cold to get undressed last night so I was able to get up in an instant and get downstairs, passing Edna on the way. Speed was of the essence because whoever had the package was alone in the shop. I greedily signed for it, whatever it was. Of course it was the teapot, nice and early, which was better than ever.

It wasn't until Edna said, 'That looks interesting. What is it?' that I realised Edna wasn't Tracey, or rather realised that Tracey wasn't here working the early shift.

'Where's Tracey? Is she all right? She isn't ill is she?' Edna pretended not to hear.

'What's in the package?' Edna specified with a finger. I pretended not to be listening and went back to bed mumbling without answering her question, because she wouldn't answer mine. I was relieved when I got up in the afternoon to see Tracey working in the shop, but she didn't see me.

I had to get it into the wardrobe without the luxury of the portal and I had to be certain Iman hadn't found out. The only thing for it was to pay my friends a formal visit that evening. I stowed the line-dancing cowboy teapot, still inside its bubblewrap and LINE DANCE PRO TIGER bag, inside a carrier bag from my shop. My plan was simple: while Will was making the tea I would ask Iman what she had bought him for Christmas. This would give her the opportunity to tell me, *would you believe it I bought this excellent teapot, but the blessed/blooming/bloody/*

251

bollocking (I don't know how strongly she'll react) *thing has broken!* If she didn't, then I would excuse myself to go to the toilet and instead switch the bags. I would have at least four minutes while the tea brewed.

As I walked up their garden path I made a mental note to remove my shoes when I got inside; it was a damp Tuesday night and I couldn't risk leaving any footprints on their bedroom carpet. I rang the doorbell. There was no answer, but the lights were on. I rang it again and waited and waited, then flipped open the letterbox just to have a look and saw Jemma coming up the hallway and I let the letterbox snap back into place.

I said, 'Hello, Jemma' just before she opened the door which was a stupid admission that I'd opened the letterbox, or that I had X-ray vision. She put her arm defensively across her chest, just in case.

'What do you want?' She peered into the night. I didn't tell her what I wanted.

'Is Will in?'

'No, he's at line-dancing. It's Tuesday isn't it.'

'Oh yeah,' I admitted, and cursed myself for not realising it was a line-dancing night by the fact that Edna had switched shifts to go. How could I be so careless when I am nothing if not thorough. I asked Jemma, 'Can I wait for him?'

'He's only just left.' Which may be true but it didn't answer my question, so I repeated it.

'So, can I wait for him or not?' Jemma paused and obviously realised that as it was not her house she was not really entitled to decide.

'Iman!' she called and then turned.

Iman came into the hallway and took charge. 'You're letting all the heat out, Jemma.' She obviously knew my silhouette (which is not surprising as it's a famous silhouette – the same as Jimmy Cagney's), and she chided me, 'You don't need to stand on ceremony Liam, come in a minute, it's freezing out there.' I went in and stood on ceremony in the hallway.

Jemma explained to Iman, 'He wanted to see Will.'

'Oh, he's line-dancing. Didn't Edna go tonight?'

I didn't know for sure, so said honestly, 'I wasn't thinking.'

'Well, he's only just gone,' said Iman.

'That's what I said,' Jemma echoed.

I looked down in disappointment and wondered what they would do if I took off my shoes.

'Why don't you stay and have a hot drink before going back out into the breach, Liam?' said Iman and I wished all my teachers had been as nice as her, size 12 pants, 34B bra. I accepted her offer by taking off my shoes.

Their house looked very different from the building I knew. Everything was warm and lit differently. I went into the lounge, Jemma went into the back room and Iman went into the kitchen and called out, 'Tea all right for you, Liam?'

'That would be lovely.'

'Don't forget me,' Jemma called in passing through the hall, then she came into the front room carrying A4 papers and a map rolled up under her arm.

'What's the map for?' I asked.

'The school Christmas play, we've had enough of nativities, too Christian.' She held the map edges up to her face, letting it unwrap and drop down, 'This is Narnia! We were just having a read through, we've written it all ourselves.' And she put down the ream of paper. 'How's your acting, Liam?'

I acted as if the question was rhetorical and didn't bother answering.

Iman carried in the tea-tray and motioned for Jemma to move the paper to make space. I said, 'Shall I be mother?' and started to pour out the tea.

'Your acting's very good, Liam,' Jemma said to both me and Iman. I think I went red, she's seen me in just a small towel after all.

'Any chance of a chocolate digestive biscuit?' I said, handing Iman her tea.

'Er, sorry, we've run out,' she lied. It had to be a lie, there was a double pack only yesterday. But this was good, I should've had a biscuit (tea and biscuits, that's the phrase isn't it?) and didn't. So, maybe that meant I didn't owe them for the chocolate digestive I'd taken yesterday? We were nearly even.

WILLIAM

THE LYING WITCH AND THE WARDROBE
By Iman West and Jemma Clare

DRAMATIS PERSONAE

THE PROFESSOR, guardian of the evacuees,
played by **Jemma Clare**
IVY, servant to the professor, played by **Rhona Law**
MARGARET, servant, played by **Iman West**
BETTY, servant, played by **Angus Law**

PETER, evacuee, played by **Ryan Law**
SUSAN, evacuee, played by **Sunetra Behari**
EDMUND, evacuee, played by **Miles Lacy**
LUCY, played by **Stacy Middleton**

MR BEAVER, played by **Ian Williams**
MRS BEAVER, played by **Blaze Fish**

ASLAN, played by **Dean Martin**
ASLAN'S ARMY of Dryads (tree women), Naiads (well-women), Centaurs, Unicorns, Bull with man's head, Pelicans, Eagles and two Great Dogs, played by **Class 2C**

THE WITCH, played by **Terry Armitage**
WITCH'S DWARF, played by **Michael Fish**
WITCH'S ARMY of Werewolves, Tree Spirits, Ghouls, Boggles, Ogres, Minotaurs, Cruels, Hags, Spectres, Toadstool People, played by **Class 4A**

Santa Claus is played by himself.

The action takes places in Narnia, where it was always winter and never Christmas, until now.

257

I was missing the line-dancing Christmas party for this, but it was going to be worth it. My scores in the diary had been too low recently to take any chances, especially so near to Christmas. Iman and Jemma had put a lot of work into this play, so it was the least I could do to come and watch it. I was a little surprised that Liam was so up for it though.

I sat back in my seat and tried to get comfortable. The stage at Iman's school is pretty impressive, but the seats were made for children. My knees were pointing upwards. The most comfortable I could get was to sit with the palms of my hands placed over my knees. At least it was nice and warm in the hall, and there was the familiar smell of freshly cleaned school floors. It reminded me of my school, they must still use the same cleaning stuff in every one.

The hall was half full, with brothers and sisters and mums and dads. Immediately in front of us was a young boy and girl, flanked by their parents. We had an ideal view of the stage over the kids' heads.

Liam opened a can of beer.

'Want some?'

'Liam! We can't drink beer in here.'

'Oh, fuck. Um; sorry.' And now he had sworn in front of the children. Liam waved the beer can around, looking for somewhere to put it. 'What shall I do with it then?' There was no easy answer to that; in fact, the easiest thing to do was to drink it.

'You'd better down it,' I said, and he obliged, and let out a near silent, gassy burp. The children in front turned round to laugh. Liam raised his empty can to their good health. Children have such excellent hearing, but at least he didn't swear in front of them again. Their parents fidgeted in their child-sized seats.

The stage set was impressive. On the left was a lamp-post. Iman told me that when this was turned on, looking like a winter moon, it represented that the stage was Narnia. (There was a note about this in the two-page programme. When it's turned off, we are to assume the stage is the world of men.) Then there were some steps up and down, to be mountains, hills, long walks, the witch's castle and the professor's house. Centre-stage was the main event, the wardrobe itself. When I went shopping with Iman and Jemma we'd not been able to buy this. The headmaster, Terry Armitage, had bought it, and he was playing the witch.

'Magnificent, isn't it?' said Liam. Again I was surprised by his enthusiasm for the project.

'Yes. I suppose it is rather an achievement.'

'Hmm?' he said like I'd interrupted him. 'I was talking about the wardrobe. Magnificent; don't you think?'

'Yes. Yes, it's rather a beauty isn't it.' But before we got to discuss anything else on the stage, Terry Armitage came out of the wardrobe, dressed as the wicked witch.

'He's coming out of the closet!' said Liam, just loud enough for me to wonder how many beers he'd had. It made the dad in front of us laugh though.

The children booed. The mums and dads booed. Liam nearly pissed himself laughing.

The witch hissed. The lights dimmed, then, the lamp-post was turned on, like a winter moon, and we were all in Narnia.

Iman and Jemma sat on the far right of the stage. Jemma was dressed as the professor. The children in the play are evacuees staying with him. It's his house and his wardrobe. Iman played Margaret, one of the professor's servants. This was their conceit, to tell it from the servants' and professor's point of view; plus, if they were on stage the kids wouldn't muck about like no one could really see them.

I watched Iman, she was an absolute fox. Seeing her up on stage, in her element, as a teacher, in something that she'd made up – in another

259

world – she was a total fox. She looked way better than Jemma – although Jemma was dressed as an old man.

Stuff happened in the play. A little girl came on stage and looked amazed to see the audience and the magical world of Narnia. She waved to her mum.

A boy came on stage and the witch got him. Liam booed like a demon. The witch gave the boy Turkish Delight from the box with the red light in it that glowed. I felt some pride as I'd gone shopping for that box. The boy remarked that he loved Turkish Delight and that his family had it every Christmas. The witch was furious. Liam laughed, he repeated what the witch said, how it was said, but in a whisper, 'Christmas! No! Always winter, never Christmas.' He laughed again.

'I don't think it's a joke,' I told him. How many beers had this guy had?

More kids came on stage and stuff.

Then it was the turn of Mr and Mrs Beaver. Their masks were pretty good. I thought Liam was going to burst. He rocked in his chair. He couldn't contain himself, every time any of the kids said Mr, or Mrs, Beaver he laughed like a car skidding.

I weighed it up. I had three options. 1: Do nothing, keep quiet, hope he calms down. After all, if I tell him to shut it, I'd be disturbing other people. 2: Tell him to go and calm down. 3: Take him outside. I chose option 2. Maybe I should have taken him outside and we could've sat in my car, but I had to see this play. Iman would want to know what I thought and I'd not even read the Narnia book, I didn't even know the story. I was never that type of child. The next time the witch came on and there was a severe round of booing I took my chance.

'Liam? Liam!' I said. He turned to me, crying with laughter between boos. 'Why don't you go and calm down a bit?'

'I've got all this booing to do.' He booed.

'Seriously,' I said. 'You're too pissed for this, you're too loud, at the wrong parts. It's for kids; beaver isn't a joke for kids. Go, calm down, and meet me back here at half-time.'

'Oh all right.' He stood abruptly. 'Half-time it is then.'

Our row was fairly empty, he didn't disturb too many people as he made his way out. The children in front of us turned and watched him leave.

The play went on nicely. Aslan came on in the lion's mask that I'd spotted in the shop. Kids got turned to stone, and nearly held their statue poses. The witch was now accompanied by a dwarf, who I recognised straight away as the guy from line-dancing. Of course; I made the connection, his daughter was playing Mrs Beaver. I'd thought the surname was familiar when I read the cast list. When he first came on there was a collective intake of breath from the audience. But soon they were comfortable with the idea of a dwarf playing a dwarf. He was a school parent governor after all.

The dwarf and the witch were worried about Aslan coming to liberate Narnia. Apparently he was on the move, the ice and snow were starting to melt. I was worried about where Liam had gone. I should've given him the car keys. Except he seemed in such a strange, tipsy mood, giving him car keys could have been a mistake. It was too cold for him to wait outside till half-time. I wondered where he was.

The play got tense. Edmund, the evacuee boy who the wicked witch had got addicted to Turkish Delight, was about to be killed. The dwarf and the witch tied him up. There was a pause, followed by another one. The father of the family in the next row coughed. There was a third and final pause. Iman prompted with a whisper, '*Ow! You're hurting me.*'

'Eh?' said Edmund, turning to face his teacher.

'*Ow, you're hurting me,*' repeated Iman.

'Hurting you? What about me? I could get killed here!' said Edmund. The audience belly-laughed.

I didn't laugh, I wasn't convinced he was playing it for laughs. I reckon he was actually scared of the witch and the dwarf, after all it's his headmaster and a parent governor. I don't think he forgot his lines, I think he was just too scared to speak, there's a difference.

As the laughter rippled away the momentum of the scene went with it. The witch improvised a little, retightening the ropes around Edmund, getting his dwarf to expose his neck ready for his head to be chopped off. Iman and Jemma looked to the edge of the stage and nodded.

261

A whole pack of kids (unicorns, centaurs, a minatour, a bird, two dogs) bundled on to the stage, shouting. They freed Edmund and generally ran around like they were in the playground. A unicorn bumped into the wardrobe, his horn crumpled and he gulped in air like he was about to cry. The unicorn looked into the darkness of the audience for his mum. The wardrobe wobbled, and slowly its door swung open. There was another, bigger, belly-laugh from the audience: a big beer-belly of a laugh.

Liam turned round inside the wardrobe to blink at the bright lights of the stage. I blinked, in disbelief, at Liam. Iman and Jemma looked at Liam, then looked at each other. Liam gave a nod of acknowledgement to the laughing audience, before reaching out from the wardrobe and closing the door. Except, he couldn't shut it tight, and had to hold it closed with the tip of his index finger still visible.

'Ladies and gentlemen,' said the witch − well, he said it in his head-master's voice actually − 'there will now be a fifteen-minute interval. Tea and orange squash are available in the canteen.'

I queued up and got two cups of tea. I wasn't getting Liam a cup of tea out of kindness, he didn't deserve that, I was getting two cups of tea so that I didn't look like I was here alone. Iman and Jemma would be busy shepherding the kids during half-time, I knew that before I came. Liam homed in on his cup of tea.

'Oh you're a saviour.' He took the plastic cup by the rim, it was too hot to hold it anywhere else. 'You wouldn't believe what just happened to me,' he went on.

'Wouldn't believe it?' I said, in disbelief. 'I saw it! We all saw it.' I circled my cup of tea around at all the mums and dads and brothers and sis-ters. I circled it so vigorously that when I stopped the tea was whirlpooling. 'What were you doing, Liam?'

'Oh yeah, that.'

'What do you mean "Oh yeah, that"? You appear, as if by magic, in the wardrobe of The Lying Witch and the Wardrobe, during a primary school play, and all you can say, is "Oh yeah, that"?' I dreaded to think what mark Iman would give today in her diary.

262

'Did everyone see me then?'

'Of course! You were on the stage!'

'I was hiding.'

'Hiding! Hiding? You were on the fucking stage, man.' I did check that there were no children in our immediate vicinity before swearing.

'I was still hiding. I went round the back, to find the toilet, after you told me to go and calm down. And after that I went and sat backstage. It's only round there,' he pointed.

'I know where backstage is! It's behind the stage.'

'Right. So, I was there. Waiting, for half-time.'

'And?'

'I saw Wesley. He saw me. So, I walked off and went into the nearest classroom. He followed me, so I kept walking, across the classroom – which had costumes hung up – and out the other door; I thought it was a cupboard.'

'Ginger Jesus Harry Christ!' There was a child, drinking squash just in front of me now, but I couldn't help myself.

'Yeah, I know. I was lucky to find anywhere to hide. Maybe he's got a brother or something in the play?'

'Maybe he's got his dad in the audience?'

We put down our cups of tea and went to the car.

We picked up our cups of tea in the safety of my front room. Liam broke the silence, 'Love the Christmas tree.'

'Thanks.' I looked at the tree and the image of the Christmas tree youth flashed into my head. I looked at our reflection in the baubles.

'It looks great. Really fucking great.' Liam bent down to look at the wrapped presents. 'That all the gifts is it? That everything?'

'Everything so far. I'm not telling you which one's yours if that's what you're after.' Liam laughed and went back to sipping his tea, he was so easy to see through sometimes. I tried not to think about the Christmas tree youth, it had been bad enough putting up the decorations. We needed to think about Wesley.

I said, 'Let's talk about tonight. It seems to me there are three possibilities. One: It was Wesley and he recognised you. Two: It was Wesley and he didn't recognise you, not for certain. Three: It was someone who looked like Wesley, say his younger brother or something.'

Liam stopped sipping his tea, so I started to sip mine to let him speak.

'Number one, it was Wesley, he did see me and he did recognise me.'

I swallowed hard on the hot tea. 'That's a possibility. But don't dismiss the other two options, or maybe even a combination of them. Say, it *was* Wesley but he didn't recognise you, he was just following you.'

'Or maybe it was someone who looked like Wesley, wasn't Wesley but did recognise me!' Liam was right, this was getting absurd. But he carried on, 'I know it was him, he looked a bit like a cricket bat. I remembered that. He looked a bit like the actor Kevin Bacon did as a kid.'

'What? How do you know?' I had finished my tea, drinking it too hot through the nerves.

Liam stared at the television, it wasn't even on. 'Maybe that's it. It wasn't Wesley if it was the actor Kevin Bacon as a kid.'

'Ok, ok, don't take the piss.'

'I'm not.'

'All I was thinking was that you didn't do much to him. You got there a bit late, he might not remember you – we were both in disguise.'

Liam finished his tea and went to make some more. The shock of seeing Wesley and the tea had really helped him to sober up.

Wesley was the past, it just wasn't like me. Maybe that risk of him seeing me at the school was as bad as this would ever get. Liam would never tell, Wesley might never be believed. If only I could accept what I had done, it could be over.

I still had to face Iman though. She would be angry with Liam, but I had to be glad he did it, glad he'd found somewhere to hide. Although I'm not sure it still counts as hiding when everyone else can see you. At least I understood his motivation – he did it for me, he did it for us.

Liam came back with the cups of tea, he'd also found the chocolate biscuits. Bit presumptuous, but we could do with a bit of comfort food. I fancied some peanut butter on toast.

'Peanut butter on toast, Liam?' I offered, as he dunked his biscuit.

'Why?' he said and stopped, mid-dunk.

'I'm having some, want some?'

He thought about it, thought about it so long that his biscuit disintegrated into his tea. He finally answered, 'Yes.'

We waited for the toast to pop.

'Thanks for hiding, Liam.' He looked slightly suspicious. 'I mean you did it for us really, thank you.'

'No problem. Iman's going to be annoyed though, isn't she? I mean if everyone noticed me, she's going to be really annoyed, angry even. That's my invite to Christmas dinner out the window. You can't tell her I did it for us, can you?'

'Of course not, but just because she doesn't know doesn't change why you did it.'

'True,' he said. 'I like that.'

The toast popped. We had a slice each and I put two more back in.

'Peanut butter?' I offered. 'It's crunchy.'

Liam narrowed his eyes, 'I'd prefer smooth.'

'I don't think we've got any.' I gave the cupboard another glance. 'Oh, hang on, you're in luck.'

He had the smooth, I had the crunchy.

'Tell you what, Liam. I'll invite you for Christmas right now. Then it won't matter about Iman's invite.'

'I was only joking.'

'We've discussed it. You're all right, you're welcome.' It was his first Christmas on his own without his dad, I dearly wanted him to come.

'Yeah?'

'Yeah.'

'What do you think I should buy Iman for Christmas?' he asked.

'If I had any ideas I wouldn't tell you! I don't even know what I'm going to get her.'

'You could get her a cat.'

The toast popped.

'That's not really on, giving a pet for Christmas, is it?'

'That's only if you're not certain. We both know she loves cats. I bet she'd like another one.'

'I don't know, I have asked if she wants a cat for Christmas. She thinks it might be too soon after Aslan. I mean he's not been dead long at all.' I felt so clumsy, mentioning the death of a cat to him like that. It was nothing to him, he'd lost his dad. I wanted to tell him I loved him and that I would do anything I could to see him through his first Christmas alone. Instead I said, 'Jemma asked me yesterday if she could get Iman a cat for Christmas, I told her no.'

'If Jemma's not getting her one that's all the more reason for you to. It's a good idea. I don't think it's too soon. It's too soon for Iman to go and buy one – that would be disloyal – but if you buy it all she's got to do is want it. I think she'd like another cat.'

It was a good idea and I could always check her diary for hints. This conversation had given my toast time to cool. I eagerly put the peanut butter on and it had gone lovely and crunchy. Crunchy toast and crunchy peanut butter, magnificent.

Liam continued, 'Get a tomcat and call it Tom. It's the name that makes sense.'

'Tom; Tommy, Tom-Toms.' I tried out the name for size.

'No! It's just Tom. Not tom-toms – that's a type of drum for fuck's sake. You should get a tomcat and call it Tom.'

'Ok,' I said, with a mouthful of toast.

'Excellent.' Liam said it with such force I wondered what I had agreed to. So I backed up a little.

'If I get her a cat, I'll get a tom and call it Tom.'

'Do it, Will. Believe me, it's not too soon after Aslan's death. I know if you could get me a dad for Christmas, I'd take it!'

'What?' I thought I'd be introducing this into the conversation, not comparing his dad to a dead cat, it wasn't right. 'What do you mean *a dad*, what about your dad?'

'Well, if you could get him that'd be brilliant!'

I was at a loss for words. All I could think to say was, 'Do you want that toast?' It was still stood in the toaster. I took it, but in fact it had gone a little too crunchy and shattered under the knife.

We moved back into the lounge. I had an Irish coffee, Liam had an Irish tea, I think he made it up. I was in trouble with Iman, a lot of trouble. I wanted Liam to be gone before she got home. But we had time, all the second half of the play and then some.

'I'm in trouble with Iman,' I told Liam.

'Why are you in trouble? I mean I know I owe her an apology, because someone was bound to have seen me in that wardrobe, but why are you in trouble?'

The full answer was that I felt some group responsibility with Liam, but that was just guilt because I couldn't explain it to her. I simplified it, 'I'm in trouble because I missed the second half of the play she's put blood, sweat and tears into.'

Liam was silent for a moment. 'If you know you are in trouble then you are not in trouble.'

'Eh?' I should've known that giving him whiskey was a bad idea, he seemed to be racing back to the point of drunkenness he had reached at the play.

'You're only in real trouble when you don't know you're in trouble. When you think everything is going ok.'

'I've missed the play though.'

'But how will she know? I mean, I've been on that stage and I can tell you, you can't see anyone in the crowd.'

'Yeah, but even so—' He cut me off and poured more whiskey into our drinks.

'Well, I read through the play with her and Jemma, the other Tuesday, when I was waiting for you to come back from line-dancing. I know what happens in the second half. I'll tell you, then all you do is mention a bit of it to Iman and she'll assume you saw the lot. You don't even need to lie.'

'That could work.'

'Of course it could. Implied knowledge – it got me through university. Ok, then, where were we in the play?'

'Edward was about to be killed . . .'

Liam interrupted, 'Edmund, it's Edmund, not Edward.' This was going to be harder than I thought. 'Yes, I remember, Edmund was about to be killed by the witch – she'd got him addicted to Turkish Delight – then he was rescued by Aslan's army, played by class 2C I believe. Then, the second half starts with . . . with . . .' Liam shut his eyes to try and remember.

'Look, how much detail do I need? Remember, like you said, implied knowledge. You just give me some facts, any facts, I'll mention something to Iman that I couldn't know unless I'd stayed for the second half and she'll assume the rest. Just like you said.'

'Ok, ok. Right then. Aslan's army can't catch the witch and the dwarf because they're standing there as trees.'

'Trees?'

'Yes, trees; they're watching Aslan's army looking for them. So they give up looking and take Edmund back to see Aslan.'

'Ok, no problem.'

'No problem! What about the fact that the witch and the dwarf follow them to find Aslan! The audience shout *behind you*! I don't know why they bother, they never see them.'

'Well, they shout that a lot at pantomimes. That's why.'

'Oh,' said Liam, it gave me some confidence, I knew more about this play than I thought, maybe this would work. 'So, they lead the witch right to Aslan. The witch and Aslan strike a bargain, that she won't kill Edmund, instead she'll kill Aslan. He sacrifices himself, gets killed, everyone worries, but then he comes back to life.'

'Resurrected?'

'Like John Travolta's career! But the witch is such an evil slag she decides to kill Edmund anyway, thinking Aslan's dead.'

'Oh.' I decided I was glad I never read this book as a boy, it sounded too far-fetched.

'You see, there's this prophesy about people coming to Narnia and taking it from the witch.'

'Do you want some more tea in your whiskey?'

'No. Listen, it's nearly over. The witch has turned a load of children, centaurs, pelicans and all that, into statues. When there's a big battle at her castle, Edmund redeems himself by knocking her wand away – and it's the wand she used to make people into statues; did I make that clear?'

I realised I wasn't listening. 'Er, yeah. That's fine.' The nerves about lying to Iman mixed with the whiskey were making me anxious. Liam had to be gone by the time Iman got in. She would be angry with him. I tried to finish up. 'Let me guess, we're close enough. Aslan sorts it all out?'

'Well, yes, he's a Christ figure and then it's Christmas.'

'All right. It's all ok in the end.'

'You need details, Will, if you only remember one thing, remember this bit. Father Christmas comes on at the end of the play.'

'Father Christmas? So, all that winter and never Christmas stuff is over.'

'Yes, but Iman got it perfect. She got the real Father Christmas.'

'How?'

'He works in Debenhams department store each year. He has a sleigh with DEBENHAMS on the side. When he comes on stage, throwing out presents, the audience go crazy!'

'That's the bit I'll tell Iman I liked most then.'

'And tell her that Father Christmas throws out sponges. Iman's been so thorough, I like nothing more than thoroughness, all the gifts he throws out are bath sponges, wrapped up in Christmas paper of course.'

'I get it, I get it! Sponges, so he can throw them and no one gets hurt.'

'And they are a good gift for a child or an adult.'

'Perfect.'

'Father Christmas. Makes me think a bit of Dad, that. You know, fathers and Christmas. Stupid isn't it?'

Not now, Liam, I thought. There would be plenty of time for me to console and support him over Christmas.

'I expect you'll be wanting to make a move soon, eh Liam? It's a bit of a walk home.'

'It's not that far,' he said, pouring us both more whiskey.

Liam didn't make it home: we finished the bottle and he stood to leave but fell over. I shut the door and left him there on the sofa. I thought about leaving Iman a note telling her he was in the lounge, but it didn't matter, she was certain to come straight to bed, it was a work night after all. I would pretend to be asleep, it seemed safest. It was all tactics. This way I could pretend she'd woken me, gain some sympathy and delay any discussion about the play until the morning at the earliest.

I fell asleep and she did wake me. I dreamed that I was being beaten about the temples, hard unforgiving blows aimed at the middle of my brain. Iman was hitting me. Not hitting me so it hurt, just hitting me so that I knew I'd been hit. I love her so much that the fact she wanted to hurt me, hurt me more.

'Will, Will! You stupid man.'

'Ok, ok, I'm awake.' I shielded my eyes from any more blows before opening them. I saw what she'd been hitting me with and my heart sank down into my balls. She was holding her diary.

'I thought we'd been through all this?' I decided not to reply, I didn't know how much trouble I was in. I wanted to know what she knew. She slapped me around the face with the blue school exercise book. 'But no, you've been through all this! How could you? After that time with the chip grease and I caught you out. You promised me, Will. What do our marriage vows mean if I can't believe your promises?' That was some leap from the diary to our marriage vows. I was in trouble – but at least I knew it. She was getting louder, I thought about Liam downstairs, hoping he was too drunk to wake up. I didn't want any witnesses to this humiliation.

I played for time. I rubbed my eyes and my cheek where the book had slapped me. How did she know about the diary? I hadn't even read it tonight. And why was she intending to write up today this late?

270

Normally she would be happy to wait until tomorrow. It didn't make sense, I thought I was dreaming.

'Am I dreaming? Pinch me,' I whispered. Iman leapt at the request and grabbed two handfuls of kidney and twisted. I writhed and pushed her away. 'I thought I might be dreaming!' I said. 'That's all. This doesn't make any sense, what are you on about?'

'You fucking fucker!' she shouted, but I forgave her, I knew for a fact she wouldn't ever swear like this in front of our children. 'You have the sang-froid to lie there and tell me that!' I wanted to check with her what sang-froid meant, but kept quiet. I couldn't understand what I'd done wrong with the diary. I must've made a mistake so I only had myself to blame. But when? And how? Then I saw it. The diary had fallen open on the bed beside me.

February 9 Highlight: 54% Talked about going to Dublin for our summer holiday, Will made a crap joke, 'Did you know that's the fastest growing city in Europe?' 'No.' 'Yeah, it's always Dublin!' Painful. I'll get Jemma with it tomorrow.

I remembered the joke, crap jokes, yet more practice for being a father. I felt some guilt that we didn't even go to Dublin. But it was the date that leapt out and hit me in the face. This was the old diary, volume one, that I couldn't find after the burglary. The one that Iman had told me, in her own good time, that she couldn't find.

I was in trouble, big trouble, because I didn't understand what was happening. I couldn't think of anything to say and Iman was silent. This made it harder for me to keep quiet. I reached out to her but she moved back. Jesus I was in trouble. I decided that I should tell the truth.

'I don't understand,' I said. No reaction. 'Really, Iman, I don't understand. You said that the diary was lost in the burglary. How could I have it?' I glanced down again at the exercise book, it was right next to me. How could that be the truth? How could I not know how I had it when it was right there? I wondered again if I was asleep. Iman walked out of the room and I thought for a moment I would hear

271

the front door slam as she left me. Instead I heard her in the bath-room.

My mind was frozen, volume one of this year's diary was just next to me. Was she testing me to see if I'd read it? (There was little point, I'd already read it.) From Iman's point of view it was difficult, she couldn't put it away without giving away its hiding place. But she must now know I knew the hiding place? But when I checked there after the bur-glary it wasn't there.

She was back and pulling a blanket out of the cupboard over her wardrobe.

'I'm going to sleep in the box room. You're too drunk and I'm too tired to discuss this now.' She turned to go, but I was up and out of the bed too quickly for her.

'It's ok, you have the bed. I'll go in the box room.' She let me take the blanket from her and I was gone. I went and got my puffa jacket too, the blanket didn't seem thick enough to keep me warm all night. Downstairs I thought of Liam in the lounge. Here I was worried about the cold and he didn't even have anything over him. I clicked on the cen-tral heating and went to bed. Also, Iman was more likely to be approachable in the morning if she was warm.

Eight steps up the alarm burst out like a bomb. How was I to know Iman had set it?

I woke up early, I didn't feel hungover (making me think I was still drunk) and went downstairs. There was the smell of grapefruit. I wanted to get Liam out of the house before Iman woke. After his stage per-formance last night he was the last person she would want to see.

Liam wasn't in the lounge and he wasn't in the kitchen or the bath-room. There was a definite smell of grapefruit. I went into the dining room and there, large as life, was my neighbour, Tim, outlining the seg-ments of a grapefruit with a knife.

'Good morning good neighbour!' he chirped. I nodded and won-dered, as the tea brewed, if I had only dreamed that I had woken up. How could my neighbour be here eating grapefruit? I never buy grapefruit. Maybe it was a dream in which Liam had become Tim. But that was bollocks. The tea was hot and strong.

I put Iman's tea beside her on the floor, she sensed it and woke up.

'Oh, you're an angel.' Obviously she'd forgotten how angry she was with me.

'Have you been buying grapefruit?'

'Grapefruit?' she squinted at me and I realised I wasn't making any sense.

'Tim, our neighbour, from the party, he's downstairs eating grapefruit.'

'Aha!' she said. 'Tim, from next door, well from Poland actually, he's Jemma's new boyfriend. We introduced them if only we'd known it. He was drinking with us after the show. Jemma and him stayed over in the guest room.'

'Oh,' I said, thinking how lucky it was I'd gone to the box room. Then I thought how a burglar alarm is no use to a house full of sleeping drunks. I'd set it off last night and no one had responded, but this was better than Tim, Jemma, Iman and Liam all descending on me like an intruder in my own house. The idea made me smile. 'And the grapefruit?'

'No idea.'

Maybe I had a few more seconds before Iman remembered about the diary and Liam and last night. I had to be quick.

'I liked the play,' I began, more smiles. 'Especially Father Christmas at the end. Throwing out sponges, nice touch, people loved it.'

Iman looked surprised. 'What about the whale song?' Shit, Liam didn't say anything about a whale song.

'What about it?'

'Well, in the book it's meant to be the songs of mermaids and mermen, we thought whalesong would do – it was meant to be on when the children were crowned, at the end.'

I nodded. 'I don't remember it,' I said, pretty neutral.

'Exactly.' Iman swung out of bed. 'The tape didn't work.' She went to the bathroom. I had a few moments, I looked around the room, the diary had been hidden away again. Good. Iman came back, now fully awake.

273

'Fucking hell Will, must you always leave the toilet seat up?'

'I haven't. We've got guests, remember?' I mentioned them to avoid all the arguments I was owed. 'Maybe it was Tim?' Maybe it was Liam, but I didn't dare mention his name.

'It's not just now, you keep doing it. You! You keep doing it!' I was in trouble, I didn't know why, but at least I knew I was in trouble.

Buying Iman a cat for Christmas was a great idea. I needed to make it all up to her. After work I went to Liam's shop, I wanted him to help me choose a cat and I'd need him to mind it till Christmas.

I looked in and saw Edna at the counter, serving a customer. The shop was light and the night dark, so she couldn't see me. I watched her for a bit. In the window I noticed a postcard, just the ticket, in the *Advertise here for £1 a week* section, KITTENS AVAILABLE, FREE TO GOOD HOMES. I went in as the customer came out. I held the door open for him.

'Hello Edna, how are you?'

'Oh, William, how nice to see you. You missed a marvellous Christmas party last night at line-dancing. Balloons, cake, everything. Everyone was there.'

'Everyone?'

'Oh, everyone, except you.'

'And Mr Fish.'

'Mr Fish?' Edna thought aloud. 'Of course, the dwarf gentleman. Can we still use that word? He's a lovely dancer.'

I went to the shop window, took out the kittens postcard and walked past the counter.

'Is he in?'

'Liam? No. I don't think he's here much at all nowadays. Must be staying with his fancy woman.'

'Fancy woman?'

'Of course he hasn't told me, but I know the signs.'

'Well, I think I'd know, Edna, if there was a fancy woman.' I walked back out the shop. 'See you next week at line-dancing,' but realised, as the shop door closed behind me, that next week there was no line-dancing because of Christmas.

I stopped at a phone box to call up about the kittens. Obviously I couldn't do it from home. I dialled carefully and the man who answered repeated the number and said, 'Hello?'

'Hello, I've rung about the kittens.'

'Not you again!'

'No,' I answered truthfully, it was my first call.

'How many times. I don't have any kittens. I used to breed chinchillas, but that was in the past. Where did you get this number?' But he hung up before I could answer.

These were strange times that I was living in. And I turned into my own drive with a heavy heart, bracing myself for the row with Iman I was owed about the diary.

Iman called out as soon as I got through the door.

'Will!' she held out the phone. 'Liam,' she said and walked off upstairs.

'How de-do-de?' he said.

'Ok,' I lied. 'Well, I've had a bit of a strange day.'

'Strange day?'

'Yeah. It started off strange, I got up to find my neighbour in here eating grapefruit.'

'No! No way. Your neighbour?'

'What do you mean no. He was here, large as life.'

'Hang on. Eating grapefruit?'

'Yes. Which I never buy. Anyway, why did you ring?'

'I was just apologising to Iman. About being in the wardrobe. I left dead early this morning to avoid her, give her time to calm down.'

'Oh.'

'Being in the wardrobe during the play.'

'I know.' I checked Iman wasn't within earshot, it was all ok, I heard the toilet flush, there was no way she could hear. 'And I've just had a strange time phoning up about some kittens advertised on a postcard in your shop.'

'My shop?'

'Yeah. I got an ex-chinchilla breeder with a persecution complex.'

'Yes,' said Liam, and I was amazed he even pretended to understand. He laughed. 'Those cards are years old. I leave a few up to build up trade, to make it look in use. They'll be cats by now.'

'Right. Well, he's obviously had a few calls about them by the way he talked.' We both laughed about it. 'I need you to help me get a cat.' Liam carried on laughing and the sound of his laughter made me laugh even more.

Iman came down the stairs. 'Did you leave that toilet seat up on purpose, Will? Just to annoy me?'

I didn't answer, but maybe Liam heard her because he said, 'I'd better let you go. Bye mate.'

'Bye mate,' I agreed.

Had I left the toilet seat up? I'd only just got in for fuck's sake, I'd been at work all day. She couldn't blame me, it couldn't even be true, Iman must be making it up, just looking for an argument.

'Are you going to answer me, William?'

William, she called me William, the full name, the works, Wil*liam*. I was in trouble and I knew it.

'What about, *Iman*?' I emphasised her name as much as I could, but cursed her that I couldn't lengthen it. I'd much rather just get on to the diary argument, forget this supporting bout about the toilet seat, but no.

'Answer me, about the toilet seat, about leaving it up to annoy me. That'll do for starters.'

It wasn't even true, how could it be? Iman was definitely looking for an argument and she certainly would not be disappointed.

WILLIAM

OUR DUMB FRIENDS' LEAGUE
(Incorporating The Cyan Cross)
ADOPTION FORM

Ref. No . . . . . .

Stray . . . .

This agreement is in respect of ...... _Smokey and The Bandit_ ......
(animal's name)

Species and description ...... _2 domestic cats, unspecific breed_ ......

Thank you for offering a new home to one of our animals. In the interests of responsible pet ownership, Our Dumb Friends' League asks you to read, sign and abide by the code below. Your attention is drawn to Clause 11.

CODE OF ADOPTION

'Every care is taken by Our Dumb Friends' League to ensure that the animal you are taking to a new home is in good health and we are happy to offer any advice you need. However, if the animal exhibits any abnormalities or illness within one month, please inform us immediately. In emergencies you should seek the advice of a qualified Veterinary Surgeon. You are responsible for all veterinary costs from the date of adoption.'

All adoptions from Our Dumb Friends' League are conditional on the following points being agreed:

DECLARATION

As the new owner:
1 I agree to give the animal a good, caring home.
2 I am willing to allow a representative of Our Dumb Friends' League to visit the animal and check on its welfare at any time. In the event of Our Dumb Friends' League representative deciding that the conditions in which the animal is kept and/or its state of health and welfare are not satisfactory, I will allow the animal to be repossessed by Our Dumb Friends' League in accordance with Clause 11 of this Declaration.
3 I promise that the animal will in no circumstances be sold, abandoned or given into other hands and that if I am unable to keep or maintain it, I will return it to Our Dumb Friends' League.

4   Should the animal go missing, I will take all practicable steps to find it as soon as possible and will inform Our Dumb Friends' League and the police immediately.

5   I understand that where the animal came to Our Dumb Friends' League as a stray and is claimed by its owner within one month, Our Dumb Friends' League may request its return. I agree to return the animal in that event.

6   I will not allow the animal, if female, to produce a litter, or if male, to sire a litter. I understand that neutering is the procedure recommended by Our Dumb Friends' League.

7   I will keep the animal fully vaccinated and de-wormed throughout its life.

8   I will not allow the animal to be a nuisance to others or to worry livestock.

9   I will notify Our Dumb Friends' League of any change of address.

10 I agree to make full provision for the animal should I leave it unsupervised.

11 I have read and understood the above and realise that I am responsible for the animal's future health and that should I fail to comply in any way with the terms of this declaration, or if Our Dumb Friends' League considers it to be in the interests of the animal to do so, Our Dumb Friends' League, at its absolute discretion, may recover possession of the animal.

Signed .... **Liam Fox** ....

Date .... **22nd December** ....

Name (please print) .... **LIAM FOX** ....

Address (please print) .... **23 LIME STREET, OAKLEY** ....

.... **SOUTHAMPTON** ....Post Code .... **SO6 9EE** ....

Signed on behalf of Our Dumb Friends' League ....

.... **Lesley van der Sar** ....

There was a man and a woman working at Our Dumb Friends' League. The man looked like Dolly Parton, if she was a man. And the woman looked like Kenny Rogers, if he was a woman. He had long blond big hair; she had a wispy dusting of grey beard. Grey hairs lingered on her face, focused on the top lip and underneath her chin. This was a change, I thought: people had been looking like movie stars, with a twist, but these people looked like country and western singers who did a little bit of acting. I was obviously getting better.

There were a lot of cats to choose from. I already knew I was going to get two. Will was meant to come with me to choose, but I was ahead of him. We decided to go on the Saturday afternoon when I knew, from Iman's diary, that she wanted him to go Christmas food shopping. Perfect, I went with his blessing and his fifty quid. Will even thanked me for helping him out. He wanted a cat over six months old, not a kitten – that was the only remit he gave me; other than that I was on my own. In his position I would have been more thorough. I was aching to ask what Tym was doing in his house. But I didn't think I could pull it off without the anxiety and desperation showing in my voice. I would have to wait and ask Tym.

At Our Dumb Friends' League you get the cats for free. The taxi there and back cost a lot, but Will was paying. Going there, I didn't get the taxi driver who looked like Tom Cruise. On the way back I avoided looking into the cabbie's face, I was reading a leaflet

281

from Our Dumb Friends' League, so I don't know who he looked like.

Smokey and The Bandit were brother cat and sister cat. Smokey was, predictably enough, grey. The Bandit was white, with a ginger spot on the top of her head and shoulders, just where Nicole Kidman has her ginger hair. I renamed them Tom and Jerry. Will would give Tom the tom like we discussed and I would give Jerry. I decided not to ask Will's permission about the second cat, I would just do it. When Iman saw how beautiful Jerry was, snowy white with that marmalade patch of hair, she would fall in love and want to keep her for ever.

Because I couldn't risk Will seeing them I would keep the cats at my house. If he came round to the flat I would tell him the cat was at the vet being neutered. I wasn't happy about this lie, and I would have to say cat, singular, but remembering would not be a problem because I'm so thorough. At least both Tom and Jerry were already sterilised which would eventually give my story the veneer of truth, and I would be careful to give Will the right change from the fifty pounds.

'Our Dumb Friends' League Information Leaflet 3: Your Rehomed Cat' is a very informative guide. *For the first two days, it may be advisable to keep your new cat in a room of its own – a utility room or equivalent is ideal.* I would lock Tom and Jerry into my bedroom. I had no alternative, but it was good to know that this was actually the right thing to do.

A cardboard box with a small hole cut in the side as an entrance makes a good cat bed. This should be lined with a blanket, or one of your sweaters – this way your cat will get used to your smell. Wholesale crisp boxes could have been tailor-made for this job. They have a perforated circle of card on one end which is pushed out to allow easy access to the crisps. I had plenty of these in the shop, I chose salt and vinegar for Tom and prawn cocktail for Jerry – because she's a lady. I considered borrowing two of Iman's sweaters to line the crisp boxes. It was tempting, and it would help them to bond, but it was a risk, too great a risk I decided. Anyway, borrowing something without the other person's permission is tantamount to theft.

To be thorough I got the taxi driver to drop me off at the shop. This way I could pick up the crisp boxes and get some cat food and cat litter from the stock room. More importantly, I could wait for the cover of darkness. I phoned my house and checked that Tym was out. He didn't answer the phone, which I had to assume meant he was out. Even the most thorough person can't account for every eventuality. I had done my best. Now it was just a case of taking a taxi to number 4, Wood Road and getting the cats secure in my room. The gods were with me, it was easy. Tym was out more than he was in these days and Iman draws their curtains early in the winter. The only shadow of doubt was due to their Christmas tree. Since it had been up they left the middle curtain open. This way everyone in the street could see the tree lights. I consoled myself with the fact it is hard to see past lights into the darkness. Since the tree was up and the presents were wrapped, and put under the tree, I had been able to get through the wardrobe again. I'd already replaced Will's teapot and I felt good about it, it was only fair, and Iman and Will would never know I'd broken it. That's real kindness, when the recipient doesn't know it; selfless.

Tom and Jerry were not very happy. They hissed at me and had to be tipped out of the Our Dumb Friends' League cardboard box. I put a folded up towel into each crisp box but couldn't persuade them in. I went downstairs and put some cat food on to two saucers. I found an empty seed tray of Tym's which I lined with a plastic bag and covered over with the cat litter. This way I could just pull up the plastic bag, cat litter, shit and all, and chuck it out. I was a bit squeamish about this part of cat ownership.

I needed to be dead dead careful opening my bedroom door from now on. It was easy on the way out because I knew where the cats were. But going in, I had to be careful. I opened it a little less than cat-width, then blocked that space with my leg and turned myself in. I couldn't use the same method to bring in the food and the litter tray, so I shut the cats in the wardrobe and brought the stuff in. Tom scratched me, but I didn't retaliate. When I opened up the wardrobe door Tom hissed. I didn't take it personally. The door was left open so they could take their own time to come out.

I put down newspaper for the cat food and litter tray. I sat on the bed reading a bit more of 'Our Dumb Friends' League Information Leaflet 3: Your Rehomed Cat'. When I read the bit about not putting the litter tray near the food I got off the bed and moved it to the other side of the room on some more newspaper. It was badly timed, Tom was just peering out of the wardrobe as I moved and he hid in the wardrobe darkness again.

I finished the leaflet, and lay still. Jerry put her marmalade-haired head out and sniffed the air. They followed their noses to the food. I watched them eat. They were beautiful eaters, if a little noisy. Afterwards they kept their backs to me and had a brief grooming session. Tom licked the back of Jerry's head, the hard to reach spot for any cat. And so to bed, but Tom went into the prawn cocktail box and Jerry went into the salt and vinegar. That wasn't right, it was blue (salt and vinegar) for a boy and pink (prawn cocktail) for a girl. I tried to tip Tom out, so I could change them over. But the opening on a crisp box is so small that he stood astride it without falling out. I didn't want to shake him out, he hissed and brayed so much I left him to it. They could change over tomorrow. The towel had fallen out of Tom's box, I tried to shove it back in and got another scratch. This one bled; I dabbed it with the towel.

Jerry was shy about using the litter tray with me in the room. I can remember being like that at school, sometimes you just don't want spectators in the toilet. Fortunately, they were both used to using litter trays from their time at Our Dumb Friends' League. The plastic-bag lining of the seed/litter tray rustled as Jerry got in position, then she just looked round at me, suspiciously. Her eyes, as well as her red hair, were reminiscent of Nicole Kidman, and I relented to that gaze, like so many studio executives must have before me. I left Jerry to use the litter tray in silence, and went to make a cup of tea.

The house was too hot. Tym must've had the heating on for hours. There was practically a heat haze on the landing. I walked down the stairs and knew that such heat was not consistent with the Red Hills of the Isle of Skye in December. Obviously, I didn't want to go too far, I didn't want snow inside, but this was tropical heat. This was as hot as Tym's secret wardrobe hot-house. I wondered if he was growing plants somewhere else in the house, but decided not to get stuck on that thought, it could lead to paranoia. I clicked the heating off and clicked the kettle on.

As my tea brewed I considered the problem of Tym's wardrobe forest of marijuana. I had painted myself into a corner. Something was happening in my house that I was not happy about. But Tym could object to how I found out, I don't want to lose him, I need the money and he is very big. The best I could come up with was to turn all the electricity off for the evening, it would turn off his lights and stop him turning the heating on too because of its electric ignition and over-ride switches. It wasn't enough to stop him permanently, but it was something.

I would need to be careful how I asked Tym about Will, I wanted answers, not a long conversation. The longer I went without seeing him the better. It was some consolation that by leaving early the morning after the play, I'd saved myself from seeing Tym in the wrong house. I'd known I was in trouble with Iman and was thorough enough to leave dead early. But I didn't know I was jeopardising everything by staying over. How could I? Thoroughness had been my saviour.

Before turning the power off I got everything I needed together: batteries for my radio cassette, a sandwich, a flask of tea, a torch, my woolly hat and winter coat and clicked off the line of big switches under the stairs. I would tell Tym we'd had a power cut. Tom and Jerry meowed.

The sound of Will and Iman's television pressed its way through the wall in my lounge. It was nearly loud enough for me to follow the programme. It was quite funny, there are a lot of funny Christmas television specials. I heard Will laugh, so loud I missed the joke. The house cooled. I put on my hat and coat. Will's coat is warmer, but mine would just have to do, and the hat would help, you lose loads of heat through the head.

I knew my bedroom smelled before I even opened the door. That was the main problem. If it smelled inside then I could put up with it, or even sleep downstairs, but Tym would be able to smell the shit from the landing. How could I casually raise the question, 'Why were you eating your grapefruit next door?' when the house smelled of cat shit?

Ideally, I needed the lights on to get into my bedroom and ensure Tom and Jerry didn't escape. But, for once, I had to compromise my thoroughness and keep the electricity off. The torch would have to do. I edged into the room and spun the torch about, hoping to light up the cats' eyes like, well, cats' eyes. I got the door shut quickly, I listened and heard Tom's reassuring hiss. I hissed back – I'd had enough of his attitude.

The litter tray was bulging. They must have really been holding it in. It looked like it had been quite a traumatic day for these two cats. I had to do something about it, squeamish as I am about such matters. My plastic-bag method worked well, both lining the tray and allowing me to pick it all up easily. I did so, and placed the bag on yet more newspaper, I filled the litter tray up again in case they needed to use it before I was back. Very thorough.

'Our Dumb Friends' League Information Leaflet 3: Your Rehomed Cat' had given me an idea. Despite the aggression Tom the tom had shown to me I would do these cats a favour. As the leaflet states, *Any new cat in an area has to establish his territory. Digging the contents of his litter tray into the soil in your garden will*

286

help him establish his own territory. It was a good arrangement for us both; I had a bag of shit to get rid of.

Now, the territory for Tom and Jerry would be centred on Will's garden. My night-time gardening had been going very well in my own garden. I had stuck to the rules: only gardening in the early hours. The cold was becoming a problem, but it was practically complete. The plants were Lord Macdonald's Forest, and beyond them, at the bottom of the garden, waves of earth were giving a good account of the sea surrounding my Isle of Skye. It was quite late, but I knew Will and Iman were still up watching the television. Although it was far, far too early for my own night-time gardening I had to go next door and bury this shit.

I opened the windows in my room, went downstairs and out the back of the house, opening windows as I went. The smell hung about. I was shaking with the cold and the fear. I put down the bag, went back into the front room and heard the reassuring sound of Will's television. He wasn't laughing any more, but I could just make out their voices.

I got my hammer and chisel and went to the end of the garden, past Lord Macdonald's Forest, walking over the waves that lapped against the bottom fence, to stand in the corner. I had too much to hold to climb over, so, after tying the handles of the bag, I dangled it over the fence and then dropped it. It was louder landing than I anticipated. I waited a respectful amount of time before climbing over myself, just in case Will or Iman had heard the noise. I didn't want to frighten them.

I thought of it like this: *what they don't know won't hurt them.* That's a phrase isn't it? That's a truism. It is true kindness to do something for someone that they never find out about, to not want thanks. This was the spirit in which I replaced Will's line-dancing cowboy teapot; I didn't have to. I'd replaced everything I took from their house: the chocolate, the peanut butter, even the diary. And, I may have killed Aslan, but I'm the one who's bought Iman two cats. That's a net gain of one cat. But my point, in the dark and

287

cold of the garden, was, so long as they didn't catch me in their garden, or in their house, or in my house, I would have done nothing wrong. In actual fact I was doing this for their new cats, helping them establish their territories.

I had got over the fence in silence. My eyes had adjusted well to the December moonlight and I saw enough of the plastic bag on my way down to avoid it, legs astride. I had a soft landing, which made me instantly suspicious. The carrier bag of shit had burst on impact. I had been too thorough! By tying the handles I had made it airtight, and as it landed it must've hit a sharp stone, thorn, or something because it had gone off like a balloon.

I looked down the garden to Will's house. All the lights were still on, this was a good sign. So long as the lights were on they would be disadvantaged if they looked into the darkness, as soon as the lights were off I would be more easily seen. I worked quickly, only tempering my rush for speed with the caveat of silence. Except, one of the stock-in-trade tools of the night-time winter gardener is the hammer and chisel. There's no other way into the soil. I chiselled out a bowl shape by pushing the hammer against the chisel (like Bruce Lee's one-inch punch) to minimise the noise, but it wasn't silent. My boots were already dirty and I decided to make a virtue of this. I pushed the shit into the hole with my boots. Ideally I would have filtered out the cat litter, but I didn't have the means or the time to do it. So once the hole was full I scraped my boots against the side and dropped the excavated earth over the surface. I pressed it down a little with my boot and it swelled like meat under the lid of a pie.

I had done my best. But there were still traces of cat litter on the plants where the bag had burst. I shook these shrubs and bushes so that the cat litter dropped to the ground. Back on my side of the fence I panicked. For one so thorough, I had made a classic error. I had, voluntarily, left a foot print as I compacted down the earth. I was tempted to go back and ruffle the surface, but my work had already taken so long that Will's house lights were off – I could now

288

be seen. I tried to think of a phrase for my predicament, but all I could muster was *discretion is the better part of valour*, which meant I should not risk it.

After putting the split plastic bag into the bin I decided my boots should follow, they were old and dirty and matched the footprint in Will's garden. It was the thorough thing to do.

Downstairs no longer smelled. I shut the windows. The Red Hills stairs no longer smelled, and I shut the landing window. This was good, if Tym came in now then the house would look and smell normal once more. If he'd been drinking it would be the ideal time to ask him about Will.

I hit upon a new tactic for getting into my room without the cats getting out: I banged and kicked the door first to scare them away. It worked well. I flashed the torch around to find Tom and Jerry shivering in a corner. I've never seen a cat shiver before and I wondered if it was from my noisy entry or the cold. I would make it up to them either way, by shutting the windows and offering the hand of friendship. Tom scratched me for the third time, drawing more blood, this time on my left hand. Again, I restrained from retaliation, although I did hiss. I opened my flask of tea and drank two cups, well one cup and one lid – you know what flasks are like.

It was the noise of my teeth chattering that woke me. I turned on the bedside light and nothing happened. I did it again before remembering all the power was off. I used the torch to see the clock; it was four in the morning. I flicked the torch beam into the prawn cocktail crisp box; empty. I was up, reaching into the box to check, nothing, not even a scratch. I tipped the box upside down and shook it; nothing. Listening I could definitely hear something, breathing, it couldn't be Will or Iman, these walls are too thick for that. I shone the light into the salt and vinegar box, it was full of Tom and Jerry, curled up for warmth. I put my coat and woolly hat on and went back to bed.

The next thing I heard was Tym coming in, stumbling up the stairs and walking into his highly polished door. He got it open at the third attempt and I didn't see him again until the following afternoon.

By mid-morning I could bear the cold no more and turned all the power back on. Ideally it would have been off when Tym got up, but I might have done enough to kill his plants anyway. He got up for lunch. I met him in the kitchen.

'Hellos, Liam.'

'Afternoon.'

'Would you like sandwiches? I'm having some rounds of sand- wich.' Tym was buttering bread. I thought that a sandwich was the ideal prop for a conversation about Will. A neighbourly chat.

'Yes. That would be very kind of you.'

'No problem. Nutella or Marmite?' Tym was obviously having the Nutella, he generously carpeted three slices of bread with it.

'Er, Marmite. Yes, Marmite please, Tym.'

'Thank you,' he said.

'Would you like a cup of tea?' I offered. Tea and a neighbourly chat would be even better. What could be more natural than to ask the lodger why he had been eating grapefruit next door over a nice cup of tea and a Marmite sandwich.

'Thank you please,' said Tym. I heated the kettle, put the milk in a jug and even warmed the pot. Tym was half-way through his second Nutella sandwich by the time the tea had brewed. We both stood in the kitchen, even after I had poured the tea.

'Liam, it's the eve of Christmas, but you have no tree or giftwrap?'

'No.' I sipped and changed the subject. 'Were you next door the other day?' Tym pointed upstairs. 'No, I mean in the next house? It's just I thought I saw you leaving there, but I wasn't sure.'

Tym sipped his tea thoughtfully. I took a big bite of my sand- wich, very relaxed and natural, folding the bread into my mouth to get the whole half in. Tym was about to answer, but I coughed, choked and gasped for air.

'What the fucking . . .' I paused, to choke and to stop myself from launching into a diatribe against Tym's sandwich. I coughed again. Tym got behind me, into position, ready to give me the Heimlich manoeuvre. I coughed and choked again, and then again, he gripped me around the solar plexus and pumped, twice. I tried to call out but he forced all the air from my lungs. I wasn't choking on food, I was choking on flavour! I wriggled and struggled free, before dropping to one knee, breathing heavily. The other half of the Marmite sandwich was on the kitchen floor, along with broken pieces of the plate. It was spread about half an inch thick with Marmite; Marmite spread as thick as Nutella. I was furious.

'What are you trying to do? Kill me?'

'No, no, now you have to thank me. In Poland that is called the Heimlich manoeuvre. It saves a man from choking himself to death. I was the registered first aid guy at the shop where I worked all summer. I can do it right. I saved you.'

'You tried to kill me – just look at that Marmite.' I pointed, but he kept on looking at me. 'You don't spread Marmite like that, not unless you want to kill someone!'

'That's peculiar,' said Tym.

'Peculiar? Have you any idea what Marmite is? What it tastes like?' We'd always stocked Marmite, I knew the product back to front.

'No. It was my first purchase.' Tym picked up the giant jar, enough for six months' regular use, or one packed lunch Tym's way. 'It was recommended me and looks like Nutella. I like that.'

I stood up, reaching out palm upwards, which should mean *give me that* anywhere in Europe, but Tym did not give me the Marmite. I wanted to point out the label instruction, I could read it from here: *Delicious when spread thinly on toast.*

'Let me show you. *Spread thinly.*' I pointed at the words. 'Thinly! Understand?'

'Thinly. Yes, of course I understand.' He looked for a moment like he didn't understand. Tym carried on talking, almost to

291

himself. 'Thinly. Thin. Thin is not fat. I see, I am a big guy, too fat perhaps. I need thin food.' How could he be so clever and so stupid?

I decided to let this attempt on my life go, but only because I had a more important question to ask him. So, after a very large glass of water, and a few sips of tea, I said, in what was still a slightly hoarse voice, 'Tym?' He looked up, dividing his attention between me and his last Nutella sandwich. 'Tym, as I was saying, about the other day and next door.'

'Sssh, sssh,' his voice was muffled by white bread.

'I'm only asking a casual question, about being neighbourly,' I said, defensively.

'No, no, sssh. What is that sound?' I listened. It was the faint mew of hungry cats. Tym stopped eating. He put his last half of sandwich on to the kitchen counter so he could listen completely. 'Is that a ghost? The ghost of Christmas past perhaps?' Tym smiled, as if he didn't really think my house was haunted any more, or perhaps he was just pleased with his Dickensian reference.

'No, I don't think so,' I said, loudly.

'Or, it could be the ghost of Christmas present,' Tym continued. 'Look, tonight's the night, it is the eve of Christmas!'

'No, Tym. I've told you, this house isn't haunted.'

'Or, it could be the ghost of Christmases, yet to become!' He sounded triumphant, pleased to have remembered all the *Christmas Carol* ghosts.

'No, Tym. I think what you can hear is my radio. Or my television. I've left them on upstairs.' I walked off towards my room.

'Television and radio?' said Tym.

'Yeah,' I said, climbing the stairs.

I locked my bedroom door behind me, put the radio on and opened the windows to let out the smell of the litter trays. The cats seemed pleased to see me, but all that stopped as soon as the food was out of the can. Tom hissed as I put down his full saucer. I hissed back, I could've sworn he looked amused with me, but that's ridiculous. Maybe he thought my hiss was funny, not at all feline. I tried again, twice, and the second hiss was so effective he stopped eating and edged towards Jerry. They shared Jerry's food, before both eating Tom's dinner.

I listened to the radio and for the first time felt a bit Christmassy. Every other song was about Christmas. Not carols, but pop stuff. I re-tuned to find something religious and soon found a carol service. It made me feel like a boy again. Will would be desperately trying to contact me, I'm sure. Telling Iman that he was phoning to confirm our arrangements for tomorrow, while all the while hoping I'd got him Tom the tomcat. Christmas was so exciting. Will needn't worry, I would make it up to him, and Iman, tomorrow. We would be even. I didn't like putting Will through such anxiety, but it was necessary; I was sure as soon as Iman saw Tom and Jerry, with her lovely ginger Nicole Kidman hair, she'd fall in love. And I was busting to go next door. Iman had wrapped the presents up so I could get in the wardrobe but since the school holidays began I'd hardly been able to get in there. Tomorrow it would all become clearer, and Will would give me that sweater. Very nice, for the first time this year, I was looking forward to Christmas. I turned up the carols.

Tym went out, leaving in his wake a haze of Alpine Breeze and a large box wrapped up in the lounge. There was a cracker on top of the box. Waves of Christmas spirit were breaking over me. Here was this big gift for me and I'd not got him anything. I told myself I'd not got him anything because of his attempt on my life with the Marmite sandwich, or, because of his wardrobe marijuana forest. But they were lies, I'd not even bought anything for Will and he's my best friend who's having me over for Christmas Day. How did I ever think I was thorough? In fact this present was probably a goodwill gesture after Tym's mistake with the potentially lethal sandwich. It is one of the most embarrassing things in the world to be given a Christmas present without being able to give a gift in reply.

I needed to know what Tym had got me. I pressed the paper down in the hope of reading the side of the box, but the paper was too thick, it was good quality. The box was about as wide as my shoulders, and I took a firm grip and lifted from the knees, back straight (pretty thorough, eh?). I put so much effort into lifting it and it was so very, very light, that I staggered back. The cracker fell to my feet. Something rattled inside.

This was a major dilemma. The gift looked big and therefore expensive; but it was very light, and perhaps therefore cheap. Now I needed to buy a gift for my Polish lodger on Christmas Eve after the shops had shut, and to top it all, I didn't know what he'd got me. (I did at least know what Will had got me; maybe it was not too late to get him something.) I knew I had to open the box.

The early signs were good. Tym had used clear sellotape, not any of that *Merry Christmas and a Happy New Year, on the first day of Christmas my true love sent to me* rubbish. All I had to do was split the sellotape and free up just enough wrapping paper to read what it said on the box. I would then assess how much the gift was worth, re-wrap it, go to my shop and find something from stock for Tym and Will and wrap them up.

I split the sellotape in two places, and unfolded the paper to reveal the top of the box: *Alpen Muesli 33% extra free*. I'd told that cunt I didn't like muesli, what was he playing at? First he tries to kill me with a Marmite sandwich and now this, adding insult to injury. Ok, I could accept that it was perhaps a mistake, perhaps he was new to Marmite, but I'd specifically told him I didn't like muesli. This was beyond belief! Unless, of course, this muesli was not for me. Even so, what a weird gift, who, with the exception of a hamster, would want muesli for Christmas? The muesli was ticking.

Maybe the Marmite sandwich was not a mistake? Maybe Tym and Will knew each other, maybe that was why Tym was round there the other morning? Maybe Will knows about the portal and maybe Tym is the hired hit-man for him? It sounded a little far-fetched but the muesli was definitely ticking. Maybe I had set off the bomb mechanism inside when I shook the box?

Luckily I knew what to do. I split the tape along the lid of the box and lifted the lid. I'd seen enough films to know that if there was a bomb inside this box I should cut the red (or was it the blue?) wire and the ticking would stop. There was no bomb, there wasn't even any muesli. There was a small box lying on the bottom of the box, no red wire visible, nothing. The small box was wrapped up in the same paper as the large box. If Tym was in league with Will then I was done for; I reached inside.

I lifted the small box carefully, just in case it was the sort of bomb you don't see in films, just in case it had a mercury spirit-level trip-switch that could explode if tipped. I was shaking so much that, by the time I put it on the floor, I was pretty confident it didn't have a mercury spirit-level trip-switch. The ticking was louder.

Using the open scissors like a scalpel, I split the only piece of tape on the small box. I unfolded the paper slowly, like petals, all the while listening to the tick tick tick of what were, perhaps, my last few seconds. My hands were shaking and I tore the paper in a jagged, nervous arc. No matter – at least I hadn't blown myself up.

Inside was a plastic box. I opened it. Curiouser and curiouser. Yes, I did need a watch, but why had Tym bought me a ladies' watch? Was this an insult? Did he not realise this was a ladies' watch? (The watch face was so small and the strap so thin, it most definitely was a ladies' watch.) And what should I buy him when he'd bought me a ladies' timepiece? I just didn't know what to do.

I didn't go to the shop until Edna had left. She and Tracey had the idea that I spent my days with a 'fancy woman', arriving at teatime made them think she wasn't feeding me right. I never confirmed it and I never denied it. I avoided it. I went to my shop, under cover of darkness, for the lastest of last-minute Christmas shopping. I didn't bother putting the lights on. If I did there was a strong chance another last-minute Christmas shopper, invariably a drunk, would start banging on the door.

I got a piece of the wrapping paper to re-wrap Tym's present. Of course I could have re-wrapped it with the existing paper, but I'd torn that a little on the piece around the watch box. I was too thorough to accept that, and luckily we stocked the same paper. I had plenty of time and it was highly unlikely that Tym would be back before me. I rolled up the wrapping paper as I walked around the shop looking for a gift for Will. I could see pretty well. A large box of chocolates, that would be good to give as a general gift tomorrow. A few cigars, Will's dad was going to be there too, he'd appreciate those. Someone knocked on the shop door. I ignored them. They knocked again. I picked up a large box of Turkish Delight (rose and lemon flavour), this would be another good thing to take. The knocking got louder and they started shouting.

'Liam! Liam! How-de-do-de mate! Come on, let me in, I'm freezing my nuts off out here!' I turned to see Will, that was a mistake, I should have just casually walked out into the stock room. How could I choose a Christmas present for him if he was watching me? This was a disaster, there were no other shops open and it was getting late on Christmas Eve. Will frightened me. What if Will wanted to see the cat? What did he know from Tym? Why had they had breakfast together? I had to brave it out, I had to cling to the possibility that Will knew nothing. I smiled and let him in. As he stepped over the threshold a drunk called out and staggered, quickly, towards the door too.

'Are you open? Ah! Just let me get a . . . oh, what was it? Can I get?' Every year this happens. Maybe not with the same drunk, but every time you open the shop door on Christmas Eve a drunk will stagger towards it like one of the Evil Dead. We were too quick for him. Will told him to 'Piss off!' as I shut the door. Will was frightening, I don't think I would have been so forthright with the drunk just in case he took umbrage. But Will was really frightening and the drunk staggered away.

Anyone who is familiar with horror films knows that a vampire needs to be invited in. It was a bit like that with Will. By successfully getting rid of the Evil Dead drunk, Will had worked his way into the shop, but I soon realised he was like the Evil Dead drunk; Will was dead drunk.

'Liam! Merry Christmas! And, and, let me be the first to wish you a Happy New Year too! I've been looking all over for you.'

'Really? Where?'

'Well, ok, you got me, not exactly all over. More like looking here and at the bottom of glasses at the Elm Old . . . the Ald Arms . . .' Will laughed at himself, stood up straight, took a deep breath and said quickly, 'The Old Elm Arms.' He laughed. 'Come on, it's Christmas Eve, I left a warm pub just to come and get you. I tried phoning but you never seem to bloody answer. Everybody's there! Iman, Jemma, Dad, Jimmy . . . er, me. Well, not me now; I was there, till I was here.'

'All right. Can I come and meet you in a while? I've got a few things to finish first.'

'It's Christmas Eve!'

'I know.'

'Oh,' said Will, deflated. 'No. Come on. What's more important than being in the pub on Christmas Eve? You don't want to be here working,' Will said, with the sharp clarity of thought that the very drunk can attain. I was stuck, I couldn't tell him I was Christmas shopping for him, in my own shop. 'Ooo! I know what else I wanted! Yes!' said Will. 'Can I see the kitten! I've been ringing for days. Are you sure your phone's working? Yes, that was it, I want to see the kitten! Unless you haven't got one.'

'The kitten? You explicitly told me not to get a kitten. You wanted to give Iman a cat. You told me to get a cat.'

'Oh yeah.' Will laughed, a lot. 'You're right, I remember, I must be a little drunk.' He moved towards the back of the shop.

'Stop!' I said with a force that surprised me. It must've been the nerves, panicking and squeezing my diaphragm. Will looked

297

shocked. Because there was no cat to see here and because it was too late for my pre-planned excuse (that the cat was at the vet's being neutered – no vet would do that on Christmas Eve) I took the only escape route there was. 'I thought we were going down the pub? You'll see the cat tomorrow. It can be a surprise.'

Will didn't answer, he just walked towards me with his hands up, like I had a gun. I locked the shop door, and put all the shopping I'd done into a carrier bag and took it with me. We went out the side door, Will walking in front of me still, hands up. We walked like this past the Evil Dead drunk, Will put his hands down, made his fingers into pistols and clicked his thumbs to shoot the drunk, who fell back, laughing like he'd been shot. This must be some of that Christmas cheer and goodwill.

Will was walking and talking fast, occasionally I had to run a few steps to catch up, carrier bag swinging. It was ok, it helped keep me warm.

'I'll tell you something Liam, you'll like this. It'll appeal to your sense of humour. I was fucking angry about it at first, but now, now I can see the funny side. Anyway, you know I'm getting Iman a cat for Christmas. Well, of course you know, you bought it, I've not even seen it yet, but thanks for doing that for me. I can't keep it at my house. I can't wrap it up and put it under the tree, for fuck's sake! Anyway, it's a good idea to get Iman a cat for Christmas. How can I be so sure? I'll tell you, I'm sure she'd like one, because she's already got one! Yeah, Candida, her mother, came round two days ago with a gift in a wicker basket. My first thought was she'd got us a Christmas hamper, very nice too, but then the thing meows! Fucking meows. Iman's face was a picture. Anyway, Candida had already named it, Grizabella – it's from that play we saw . . . what was it called? . . . *Cats*!' Will laughed heartily at this. 'So, Iman's taken to her new cat like a duck to water, she calls it Bella, short for Grizabella.' Will stopped walking, stopped so abruptly that I overtook him slightly. I turned to face him. 'What shall I do, Liam? It's ten o'clock on Christmas Eve and I haven't got my wife a proper present. Well, I've got lingerie – but that's next to nothing.'

'You have, you've got her a cat, a tom called Tom, like we said.'

'I can't give her that. She's got one. A pedigree kitten with a ballerina's name.' He looked close to tears.

'Of course you can. This cat's special, believe me. You have to give it to her. She loves cats.'

'You think?'

'Yeah.'

'Two cats?' Will said, trying the idea on for size. 'Yeah, two cats. Why not?'

'Yeah, if one, why not two? If two, why not three?' I said. Will looked at me, bewildered. I laughed and he joined me. We walked on, just in time, as I was beginning to get cold standing still.

'What's in the bag, Liam?'

'It's a surprise!' Now I was leading the way, ever so slightly. The exertion of walking was taking its toll on Will. He was more drunk than he was fit – and he couldn't keep up the high walking pace for long.

We caught our first glance of the Old Elm Arms, there it was, a beacon against the winter night sky. Will was slowing up and I pointed out our destination to him.

'Look, Will. We're nearly there.'

He stopped to look. 'Fantastic. Bloody fantastic.'

I stopped and tried to get him started again. 'Come on, I've got some catching up to do.'

'Hang on son, hang on. Before we go in there – it's very loud; karaoke – before we go in, I want to tell you, well, thank you, for getting the cat for me.'

'That's fine. You're welcome. Thanks for inviting me over for Christmas Day.'

'Well, yes. That's the thing isn't it. You are alone, no, not alone, but alone for Christmas. What I mean to say is, it's the first Christmas without your dad, and I want you to think of us as

299

your family this year. I've always thought we've had a brotherly bond; beyond friendship. I've got Iman, and she welcomes you too this Christmas. Christ, even Jemma's got her new man, my fucking neigh-bear – boy can that man drink, I've bought him three pints tonight myself; fair play to him though, he's bought his rounds, paid his way. But I want you, I'm glad you're coming tomorrow.' He moved in and hugged me, catching me unawares and crumpling the wrapping paper in the carrier bag.

I was lucky and unlucky in equal measure and I could not move. Tym and Jemma! Jemma and Tym! It made no sense and it made sense. They were a really unlikely couple; I was so unlucky. But I knew I was lucky that Will had mentioned it out here in the dark and cold, rather than walking into the Old Elm Arms on Christmas Eve and seeing Tym and Jemma with everyone. I would have been done for. At least this way I could avoid them, but for how long? One of the threads of my life was there dangling in front of me, and if it got pulled everything would unravel. I could think of nothing and I could think of nothing else. I must not go into that pub, that much was certain. Will started to lead the way, I was rooted to the car park, my resolve as strong as the weeds that push through tarmac. What if Will already knew? What if he knew Tym (they'd had breakfast together) and this was the set-up?

'Come on, Liam! You're lagging behind. What's up? You worried you'll get to the bar first and have to get them in?' He walked back to me. 'You look eighteen son, I reckon you'll get served.' He laughed, and stopped when I didn't start. 'What's up? Shouldn't I have mentioned your dad? Look, sorry Liam. It's Christmas, you've got me, I love you. I know you've been under pressure, I mean what was that job application about? I'd have been better off going for a post like that. What was the money like? No, don't answer that. Let's talk about you, grief, I mean all that sitting in the dark you've been doing, not answering the phone. I've wanted to reach out, but sometimes I thought you wanted to be alone, even if it was in the dark.' Will had talked himself out, and, lost for words, he moved in to hug me again.

When cornered there is only one thing to do. It was taught to me as the way to escape if someone starts beating you up. Even if they've got you in a clinch, this works, or so I heard. Social workers get taught this, as the ultimate way to escape. The police don't use it though.

I started to retch. I rasped and rumbled and gagged and bellowed. I flexed my neck like a swung swan. Will stood still. Then, it happened, and the fear had helped: I puked. It worked, just as it does for a cornered social worker, or a youth caught by the throat; Will backed off, it's only natural, everyone is repelled by vomit. Now he was more shocked than me, now I knew what was going on and not him. I ran. Will didn't.

'Liam! *Liam*! See you tomorrow then!' he called.

Funny how the mind works in a crisis. The night air was too cold to run far, it cut into my raw throat, but what I was worried about all the way home was that Will's hug had crumpled the wrapping paper. Hopefully not so much that I couldn't use it. The rest of the picture was clear. I had to go to number 4, Wood Road. Yes, there was a chance that Will knew about me living there, but he definitely knew I lived in the flat over the shop. At least this way I had the chance of remaining undisturbed. I had to get back for the cats and to re-wrap the present, the present that Tym had obviously got for Jemma.

Mrs Price was in, but there were no lights on in our building at all, not even Iman's Christmas tree lights. First things first, after putting the kettle on and making a cup of tea, I started repairing the damage I'd done to Jemma's Christmas present. The torn paper on the watch box was the biggest problem. Will had crumpled up all the wrapping paper, I found the flattest bit for the watch box, but it wasn't perfect. As for the rest, if surgeons made bombs they would assemble them with the care I used to re-stick the wrapping on that gift. Every piece of tape was the perfect size to mask the split in the piece below and every crumple in the paper was smoothed out; like repairing an egg. I did my best, hardly touched a drop of tea, so I made another cup and put the present back in the exact spot in the lounge where I'd found it.

I didn't put the heating on, but I didn't turn the electric off. I kept my hat and coat on. The cats were almost pleased to see me, I was pleased to see them. The bedroom curtains were open and the room was well lit by moonlight, even better once my eyes adjusted. I couldn't risk burying the contents of their litter tray in Will's garden tonight, so I just chucked the lot out the window. Fact was, I didn't even want to leave the room. There was nothing to go out for. As a compromise I found Lord Macdonald's Forest on the map of the Isle of Skye that I'd enlarged and photocopied for my wallpaper. It was just above the double radiator. I went and sat there, it wasn't as good as the real thing, wherever that was, and the radiator wasn't even on. But it was something. It made sense. On a cold winter's night it makes sense to sit in front of the radiator. And if you can't go out it makes sense, if your garden is Lord Macdonald's Forest surrounded by the sea, to find that point on the map and go there. Whoever had been in this house before me, and whatever they'd done on the Isle of Skye that made them paste the map on to the wall, it had to mean something.

I shut my eyes and hung my head to rest. My body was tired, but my mind was racing. I couldn't focus on any single thing, and I couldn't focus on nothing. What I needed was someone to talk to, a best friend or a father would be ideal. I attained an anxious sleep that could have been a dreamlike waking.

Something touched my knee – I leapt, and for the first time in my life shaped my hands into a karate pose. (Judo as a lad, yes, karate, never.) I was just quick enough to see Jerry recoil and run away. She'd tried to touch me, she'd reached out her paw to me as one

302

sentient being to another and how did I repay her? With a karate threat.

'Oh no. Sorry. Sorry, little cat.' I reached out, softening my hard karate hands and trying to touch her marmalade head. She winced, sniffing my hand. Remembering the non-threatening cat body language I'd used on Aslan, I blinked. It was dark, but not very dark to a cat. It worked, and after a brief tickle under the chin, Jerry walked on to my lap. She revolved twice and came to rest in the basin of my crossed legs. I stroked her. Tom watched from a safe distance.

I kept on stroking Jerry, tickling her Nicole Kidman patch of red hair and blinking whenever our eyes met.

'It's not so bad, is it?' I whispered. 'It's not so bad.' Jerry purred.

If Will knew Tym then maybe he knew about me, as his landlord. This was bad. If Tym knew about the portal, or if Will knew about the portal, then maybe I was living in the last days. Anything that could break my friendship with Will was life-threatening. The Marmite sandwich was a far-fetched way to exact vengeance, but it seemed real at the time. I tried blinking at Tom – no reply.

It took Tym several moments to open the front door. He was a long time finding the right key. The key was a long time finding the lock. He was a long time turning the key. I listened for his foot on the stairs and it sounded like he was staggering, at times one step up, two back. There was a light, feminine giggle, almost nothing, but quite definitely something. Someone was with him, it had to be Jemma. I eased Jerry off my lap, and, instinctively, made my karate hands again. Keeping my hands in their karate position I shaped a ssshh to the cats against my lips. It wasn't terribly clear but maybe they knew what I meant, they were both silent anyway. I was under siege.

'No!' Jemma laughed.

'Ssshhs,' whispered Tym, and they both laughed again.

'No way!' said Jemma, sounding drunk and incredulous.

Tom looked disturbed by the new voices, or maybe it was the smell (Alpine Breeze, beer and smoke). Either way he started to meow.

'I've never seen Iman as drunk as that!' That clinched it, it was definitely Jemma.

'Ssshhs. Can you hear that?' Tym interrupted.

'What?' said Jemma.

'Are you a believer in a ghost?' said Tym.

Jemma laughed, stopping suddenly and saying, 'No! Of course not.'

'Well, what is that?' said Tym. They were outside the door on the landing, but sounded closer. Whenever anyone comes back from a night out they sound so very loud to the people at home. It's true; babysitters must know what I mean.

There was a moment's silence as Jemma listened. I looked at Tom, blinking my eyes in an over-friendly way. He shaped like he was going to meow again and I went for him – forgetting that my hands were in karate formation – and he just hissed. I was so angry I hissed back without thinking. I cupped a karate hand to my mouth, what had I done? What I needed was planks of wood to nail across the door. But even if I had them the noise would give me away. I could lock the door, but Tym could open it, his bedroom door key was identical to mine.

'That's only a cat, silly,' Jemma reassured Tym. 'Two cats at most.'

'Two of cats! We don't even have one cat. There are no cats in this house. Cat ghosts? Don't you see, it cannot be!' Tym was close to drunken tears.

Tom meowed, and I finally understood him, he was stood by the saucers. He wanted to be fed. Now I was worried that this meow provoked no comment from outside the door, I imagined they just looked at each other. There was a fractional sound, not words, perhaps the sound of someone grasping a door handle, a mechanism beginning to grip itself. I stared at the door handle, and maybe it was the moonlight, but maybe it wasn't. The door handle flickered. I am too thorough to take a chance.

I moved, quick and quiet, scooping up both cats by the scruff (they were young enough and small enough to go limp on instinct) and dumping them into my coat pockets. I had the element of surprise on them. I slid open the wardrobe with my foot, and, remembering it is very foolish to shut oneself into any wardrobe, I shut myself in. The cats wriggled, I tightened my grip on their scruffs until they were silent and still.

The edges of the wardrobe lit up as the bedroom light went on.

'Jemmer! Jemmer! You cannot go in there,' said Tym, but he followed, 'Mr Jesus Christ! Look at these walls.'

Jemma whispered back, 'Never mind the walls, look at the ceiling!'

I kept hold of Tom's scruff and let go of Jerry's, keeping my elbow over the pocket flap. Using this free hand, I moved back the bowling ball (still in its box) and flipped back the loops of fishing wire. Fear kept Jerry still, we'd bonded, she leaned into my side through the coat pocket.

All that was left now was the brick plug. It was too heavy and broad to move with one hand, but I had to try (Tym and Jemma were moving around the room, between each anxious breath I could hear their feet on the carpet). My fingers grappled with the top brick, it fell forwards, landing on the bowling ball (still in its box). The sound was atomic. I knocked forward the laminate board and shoved the cats through, letting go of their scruffs on the other side. I followed, turned, grabbing and reinstating the brick portal and the laminate board.

The cats meowed, it was a low, long, fearful sound. My fingertips hurt, putting them into my mouth I tasted blood. By the end of the cats' long meow I'd located them both (there's nowhere to hide in a wardrobe) and scruffed them back into my pockets.

Tym and Jemma's voices followed me through the wall, faintly.

'It's empty! There's nothing there!' Jemma didn't seem to know whether she was pleased or disappointed.

'But you were hearing it, the thing, as I was hearing it, the, it, thing!' Tym's English deteriorated with the anxiety and alcohol. Then maybe they shut the wardrobe door because the rest of their conversation was too faint to make out.

Sleep is rarely silent, and, as my own breathing calmed, I heard the rise and fall of Will and Iman's dreams. Tom gave a low, reed-thin growl. I shook his scruff. He did it again, and I loosened my grip, gathered more of the scruff into my hand and felt him go limp. This was the busiest Iman's wardrobe had ever been. Will snorted, then coughed. I held my breath.

In the flick of a switch the wardrobe became fractionally lighter – Will turned on his bedside light. He shuffled to his feet, I heard the bedroom door sshh against the carpet and guessed he was going to the toilet. I had a chance. A thin sliver of opportunity to make a run for it. Iman was the unknown. What if she was awake? What if she wasn't even in bed yet? I breathed a sigh of relief, not because I knew anything about Iman, but because I remembered about the burglar alarm. It could be set at night with the landing and stairs as a walk-through zone. If I ran down the stairs the alarm could sound and I would be locked in. No way.

The toilet flushed and Will was back (he obviously didn't bother to wash his hands, he wasn't gone long enough). As the toilet cistern filled up, Tom started his low, reed-thin growl again. He was moving too. It was a straight race, the noise of the cistern masked the noise of the cat in the coat in the wardrobe, but which would stop first?

My life was not so much flashing before me as unravelling. This was it. If I was found now, here, with these cats, Will would disown me. Maybe he would beat me as an intruder, but once he knew it was me, once the swelling went down and the blood was wiped away, if I was still alive – he would disown me. The toilet cistern was full and silent. Tom hissed. I didn't hiss back.

In the flick of a switch the wardrobe became fractionally lighter again as Will turned his bedside light back on.

'Iman,' he whispered. 'Iman! Did you hear that, Iman?' No answer.

I heard him stand and the bedroom door sshh shut against the carpet. I put my ear to the wall and heard the voices in my bedroom. I couldn't go backwards and I couldn't go forwards.

Instinctively I moved back as far as I could in the wardrobe, but it was inches at the most. The hairs standing up on the back of my neck met the lush fur on Iman's fur coat at the back of the wardrobe. I could retreat no further. The only thing I could think to do, the only thing that even slightly increased my chances, was to put on the fur coat. It was so dark, it absorbed so much light that maybe, just maybe, it would cloak me in darkness if Will opened the door.

I let go of Jerry and she didn't move (dead?) then, one-handed, I unhooked the fur coat from the hanger (which had the cowboy clothes we'd used for Wesley on it) and put the coat over my shoulders, doing up the top button like a cape. I daren't let go of Tom. I tickled Jerry's neck before re-gripping her scruff again.

There was a knock on the door.

'Who's there?' said Will, answering his own knock.

I held my breath. Tom did his reed-thin growl again.

The door started to open, light flooded in. Then there was a pause, and again Will said, 'Who's there? I'm warning you, I've got a baseball bat.' I didn't think he had, I'd never seen one. The door swung back. I'd have needed to be covered in black fur from head to toe to absorb that much light. He could see me, but he looked like he couldn't. He swung the door half-shut and fully opened it again. He rubbed his eyes. He peered. Tom growled again, Jerry meowed in response, and – funny how the mind works in a crisis – I was relieved that she was still alive. I tickled her neck and she meowed again. Tom meowed in answer.

Will raised a finger, like he was going to speak, but it was a further two meows, one from each cat, before he spoke. 'Er, der, ber: Liam?'

'Ignore me,' I said. 'I'm a coat, an old fur one. I'm a family heir-loom.'

Will opened his mouth, twice, nothing came out. I saw my chance, let go of Jerry and punched Will in the face, so fast and hard that I had my hand back round her scruff before he hit the floor.

A sweet shop is not a good place to avoid people, unless of course it's Christmas Day. My only other thought was to book into a hotel, as a prelude to disappearing, but the hotels were fully booked – it's Christmas. The shop was a stupid and clever place to be. It was where Will could find me, but it was very secure. Everything shuts on Christmas Day, so my alternatives were my house, my invitation to Will's house, or outside – which was far too cold.

It was not very fair to the cats to bring them to the shop. They were having a difficult Christmas. All the groundwork I'd done to get them settled in Wood Road, burying their dung to introduce them to the area, was wasted. It's funny how quickly my thankful-ness at being alive, my joy at surviving Tym's assassination attempt and Will finding me in his wardrobe, was replaced by annoyance at missing out on Christmas. I had cats to give.

It was a mess. Stuck in the flat, with all Dad's stuff. The phone rang. A dilemma. Chances are it was Will. If I didn't answer Will might come round instead. If I did answer I would have to explain myself, and I couldn't. I let it ring. Will was persistent. So I answered, partly because if I spoke to Will on the phone he couldn't hit me, but mainly because I just wanted to hear his voice. I was lonely, and even an argument is something, so I was sur-prised by his friendly opening.

'How-de-do-de? Merry Christmas, Liam!' He waited for me to respond.

'What?'

'Are you fully recovered?' He sounded so friendly, so concerned.

'What?'

'From last night. Your chunder blunder? That tiger you parked?'

'What?'

'Outside the pub. Blimey Liam, most people at least drink heavily before puking on Christmas Eve. It's traditional.' He laughed, but in a friendly way.

'Yeah?' It was all I could do not to say *What?* again.

'Yeah. Anyway, I've been putting crosses into the stalks of brussel sprouts – what time are you coming over?' Did he really mean I was still invited over for Christmas dinner? After what I'd done?

'Er?' It was ok to say er, even before I'd hit him we'd never specified a time for me to go over.

'The sooner the better. I need that thing.'

'Thing?' Now what did he mean by that? Either he was still my best friend and forgiving me, or I was being set up.

'The gift.'

'The cat?' Maybe he needed the cat more than he needed to kill me for being in his wardrobe and punching him. I know it's desperate to wake up on Christmas morning without a gift but this was extreme.

'Exactly! Anyone would think it was you nursing the hangover. I didn't even make it into bed last night!'

I could bear this no longer, I had to be direct. 'Will, are you all right? No nasty blows to the head or anything?'

'No, I don't think so. I woke up with a pumping headache, right on the forehead, I suppose I could've passed out and hit my head?'

'Really?'

'Maybe. I don't know, I was drunk! Actually, I did have the strangest dream. I was just telling Iman, really lucid. It wasn't until I said it all to her that I realised it couldn't be true. I was going to kill you!' That was more like it.

'Well, they say dreams are the highway to the subconscious. Do you want to kill me?'

'No! This dream was nothing to do with the subconscious, I can explain the lot. I dreamed that you were in my wardrobe! Now that's just because of the thing at Iman's school play where you were in a wardrobe.'

'Yeah?'

'Yeah. I was really drunk and I vaguely remembered you were in this wardrobe. If it wasn't a dream it was a hallucination.'

'On beer?' Hallucinating on beer didn't make any sense.

'And shorts! But it had to be a dream, Iman said so. Look, when you were in the wardrobe you meowed!'

'Meow?' I said it in such a high-pitched nervous voice it sounded like a meow.

'That's it, exactly. But that's just cos I know about the thing.'

'The gift?'

'Exactly. And the clincher, that Iman pointed out to me, because she doesn't know about the thing, was that you . . .'

I interrupted just to check, 'In the wardrobe?'

'Yeah, in the wardrobe, you were wearing Iman's great-grand-mother's fur coat.'

'Like a cat?' I said, trying to firm up the realism of his dream analysis.

'Possibly. But you said it was an heirloom. So, you said something you couldn't possibly know! Weird or what?'

'What?' Fuck! The diary. My cheeks flushed red with embarrassment, but it was ok, we were on the phone.

'So, when can we expect you?'

I was nearly out of the woods, but I had to be certain, 'Who's going to be there?'

'Me, you, Iman, oh and my dad.'

'No one else?' I checked.

'No one else. Except the thing.'

'Tom the tom?' I double-checked.

'Exactly. And a turkey.'

We agreed I would go round to Will's at lunchtime, it made the most sense. As I put the phone down I felt fireworks going off

310

inside my head, I could have a Christmas! It was really going to happen, I was breathless with excitement.

It was a lovely Christmas dinner. Will's dad did the washing up. Will was pleased with Tom the tom. Iman was even more pleased. Tom hissed at Grizabella.

I left Jerry at the shop. It would have been funny to give Iman another cat, but I liked Jerry and Jerry liked me. Iman had enough cats. That meant I only took a few general gifts from the shop: the box of chocolates, the Turkish Delight and cigars. (But in a way I gave Will the line-dancing cowboy teapot that got used after dinner; it did make him smile.) I had taken the cigars for Will's dad, but he gave me cigars too so our gifts cancelled each other out. Iman wasn't interested in the chocolates or the Turkish Delight or the cigars, so I hadn't got her anything. She didn't seem to mind, maybe nothing was better than an extra cat. I realised what exceptional people Will and Iman were as friends, I'd not got any proper gifts to give and they didn't mind. If only I'd known earlier that Iman loved fizzy sherbet flying saucers I could easily have brought her a box from stock. Will still gave me the sweater, and I was right about how warm it would make me feel. But I couldn't help thinking it would have been nicer to get it as a surprise.

Jemma and Tym had gone to her family for Christmas Day and Boxing Day. It gave me some breathing space. I could never have foreseen them getting together, it was nothing to do with being thorough or not being thorough, it was unexpected love. Even Iman remarked that they were an unlikely pair. She remarked on it when we were talking, I don't know if she wrote it up in her diary. I wonder what Jemma and Tym made of my Isle of Skye bedroom? Maybe Tym would be too embarrassed to mention it; I was.

Of course I would do all I could to stop Will finding out I was Tym's landlord. With caution and thoroughness I might get away with it, but it would be close. I consoled myself with the fact that

311

even if Will found out, all he would know was that I had lived next door. That's not a crime. If needs be, I could make out I was simply the landlord. He need never know that I punched him in the face. No amount of thoroughness could have planned for the level of luck that saved me.

Sitting in Will's house on Christmas evening, smoking cigars, I decided what to do. The shop was more than enough for my dad, so surely it would do for me, for a time at least. And Jerry, Jerry was a lovely cat, I'd keep her for me and the shop. There would always be people around, Jerry would like that and I'm sure the Crabbe sisters would love her, Jerry was my dad's name after all so it was the right thing to do, it made sense.

IMAN

January 1
D.D. welcome to another year in the life of me. I predict changes!
As is tradition, here are my New Year Resolutions:

1. *To move house*
2. *To get more music*
3. *To be happier and happier*
4. *(The traditional closing resolution) To keep this diary for the twelfth year.*

Highlight: 99% When we were in the January sales (Debenhams) I talked about moving to Will. He agreed. If we move now we should make about nine grand profit. I've had it with the burglaries here. I don't think they've beaten me, everything is as it was, but different. Will said he'd been thinking about moving too, we are so in tune, it's perfect. We shook on it and hugged on it, in Debenhams' cookery department, just perfect.